Charly Dorn had it made. He had survived the war and now he led the good life in the posh New York/Southampton scene.

Karl-Heinz Dorn was a Nazi. He also had survived . . . by making himself indispensable to the Third Reich.

And now the world was about to find out that Karl-Heinz, the Nazi, and "good old" Charly Dorn were one and the same . . .

FRIENDS IN HIGH PLACES

"Fascinating . . . hard to put down."
—**PUBLISHERS WEEKLY**

JOHN WEITZ

FRIENDS IN HIGH PLACES

CHARTER BOOKS, NEW YORK

This Charter Book contains the complete
text of the original hardcover edition.
It has been completely reset in a typeface
designed for easy reading, and was printed
from new film.

FRIENDS IN HIGH PLACES

A Charter Book / published by arrangement with
Macmillan Publishing Co., Inc.

PRINTING HISTORY
Macmillan edition / 1982
Charter edition / August 1983

ISBN: 0-441-25313-X

Charter Books are published by The Berkley Publishing Group,
200 Madison Avenue, New York, New York 10016.
PRINTED IN THE UNITED STATES OF AMERICA

For Susan

I OWE THANKS TO:

MILLARD A. RING, ESQ., whose knowledge of
immigration law was invaluable.

MAYOR L. C. STILES and MR. HANS R. POETHIG
of Roswell, New Mexico, both of whom were kind enough
to give me their efforts and time.

DR. JOHN KEUHNELIAN who was kind enough
to research some medical facts.

BARBARA KHOURY for many hours of help.

CONTENTS

FRIENDS IN HIGH PLACES

NEW YORK

1954

CHARLY DORN—christened Karl-Heinz Dorn in Berlin some forty-two years before—driving the new, open Brunzig 190R, turned right at the Irving House, a large white wooden structure and Southampton's only real hotel. Then he headed toward the ocean, past large summer homes, smaller sisters of the hotel, white buildings in the New England style, set back from the road behind wide lawns and rose-covered split-rail fences. In driveways, under porticos or peeking out of open garage doors were Rollses, Bentleys, Packards, Lincolns, and Cadillacs. Bicycle-riding tennis players, raquets tucked into saddle baskets, lazed along, in no hurry to get to the courts. The street was sun-dappled under flanking oak trees and maples. He could smell new-mown grass and a touch of ocean salt on the breeze from the south. Starched, imperious

1

nannies pushed baby carriages and gave him fierce, defensive looks. A small single-engined plane droned overhead in the sky. Paradise!

Where the road met the beach he turned left, past an old dark red church backed against the dunes. Finally came the low buildings of the Beach Club. He parked the 190R in the lot, buttoned a tonneau cover over the open cockpit, and walked into the club.

"Mrs. Allery, please. My name is Dorn." Dorn spoke almost perfect English, pronouncing each word correctly, but, because of his German cadence, still sounding slightly foreign. This, and the fact that he had been in the *AfrikaKorps*, had made him an interesting, though slightly menacing, addition to the New York-Southampton scene.

"Yes, sir, she's expecting you." The receptionist was a young girl with sun-bleached hair, tan face, and blue eyes. She looked splendid. The SS would have requisitioned her at once! The perfect Aryan specimen! *Bad joke. For one split second, he felt that slap of guilt, of complicity. It stung and left as quickly as it came.*

Marge Allery was an overweight, overwealthy widow in her early forties. She still had a beautiful face, magnificent blond hair and enormous mouse-gray eyes. It was all that remained of her once-famous good looks. Yet, despite many marital disappointments, which, as she readily admitted, were mainly due to her own bad judgment, she was optimistic, cheerful, and generous. Dorn had met her the previous summer and they had become friends. He liked her enormously, and she had adopted him, though not as a lover. He could not qualify. He was too old, too bright, and made too good a living. She still had a busy sex life, but always with beach kids, boys she rewarded either with jewelry or money. None of these adventures was sad or sordid to Marge. She enjoyed her lovers, her money, and her freedom to choose. She no longer fell in love, but she offered and gave friendship. She was as free with advice as she was with gifts, but in both she never spent beyond her means.

Marge was a member of Southampton's two main clubs and a perennial guest at all parties. Outsiders whom she introduced were soon integrated into the resort's clublike life. She was too intelligent to bring her various paid lovers, and she made sure they remained back at her house, swimming in her pool, playing tennis on her court, drinking from her bar.

When Dorn entered, most Beach Club members were taking their morning cocktails on a wide terrace facing the ocean. Marge was on the qui vive for Dorn, and she signaled with a flabby arm as soon as she saw him. She introduced him to the middle-aged couple she was with. They were tall, tanned, slim, and wrinkled. They looked more like brother and sister than husband and wife. Their name was Crutchley. The man immediately said, "Call me Tom. My wife's name is Kathy." Like many Europeans, Dorn found it difficult to be this familiar at first meeting, but he admitted the advantage: It was easier to remember first names.

Tom said, "We're from California, Santa Barbara. Have you ever been there?"

Dorn said, "No."

"You ought to come out," said Tom. "Marge told us you're German."

"Right. From Berlin."

Being German was no longer taboo, especially if you were a German from Berlin, ever since the 1948 airlift when Harry Truman had "shown the Russians what was what." Suddenly Berlin was converted from unworthy to worthy, and Berliners from defeated barbarians into upstanding heroes. Dorn had learned that American opinions were volatile.

"Oh? We've never been to Berlin, but we used to go to Munich before the war. We skied in Garmisch and Berchtesgaden. Great places. Been there?"

Yes. He had been there. No use bringing up why.

"Only a little while, and in the summer."

"Must be great scenery in summer . . ."

"Great." *The Berghof in summer! Time to get off the subject. Besides, he did not like Bavaria. He had never been comfortable with Bavarians. He found them phony. But that, too, had no place in this conversation. How could the Crutchleys know the Bavarians called Berliners "sow Prussians"?*

He said, "I'm glad you liked Germany."

Tom said, almost as an apologetic explanation, "Fortunately, I was not in Europe during the war. I skippered a D.E. in the Pacific."

"D.E.?"

"It's like a destroyer. Only smaller. I did some sailing

before the war, so they gave me a commission. We got sunk by Kamikaze. I got home early.''

His wife said, "Good thing, too. His golf was way off.''

Some upper-class Americans were like the English, always understating. Affected and silly, thought Dorn. She couldn't possibly mean it. Golf couldn't matter that much. And yet, maybe she really did mean it. *Na, ja*—the German way of saying, oh, well—on the other hand, they seemed pleasant. He was finally learning to accept people. Stop analyzing, judging, he told himself. It all doesn't matter that much!

Marge led them all to the dining room, her magnificent head above the crowd, unbetrayed by her waddling body. They settled at a large table.

"I'm expecting Will Simms," she said.

"I know.''

"You don't like him?''

"Who does?''

She laughed. "You're right. But behave! He's only here because he did me a favor.''

"I also know that.''

"Oh?''

"He brought out your other houseguest, Carla Roselli.''

"Charly, you *bastard*, they're *right!* You're really a spy!''

"Not quite. I met them at Shinnecock on the drive out. We had breakfast together. She's, as we say in Berlin, *Prima!*''

"Not bad, eh?''

"Great girl, judging from the twenty minutes I saw her.''

"You judged right. Did you know her family?''

"Textile mill people I think, from the north. I heard that their factory got bombed out and they rebuilt it. Anyway, she has two brothers I once met. Good race drivers. We got that far when Simms had a fit and broke up the conversation.''

"A fit over you?''

"No. Some boy at the next table made eyes at Carla, and Simms started bellowing.''

"Be good, Charly, for my sake. Here they come!''

Carla and Simms were introduced to the Crutchleys and settled at their table. The Italian girl, beautiful and dark-haired, looked upset. Her face was so open, so easy to read! She looked at Dorn silently, while Simms spoke to Tom Crutchley, and meaningfully shook her head. Obviously, he had been all over her.

Now Simms said, "And Charly over there is going to sell me one of his Blitzkrieg buggies, aren't you, lover boy?"

"We'll talk about that tomorrow."

"You're flippin' well right we'll discuss it. I want me one of those thingamajigs."

Dorn looked at Simms and thought, *Kick yourself in the ass! You'll get your 190R. I won't lose the sale. But you'll get it when we're good and ready.*

The 190R was Brunzig's newest, most expensive model, the sports car that had beaten all competitors in the Le Mans and Mille Miglia races. It was the most advanced design in the world. Dorn's job was to sell the first batch of 190Rs which the Brunzig factory in Stuttgart had allotted for the American market. He was national manager of special sales, which meant he sold only the newest cars the company made.

Carla seemed relieved to have Dorn there. Wasn't Southampton *stupendo?* And wasn't it amazing how few Europeans knew about this place? Everyone would come here soon, *vero?* She now prattled happily, her long hands sweeping the hair from her face every few sentences. Relieved of Simm's solitary company, she sent out warmth and good feelings.

A light wind coming up from the ocean across the wide beach and over the thumping surf carried snatches of words from sunbathers and children at play. *It was all so familiar, almost exactly like the North Sea beaches. But for the missing basketweave beach booths and hundreds of little pennants snapping in the wind, this could have been Sylt or Föhr. A woman at a nearby table wore Arpege, and he could never mistake the scent. It was Hilde's favorite. Often he thought of Hilde; what they once had and could have had again if only they had been given another chance. Hilde would have liked Carla Roselli, he was sure.*

Marge Allery said, "The Crutchleys are looking for a house here."

"We love Southampton," said Kathy Crutchley. "But it's not at all like Santa Barbara, except in one respect: The Jews haven't gotten here yet." She spoke quite matter-of-factly. The others nodded, except for Carla, who looked up suddenly, startled, and found Dorn's eyes. She began to say something, but stopped herself.

Simms boomed, "I'm starved. Let's order." He put his arm over Carla's shoulder and tried to pull her over toward

him, but she shrugged him off. He seemed hardly to notice.
He said, "What do you say, Carla? Can't guarantee how
good the spaghetti is in this place. They don't have any
Italian members." He roared with laughter, pleased by his
own wit.

After lunch Dorn excused himself and drove east along
Montauk Highway toward the village of Bridgehampton a few
miles away, where the sports car crowd was preparing for the
annual road races.

The races at "Bridge" were run on open country roads and
through potato fields, past old farmhouses and barns and a
tiny red schoolhouse. The event was for charity, and the
drivers were wealthy amateurs. Competitors and spectators
were socially interchangeable, just as they were at polo matches,
club tennis tournaments, and sailing regattas.

The weather was holding, warm, with a light breeze and a
few puffy clouds, cheerful lambs on a field of blue. Dorn
drove past potato farms, slab-sided stone barns, and roadside
inns. Here and there the asphalt was smeared with dried mud
from tractors, and just before Bridgehampton he passed through
the stench of a duck farm alongside the road, where thousands of the fat white birds quacked toward their predestined
future on someone's dinner table. He was fond of this piece
of old countryside, which was still simple and unchanged.
Much of America looked as if it had just been born. This did
not.

He thought back to the conversation at lunch. Carla Roselli
was obviously taken aback by Americans making anti-Jewish
remarks. Dorn no longer was, because he had heard so many
of them. One had to expect such remarks wherever rich,
Christian Americans gathered.

At first he, too, had been shocked. He was sure that
America had no anti-Jewish prejudice. He knew Americans
were hard on Negroes. But Jews? In Germany it was now a
crime to make remarks against Jews. In Germany! But in
America it seemed quite acceptable to people like the
Crutchleys.

The 190R was a dream to drive. Straight as an arrow, and
when he wanted power the engine came in with a tremendous
surge. The Southampton sports car crowd would love the
190R, he knew that. He rather liked those people, although

they were often ridiculous, spoiled and superficial. *Na, ja,* that suited him for now. This was not his moment to think hard.

Bridgehampton came into view. He drove slowly through the center of the large village and turned right at its end near a war memorial. Then he followed the oak-flanked road past a small golf club to a widening, where a temporary pit area was being built on the edge of a potato field. Parked on the shoulder of the asphalt were dozens of sports cars, from Alfa-Romeos and Bugattis of the pre-war years to the latest MGs, Nash-Healys, Allards, Jaguars, and Ferraris. Hundreds of people milled around, raising dust, some gawking, some trying to set up a temporary depot for their cars and supplies. It was a cheerful crowd: college boys in chino slacks, mechanics in overalls, and dozens of pretty girls with long bare legs. They all made a great show of efficiency, stacking spare wheels, lugging canisters of gas and oil, unloading jacks and tools from station wagons and panel trucks, pasting large decal numbers onto the race cars, checking spark plugs and oil levels. Above the entire scene there hung the scream, roar, and boom of various engines being warmed up and tuned.

The din was ear-shattering.

When Dorn drove into the area, it was as if someone had signaled a sudden halt to all activity. Engines were shut off, crew members stopped in mid-work, and all eyes were focused on his arrival. It was the first time most of them had seen Brunzig's 190R. The pancake-flat, shark-mouthed, steel-gray convertible with its aluminum racing wheels and winged hubcaps looked gracefully low and savage. Dorn stopped across from the middle of the pit area and within seconds was surrounded by a crowd. A deluge of questions descended on him. After ten minutes he started the engine and slowly drove back toward the center of Bridgehampton. He had given them a quick look. Enough for now.

Two hundred yards down the road, a lovely Bentley sports sedan came into view heading for the pits. The driver blinked his headlights and stopped, as did Dorn. He knew the Bentley, which belonged to Al Perrin, one of the wealthiest sports car drivers in America. There were two other men with Perrin, also middle-aged sports car enthusiasts.

"Charly," Perrin said, "so *that's* your new monster? Great body!"

"Thank you. Glad you like it."

The three men walked around the Brunzig, inspecting it like horse lovers at a yearling auction. They stopped, squinted, squatted, looked at the suspension, leaned into the cockpit, felt the tread of the tires, softly tapped their fingers against the fenders, and did everything but pat the 190R's flanks. Dorn pulled the hood release and revealed the radical new engine. They made small, admiring noises. One of them whistled softly. They were hooked.

Perrin said, "Charly, put me down for one of these, will you?" He didn't even ask the price.

"Okay."

"When can I get the darn thing?"

"I'll have to let you know. We're quite a bit behind. Ever since Le Mans."

"Okay. Let me know. And for them, too." The others nodded.

Everyone was impressed by the 190R. Everyone wanted the first one. Could they drive the car around? Yes, but not until Monday. Then the outsiders were back in New York. The roads were emptier.

And so three middle-aged and wealthy men canceled their Monday business schedules to drive around for a short time in a new sports car. Why not? Dorn admired their self-indulgence. Typically American! The whole idea that "there's always more where that came from" appealed to him. To a German, trading play for work would have been inconceivable.

Some of the executives at Brunzig in New York were contemptuous of their American clientele, partly because of this easy acceptance of obstacles created by Brunzig. Some were created artificially, but, of course, no one at Brunzig would admit it. The New York staff understood that Americans loved the scarce, the hard-to-get.

Dorn had actually improved his sales leverage by postponing the test drives for a day. German customers would have insisted on suiting their own convenience. The ease with which Americans could be handled disturbed him. Much though he loved them, he wished they were less masochistic.

He headed back to Southampton and Marge Allery's house. His day's work was done.

•   •   •

Charly Dorn was a slim man who looked ten years younger than his age. He was six feet tall and had black, graying hair, a ruddy complexion, and high Slavic cheekbones like so many people from the Brandenburg province around Berlin. His nose was short, high-bridged, and straight. He had gray-green eyes which looked out from under black, arched eyebrows. Dorn was attractive to women because of his taut, lanky figure and symmetrical face, but mostly because of his friendly and calm ways. Outwardly, he seemed passive. He listened well and smiled easily. He had quickly adjusted to New York life. Like all Berliners, he was a city boy. New York and Berlin were much alike: both were nouveau riche, both filled with vulgarity and display, both constantly changing their values with each latest fad.

There was no one woman in Dorn's life. Occasionally there were one-night stands, when the urge, the mood, the opportunity, and the desire were mutual. Some were genuinely friendly and amusing adventures. Others were drunken screwing bouts, which ended before dawn. He lived the bachelor's life, and there seemed to be no reason and no person to cause him to change it. Some of his bedmates remained his friends, good for rational advice and rational sex. But mostly they were women he could live without. *The other love, the real love, the one that had owned him and was part of him, that was long gone. Not even grief was left. Just a happy memory, as if Hilde had been his in another life.*

But now, the closer he got to Marge's house, the more he looked forward to seeing more of Carla Roselli. For that, he was a bit angry with himself. After all, he was not a schoolboy.

From the outside, Marge's two-story saltbox house looked deceptively small. Originally built for a wealthy, nineteenth-century sea captain, it made use of every inch of interior space. Most of the old furniture, designed by ships' carpenters, were still in use. There were eight small bedrooms, and a master suite. To modernize chamberpotera facilities, Marge had installed several bathrooms. The outside of the house was wood-shingled and had weathered to a natural gray. Window frames and doors were painted white, with the exception of the front door, which was bright red. Marge had enclosed the pool, cabanas, and tennis courts behind the house with huge rhododendrons that bloomed in pink and red. The stable at the front of the estate had become a three-car garage and gardener's shed, as well as her chauffeur's quarters.

Vivier, her Haitian butler, was homosexual and almost seven feet tall, with chest, arms, and thighs to match his heroic height. He dressed year-round in loose white smocks and black trousers. In summer he wore Japanese sandals and in winter felt-soled Chinese slippers. Marge and he communicated in French, which Vivier spoke with his soft island patois. Marge massaged the language with a touch of South Carolina, her native accent. A Parisian friend once said, ''Marge? She speaks perfect French, *without the trace of a French accent!*''

Casey, the chauffeur, was New York Irish. He ministered to her Chrysler Town and Country convertible and a small, vulnerable Bentley R4 sedan. The Chrysler took the brunt. The Bentley was reserved for the city: theater and shopping.

Both Vivier and Casey made sure that neither harm nor discomfort came to their beautiful, bloated boss.

When Dorn pulled into the driveway and stopped at the front door of the house, it swung open as if by some silent signal, and Vivier appeared.

''*Bonjour,* Monsieur Dorn!''

''*Bonjour,* Vivier.''

''*Quelle voiture exquise!*'' He was obviously bewitched by the 190R.

''*Merçi,* Vivier.''

''*Elle est épatante!*'' Then Vivier took the leather duffel bag Dorn handed him and the folded blazer, and led the way into the guest room, a small, square chamber on the ground floor that smelled of floor wax and freshly laundered linen. Its walls and ceiling were papered with a farm print in green tones. The floor was polished oak with a round, white, hooked rug covering the center. The wooden sleigh bed was made up in gingham sheets and pillowcases to match the green in the wallpaper. Two paneled windows opened directly into a cutting garden of riotous zinnias.

Dorn had stayed in this room before. He loved it, because it was in the back of the house, away from the pool and its commotion. A red-throated finch came to say hello each morning and to collect his share of the cookie that accompanied the English-style wake-up cup of tea. Marge was an exquisite hostess.

Having unpacked, Vivier said, "Monsieur Dorn, I'll bring you a drink. What would you like?"

"A Dubonnet. Did Signorina Roselli come back from the club?"

"*Oui*, monsieur. She and Madame Allery"—he pronounced it to rhyme with *gallérie*—"have returned. Madame Allery is taking a nap, but I think the Italian lady is at the pool."

There was no sound behind the rhododendrons from the pool area, but when Dorn rounded the bushes he saw Carla lying on a towel, sunbathing, eyes closed, her stretched-out body wearing the sort of bikini one often saw in Europe but never in America. To avoid startling her, he quickly said, "Hello!" in a stronger voice than was necessary, and she rolled over, rested her chin on her fist, and smiled. "Hello!" she said, and he almost felt nervous, like a *Primaner*, a high school senior with a new girl. He was about to speak when Vivier brought a tray with glasses and a bottle of Dubonnet. At the same moment, the phone rang back in the house, and Vivier left to take the call.

Dorn offered her a Dubonnet, which she refused. He began to talk about the scene at Bridgehampton when Vivier returned to fetch Carla to the phone.

"A call from Milan, mademoiselle."

She shrugged her apologies and left. He looked at her departing back and at the way its tiny muscles moved the skin. which was nude but for the back string of her halter brassiere and the top of the triangle bottom below the hollow at the base of her spine. He was stirred, excited. There were many pretty girls with beautiful bodies whom he saw and appreciated, but who did not rouse him. They were *Pipimädchen*, commonplace.

Dorn stretched out in a beach chair and looked into the blue-tinted rectangular pool. Should he get into a swimsuit? No. It was late in the day, and Marge probably had plans for cocktails. He was too lazy. He watched a dragonfly settle on a floating oak leaf and there was no fish to threaten the tiny sailor. He began to drift, thoughts without focus. Then he heard steps on the grass, and she was back.

All of her appeared: voice, sweeping black-brown hair, perfume, tall, loose body, gesturing hands.

"*Scustate!* A call from my brother Umberto."

He asked, "Is everything all right?"

"Yes, sort of. Umberto sends his best to you, by the way. He remembers you. . . . They have a *sciopero* coming up, a strike! It is *ridicolo!* We are a company that really cares about its workers. . . ." She poured herself a Dubonnet before Dorn could help. "We have hospitals and insurance and a school for the *ragazzi*, the kids. *Tutto* . . ."

"Communists?" said Dorn.

"*Si* . . . and *no!* In Italy we have a lot of Communists, but they're Italian. You know . . . *differente*, not like the Russians or the Czechs or the Balkans. We haven't got the *dullness*."

Dorn knew. He used to look down on the "Spaghettis" in those Africa days long ago, until he found out that the Italians were right and Berlin was wrong.

She continued, "But Italians, when they feel they have a complaint, they get dramatic. And a strike is dramatic."

"Even if it hurts? Even if they can't support themselves?"

"Even then. *Come gli ragazzi*, like kids."

Dorn shook his head. Hard to believe, but Italians had always been hard to believe. Until now.

Of course, Marge had plans for that night. She always had plans. The stocky, smiling Casey drove the three of them to a cocktail party that was held on an enormous beachfront estate called Mon Plaisir, and for all its pomposity, the name suited the place. Its front was part French, with terraced gardens and fountains, and its rear Hollywood-1930s with an oversized, old-time swimming pool and a lawn that led clear up to the dunes and looked like a giant billiard table.

The estate had been rented for the summer by a Chicagoan in the liquor business, who was so wealthy that he could afford to shrug off allusions to his past in the bootleg era. He and his wife adored Marge, had used her for social entrée in the Hamptons, and would reciprocate by offering her the hospitality of their homes on Lake Shore Drive and in Cannes.

As Marge said, "They couldn't be nicer. I don't mind their social climbing. Half the people I know in Southampton were social climbers a few years ago."

"And now," said Dorn, "they've got nowhere left to climb?"

"The hell they don't." Marge laughed. "Now they're

tackling Lyford Cay and Deauville. Wherever the Duke and
Duchess of Windsor are!''

Carla wore a shocking-pink Pucci dress, a simple silk
sheath with tiny shoulder straps. It touched her body in places
but did not cling. Her hair was loose, thick and shiny, and
she was surrounded by a cloud of scent, a new Italian perfume,
she told Dorn. It riveted him. He felt strangely proprietary toward
her, even accustomed to her, although they had known each
other for less than a full day.

Marge, dressed in one of the figure-hiding, voluminous silk
creations they fabricated for her in Paris, was obviously
pleased by the effect her two houseguests had on each other.
Marge was a romantic, even though her own love life had
become so matter of fact. She had no escort, but she was
never averse to opportunities, and she could always pick up
someone later. For now, it pleased her to act as duenna for
the beautiful Italian and the tall, handsome German.

Most of the party took place behind the mansion around the
pool. They walked through the white-stuccoed circular main
hall with its black-and-white checkered floor, and out onto
the wide terrace, facing the ocean, where a small band played
Cole Porter and Gershwin tunes in the strict dance rhythm
known as "society beat." Below, on the lawn, were more
than a hundred guests, some dancing on the white stone deck
around the pool, others gathered in small groups, talking in
the high-pitched chatter that is part of a summer resort's
weekend.

The women were in bright colors and prints, and the men
wore blazers, madras jackets, and cotton slacks. Southampton
was developing a style of its own, more worldly than Palm
Beach, which had become quite midwestern.

The young waiters and waitresses, probably local kids,
were passing trays of drinks with a certain desperation. This
was a drinking crowd. The lawn was floodlighted from the
roof of the mansion, and guests looked shiny with fresh
suntans. The dark, star-dotted sky served as a stagelike
backdrop. Dorn spotted familiar faces: a Hollywood actor
who was considered "social" and always spent much time in
New York. Three years before, he had bought an expensive
Brunzig, one of the first in Beverly Hills, when buying a
German car was still considered unacceptable among Jewish
film executives. By now many of them had bought Brunzigs.

Standing a few yards away were Dorn's three new clients from Bridgehampton, with whom he had scheduled the test drive. They waved at him. "See you Monday!"

There was a squeal, and a blond debutante Dorn had dodged a few nights before at the Stork Club descended on him.

"Charly! Charly Dorn!"

Dorn did not remember her name, so he said, "This is Carla Roselli, and, of course, you know Marge."

"Sure I do. Mummy and Marge are practically sisters." She turned to Marge. "Thanks for the invite."

"That's all right," said Marge. "Your mother and I go back a long way. Where's your fiancé?" She did not sound overjoyed to see her again.

"There he is," said the girl, as a blond giant lurched over, obviously quite drunk.

"Hey," the boy boomed. "Charly, my Kraut friend! How are you, buddy? Burned any Jews lately? If you have, you've got my sincere congratulations!" He slurred his words.

Marge Allery took instant action. One look at Dorn and his darkening face, and she told the girl, "Take your young fellow and get him out of here. I won't allow him to be rude to my friends."

The girl, wide-eyed, realized that Marge was incensed, and one did not cross Marge Allery, not in Southampton.

She quickly said, "Okay, okay! Come on, darling!" grabbed her burly fiancé's elbow, swiveled him around, and dragged him away.

"What was that all about?" asked Marge.

"I was at the Stork Club the other night, and the two kids were there. The girl was paying too much attention to me, probably to make her fiancé jealous. Nothing serious. She's an empty-headed little fool. But her boyfriend got annoyed, so I left before there was a fight."

"Now I understand," said Marge, and steered them toward the bar behind the band to get a drink. Soon Carla and Dorn decided to dance. They were perfection. Like many Berliners, Dorn was a very good dancer, and Carla followed his every move.

"*If they asked me, I could write a book* . . ."

"*I get no kick from champagne* . . ."

"*In our mountain greenery* . . ."

They danced until the band took a break and Marge said, "I'm starved. Vivier has reserved a table at Herb McCarthy's. Let's go."

Casey was waiting out front to drive them to the inn.

McCarthy's was a rambling Victorian restaurant in an unfashionable part of the village. All of Southampton went there after its round of weekend cocktail parties. Herb McCarthy, a redheaded man in his thirties, always wore a white busboy's jacket, as if to insulate himself from his boisterous clientele. He was a stern disciplinarian, unimpressed by family or wealth, willing to eject drunks and brawlers, no matter who they were. Like Billingsley of the Stork and John Perona of El Morocco, he ran his saloon "the way he damned well pleased," as he would tell anyone who dared to complain. Marge was one of his great favorites, and he immediately piloted her, Carla, and Dorn to a ringside table near the tiny dance floor. A waitress brought them drinks, but normal talk was impossible over the din of alcohol-boosted voices. They tried several times but then gave up.

Marge, emphasizing her words with hand signals, shouted, "Shall we go home? Vivier can fix up something to eat."

"*Brava!*" Carla applauded, and Dorn nodded his agreement.

Herb McCarthy was at the door near the packed bar, directing traffic. "Anything wrong, Marge?"

"No, Herb. Too noisy! See you tomorrow."

"Don't blame you." He shrugged. "I'm only here because I've got to be." He grinned and waved good-bye.

Casey had read their minds.

"Figured you might not stay!" he said.

They got into the Chrysler, and as Casey started the car, his path was suddenly blocked by Simms's Ferrari, which streaked toward the front of the inn at high speed. The red sports car slid to a halt until its flank almost touched the front of their car. Simms jumped from behind the wheel and, seeing Casey in his chauffeur's cap, howled, "You fucking flunky! Who taught you how to drive?" He obviously had not recognized Marge's Chrysler. Casey, trapped in his uniformed role, recognized the man as an acquaintance of Mrs. Allery's and could say nothing. Simms grabbed Casey's shirt front and tie through the open window. From the seat next to the chauffeur came Dorn's cutting voice: "Get your goddammed

hands off this man, you shit!'' and he stepped out of the car.
He had been pushed beyond his usual constraint, and now he
was angry to the very edge of self-control. ''All right, Simms.
You heard me!''

Simms immediately let go of Casey. This was a Dorn he
had never seen before. The tall German's face was drawn
with anger, and suddenly all the wild stories Simms had heard
about Dorn, the Nazi, seemed true. He was willing to take on
a chauffeur, but not this threatening figure. He mumbled,
''Hell, Charly, I didn't know he was with you. You could
have gotten hurt.''

He pointed, showing how close the cars were. Then, a
cowed man, he got back into his Ferrari and drove slowly
toward the parking area.

Dorn stood, staring after him, cursing to himself, *''Du
verfluchtes Schwein, du! Du Drecksau! Du Kotzmittel!''*

Then he got back into the Chrysler.

''Thanks,'' said Casey, admiring the way Mr. Dorn had
handled things. *Goddamned Simms had nearly shit his pants!*

From the back seat, Marge said, ''Good boy!'' And Carla
put her hand on Dorn's shoulder, silently applauding him.

For the moment Dorn was pleased with himself, but then
again, *na, ja,* he had acted like a fool. What was the point of
blowing his top at that silly drunkard? Was he showing off for
Carla? Perhaps, he was not showing off, just reacting to her
presence. Still, to get this furious? Stupid! As they said in
Berlin, *''Junge, mach dir kehnen Fleck!* Don't wet your
pants, chum!''* Berliners had a graphic way with heroics.

Back at Marge's house, the night was crystal clear. Over
toward Southampton the glow of electric lights reached into
the sky, but behind the dunes everything was blue-black
velvet. After the din of McCarthy's, the calm was soothing,
and crickets gave choral performances backed by a gentle
surf.

Carla made a wide gesture and said, ''This is what I really
want. I love the style. It's so American. Our country houses
are all so *pomposi, pretenziosi!''*

''Well,'' said Marge, ''come on now. Your houses have a
right to be pompous. Most of them were built two or three
hundred years before this place.''

''I would like to spend more time here,'' she said. ''And

my brothers, too. They were at Sebring last year for the races. Then they visited New York and everyone was so nice to them. But they have never been out here. They would absolutely love it. Will you help me find a place?''

"Of course," said Marge.

Dorn said, "I know just how Carla feels. I have been here a few years, and I feel more and more at home. In fact . . ."

"In fact, what?" said Marge.

"Well, I was thinking of taking out citizenship eventually. But"—he held up a hand—"that's confidential. So please . . ." He knew Marge, of course, but Carla? *Schon gut.* He instinctively knew his confidence would be kept.

"How did you make out over in Bridgehampton?" asked Marge.

"Sold three cars."

"Marvelous! To whom?"

"Al Perrin and two of his friends."

"Oh?" Marge sounded taken aback.

"Anything wrong with Perrin? He's a nice fellow and a good sportsman. And he can certainly afford the car."

"No question about that! He's rich as Croesus. I'm just being stuffy."

"Stuffy?"

"You know, he's a Jew. He's got a big house out here, but of course he can't join the clubs."

"Perrin? Doesn't sound like a Jewish name." Dorn was puzzled. Most Jews in America had German names.

"Well," said Marge, shrugging, "God knows what his name really is. Someone said Pearl or Perlman or something like that. Anyway, he sure can afford the car. Congratulations, Charly, my boy!"

Dorn and Carla exchanged looks.

Carla said, "Marge, I don't understand. What's all this *commedia* about the Jews? Those people from California. And then that drunk young man at the party. And now you. I mean, even you."

"Baby," said Marge, "that's par for the course in our country."

"Par for the course?" Carla did not understand the phrase.

"Normal, that's what that means. In America everybody calls everyone dirty names. You can't imagine what it must have been like here in Southampton. The Irish Catholics once settled here for the summers because when it came to Newport or the resorts in Maine they didn't have the chance of a snowball in hell.''

Carla laughed. She said, ''I love your expressions . . . *snowball in hell*? Tell me, what was wrong with the Catholics, the Irish?''

''Well, when the Irish immigrants first came over, they didn't have a penny. They were often illiterate. What's more, they landed mostly in Boston, where the old families were Protestant and hated Catholics. We only have one Catholic state and that's Louisiana. But up here in the Northeast the Catholics once had a tough time. They got called a lot of dirty names. I'm speaking of the grandparents of the people you met today at the club and at parties. Many of them are Irish. Now, of course, they're all set.''

''How about when that young fellow made the remark to Charly about burning Jews? I mean that *was* in terrible taste!''

''I wouldn't worry about Charly,'' Marge said. ''In another four or five years it will all be forgotten, the whole business about the war and the Germans.''

''*Vero?*'' said Carla.

''*Vero,*'' said Marge. ''Now, if he were a Jew, that would be different.''

''Why?'' said Carla. ''I have Jewish cousins in Italy. They are old and distinguished and aristocratic. Some of them were killed in a concentration camp.''

''I wouldn't talk too much about it. The Jews in America are still treated like the Irish used to be. They're different. People say they're pushy and crude. Of course, that's only partly true. But you see, New York is nearby and there are so many Jews in New York that if you let them, they'll just take over. It happened to places like Forest Hills and Cedarhurst and Lawrence, where there used to be lots of Christian families. Now they're like ghettos. Nothing but Jews.''

''But the Irish thing changed,'' said Dorn. ''You said nobody is against them anymore. . . .''

''Yes, that's true. But the Irish are at least Christians. They're not absolutely *strange* like the Jews. The Jews might as well be Mohammedans or Buddhists. They've got a whole different language. No one can understand their prayers. Their churches are open on different days. They wear hats to services. They're just too goddamned *different*. Hell, I know a lot of them and I'm quite comfortable with them. I don't know if I'd like to spend my whole life with them, but that's my right. I can pick and choose whom I want to be with. We have a free country. Right?''

"Yes," said Carla, "I guess you do. But to some of us Europeans that sort of separation seems strange. We have *class* separations, you know, people you don't see because they are lower-class or crude and vulgar, but not just because they're *Jewish*. Of course, Jews are different. But we are *used* to them. They've been in Italy for a thousand years. Now, your Italians here in America, that's quite another matter!''

"How?" said Marge.

"Because most of the ones I have met, their parents came from the south, down in Calabria or Sicily. When they try to speak Italian—and the last Italian they heard was probably from their grandparents or parents—it's absolutely atrocious, like illiterates. Now, with them, I would have troubles, just instinctive troubles.''

"You see," said Marge, "everyone gets laid differently. Whoopee!" She raised her finger and made circles, like a kid twirling a rattle. She was beginning to feel her cognac. "I notice our Charly has been very quiet during all this." She patted Dorn's hand, as if to assure him that she understood his silence.

"What do you want me to say?" He shrugged. "Obviously I come from a country that was terrible to the Jews. Obviously I know about it. But that doesn't mean I feel that way now. Or even that I felt that way then. Don't be angry at me, but I just can't discuss it. Darling Marge, I think you are, as we say, *prima*. First-class. But there is a lot you can't know about me.''

"True!" Marge agreed.

"And Carla," said Dorn, "we have only just met."

Carla nodded. She knew they were on dangerous ground. She raised her glass. *"Cin-cin!"*

"You two characters must excuse me," said Marge. "I'm off for fun and games with the locals."

"Locals?" Carla asked. Dorn did not have to ask. He could guess where his hostess was going.

Marge, straightforward as ever, explained to Carla, "A

little kid I saw parking cars at Mon Plaisir. Great bod! We've got a late date at a joint on Montauk Highway.''

Dorn said, ''Shall I drive you?''

''Hell, no. Casey knows the place, and he sure as hell knows me!'' She waved and walked off, looking like a bouncy blond balloon in a Paris gown.

Dorn and Carla were left sitting alone at the pool. He asked, ''Another drink?'' Carla's glass was empty, but she shook her head.

''Marge is so nice,'' said Carla, ''and she is so *generosa* about people.''

''Yes. She is very kind, if you overlook that Jewish business. Very American, that. Hard to understand. Sometimes America is not at all like the place I expected. I remember how we used to feel about Americans when I was a kid in Berlin.''

''How?''

''We thought they were all glamorous, exciting, full of adventure, and rich, always rich. We loved their jazz and all their dances like the foxtrot and two-step. In the Eden Hotel in Berlin there was a jazz band, all Germans, but they only played American *Schlager*, hit tunes.''

Carla nodded. ''*Vero!* And the films. Robert Taylor and Clark Gable and Tyrone Power.'' She pronounced it *Teerhone*.

She stretched out, lolling back in her chair, long legs extended and crossed at the ankles and hands folded behind her head. He could see the nipples of her breasts touching the silk, not like American girls with their padded bras.

She shrugged away a little shudder. ''It's getting cool. Can we move inside?''

They settled into two flower-printed, upholstered armchairs in the living room, and now Carla wanted a brandy, which he poured. Vivier came in to ask if they needed him, and when they said ''no, thanks'' he excused himself. It was nearly midnight by Dorn's old wristwatch, which had gone through the desert campaign and prisoner-of-war camp and was still true as ever. Carla, completely at ease, cradled the little brandy snifter in her cupped hands and looked at the ceiling, deep in thought.

Fantastisches Mädchen! Dorn did not want her to speak. He just wanted to look at her.

''Charly.'' She startled him, having caught him in mid-inspection. She grinned. ''Stop staring like some *paparazzo*.''

"What's a *paparazzo?*"

"They're a new kind of *creatura* we now have in Rome, photographers who came with the new film business at Cinecitta. *Ecco,* they stare and wait until one bends over or shows too much décolletage. Then they go click-click and take a picture, particularly if one has a name people know. They sell the photographs to the cheap newspapers. Last month that happened to me."

"How?"

"There was a photograph of me on a front page with my left bosom exposed."

"You did it on purpose."

"Idiot!" She laughed and balled up a paper napkin, which she threw at him. "Don't be *pazzo!* That *paparazzo* was somewhere in a building over me, photographing a restaurant where a bunch of us were having *gelati* on Via Veneto. You know Rome, don't you?"

"I was there once, just before the war."

"Do you have any friends there?"

"Used to. A man called Navone. The Marchese di Navone."

"Oh, we know the Navones. Friends of my parents. One of them was killed in Africa. He was the same age as my brothers."

"That's the one I knew."

"What a coincidence. How did you meet?"

"Long story. Someday I'll tell you. Not now."

"Of course."

"For now, how about another conversation?"

"*Come?*"

"About men and women and what they find sexy about each other."

"That's a good subject. But not now." She mimicked his German accent.

She stood up, walked over to his armchair, quickly kissed his forehead, and turned to go. Over her shoulder she said, "*Ciao.*"

Sunday morning, Dorn rose early because he wanted to show off the 190R once more at Bridgehampton. He dusted it off and warmed up the engine, which, fortunately, purred smoothly, unlike a Ferrari or a Jaguar, which would have awakened the household. In the distance he could hear racing engines on Montauk Highway, cars on their way to the track. It was an exciting sound. The morning of an automobile race was always electric, no matter if it was an international grand prix or a local sports car event.

Paul Stern, Brunzig's director of public relations, had left two pit passes for him in the glove compartment of the 190R, cards in plastic containers with pinbacks. Dorn stuck one on his sweater, because there was no other way to get past the usual cordon of state police, local cops, and volunteer firemen who always guarded the pit area with the fury of troops preventing a riot. He was used to it. He had been shoved around at many races: by the *gendarmes* at Le Mans, the *carabinieri* at Monza, and the *Verkehrspolizei* at Nürburgring. Somehow, automobile racing brought out the beast in local policemen, probably because the deification of reckless drivers shattered their basic beliefs.

Earlier that year, at a race in Mexico, England's champion race driver had to beg on bended knee to be readmitted to the pits, because he had forgotten his credentials. The *Federales* almost threw him in the clink. He tried to explain that he had left the pits, as he tersely put it, to avoid "committing a blunder of the bladder." *Dorn admired English humor. During the Africa campaign, near Kasserine, an R.A.F. Hurricane fighter crash-landed in a huge cloud of sparks and dust with the screech of tearing metal. When the plane finally ground to a halt, the pilot hoisted himself out of the cockpit, his face bloody and one broken arm hanging straight down. He then limped up to Dorn and some other* Panzer *officers who had watched the whole horrifying sequence, saluted with his good arm, grinned through broken, bloodied teeth, and said, "I say, chaps, is there a local Lloyd's office? I seem to have bent an aircraft." They took the man prisoner and then poured him several tall glasses of (captured) whisky.*

Vivier loomed in the doorway. "*Bonjour*, Monsieur Dorn. *Du mauvais temps?*"

"No, Vivier. I don't think it will rain." But the Haitian's instincts were right, because heavy clouds were rolling in from the west and the breeze had picked up. Then Vivier gestured him back into the house for breakfast in the small, low-ceilinged dining room.

"A boiled egg, please?"

"*Oui, monsieur. Du café?* Toast?"

"Parfait."

Carla came in. She looked scrubbed and brushed. Her face was without makeup, and a few drops of water from her shower were still in her eyelashes and on her forehead, like dewdrops. She wore a boy's shirt in pink cotton, tucked into slim maroon corduroy slacks, and there were tan suede moccasins on her feet. She was obviously glad to see him.

"Can I come to the race with you? I promise I shall not be a nuisance."

"Of course! *Certamente!*" He was delighted. This was a bonus he had not anticipated. "How could you be a nuisance? You've probably been to every big race in Italy."

"*Naturalmente!* With my brothers. I was usually on their crew until my father dissolved the *Scuderia* Roselli. One day, after a friend of Paolo's got killed at Monza, Papa told us *basta,* and the boys moaned and groaned. You know Italian men and their sports cars. Now, the only thing they do is to waterski with our Riva. And also a few *indoor* sports." She arched her eyebrows until her eyes looked innocent, round as saucers.

He nodded, grinning.

Because of the darkening sky, they put up the 190R's convertible top. She was very capable and helped him without a hitch. They left a note for Marge, who was still sleeping. It must have been a very late evening, because Casey was still asleep and he was usually up before anyone, washing the cars.

"Vivier, we'll be at the races, and we'll call later. Will madame be joining us?"

Vivier's large eyes were noncommittal. "I don't know, monsieur."

The first raindrops fell as they turned onto Montauk Highway, and from then on there was a constant drizzle.

Despite the wet weather, the 190R was the focus of attention amid the dozens of sports cars going their way. They were stared at by curious drivers until they got to the barrier near the village of Bridgehampton which said "Pits" and which was manned by a giant local cop. They showed their badges and were waved through while the other cars had to creep toward assigned public parking lots through a swarm of pedestrians.

The rain had changed the pits since Saturday. Tarpaulins

covered spare parts and tires. Tents had been erected for the crews, and race cars stood in the drizzle with tonneau covers in place. It was a dismal scene. Everything about Bridge-hampton said "beach resort," and what is more baleful than a beach resort when it rains? Dorn drove slowly, waved on by men in wet raincoats with "Steward" armbands, until he was hailed by someone in a green Brunzig touring coupe, which was parked under an enormous oak tree. It was Paul Stern. He got out of his car and waited, hands stuck deep into his old-fashioned Burberry trenchcoat, his gray hair hidden under an old tweed cap.

Stern said, "Charly, boy, I knew I couldn't trust you, you bastard. How the hell are you going to sell any 190Rs in this stuff?" He held up his hands in the drizzle. He spoke perfect American slang with a residual German inflection.

"*Na, ja,*" said Dorn, "the cars are already sold. I sold three yesterday and that's all we can get next month anyway. Now, can I introduce you to this lady? Signorina Carla Roselli. She's a visitor from Milano."

Stern made a short, Germanic bow, brought on by the presence of a European woman. "*Piacere . . .*" he said, ever the internationalist.

"Thanks for the pit passes," said Dorn.

"Would I forget my favorite *AfrikaKorps Lantzer?*" said Stern.

"*Du Arschloch,*" said Dorn with good humor. They were both Berliners, and they often exchanged cheerful Spree River vulgarities.

A girl emerged from the touring Brunzig, very young, with a freckled nose and sun-streaked blond hair. She looked like a college kid, but Stern introduced her as "Nellie, who brought me ham and eggs this morning at the Alhambra Coffee Shop in Hampton Bays." Stern was usually inclined toward waitresses, manicurists, and hatcheck girls, whom he could cover with gentle insult without any fear of being understood and, therefore, resented. Stern's girls were interchangeable. Dorn accepted the introduction and promptly discarded her name. He would probably never see her again after this day. Carla also got the drift of the relationship. She gave out a thin smile of acknowledgment, not of acceptance.

"Snob!" Dorn whispered to her.

"*Assolutamente!*" Carla agreed.

Ten minutes later the road was closed for racing practice, and the first cars began to lap around the three miles of interconnected roads that comprised the temporary racetrack. They howled past, in thick clouds of spray, their wheels throwing up fountains of water. Simms, whose pit was nearby, made a hasty stop, and they could hear his angry voice complaining about his tires.

Al Perrin's Bentley was parked under a nearby tree. He waved at Dorn. "Tomorrow?"

Dorn nodded.

"Right here at ten?"

Dorn signaled okay by making the American-style "O" with thumb and forefinger.

Stern asked, "Is that one of your customers?"

"Yes. Al Perrin and two of his friends."

"I know who Perrin is" said Stern. "Mighty rich fellow. You're a good man, *Hauptmann* Dorn!"

Dorn, who had not heard his old army rank for a while, grinned and extended his center finger in the old Italian-American gesture, which Carla saw. She grinned and shook her head. A half hour later practice stopped temporarily and Stern said, "Let's get out of here. I spoke to all my press contacts. We'll have a drink in East Hampton."

Stern was a naturalized American. He looked like an ex-U-boat commander, but he was half Jewish and had come to America as a refugee. Before Pearl Harbor he worked as a young press agent in Hollywood and New York. Then he joined the United States Army. He knew his way around the celebrity circuit and made full use of his open-sesame expense account. He got along well with the Germans who ran Brunzig in New York, and he insisted on speaking Berlin-broadened German to them, although they, like Dorn, had fallen into the everyday habit of English. Stern's devastatingly Teutonic appearance appealed to New York foreign car fans.

In the late 1930s, when Stern was part of Austro-German-refugee Hollywood, many famous exiles worked in movies and conducted a raucous marathon kaffeklatsch under the palms alongside their employers' swimming pools. The old Hollywood bunch, who all knew his part-Jewish background, had taken to calling him "von" Stern to his face.

Stern was the perfect spokesman for Brunzig. Even those

who had known him for years sometimes forgot that he was the grandson of a rabbi from Breslau. Dorn and he shared a bottomless well of pornographic German limericklike poems, and they could also exchange the punch lines of Berlin stories so hoary, that it was no longer necessary to tell them. The punch lines would do. Like the Hollywood crowd, Dorn sometimes called him "von" Stern.

Stern held no malice. Unlike other refugees, he found it easy to work with Germans of the Nazi era. When he was an American soldier during the war, he had made up his mind that German girls were attractive, that German was his mother tongue, and that German humor was still familiar. Besides, what remained of the German *Wehrmacht* was pitiful—with the exception of the SS.

Stern served as an interrogator, a staff sergeant, with an infantry company. He received a light shrapnel wound near Augsburg, recuperated in Bavaria, and then returned to the United States as soon as his Purple Heart and three battle stars gave him enough points, the system through which soldiers got home.

He returned to America with some regrets. He was aware that it was his new home, but he would miss German girls and German wit (even Bavarian wit!), and he loved the special status of the American soldier who spoke German and could think as a German. Defeated Munich, where he spent the last months of his convalescence, was filled with Berliners who had run away from the Russians and toward the Americans. Most of Germany's old movie industry was there—actresses, directors, writers—and the Geiselgasteig Film Studios were about to reopen. There were endless parties, with biting postmortem humor about the Nazi years. Munich's top people tried frantically to please Americans, even lowly sergeants like Paul Stern. Villas were reopened, dinner tables were set with black-market food, business deals were initiated, and some film production had begun.

Several of Munich's movie people knew that Stern had worked in Hollywood, so they cultivated him for future use. One of them, an old friend of Brunzig's chairman, recommended Stern to him. (As Stern had said to Dorn, "After all, didn't I help you to get the son of a bitch's house back for him? And didn't I lay his ugly mistress? And wasn't that enough reason for him to tell Brunzig that I was absolutely brilliant?'')

Dorn began to follow Stern toward East Hampton, but first he stopped at a gas station and called Marge Allery. Cheerful as ever, she told him that she'd be "busy through dinner," which meant that her little car jockey was there. Dorn said he'd call later in case she might want to join them.

"Not likely," she giggled and hung up.

He and Carla continued along Montauk Highway to East Hampton, the most distant of the Hamptons, and the most beautiful. They pulled into the parking lot of the Sea Spray Inn, a low wooden hotel right on the fog-shrouded beach. The inn's bar had just opened, and it was already crowded with people consoling themselves for the bad weather. They were a boisterous young crowd, the handsome sons and daughters from local estates mixed with lifeguards, carpenters, gardeners, and electricians. Their mood was infectious, and soon Dorn, Carla, Paul Stern, and his girl found themselves part of this laughing, loud-voiced group.

A pretty brunette asked Dorn, "Great accent you got. Swedish?''

"German.''

"German? Kraut? That's what my dad calls 'em, 'Kraut.' He was in the war." The girl looked eighteen, which made her three years old when the war started in Europe.

"Kraut. That's okay," said Dorn, smiling at the term he had not heard since P.O.W. camp. *You fuckin' Krauts! Get your fuckin' Kraut asses moving!*

"Is it a nasty word?" she asked. "What does it mean, anyway?''

"Cabbage. Like in sauerkraut. We Germans are all supposed to eat a lot of sauerkraut.''

"Don't you?''

"No. I hate it.''

Carla had stayed close to Dorn, taken aback by the cheerful aggressiveness of these young Americans. He knew exactly how she felt. Upper-class central Europeans were slow to loosen up with strangers. He took her hand and squeezed it to reassure her, and she returned his grip and looked into his eyes to smile her thanks. Her hand was strong and dry, and he thought it felt very good in his. She pulled Dorn away.

Paul Stern followed them, his blond girlfriend in his wake, like a yacht towing a dinghy. "I'm off to New York, *Herr Sales Director!*" he said as they left.

Dorn and Carla had lunch at Marge's house. It was still raining. Marge was nowhere in sight, and they thought it better not to ask for her.

Afterward, they walked on the beach, like two people in a cloud, because the mist made a half-dome around them, fifty yards along the shore in each direction, up to the dunes and a little way out to the flat gray sea and twenty yards overhead. They were wrapped in a cool cocoon, not at all unpleasant, accompanied only by sea gulls and terns. They picked up shells, from tiny pink scallops to the football-sized armorplate of horseshoe crabs, and Dorn skimmed flat pebbles three or four bounces and, if the waves were right, five. They borrowed bicycles from Marge's garage, rode the lanes through the fields, and, finally, returned for dinner, still alone, Marge still incommunicada.

For dinner, Vivier served them ceremoniously in the dining room. They had a sort of Caribbean bouillabaisse made of local fish.

Carla raised her glass of wine. "A German. Papa would not have believed it!"

"What's wrong with Germans?" He touched his glass to hers, and they drank.

"We used to hate them."

"Why not?" said Dorn. "It seems everyone else did."

"I was only fifteen when things really went wrong, when Mussolini, the *Duce,* was arrested, when the SS took him to Germany."

"I had forgotten," said Dorn. "They rescued him and flew him to meet the *Führer.*" *He remembered: SS Colonel Telesty, the huge Austrian who had snatched Mussolini from a mountaintop where he was held by Italian Partigiani.* He laughed.

She asked, "What are you laughing about?"

"About the SS officer who grabbed your precious *Duce* and flew him to Germany."

"What's so funny about him?"

"The colonel's now one of our biggest Brunzig distributors. He has all of South America, and he's making a fortune."

"Sad."

"Why? He did his job, that's all."

"Do you really believe that?"

"Yes and no. I doubt if he had any deep political convictions. He was an opportunist."

"But he was in the SS. . . ."

"In the *Waffen*-SS. They were like soldiers, mostly."

"You mean he was not a Nazi?"

"Some were, some were not. I knew Telesty quite well. I doubt if he was politically involved. He was just ambitious. A lot of people joined the SS only because it was prestigious."

"Carlo, tell me. *Veramente*. Were you a Nazi?"

He liked her calling him Carlo instead of Charly.

"We haven't talked politics. Why start now?"

"Because we are here in America. Because I like it here. Because I like you. Because sooner or later, as an Italian, I always have to ask my *own* questions."

Dorn knew she was right. He asked, "Were your brothers in the *Ballila*?"

"Yes. They were in the Fascist Youth Movement like all kids."

"Well, then, in *that* sense, I suppose I was a Nazi. But not the way they see it here. To Americans every German who did his job and was loyal to his government was just like Joseph Goebbels. I did what it was my job to do. I never harmed anyone. I never sent anyone to a concentration camp. I worked for Brunzig. Then I joined the army. Then I was taken prisoner and sent to America. *Basta!*" *He remembered the word. How many Italian P.O.W.s had used it that incredible week in Bizerta, when there were hundreds of thousands of them, Germans and Italians, all prisoners. Basta. Done. Over with.*

"What," said Carla, "about the officers who tried to do away with Hitler? What about them?"

"Many were wonderful men. Some were opportunists. Maybe they were just fed up with the way Hitler ran the war and wanted to stop things before Germany was destroyed. Who knows? I was very close to some of them. There were some famous old family names among them. Anyway, I was a P.O.W. before the assassination attempt in 1944. I only got closely involved with it once, for a little while."

"How?"

"Someday, when we know each other longer, I'll tell you

much more about my years before the war. But not now. It wouldn't be fair to you.''

"Not fair to me?'' She was puzzled.

"Please, let it go at that.'' He changed the subject. "You never told me what you disliked about Germans.''

She said nothing for some time, staring out at the wet, dark garden. Then she began: "My brothers were pilots. After Mussolini was kicked out, they were ordered by the Italian High Command to surrender to the English. My mother and I were at home in Como. The Germans came to our villa, told us that we were under arrest because my brothers were traitors. They were very insulting. They said they were coming to take over the villa the following day and that we were to be packed and ready.''

"What sort of Germans? Army?''

"No, SS. Some sort of staff people from Milan. Anyway, that night our old gardener took us to his village in the mountains, and the villagers hid us until the Allies took Como. The SS beat our stable boy until he was crippled, but he wouldn't tell them where we had gone.''

"No reason to hate all Germans, just because of a group of miserable SS people?''

"No. It was more. Most of us thought that Germany had pushed the *Duce* into the war. Everything was fine until the *Duce* went to Munich in 1937. The government people wanted Papa to go with them, but he said he was ill.'' Carla paused to light a cigarette, then she continued. "When the *Duce* came back to Rome, everyone said he had sold his soul. Then Hitler came to Rome. My brother Umberto was part of the escort party because Prince Colonna, the governor, ordered it. Umberto was horrified. He said the Germans would have us in war up to our necks. He was right. At first, the Germans who came to Italy were very polite. But after the war started, they got more and more arrogant. We would see them at parties everywhere. Some German officers even had a fist fight with my brothers because they said Italians let them down in Africa.''

Dorn asked, "And the *Duce?* Wasn't he aware?''

She shook her head. "He was vain. He was deluded!''

Dorn reached for her hand and she gave it to him. "Your family,'' he said, "they seem to have come through it all right.''

"All right?" She shrugged. "My cousin Giulietta, she was married to the Forlaris, an old Florentine Jewish family. They were all killed at Belsen; so was she."

"Your brothers," said Dorn, "they now seem very happy and well?"

"Yes. After they worked with their hands, right alongside their men, to rebuild the factories. Sure they're playboys. They're Italians. . . ." She smiled. "But they slaved to get back their position. And now they are going to have a strike. What an injustice! Without my brothers those workers would have no jobs. . . . Depressing! Carlo, I'm getting sleepy. Please excuse me." She gave him a hug and left.

Something awakened him. He looked at his wristwatch on the table next to the bed. One A.M.! When he fell asleep, a steady drizzle still brushed against the window. Now it had stopped and the deep dark of the room had given way to patches of moonlight; perhaps these things had nudged him awake. He tried to ease himself back into sleep, but he soon gave up, because he was fully awake.

He put on his robe, lighted a cigarette, and walked through the dark living room, opened the door to the outside and sat down on a garden chair after wiping away some rainwater with the edge of his hand. There was a massive concert of crickets, almost overwhelming after the silence inside the house, which was still shuttered against the rain of the night before. Then, after a few minutes, the chirping toned itself down and blended into the other sounds of the night, along with the wind in the branches of the elms overhead and the permanent surf to the south. The dark sky was clear of clouds, and overhead were those same stars he had always known. Berlin, Africa, New Mexico, New York—the stars never changed.

Did he finally feel at home here? Yes. Like Germany? No. But then, perhaps *that* Germany he had known was no more. The words of the *Deutschlandlied* came to him: *Deutschland, Deutschland über Alles. . . !''* "Germany, Germany above all others!" What an arrogant song. (A Berlin cabaret comic once suggested, *"Deutschland, Deutschland, nebenbei auch."* Germany, Germany among others.) And yet, being German *was* special—capable, dependable, skilled, involved. In so many ways Germans could be thankful for being Germans, and yet they were so often despised. Like—the Jews? Could one make that comparison?

Nazis had always focused on Jewish ugliness—bulging lips, hooked nose, kinky hair, sallow jowls, fat belly. Yet none of the Jews he had known fit this parody.

Germans always fancied themselves as tall, blond, blue-eyed, Nordic, handsome, but neither was this the truth. Germans looked like everyone else. So did Jews. Still, many American films portrayed the fat-necked, bull-faced, shaven-headed German. That, too, was a sham!

Eight years since the Nürnberg trials, and here, in the middle of Southampton, all this anti-Semitism! *Had these Americans learned nothing? Did Hilde die for nothing, and all the other Berliners who had risked their necks for the Jews at the very end in forty-five?* So many people here tried to make him feel guilty for being German. Or perhaps they did not even have to try! Perhaps he actually felt guilty. Dammit, these *Scheiss*-Americans hated Jews as much as the Nazis did. Hypocrites! He'd bring up the subject with Stern, the big expert on America. What was his explanation for all this? *Na, ja,* Stern should have some interesting answers!

He could hear the drone of a plane overhead, four engines, the same sound as a big bomber. Then he saw it, tiny lights blinking, very high and heading east-northeast, following the Long Island coastline, probably on its way to Europe. Long Island pointed straight at Europe. In Southampton he was 160 kilometers closer to England, to Berlin, to Rome.

Was Carla sleeping?

He had a fantasy: If he went back to his room, she would be there, in his bed waiting for him, as hungry for him as he was for her. He could still feel her hand in his. And he knew, absolutely knew, what her body would feel like: dry, warm, strong. He thought of her hand on him, everywhere—stomach, buttocks, groin—and it excited him. The mood came to him to make love to himself, as soldiers had done always, as prisoners do, to prove that they are alive, ejaculating life. He looked around to see if he was alone. He was not. Carla stood a few yards behind him.

She wore a white robe, cut like a man's, its collar up, her hands deep in the pockets. He started to stand up, but she gestured for him to stay seated and she quickly wiped off the chair next to his.

"I cannot sleep," she said.

He nodded. "I know how you feel. I woke up and that was that."

"Beautiful." She pointed at the stars.

"Beautiful," he said, looking at her. "Very beautiful."

She was pleased that he meant her, and she reached for his hand and carried it to her lap, where he could feel a thigh through the soft silk robe. He turned his hand onto the curve of her leg until her muscle tensed. She leaned forward, her face in front of his, and put her lips onto his. Her mouth was warm and generous, and she used her strong, probing tongue. There was no hesitation in the way she kissed him, no doubt, no question.

He reached for her breasts under the robe and touched her nipples, which rose like sweet, strong knots. She breathed quickly now, and they both knew their way. Linked closely, arms binding them together, they walked back to the house and into his room, where they lay down on the bed and she shrugged off her robe and he shed his. He kissed her everywhere and kept from entering her, postponing that moment until she begged, demanded, *"Prego, prego, amore!"*

Then they made love, gently, sometimes not moving at all, feeling only the pulse and the contraction where they were most closely linked. They came to climax together, exactly together, and they spent the rest of the night in each other's arms.

On Monday morning, Perrin and his friends drove the 190R and were ecstatic.

What handling! What acceleration! What braking! What quality!

Dorn left them at noon, returned to Marge's house, and packed his gear. He gave Vivier fifty dollars. The exchange of money was smooth and dignified. The tip was slipped into Vivier's enormous hand, whence it wandered into a pocket of his vast burnoose. The mumbled *"Merci, infiniment!"* could barely be heard.

Marge was finally awake and alone. "Charly, you bastard, why can't you stay the week? Or should I send you Carla? Casey can bring her tomorrow." Marge was aware that her guests had become lovers, and she was enormously pleased.

"Could you? If Carla wants to . . . ?"

"Of course. She can stay at the maisonette." Marge owned a four-story, street-entrance apartment at Park and Seventieth Street, ten bedrooms and even a small ballroom. There she had brought up four husbands and six children, not to mention a platoon of lovers.

Carla was enthusiastic about the plan, and agreed to meet Dorn at Marge's apartment the next day. As he drove into Manhattan, he picked up a short race with an open Cadillac on Northern Boulevard. The 190R easily outpaced the battleship-sized car, but both drivers enjoyed their joust. Americans, all in all, were good road drivers, not as erratic and jerky as most Germans. Germans did everything with convulsive urgency. Passing through a crowd, crossing a street, getting into a bus, Germans moved with angular haste.

When Dorn reached New York, he drove the car to the Brunzig showroom, where he put it into the care of old Zummer, a mechanic he had known since their days at the Berghof.

After handing over the 190R, Dorn walked into Stern's office over the showroom and told him about the test drives that morning.

"Looks as if 190R is our new *Wunderkind*."

"Yes," Stern agreed, beetling his brows. "We've struck again! Today New York, tomorrow the world!"

"*Arschloch!*" said Dorn, laughing. He went into his own office to fill out the order forms. He could place bets that he would not lose a single sale. Not with Brunzig, not with the 190R. Then he called Stern. "How about dinner?"

"Great."

"Al Schacht's? Steaks?"

"Perfect."

Dorn went home to shower.

Stern was prompt. Al Schacht, a former baseball star, ran what they called a sportsman's restaurant, its wooden walls covered with photos of sportspersons, catering to that mixture of horse, boxing, baseball, and football fans found in New York. It was crowded and noisy. Neither of them was hungry, so they drank for a while: martinis for Dorn, Scotch and soda for Stern.

After his second martini, Dorn said, "Paul, yesterday in Southampton I met some nice, normal people from California, obviously quite wealthy. They made a tough anti-Jewish remark, and nobody said a word about it.''

Stern slowly drank his whisky. He looked down at the glass on the table between his two hands and said nothing.

Dorn continued, ''First I thought that, because I am German, certain Americans want to somehow *please* me in some crazy way by saying these things about Jews. But even when no one *knows* I'm German, I hear anti-Jewish stuff.''

Still no response from Stern, who waved at the waiter for another drink.

''In Germany today,'' said Dorn to finish his point, ''you can go to jail for an anti-Jewish remark made in public.''

Then Stern reacted. He was furious.

''So you didn't know?'' he said. ''Come on! You can't be that naïve! You didn't know that here we are in the nineteen fifties and that most good apartment houses on Fifth and on Park won't rent to Jews? That the best clubs bar Jews from membership? That most good private schools have quotas for Jews? This fucking country of ours is riddled with anti-Semitism. In New York it's not so bad. There are millions of Jews here. But outside?'' Stern shook his fist and his head. ''Americans are like everyone else. They love to have someone to kick around. Look at our Negroes, and how we treated the Japanese Nisei out West when the war broke out. What's more . . .'' He was red-faced. ''I'm as guilty as everyone else. I make cracks about 'spades' and 'guineas'!''

Dorn, taken aback by Stern's violent response, said lamely, ''Even after everything that happened? After the Nürnberg trials?''

''Yes, even after what happened.'' Stern looked him straight in the eyes. ''You and I, we know a bit about human nature, don't we?'' He grabbed Dorn's forearm and said slowly, ''But there's one difference in America, one super-fucking important difference, my friend: Kicking around Jews or Negroes or anyone else is not licensed by the law! *It's not government policy!* In Nazi Germany it was the law, *Stimmts?*''

''*Stimmt.* You're right,'' said Dorn. ''It was the law.'' Then he shrugged. ''Look, I should admit something to you: I keep on hearing about all the sins that were committed in the National Socialist days. I admit that they were terrible, but it hurts to think that it all happened. And so, sometimes I try to get my own back. . . ." He stuck out his right hand. "I'm sorry, Paul. Forgive me!"

Paul Stern looked at the man in front of him and felt no anger. He always found it impossible to hate Germans like Dorn. He shook his hand and said, *"Genug, schon!"*

Then they ordered dinner.

Stern had put his finger on the vital difference, Dorn realized. More than ever, he now knew he wanted to stay in America. When he got home, he called Carla in Southampton and told her of the conversation. *"Assolutamente,"* she said. "Of course, that's the difference! Your friend Stern is so right. That's what happened with us. Every Italian is a little *pazzo*, crazy. But when the *Duce* made it the *law* to behave like you are crazy, that's when everything went wrong." Her voice softened. "I miss you, *amore!*"

"Tomorrow night?"

"Domani!"

Brunzig, *Hubertus Brunzig A.G.* of Stuttgart, was the oldest automobile manufacturer in Europe. Perversely, in the depth of Germany's depression, Brunzigs, driven by amateurs, began to win international races, and soon the vast two-seater Brunzig supercharged tourers became fashionable on the Riviera, in Hollywood, London, and Paris.

In 1933, Adolf Hitler personally propelled Brunzig beyond any competitor in Germany. The *Führer* decreed that all his personal and staff cars would be Brunzigs. Many of the tens of thousands of photos and films of the new Reichs Chancellor were also photos of his Brunzigs: black, open eight-seaters.

Brunzig's first postwar chief in the United States was Helmuth Erdmann, an elegant Stuttgart veteran. He was shy, white-haired, of medium height. He stayed behind the scenes, commuting to Germany monthly. His superiors knew that breaching the American market was a delicate task.

Dorn had just arrived in his office when the phone rang. German firms begin early. It was eight-thirty.

"Herr Dorn?" Dr. Erdmann's secretary was an old spinster he had brought over from Stuttgart, who maintained all office formalities. Although she was bilingual, she usually spoke German to the German staff members.

"Jawoll!" said Dorn, snapping it out Berlin-style.

"Can you please come to see Dr. Erdmann at your earliest convenience?"

"How about now?"

"Excellent," said the secretary.

Dorn had a small office, decorated by a German design firm that did the interiors of all Brunzig offices. It was Italianesque: shiny black leather upholstery, steel-gray carpet, chrome and black glass desk, and white ceramic tile walls. Contrasting with these stark colors, there was a bright yellow desk lamp, a red phone, and a large red poster of the "Knight's Sword," the world famous Brunzig symbol that appeared on every radiator, engine, steering wheel, and hubcap.

By contrast, Dr. Erdmann's office seemed to have been transported intact from Stuttgart. Soft upholstered chairs and couches in brown leather clustered around a low marble-topped coffee table on oriental rugs that were scattered over wall-to-wall beige carpeting. There was a heavy wooden desk facing an inside wall, but Dr. Erdmann did not believe in using it for anything but his paperwork. He preferred the informal mood around the coffee table, where he and Dorn now settled into armchairs, while Dorn told his chief about the 190R and Southampton.

"*Herr Doktor*, they loved it! I have never had such an easy presentation. It was what the Americans call 'duck soup.' "

" 'Duck soup?' *Entensuppe?* What a funny term," said Dr. Erdmann. "Why ducks?"

Dorn laughed. "I don't know, *Herr Doktor*. It's a gap in my American education."

"Anyway," said Dr. Erdmann, "I want to talk to you about some other 'duck soup.' You know I just got back from Stuttgart. There we had long meetings about our American business. It has grown tremendously, and we need a national sales manager for this country. They offered me a very experienced man from Stuttgart, but I told them to wait. I had another idea." Dr. Erdmann paused and cleared his throat. He was a shy man, worried that his proposal might not be acceptable to this nice fellow Dorn, but he plunged ahead. "I want *you* to take on running all our American sales. I think you would be very suitable."

Dorn was totally surprised. He had gone along doing his specialized sales work because he enjoyed it. It had not occurred to him to want more responsibility.

"At the risk of seeming to brag: Yes, I think I can do the job."

"Good." Dr. Erdmann was pleased and relieved. He was over this hurdle. At heart he was an engineer and hated human unaccountability. "I'll inform Stuttgart. They will come up with a new salary and other perquisites. I am sure you will find them generous. They usually are."

"I know," said Dorn. "I've been with Brunzig since thirty-six."

Dr. Erdmann tapped his forefinger to his head. "Of course. How stupid of me. I keep forgetting that you are an old Brunzig man. Forgive me."

Dorn smiled. He raised a hand—"*Bitte . . .*"—to forestall any further apologies. "One thing," he said, "which may or may not present a problem."

Dr. Erdmann waited.

"*Herr Doktor,* I served in the war. I lost my wife in a bombing. I was taken a prisoner. You know I did my duty as a German."

The older man nodded.

"Now," said Dorn, "I want to apply for American citizenship. It will still take five years, but I wanted to tell you now. Will that hinder your decision? Or Stuttgart's?"

Dr. Erdmann responded at once. "Absolutely not," he said. "Nor do I believe Stuttgart could object. There are many wonderful *Deutsh-Amerikaner*. It would make no difference to the company. I understand you completely. You know, when I was a young man—before I was married, long before the National Socialist time—I wanted to come here to America. I too would have become an American citizen. Now"—he shrugged—"it's too late." He smiled, and the meeting was over.

That afternoon, Dorn watched them unload the 900K, the great 1936 Brunzig Stuttgart had sent over to help promote the new 190R in the American market. The splendid old car had just arrived at the Brunzig service garage from the nearby docks. Now it was being uncrated by Zummer, the head mechanic. He pried away the planks with a crowbar. Then, with the care of a museum curator unpacking a priceless antique, he pulled off the blankets that covered the body.

Slowly, the majestic 900K convertible emerged. First there

was the endless hood, flanked by mighty, winglike fenders. On the right side were four gleaming outside exhaust tubes. Then came a low, slanted windshield, and a smooth convertible top that swept into the sloping, graceful rear deck with its twin spare wheels. Finally, when the lower boards were removed, there were the huge spoke-wire wheels shod in gleaming new black tires with their distinctive prewar tread. The body was all white, the wheels red.

The sheer size of the 900K was startling, because European cars had shrunk since the war. This classic Brunzig was even larger than modern American luxury convertibles. Dorn opened the heavy door and slid onto the soft red leather seat. His hands went to the familiar slim-rimmed wooden steering wheel, his eyes to the Knight's Sword on the horn button and then to the same symbol yards ahead on the chrome radiator cap. Everything was a memory, even the smell of the car. The mixture of leather and metal.

Oil, water, and gasoline were added. It was time to coax the big engine awake. With the wood-knobbed gear lever in neutral, Dorn turned the key, depressed the stiff old-fashioned accelerator, and pushed the starter button. The starter whined and the massive eight-cylinder engine found its heartbeat. Dorn stepped out of the car, walked around to its back, and listened as the exhaust sang its *basso profundo*. Out on the road this tune could change into a banshee scream when the supercharger button was engaged, but for now the car rumbled at rest, content, like a drowsing tiger.

Side by side in the Park Avenue showroom, the 900K and 190R would demonstrate brute old-fashioned force and modern streamlined technology. Brunzig had already shown both models in Zurich at the International Auto Exhibition and caused a sensation. Stern planned a press party where writers and photographers would have a field day.

It was a miracle that the old car was found. Stuttgart received an anonymous letter directing them to a hidden mountain cave, southeast of Munich near the Chiemsee Lake. They found the 900K, blocked from view, crated and in showroom condition, and they bought the car from the German government. A check of engine and chassis numbers soon revealed the last prewar owner: Nadia Sordan, Latvian film star of the National Socialist days, one of Dr. Goebbels's mistresses. The Reich's Propaganda Minister had gifted her

with the 900K. Brunzig's management decided to bury this
information. They disliked the freaks it might have attracted.

For Dorn everything had begun with a 900K in 1936, the
year of the Olympics in Berlin. He slid his hands along the
fenders, doors, and rear deck like a man patting a fine hunter.
Zummer attached dealer license plates to the front and back,
then looked at Dorn and gestured toward the car with his
head. *"Los,"* he said. "Get going."

The garage door slid open onto the empty side street. Dorn
got into the driver's seat, put the car into gear, and slowly
drove out. He aimed for the West Side Highway, where he
joined northbound traffic. The car settled into its narrow, stiff
gait, the vast engine barely turning at two thousand revolutions.
When he got to the Taconic Parkway, after rounding Haw-
thorne Circle, he dropped the car into third gear and kicked in
the supercharger. There was the great scream under the hood
and then the sudden acceleration, the kick-in-the-tail of 280
horses. He laughed out loud, he sang out loud. *"Das giebst
nur einmal, das kommt nicht wieder. . . ."* The kitschy old hit
song—"this feeling comes but once and never again. . . ."
Within seconds, the speedometer was at 150 kilometers an
hour and he lifted his foot, cut out the supercharger, slowed
down, and then shifted to high gear. Now the big car settled
down. Other drivers pulled alongside, stared, admired, gestured.
Dorn was used to driving unusual cars. The 190R fascinated
people, but nothing prepared him for the way people stared at
the classic 900K. Something about it, perhaps its sheer brut-
ish size or the deep roar of the engine, magnetized them.

Leaving the parkway, Dorn turned west toward the Hudson
River. Near Bear Mountain Bridge he turned off and drove
onto an empty parking lot overlooking the vast Hudson Valley below. He shut down the engine and leaned back, listening to the sounds of the mountains, the airplane high overhead
on its way into the city, the horn of a tug below on the river.
*It had been eighteen years since he saw the first 900K in front
of his apartment house in Berlin, eighteen years since Hilde
and he were newlyweds and lovers.*

Now that the pain was no longer fresh and life was not a
daily effort, Dorn had once more begun to feel whole. It was
in his nature to face each day with the best of expectations. It
was part of him to assume that patience and hard work were
restoratives. At last it had happened: a new job and, perhaps,

a new love. And then, in five years, he would have a new country.

He stayed there, quietly stretched out in the armchair depth of the driver's seat, quietly thinking, for some time. Afterward he drove the Brunzig back to New York, where Zummer anxiously sat waiting. The 900K was to be in the showroom on the following day. And shortly after that, Dorn was to be in Miami to meet the Brunzig racing team.

The noise of home-bound traffic outside on Park Avenue was muffled. Paul Stern sat in the dark showroom, alone with the Brunzig 900K. *Old friend,* thought Paul, *you and I go back a long way.* Of course, he did not mean this 900K. He meant all 900Ks.

The conversation with Dorn would not leave his mind. For the first time in years he thought back to the frightened, teenage Paul Stern he once was, how he quaked whenever marching columns of brown-shirted S.A. storm troopers bellowed their bloodthirsty songs while their boots crashed down in cadence.

Late in thirty-six, the Sterns finally left Berlin for America. Paul was fifteen, isolated from most of his friends by race, school, Hitler Youth membership. The tough and athletic small boy had become a frightened young man.

Was he really the inferior being *they* said he was? Was Jewish blood like a disease? Was his father second-rate, and had his Christian mother been sullied by giving birth to a halfbreed? He knew it had to be untrue, but then, truth was a vulnerable bulwark for his immature convictions. Nagging doubts were close to the surface, ready to emerge at the slightest signal.

To Jews, a Brunzig 900K had become such a signal. When a black, open, eight-seater pulled up to someone's house, it meant SS, Gestapo, *trouble.* To Paul it also meant: "What have we done wrong?" It took him years to overcome the boyhood assumption that there was something wrong with him.

Sometimes he thought that his mixed blood brought him special penalties, but many full-blooded Jewish boys he knew had this sense of guilt, as if they were to blame for their own troubles. Not so with Jews from Eastern Europe. Many people he met later in Hollywood, Jews from Poland, Lithuania,

Latvia, Hungary, Roumania, were different. Guilt? Hell, no! They felt superior. Anyone who was not Jewish had to be a shmuck or at least a bit slow on the uptake.

Eventually, Paul had decided that the seeming security of the "assimilated" German Jew had been the gap in his armor, the reason why the German Jew, and Paul himself, had been vulnerable. He could never again, he realized, devote himself completely to any one nation. He became a U.S. citizen and an American soldier, and thereby repaid the country that had given him refuge. Beneath his joviality, he was a wary man. Dorn's story of American anti-Semitism was no news to him. Americans could be prejudiced, race-conscious, and often unjust. But, *na, ja,* Americans could often be the most moral of people.

He went to the bar at the back of the showroom and poured himself a large shot of Scotch.

Then he raised the glass to the 900K and said, "Here's looking at you, kid." It was probably the worst Bogart imitation ever done. What's more, it was said with a Berlin accent.

The street lights outside on East Sixty-fifth Street sliced through the venetian blinds and painted a blue-white grid against the ceiling of Dorn's bedroom. It was late, but Carla was not ready for sleep; rather she was excited, elated to feel so much at home in this strange room and with the man lying in the bed.

After they had made love, he had fallen asleep, suddenly much younger-looking, almost helpless, his slim face nestled against his shoulder, one of his arms cradling a pillow. She sat at the foot of the bed, hugging her legs, her chin resting on her knees. She was nude, and their lovemaking had primed the scent of her perfume, so the room was filled with it.

She was riveted by his long body, the flat flanks, slim thighs, and runner's calves. Her eyes searched him, discovering new things: the tiny mole next to his navel, the scar over a shoulder blade, the drop of moisture in the corner of his mouth. His eyeballs moved under the closed lids. He was dreaming.

She stroked his penis and it rose, excited by her touch, and she wanted him once more but let him sleep. So she moved her hand onto herself and soon she came, a gentle orgasm, not like those they had shared earlier in the night.

This man would be hers, completely hers. He had to be. She would never again want another.

The clock on the night table showed five in the morning. She lay down next to him, and, through his deep sleep, he reached out and held her close to him.

Dorn was at the Miami airport waiting for the Brunzig racing team to arrive from Mexico, where they had been preparing for the Carrera Panamericana, the Mexican Road Race. He was taking them to Sebring, where they would check out the track before Brunzig entered the Twelve-Hour Sebring Race. The company believed in thorough preparation.

He spotted rotund "Papa" Hoegel, the Brunzig racing manager, and with him, three young fellows dressed in sport shirts and cotton slacks, like college boys on a vacation, loaded down with camera cases and cloth duffel bags.

Dorn and Papa went back many years. When Dorn first joined Brunzig, Hoegel was already a legendary figure. The great prewar racing stars at Brunzig cowered when they heard his voice, but blessed him for his attention to detail. The man had to be at least sixty-five, but he seemed unchanged. Hoegel introduced the others: one was Erich Feyl, Germany's best driver, the other two were engineers. They all got into Dorn's Brunzig sedan and aimed for Palm Beach, where they would spend the night. Soon it became clear that this was a new Papa Hoegel, no longer the booming-voiced disciplinarian of old. He coddled his young charges, particularly Feyl. What a contrast! Dorn could remember one evening before the war when a horny young Brunzig driving star was told by Hoegel, "Tonight you'll screw nothing but your bedsheets. You're racing tomorrow, and I don't want your *penis erectus* to get in the way of your steering wheel!" All this in Hoegel's booming voice in the crowded lobby of Monaco's Hotel de Paris. *That* was the Hoegel of old.

But with Feyl, he was totally solicitous. "Are you all right? Do you have enough room? Would you rather sit up front?" He had become "Grandpa" Hoegel.

They drove north along the ocean, past masses of gaudy hotels and motels, through Fort Lauderdale, and then finally into Palm Beach. There they checked into the Colony Hotel, still empty since it was before the season.

Hoegel, who had said little, had his bags sent straight to his room and aimed for the bar. His young charges put on their swimsuits and disappeared toward the beach, but Dorn joined Papa.

"*Na*, Dornchen, I'm happy to see you," said Papa, his vast hand descending on Dorn's shoulder blades. "I guess I was on my way to Tripoli the last time I saw you in Stuttgart. Must have been the last race before the shit."

"*Genau*," said Dorn, "you're right, the Tripoli Grand Prix. You know, I was there a few years later with Rommel. We had our own little race with the English and with the Americans. They won."

Papa nodded. He knew what Dorn meant. "By the way," he said, "I was sorry to hear about your wife. Knew her since she was a little girl. Terrible. Happened in Berlin, didn't it?"

"Yes." Dorn didn't feel like talking about it. He had forgotten that Papa, like Hilde, came from Nürnberg. He changed the subject. "Papa, *Alter Freund*, what's happened to you? You're so gentle."

"Gentle?"

"Yes, with that young Feyl boy. You treat him like he was a raw egg. I can remember when you used to chew up kids like that."

"*Na, ja*, things have changed," said Papa. "In the old days *we* decided who would drive for us and who wouldn't. When you drove for Brunzig, that was it! You were with the best team in the world. Today the others have the money. The Italians and the English can get any driver they want. We're not yet back in the big leagues, no grand prix races, only sports car stuff like Le Mans or Mexico or Sebring. Not great races, but these events are good for the sports car customer. After all, we want to sell cars."

"Didn't we also want to sell cars in the old days?" said Dorn.

"Cars? Did you say cars?" Papa's bulbous middle started to heave with guffaws, and he slapped his right knee as if he had just heard a great joke. "No. We were trying to sell *ourselves*. Besides, we were selling Germany! We didn't give a shit about selling cars. The factory was churning out stuff for the *Wehrmacht,* and we never cared much about export. We didn't have to.''

"I never knew much about it," said Dorn. "That's not what I was involved with.''

"I know what you were involved with," said Hoegel. "You were doing your job and enjoying it. Nobody thought we were doing anything wrong. And''—his huge face was sad and now much older—"I'm still not sure all of it was wrong.''

He stood up, suddenly tired, and a bit tipsy after only two drinks. "I think I'll go upstairs and take a nap before dinner. It's been a long trip from Mexico." Dorn signed the check.

After dinner Dorn and his colleagues walked along shop-lined Worth Avenue to the yacht docks and then back to the Colony. The young Germans were stunned by the opulence, the sheer wealth of Palm Beach. No one in Europe owned vast, fully staffed yachts, and few European resorts had shops like these. The war was still so close. . . . Then Papa and the two engineers went to bed. Feyl, the race driver, and Dorn stopped in Taboo, a bar on the Avenue.

Feyl was short and very slim. He had a slender face, with shy blue eyes under long lashes, a long straight nose, and soft blond hair that often fell over his eyes and grew over the back of his collar. His ears were very small, without lobes, and his cheeks barely showed any beard. His slim-fingered hands were strong, and he had a nervous habit of massaging his eyebrows and jaw. He looked unlike any race driver Dorn had ever seen, and yet, if Hoegel had hired him, Feyl had to be first class.

"How long have you been here in the States?" said Feyl.

"Three years. I was a prisoner of war here. I went back to Stuttgart when the war ended and they sent me to New York. I used to work for Brunzig before the army.''

"With the racing team?''

"Not directly. Why do you ask?''

"Because you knew Hoegel, and because you called him Papa. Everybody seemed to call him Papa in the old days.''

"Don't you?''

"No. We don't. Anyway, I really only met him last year, when I was driving for Porsche. He got me to join Brunzig.''

"You must have been pleased.''

"Why do you say that?"

"To drive for Brunzig . . ."

"*Na, ja*, that really didn't enter into it. It was frankly a matter of, well, *money*. Brunzig paid more." He brushed the long blond hair off his forehead.

Dorn found the answer annoying. He said, "Is it all only a question of money?"

Feyl shrugged again and said, "Not entirely. Money doesn't do much good if the cars are lousy. But their 190Rs are very solid machines. So I suppose it isn't *just* a question of money. Also, it looks like Porsche won't have Formula One cars, real racing machines, and that's what I really want. I think Brunzig will build them soon. This sports car shit is okay, but it's better for the factories than for the drivers."

"How do you figure that?"

"In sports cars we drivers get a little money, but the manufacturers get the prizes. In grand prix racing, the drivers make real money."

Dorn found it difficult not to show his annoyance with the young driver's attitude. No pride, no sense of accomplishment, only money. He looked at his watch and said, "We have to be up early to drive over to Sebring. Maybe we'd better break it up."

Feyl swiveled on his barstool until he faced Dorn. He said, "Look, don't shit me. I know what's on your mind. All of you old *Kerle* seem to have the same idea."

"Like what?

"Honor, country, Brunzig, *Deutschland, Deutschland über Alles*, that sort of thing." He spoke very quietly, like a man trying to explain a simple fact to a slow learner. "Let me tell you something, and perhaps you'll change your mind."

"You have my full attention," said Dorn, a bit sarcastically.

Feyl overlooked Dorn's tone. "First of all," he said, "and this is *not* for publication, my name is not Erich Feyl. My full name is Count Hans Edward Maria Erich von Feyl und Statten. I am only mentioning this to explain that there is a very old and broken-down family castle in Westphalia, which had the shit bombed out of it during the war and where there are now my parents and my grandparents and three uncles and two cousins—all with old titles—plus twelve old family servants. They live there on top of each other. Between them they don't have ten marks. First I sold off every square meter around the castle to industrial people and the local *nouveau riche*. That staved off disaster for a while. Then I started racing and became good at it, so as soon as possible, I did it for money. When Brunzig's offer came, I grabbed it. Every penny I make goes home to *Schloss* Statten.'' He stopped, obviously displeased by himself and Dorn for telling these confidences. He went on. ''As for patriotism and all that bunk, you don't know Germany today. People like me are getting kicked in the ass for things that were done when we were still kids. There isn't a foreign race team that will hire me. An English team wanted me, and their company directors turned me down. Can't blame them. Too many English towns were bombed. They bombed ours too, but *we* lost.'' He stopped, shaking his head.

Dorn took his time. Then he said, ''I'm sorry. I misunderstood. Don't blame me. It's hard for me to know your generation. We were so different.''

Feyl nodded. ''I know you were. That's the whole trouble. Take Hoegel—Papa, as you call him. He doesn't begin to understand me. He knows my full family name and he would love to use it if I let him. To him it would sound very aristocratic and *Treu Deutsch*, and he can just taste the publicity: 'Young German Count Wins Race!' So I try to tell him that's the last thing we need. That sort of shit got us into trouble last time. By the way, Hoegel doesn't know the whole story about my family, so I'd appreciate it if you shut up about it. I don't know why I told you in the first place, but you seem more human than the old fart, and at least you live here and can breathe some fresh air. In Germany we still have a whole older generation who never learned. They're as stuffy as ever!''

Dorn understood. ''Okay. Let's shake hands. And let's have another drink.''

Later, Dorn had trouble falling asleep. This was a new breed of German. He liked Feyl's honesty and straightforward way. He also understood the boy's anger for having to justify actions that were not of his doing. But then, were they of *Dorn's* doing? Or *Hoegel's*? What did Feyl say about *losing* the war being the problem? Perhaps it was true, but somehow he could not swallow that. The Nürnberg trials, Auschwitz, Dachau, and all the rest, the revelations of outrages that horrified him as they had to horrify anyone with an ounce of decency. How could they all have happened?

The next morning they drove to Sebring in the citrus belt of central Florida and Paul Stern flew there to meet them. The Twelve-Hour Race was held on an abandoned wartime airfield. Stern's chartered plane touched down on the track and taxied up to where Dorn, Hoegel, and Feyl stood in the glaring sun. Stern had brought three reporters and two photographers. From then on, their every moment was accompanied by the clicking of shutters. Feyl was the main target, and he answered all questions with the blasé calm of a professional. *Yes, he liked this track. Yes, it was easy compared to, say the Nürburgring or Monza because it was an airport. Yes, he had seen the back portion, and yes, that was more like a road track in Europe. No, he had not yet raced the 190R, but he had practiced in it.*

Then the questions hit closer. Did he feel he had a great tradition by being a German driver? *No, he was a race driver, like any other.* Did he know any of the famous old drivers? *He had met them, that's all. They were very nice to him.* Did he think German cars would again predominate? *If they were good, they would.*

Stern was delighted. Dorn was impressed. Hoegel was relieved. He was afraid that his new *Nummer Eins* would be pouty and sullen. But he was fine. Papa pulled Dorn aside and said, "You've got to be lucky. I thought the little shithead would screw up these interviews. In Germany he sometimes refused to talk to the press. But the goddam reporters love him anyway. How did it go last night? You had a drink with him. How did you like him?"

"I'll tell you later," said Dorn. He would have to be careful not to hurt the old man or to compromise Feyl, he realized. The reporters then descended on Papa, with Stern interpreting.

Soon it got boiling hot on the white runways and, after the engineers were through with all their measurements, they were eager to call it a day. Hoegel, Feyl, and the engineers took off for Miami in the sedan. They would then fly back to Stuttgart via the Bahamas. To Dorn's relief, there was no time to speak to Papa about Feyl.

Dorn and Stern and the five press people took the chartered

plane back to Palm Beach, where they boarded a commercial flight to New York. They settled down in the first-class lounge in back of the big droning four-engined plane and Stern ordered drinks. Pink and jade Grand Bahama Island was disappearing off to the east, and the evening sky was bright orange through the left-hand windows. Stern downed his Scotch and ordered another while Dorn sipped slowly. The stewardess who served them yawned. She was suntanned and very pretty, and she had obviously had a busy Florida stopover. Stern, perpetually horny, eyed her for a while, then turned his attention to Dorn.

"It was funny to meet Papa Hoegel."

"I thought you knew him."

"No," said Stern. "I've seen hundreds of pictures of him ever since I was a kid, but I never actually met him. He looks the same, but I have my doubts."

"About what?"

"About his future. I don't think he'll last."

"What makes you think so?" said Dorn. He had come to the same conclusion after that evening with Feyl.

"Well," said Stern, "the old guy just hasn't kept up. Take the press: Feyl was great. But when they wanted some comments from Papa, he sounded—I hate to say so—like an old press release from the Goebbels days."

"What did he say?"

Stern shrugged. "He spoke about 'the iron steeds' of Brunzig and 'the courageous young carriers of the Knight's Sword.' I had to squelch it. Fortunately, the reporters didn't speak German. He never knew I didn't translate. I edited."

Dorn shook his head. "Funny thing. Papa is the most straight-talking man with old friends. He probably would have given you a hell of an interview if we had all gotten drunk. I guess he just had too many years of the *Reichs Propagandaministerium*."

Stern took another long swallow as the plane began to bounce in some high clouds. He said, "Tell me, Charly, surely the Goebbels people didn't write Brunzig's press copy?"

"No, they didn't," said Dorn. "But the Goebbels *Scheisse* set the style for all German press writers. I ought to know. It was part of my job at the time. Later it came to haunt us in

Africa when we were getting the shit kicked out of us and we kept reading *Wehrmacht* communiques about our 'brilliant and heroic evacuations.' "

Carla returned to Milan at the end of that summer. She had found an attractive house in Southampton and a small brownstone on East Sixty-eighth Street in Manhattan, and she wanted to describe both to her brothers. She also planned to prepare her family for Dorn.

They could rent part of the town house if Carla's brothers agreed to buy it. Some Roselli money had stayed in Switzerland during the war, held in the usual privacy. Now they could use it to buy these American houses. She planned to return in November so they could marry before Christmas.

On the first of September Dorn filled out the naturalization papers, which, as they formally stated, "declared his intention" to become a United States citizen.

That Indian summer day in October 1954 began quite innocently. Dorn went to a supposedly routine interview with the U.S. Department of Immigration and Naturalization, which soon became a nightmare.

In a dull, shabby federal office in lower Manhattan he was told by a middle-aged official from Washington that information had been received that would hold up the process of his naturalization. They would, of course, reveal the charges to him, but they suggested that he provide himself with legal counsel.

The charges: "False statements on the original application for an entry visa and work permit." Similar discrepancies on the "Declaration of Intention." Also, certain other damaging evidence would have to be considered. Should all this prove to be correct, "it could result in the cancellation of his permission to reside and work in the United States." Deportation!

Dorn sat on the hard wooden chair in front of a steel government-issue desk facing the man from Washington and two New York federal officials, one a woman in late middle age, the other a heavyset bald and sweating man. The defective fluorescent light overhead flickered. A smiling portrait of President Eisenhower mocked him with its joviality. A frayed sign glued onto the glass partition to his right said, "Do not waste paper."

For a long time he just shook his head. Finally, he asked if he could know some of the evidence they were talking about. They said that he would be told everything in Washington, D.C. Transportation would be provided. They also advised him that he had been placed under federal surveillance and that he was not to leave New York City without express permission.

"Does my company know? Have my people at Brunzig been told?"

"No."

"Will they be told?"

"They may have to be advised later." For now, the matter was between the United States government and Karl-Heinz Dorn, a citizen of West Germany, resident in the United States as a registered alien.

Dorn told no one, not even Stern. Nor did he hire a lawyer. He felt he had nothing to hide. He was absolutely sure he would receive just treatment. He asked Dr. Erdmann for a day off. Then he fixed an appointment in Washington at the Department of Immigration and Naturalization. The meeting took place in a modern, wood-paneled government conference room. The senior immigration officers who confronted him (the man from the New York meeting was one of them) were surprised that he was without a lawyer. They advised him again that he had the right to counsel. He told them he did not need a lawyer because he had nothing to hide. They asked him to sign a paper to the effect that they had not deprived him of his rights, and he did so. First, they showed him a photostatic copy of his visa application, filed in Stuttgart, which did not mention his Nazi party N.S.D.A.P. membership. Then the room was darkened, and a projector began to flash photos onto a large screen. In the silence, broken only by the buzz of the cooling fan inside the machine and the click-clack of changing film slides, he saw several color shots of himself in the black N.S.K.K. uniform standing near a group around the *Führer*, walking behind SS General Dietrich, standing among officers clustered around the *Duce*, Benito Mussolini. There were also photos from the *Führer*'s retreat on the

Obersalzberg. They were all quite authentic, old-fashioned Leica slides.

"Do you deny that these are actual photographs of you?"

"No."

"Will you sign an admission to that effect?"

"Yes. Why not? I am in the photos."

"Were you in the SS?"

"No."

"But you're wearing an SS uniform."

"No. It's an N.S.K.K. uniform. Quite a different organization."

"Is that a part of the Nazi party?"

"Yes."

"Then you were a member of the Nazi party?" The questioner, a short balding young man with a button-down Brooks Brothers shirt and flannel suit, shuffled some papers in front of him. "I mean," he said, "to put it correctly, were you a member of the N.S.D.A.P.?"

"Yes."

"What was this N.S.K.K.?"

"It was the National Socialist Motor Corps. A lot of people in the automobile business belonged to it."

"Because you had to?" The Brooks Brothers man raised his eyebrows ironically.

"No, one didn't have to. But in certain jobs it was considered correct."

"What jobs? And by whom was it, as you say, considered correct?"

"By those who had important jobs or who were in the process of getting ahead in the industry."

The Brooks Brothers man snorted. "That's one way of putting it," he said. "Getting ahead!"

At this point, an older man, who had so far said nothing, interrupted. "For the time being, Mr. Dorn, that's all we want to pursue. We would suggest that you return to your job in New York. It is up to you if you now want to inform your superiors. We shall initiate proceedings against you based on the evidence we have presented to you. I must still advise you to seek legal counsel. Let me inform you once more"—and he pointed at the man who had first confronted Dorn in New York—"as you were told in New York, that you are now under federal surveillance. Please hold yourself available at all times.''

The meeting was over.

He landed back in New York that night, frightened and alone.

Carla was in Italy. Stern? Why get him involved? It would have been unfair. Sooner or later, Dr. Erdmann had to be told, but not yet. Erdmann would have to advise Stuttgart, and they might react rashly. Now, finally, Dorn knew he needed a lawyer. There was no question about it. Perhaps, just perhaps, he could explain the circumstances of the photographs and why he never felt it necessary to list his token membership in the N.S.D.A.P. He called Marge, although it was nearly midnight.

''Marge, who's your lawyer?''

''Whazzamadda, baby?'' Marge was loaded. ''You get someone knocked up? I can find you a doc. . . .''

''No.'' He laughed despite his miseries. ''I need some routine work in connection with my citizenship.''

''Tha's better.'' She got herself together and gave him the name of her lawyers.

The partner who handled Marge's business suggested the best immigration lawyer in the city, one Aaron Kornberg.

Kornberg, a man in his sixties, was a creature of the Great Depression, of Brooklyn and CCNY, and of the time when unions fought goons and the Lincoln Brigade fought Franco. Internationally, his views were the simplistic ones of New York Jews of the Roosevelt era: Franco was the devil. Stalin was not so bad until he had made a deal with Hitler. Roosevelt was God. Chaim Weizman was God. As a Russian Jew, he thought all German Jews were bastards, except refugees, who were *poor* bastards and whom one had to help. Harry Truman was okay. Didn't he once have a Jewish partner named Eddie Jacobson? Therefore, Korea was all right; therefore, MacArthur was a bastard. Ike was okay because he was on the side of Israel, but Adlai would have been good because he was so . . . *intelligent*. To Aaron Kornberg there were no nuances. His view of international politics was like a simple Hollywood script: Nazis were always villains in black uniforms. Yet he was, first and foremost, a lawyer. He might hate the clients he defended, but he did not presume to judge them, and he saw that they got every advantage the law permitted, every break, every obscure chance.

Dorn would have been shocked by the revulsion and horror with which this stooped, thin, curly-gray-haired, unkempt man viewed him. As soon as Dorn had phoned for a meeting, Kornberg called Washington and learned the details. He was almost ready to turn down this case, but he was a man of professional principles.

When Dorn stepped into his office, Kornberg pointed to a worn leather couch. He hated this *goy* on sight. Without a greeting, he said, "I have been told the details of the charges against you. I have also been told that you have admitted everything you were charged with. Why, then, do you come to me? What is it you are trying to achieve?"

Dorn looked into the lawyer's dark, clear eyes, and said, "I have learned to appreciate this country. I wish to remain here and become a citizen. I am also in love with a woman, a European, and we want to make our home here."

Kornberg stood facing the window, his back to Dorn, and nothing was said for a long time. Then he turned and sat down on the edge of his large desk, put his hands on the knees of his rumpled flannel trousers, and said, "You were a member of the National Socialist German Labor party. There are photographs of you with Hitler and with Mussolini. How the hell do you expect this country to let you live here? And worse, how do you ever expect to be awarded citizenship?" His voice cracked in anger, and his face was red.

Dorn waited for the heat to subside. Then he said, "I was a party member, but I was a not a National Socialist, a Nazi. I was in uniform, but I did not belong to a dangerous political organization like the SS. You will have to believe the first statement because it is true. The other part, about the uniform: Any expert on National Socialist Germany can tell you that the N.S.K.K. was not like the storm troops. The very name N.S.K.K. means National Socialist Motor Corps. It had no functions that could be considered criminal."

Despite himself, Kornberg was impressed. Something clicked, something this Kraut bastard had said, which had to do with party membership. During the Hollywood blacklist trials in Washington, he and some fellow New York lawyers volunteered to help with the defense of movie people accused by the House Un-American Activities Committee. One night a film writer, a man who had "taken the Fifth" during a full day of questioning, said in the privacy of his hotel room, "Yes, I was a card-carrying party member. But I was never a Communist!" He told how he had joined the party to please someone and how he had quit a year later.

Then should one accuse this man Dorn of being a real Nazi? Could one then accuse *all* Germans of complicity? If so, why the Berlin airlift? Why the new friendship with Germany?

For once, Kornberg was counting moralities, not legalities. Kornberg was a *Mensch*, the word that means the same in German and in his beloved Yiddish.

There was another factor Kornberg had to balance. This German could not know who had started the case against him: a brilliant young congressman, a Jew from New York, whose staff assistants had provided the damaging material. Recently, the congressman had rooted out several former Nazis. Kornberg admired the effort but knew the degree of personal ambition that fueled this vendetta. The congressman was aiming for higher office.

"Tell me," Kornberg said, "tell me, Dorn, how you joined the goddam party. . . ."

GERMANY

1931

KARL-HEINZ DORN'S father, Herbert, was an exemplary man. He had loved his late wife faithfully, and he worshipped his son. He was a loyal employee, and he had been a steadfast and courageous army officer, serving in the Great War, as they called the 1914–18 one.

He was born in the village of Pleskow west of Potsdam, the old Prussian capital. His parents were grain millers, and he was sent to Berlin at fourteen to attend upper high school. Berlin schooling meant a great advancement in *Stand*, in class. Prussia was not like the old Catholic German kingdoms and duchies, where a man was penalized six generations for coming from peasant background. Old King Frederick of Prussia, *der Alte Fritz*, had seen to that. Every Prussian carried a bit of the Old Fritz in him.

Herbert Dorn was shocked by Berlin, the raucous, rude, and fierce city with its biting, ironic humor and its unending haste. He moved in with friends of his parents who were also in the grain business. When he complained about Berlin, his surrogate father, a witty man, pulled out a book of the great poet Goethe's letters. Goethe wrote about Berlin, "I see by everything that this city is filled with such an impertinent species of mankind that one does not get far by using delicacy with them. To keep above water in Berlin, one has to be somewhat coarse oneself."

Soon Herbert cursed, cracked jokes, and yelled insults like other Berliners. He developed a *Berliner Schnauze*, Berlin "lip."

Even the revolutionary days after the war could not shake his humor or his faith. As a former reserve officer, he was shocked when a group of ex-officers assassinated Rosa Luxemburg and Carl Liebknecht, two Communist intellectual revolutionaries. He hated Communists, but he could not condone murder. When another group of ex-officers assassinated the German foreign minister, Walter Rathenau, Herbert Dorn was in mourning, because Rathenau, a Jew and a millionaire, had served his country with great honor.

Dorn had known some Jews for years. There was Lieutenant Simon from his old regiment. There was Schmidt, a friend who was a buyer at the KaDeBe department store, and there were others. He never thought of them as very different from him. He had a Jewish neighbor on Mommsenstrasse in Berlin, a lawyer, who lived in the front house of their building in a large apartment, a very polite man with a cheerful wife. His two children had gone to *Grundschule*, elementary school, with Karl-Heinz. Good people. No different from anyone else, except that instead of church they went to the synagogue on Fasanenstrasse a few blocks away. He often passed it, a beautiful structure a bit like a church, but he had never been inside.

He knew about *Koscher*, as the Jewish restaurants called it. That had always seemed odd because Jews could not eat *Eisbein*, a pork dish traditional in Berlin, nor would they eat venison. A pity for them! Nothing could beat hare or deer properly aged and prepared. Anyhow, how could you tell a Jew from anyone else? Their names were German, except for those called Kohn or Levi. The *Stürmer*, the Nazi newspaper published by Julius Streicher, which was really crude (everyone admitted that), caricatured Jews, and it was true that many Polish Yids in Berlin looked like the ugly drawings in the *Stürmer*. But for the most part, German Jews looked just like other Germans.

How did he actually feel about Jews? Did he hate them? No. He could never have hit one, kicked one, seen one get hurt. Did he hate them because he was a Christian? Did the Jews kill Christ? Maybe yes, maybe no. It did not matter that much to him because he was not devoted to religion. Perhaps the Catholics were more rabid on the subject, but most Berliners were Evangelical Protestants.

Did the Jews cause all of Germany's troubles? He could not believe that. Perhaps foreign Jews did. But he was sure that German Jews had nothing to do with any harm done to Germany and that they could prove it. Anyway, he was sure no one would really harm them. He had read the anti-Jewish Nazi party statements, but he was certain that if the Jews in Germany could prove they were first-class members of the German community they would be fully rehabilitated.

Karl-Heinz Dorn, his only child, graduated from a Berlin high school, a *Gymnasium*, at eighteen by passing the fierce *Abitur*, the dreaded final examination that plagued all German upper school students. But there was no question of going on to university. In 1930, young Germans of the middle class were lucky to get a job because the country was in a deep depression. Six million were out of work. That year, his father lost his job as a sales manager in a printing firm that went bankrupt. Now he was eating up his small savings. Luckily, through his friend Schmidt, he got Karl-Heinz a job at KaDeBe, Germany's leading department store. The name was a contraction of Kaufhaus der Berliner, store of the Berliners. It was owned by the Goldners, Rhineland Jews who came to Berlin during the reign of Frederick the Great and started their first little shop.

Herbert Dorn's friend Siegfried Schmidt, a head buyer, liked Karl-Heinz, a handsome kid. Young Dorn arrived at the store each morning at seven and left at ten each evening. For the first six months of his apprenticeship, he actually worked seven days a week and brought home every penny he made. Herbert Dorn was sad to see the boy cut himself off from all fun, but the older man was whipped: a lost war, wounds, inflation, the loss of his wife, national depression, and unemployment.

He was not alone. Many decent people were at the end of their endurance. Every rule they had ever learned was there to deceive them. Work hard, obey the law, go to church, and what do you get? Shafted, screwed, reamed, *beschissen*, shit on, ruined! Who was to blame? Who knew? The government fumbled and promised and argued while the Communists roamed the streets and demonstrated and had bloody fights

with the Nazis. Banks were closed temporarily by the government to get things straight, but that had brought the end to
even more businesses! Decent middle-class men were begging
on the Kurfüstendamm while foreigners ate caviar in the
Adlon Hotel and bought expensive villas in the wealthy suburbs.
In the election that year the Nazis went from two hundred
thousand to one million. Somehow they made more sense
than the others, except for their slams against the Jews. That
was *Quatsch*, bunk! After all, KaDeBe was owned by Jews
and they hadn't thrown people out of work. And Siegfried
Schmidt was Jewish and a great guy, *ein richtiger Kerl!*

Herbert Dorn knew that one Jew, Simon, his fellow officer
who was wounded in Belgium in 1914, still limped around
Berlin with a cane. He was in the garment business now.
Maybe he'd give Simon a call. Maybe Simon could get him a
job. Anyway, *these* were good Jews. One had to admit that a
lot of Yiddish-speaking Polacks had come to Berlin since the
war. They didn't exactly make themselves beloved with their
side curls, caftans, and waving hands—not to mention their
crooked ways. People said they were behind the high dairy
and meat prices. Obviously, they were thieves, and by God
they looked it. But those weren't *German* Jews.

Herbert Dorn went to the savings bank each week and tried
not to use the money his son brought home, but that was
almost impossible. They both had to eat. Every day he read
the ads and went to the *Stammtisch* at his little coffeehouse to
listen for the chance of a job, any job that was suitable to him,
because he could not be seen doing manual labor or working
as a night clerk in a hotel. After all, he had to keep some
semblance of dignity, as a former reserve officer, a former
sales manager. *It would have done harm to the boy if his
father had come down in standing.*

He was not an arrogant or a stupid man. He was just part of
his time. He was the salt of Central Europe, the middle-class
German, head and shoulders above most other Europeans in
diligence, application, honesty, and ability. He was like a
fine sailor on a foundering ship, and he deserved better, much
better.

One night he went to the *Sportspalast*, Coliseum, with ten
thousand others to a Nazi rally. After noisy and strident
introductions from party bigwigs, Adolf Hitler mounted the
podium and began to speak. The voice was quiet, persuasive,

and urgent, not like the screaming Hitler he had expected. It came over the loudspeakers of the huge hall with amazing intimacy as if the man stood only a meter away.

Hitler said, "They humiliated us. Our enemies took away everything we needed to keep our dignity and our manhood. Besotted with looting, greedy for booty, they put the knife to our throats and stole and plundered our industry, our land, our resources. Through their own blundering, they then plunged us into their economic depression, and handed us over to every crook, every Jewish gangster who wanted to come here and rape our nation. And I say to you: *Enough!* We are men and women of dignity and honor who can outwork, outproduce, outthink, and outcreate anyone in this world. And yes, we can outfight them as well! The greedy hand which reaches for our throat will be sliced off. Because we are *Germans*. Let that never be forgotten, *Germans!*"

Herbert Dorn applauded because the man was right!

Hitler continued, "For fourteen years we have suffered the shame and agony of the Versailles dictates after losing a war because of the treachery in our midst. And again I say to you: *Enough!* We will root out the traitors in our German land. We will build a new world, a German world in which we can work and produce and raise our children as decent beings, free from the Jewish filth and smut of cabarets and homosexuality, free from the insult of so-called modern art and the debauch of pornography and cocaine and all the other things with which our enemies hope to keep us drugged, subdued, and confused. German men! German women! Give me your hands! Give me your hearts! Let us now rebuild our great Germany together! Let us throw out the so-called democratic governments, the fools and weaklings who have cost us our daily bread."

Then his voice rose to the sound of thunder and slowly, distinctly, he shouted, *"Germany, wake up!"*

There was pandemonium. Hitler had reached into the heart and soul of every sad and downcast man and woman in the huge hall. Now there was hope. Here was one man who spoke with their voice, who neither hedged nor held back. He wanted to achieve what they needed by breaking the bonds of the Versailles Treaty, by regaining Germany's natural resources, by rebuilding German's military might, by giving them unity and purpose. And he did not speak about the far-off future.

He meant *now!* Of course, he was also right about the smut
that had invaded Berlin, the disgusting cesspool in the heart
of the city: pansies in women's clothes soliciting on the
Kurfürstendamm, lesbian nightclubs open twenty hours a day,
cocaine and opium dens in middle-class Charlottenburg. The
mayor of Berlin caught in a huge swindle over police and fire
uniforms! The police commissioner implicated in the murder
of a foreign soothsayer who used to tell his fortune! This was
not the Germany they wanted!

They wanted a new Germany, as clean, as decent, and as
honorable as the old kaiser's Germany.

Hitler had also blasted the Jews. But again, Herbert Dorn
was sure he did not mean Jews like Simon and Schmidt, not
decent German Jews, but the international trash, the Jewish
gangsters from the East and from Paris and New York and the
other places full of pimps and crooks.

That night he went home to their apartment, and he had
made up his mind.

Karl-Heinz was already there when Herbert Dorn unlocked
the front door. The boy had worried about his father, who
was always home in the evenings, listening to the radio and
reading the *Abendblatt*. He had bought cigars for his dad and
also two bottles of *Pilsner Urquell* beer, which they both
loved. He had also picked up some salami and *Landjaeger*
sausage in the food section of KaDeBe, where the assistant
food buyer was a friend of his and he got a discount. Now he
was relieved that his dad was all right. The old man had not
looked well.

Karl-Heinz set the table, and they had their beer and sausage and bread while Herbert Dorn told his son about the
Sportspalast and Hitler's speech.

"Karlchen," he said, "I've made up my mind. On the way
home I thought and thought, and now I know where I stand.
Hitler is the man for me!"

Karl-Heinz looked at his father's tired face. The skin hung
under his chin in ripples. The blue eyes were watery and
red-rimmed, the stiff brownish-gray hair was still cut in the
side-shaven military style of the old days. Sitting in a huge,
overstuffed, leather-covered armchair, his dad looked frail,
dwarfed. Their apartment was filled with the remainder of
clumsy kaiser-era furniture, bought long before with his
mother's dowry, the proud contribution of every middle-class

German girl. The pastoral paintings, the hunting scenes, and the small heroic bronzes, the bound sets of Goethe's and Schiller's works on the shelves, books that were meant to be passed on to Karl-Heinz for *his* home. The son felt indescribably sad, remembering when his father was a vital, sportsloving, cheerful man. His school friends had always envied Karl-Heinz his father. His mother had died when he was four, so his father had hired nursemaids from the local Spreewald delta, who wore colorful folk costumes with large, square headgear.

Occasionally, Karl-Heinz visited his maternal grandparents, who lived in Neükolln, on the other side of Berlin, but his father never left him there. They hiked, sailed on the Havel River, and went to the Avus automobile races.

When Karl-Heinz had trouble in school, his father would always help. When the boy was sixteen, his father bought an Opel car, a little four-seater with a sliding convertible roof. Now their life became even better: long Sunday drives into the flat farm country around Berlin and vacation trips up north to the sea. Best of all, Herbert Dorn taught his son how to drive.

Only four years later Herbert Dorn was like an old man.

Until that night after the Hitler speech!

Now there was something new in his eyes, something Karl-Heinz had not seen there lately. Of course, Karl-Heinz knew of Germany's political struggles. Who didn't? He read the papers and listened to the radio. He saw the demonstrations and the posters that were plastered all over Berlin. But at KaDeBe there was no time for politics. He worked and paid attention to his job. Besides, KaDeBe was owned by Jewish people, and there were other Jews like his boss Schmidt, so he avoided discussion about the Nazis. Karl-Heinz enjoyed his work and liked old Schmidt, who looked fierce, like the first sergeant in a Prussian Guards regiment, but was really very kind to his newest protégé.

Karl-Heinz's father was joining the N.S.D.A.P., and why not? It had already boosted his spirits. Perhaps these Nazis were not so bad. After all, if men like his father joined the party, other good men would also join, and these decent people would make a difference! Sure, the Brown Shirts on the streets were rowdies, but they were laboring-class men, simple fellows. Men like his father would change the party.

Right now things were rough out there in the streets, and perhaps the Brown Shirts were needed to fight the Communists. The Commies were worse!

A week later, Herbert Dorn's party badge and membership card arrived by special registered mail. From then on, Karl-Heinz would never again see his father without the small, enameled, red-ringed swastika on his lapel. Herbert Dorn attended monthly party meetings, subscribed to the party newspapers, the *Völkische Beobachter* and the *Angriff*, and he found a job as purchasing manager for a publishing house. The company belonged to an old-time N.S. party member, and they printed special books for various N.S. organizations. Now Herbert Dorn had a new chance.

He died of an embolism on his way to work on December 3, 1934, and he was buried next to his wife in the old cemetery behind the village church at Pleskow where the farmers and millers Dorn had always had their graves. Karl-Heinz was shattered. He turned to Siegfried Schmidt, and Schmidt understood. Shortly after Herbert Dorn's death, Schmidt took Karl-Heinz on his first buying trip to Paris and London. He felt quickly at home in both cities, and years of schoolboy slavery in both languages finally paid off. Schmidt was impressed.

One night Karl-Heinz discovered Scotch whisky. In cold, gray, drizzling London, whisky tasted like good cognac. He and Schmidt went to Walton's restaurant to join a group of Germans. Karl-Heinz tried hard to speak coherently and, oddly, he had more success in English than in German. The others were waiting, and he sat down next to a tiny, dark-skinned, blue-eyed girl with pitch-black short hair. He immediately fell into tipsy English, but she refused to play along. She spoke German with a southern singsong because she was from Nürnberg in Franconia. Her name was Hildegarde Antmann. She was twenty-two and a secretary at the German Consulate General. When she saw that Karl-Heinz was high, she was not at all amused. In fact, she was sick and tired of German businessmen who arrived in London and went wild because they were abroad. Hilde was no prude, but she would not put up with boors, so she gave this handsome young halfwit a cool reception.

Fortunately, Karl-Heinz just giggled and admitted that he was tipsy, that he loved the feeling, that he was having a

great time, and that he promised not to be a nuisance. She
was almost charmed, but she left early.

The next morning during a break between his meetings he
phoned her at the consulate.

"*Fräulein* Antmann? Dorn here."

"Who?"

"Dorn the drunk. The Berliner who spoke slurred German.
But wasn't my English brilliant? Why do I speak better
English when I'm drunk?"

"Who says you do?"

"I do."

"Who did you say you were?"

"Hilde, let's make peace."

"Oh, all right. *Frieden.*"

"Dinner?"

"When?"

"Tonight."

Her flat was in a small building on South Grosvenor Street.
He groped his way up the dark stairs, pushing mistimed
automatic light buttons along the way, devil instruments designed to shut off the lights before he reached the next switch.
When he finally reached her floor, she was ready to leave and
he had to turn around and perform the whole journey in
reverse, with Hilde in his wake. Fortunately, this time he was
sober. During the remaining days of the business trip he
became well acquainted with that staircase.

Hilde was an official in the passport section of the consulate.
She knew the name of almost every German citizen who lived
in Great Britain and was of great value to the consul general,
who had promoted her beyond her seniority. Besides, she was
almost totally quadrilingual. Only minuscule verbal errors
stayed with her. For instance, she could say "wid" or "vith,"
but "with" defeated her. She also pronounced "fingers"
with a soft unspoken "g" like "singers" and she sometimes
hardened the "ow" sound so that "plow" rhymed with
"*Frau.*" These tiny flaws made her sound German to those
with finely tuned ears. To all others, her English was perfect.

As a Nürnberger, she became the object of special attention
from several consular officials. Nürnberg had been chosen for
the annual National Socialist Party Rally and *Reichsparteitag*,
which had Mecca-like importance for ambitious party members.
If one attended the Nürnberg Rally, it was wise to be friendly

with an established Nürnberg family, for social prestige, living quarters, and restaurant reservations. Nürnberg was proud of this lofty new position in the hierarchy of German cities. Its narrow, medieval streets and bridges, its guard towers and castle walls now resounded to the click of boot heels, the drums of marching bands, and the loud laughter of strolling Nazi officials. During Rally Week the large hotels near the railroad station were filled with Hitler's closest associates. Coffeehouses, beerhalls, and the vast fifteenth-century market square were a sea of brown and black uniforms. Albrecht Dürer's sixteenth-century home near the castle became a place of pilgrimage, dictated by a self-congratulating and braggart sense of "Germanism." Barrels of Frankenwein, the semidry white wine of the region, gallons of local beer, and carloads of local roast sausages provided the culinary back-up for this flood of supernationalism. Berliners who visited Nürnberg during Rally Week, even Berliners in full party uniform, were usually in a state of high amusement: What fools these *Spiesser*, these provincial bumpkins from all over the Reich, could make of themselves!

Yet the same Berliners were secretly delighted that Nürnberg was chosen over the capital, because this bombastic week would have been hard to carry out in cynical Berlin. Everyone knew that the *Führer* was uncomfortable with Berliners. Berlin and he had a sense of mutual respect but not the hearty affection that was obvious in Munich or Nürnberg. To the *Führer*, Munich was the real cradle of the Nazi movement, while Nürnberg, with its ancient walls and its brilliant history of arts and crafts, was the perfect stage. Also, Nürnberg had the *Zeppelinwiese*, the huge airship landing field on the edge of the town that became the parade ground where hundreds of thousands of uniformed men assembled in gargantuan cadres before their *Führer* and the other leaders of their country. This is where they established their "blood bond," with long speeches, oaths of loyalty, and banners, blessed by the sacred hand of Adolf Hitler. Storm troopers, Labor battalions, Hitler Youth, *Bund* of German girls, the SS, there were millions of them. At night, towering red swastika banners guarded the vast perimeter like tall sentries, accented by vertical floodlights, icy pillars reaching toward the dark sky. Hundreds of thousands of men saluted with lighted torches, shouting their oaths of allegiance.

To the party faithful from all over Germany, this had become a sacred annual act, one even the Berlin party people had to go along with. And then, after all, a lot was being achieved and this bit of theater was probably necessary to please the hicks. One could always get drunk and maybe, just maybe, there were a few pretty girls among the B.D.M., the Hitler girls, although most of them were staunch, chaste, athletic, and unperfumed, with unshaven legs and armpits.

Hilde's family, the Antmanns, had been lithographers, painters, and printers for generations, and were famed in the world of art. One of her ancestors had even worked with Wolgemut, a contemporary of Dürer. Her parents were absolutely baffled by the style, and contemptuous of the substance of National Socialism. Hilde had grown up with prejudice only against stupidity and narrow-mindedness. Yet the Antmanns, proud of being German, had fought in Germany's wars, had taught in Germany's universities and had represented Germany at international art congresses.

Hilde, schooled in London, Paris, and Florence, had a talent for languages. She was also a monumentally efficient organizer.

The first thing that struck Karl-Heinz was that this tiny girl kept looking straight into his eyes, probing, questioning, leaving little room for the sort of minor lies that were part of the pattern of courtship. In fact, she was, in her own beguiling way, a damn nuisance.

"Where did you study?" she asked.

"Berlin."

"University of Berlin?"

"Well, no."

"What do you mean, 'well, no'?"

"I did not go to university."

"Why didn't you say so? When I said study, I meant university, of course."

"I only took my *Abitur*. Then I went to work as an apprentice at KaDeBe."

"And now?"

"I'm doing work I like and working for someone I like."

"Was that *Herr* Schmidt whom you were with at Walton's?"

"What a memory!"

"That's my job. Have you known Schmidt long?"

"Since I was a kid. He was a friend of my father's."

"Then you know."

"Know what?"

"That Schmidt is Jewish."

"Of course, but how do you know?"

"Again, that's my job. We know about every German who comes here."

"Schmidt is a wonderful man."

"Who said he wasn't?"

"I thought . . ."

"Because I said he is a Jew? That's got nothing to do with it."

"Then why did you mention it?"

"Because I wanted to get your reaction."

"And?"

"I got it."

"He's been my best friend since my father died."

"Your father was in the party."

"*Na, liebe* Hilde, how the devil did you know that?"

"It's my—"

"I know. It's your job. Yes, Father was a *P.G.*, a party member. But he admired Schmidt. In fact, Schmidt got me into KaDeBe."

She shrugged. "Karl-Heinz," she said, "you don't have to explain to me. I happen to respect your loyalty. It's quite rare these days."

"And you don't think I'm offending, against acceptable attitudes?"

"I don't think that being loyal makes you into a bad German."

"Don't you feel you're taking chances?"

"Chances?"

"Talking this way to a complete stranger."

"No. I am a good German. I do my job at the consulate, and I intend to stay a good German. But, I also intend to keep my family's tradition."

"What's that?"

"For being *gerecht*—what the English call fair. I'll oppose anyone who is bad for Germany, and I'll defend any good German."

Quite a girl, he thought. *Donnerwetter!* Quite some girl, an extraordinary girl, unlike any other he had ever known. How natural that he dropped all the fake, flimsy chatter that had usually brought him success—bed—in the past. Hilde Antmann was different.

How right he was! Hilde Antmann had made up her mind about Karl-Heinz even as he was discovering her. This tall, dark-haired boy with the gentle, slim face was for her. He might as well have resigned himself there and then to life with her, although he had not the vaguest notion about her feelings. To the contrary, he was quite sure that he would never pass muster, that she was untouchable and would remain so. He was wrong even there.

She was no virgin. But she had not slept with many men. Her first affair, at fifteen, was with an art student, a shy and sad boy whom she took to bed because she wanted to comfort him and make him feel reassured. Since then, there had been a few others, but they were never fools and it was never without warm affection. On their third night together, Karl-Heinz and Hilde became lovers. She took him to bed. He was surprised by the lack of strangeness and equally surprised by the explosive degree of their passion.

Hilde had a difficult year. She was doing work she should have enjoyed and for a man she respected, but still she was troubled. And she was not alone. Her superior, the consul general, a man in his late fifties, and a foreign service professional who predated the new regime, had served all over the world, bailing German nationals out of trouble and issuing visas to foreigners. He had represented Weimar-time Germany at many international conferences, all too often on the losing end of discussions. Before Hitler, German consulates were not bases of power, but now people were anxious to accept invitations to German consular parties, and German prestige rose considerably.

All this should have brought him great satisfaction, but the consul general was distressed.

The cause of it all was the group of German émigrés in Great Britain. Each year there were more, most of them Jews but still technically German citizens with German passports and a few remaining rights, though these were fast eroding with every new memorandum from Berlin.

If the consul general could only have considered these

refugees harmful or criminal . . . but he had known many of them personally, and others by their high reputations. They were businessmen, actors, authors, scientists, lawyers, artists, doctors, and some were just ordinary middle-class Germans, indistinguishable from their Aryan contemporaries back home. The consul general was pleased with Germany's (and his own) new station in the international world, but he was sure that the loss of this émigré group would harm Germany, and that the indiscriminate laws that drove them from their homeland were flawed.

Yet he would not speak out. First and foremost, he was a loyal official. He had always disliked the selfish and egotistical style of certain British, French, and American diplomats, who betrayed their superiors and national interest to the press. That was not his style, but then, he had never before faced a conflict with his conscience.

Besides, a new group of foreign service people had recently been assigned to his consulate, most of them party members and several SS. They seemed capable, but lacked experience and diplomatic sensitivity, and so they caused some friction. For instance, one of them had worn his SS uniform for a consular party, raising eyebrows among the French, British, and American guests. Even the Italians, who had resisted their operatic impulse to wear their party uniforms, were shocked. Fortunately, the Italian consul general made a rather snide remark about "teaching us, the poor crude Italian Fascists, how to wear political opinions proudly." The young SS man soon excused himself and came back in correct pinstripes.

The Jewish refugees meant nothing to these new officials, and sympathetic comments about them would have been misunderstood.

The consul general had not yet joined the party, though he was considering it. He was loyal to his fatherland, but something prevented him from making a total commitment to this new political movement. It was his nature as a diplomat to remain objective, to wait and see.

Although the new officials were polite and correct, he detected an occasional near-impertinence, a subtle form of insubordination. Perhaps his lack of party credentials was beginning to undermine his authority, and he had to consider the matter of party membership with more urgency.

He had just received an invitation to attend a dinner at Oxford, but one of the guests of honor was Professor Eintmann, the Nobel Prize-winning philosopher, a German Jewish émigré now teaching at the university. He knew and admired the professor, but he feigned an excuse and declined the invitation. He wanted to establish some distance, to gain some objectivity about the conditions produced by the new German laws and his own quandary.

The consul general always reminded Hilde of her father. His views of most things were similar to her family's, so when she overheard some of the new people call him the "Weimar holdover" and the "antique" she resented it and told them so.

Hilde knew many of the refugees because of her frequent official contacts with them. They would come to the consulate to ask "that nice *Fräulein* Antmann" if their aunt Emilia had received her exit permit from Frankfurt, and had cousin Emerich received his? The official attitude toward the émigrés was cold. Berlin pointed out that they were undesirable elements. Yet the more Hilde knew about "undesirables," the stronger became her doubts. She was an Antmann, and it was in her family's tradition to ask questions.

One morning when they were alone in the consul general's office, she brought up the refugees. He diverted to other matters, but she would not give up.

"*Herr Generalkonsul*, I am sorry, but I must get back to the question I asked."

"Namely?"

"Namely the emigrants. We are told they are scum. But you and I know that many are wonderful people. Like Professor Eintmann. Or like the Lakischers who are here in London."

"Who are they?"

"Art dealers from Nürnberg. Very old friends of my family."

"Have you seen them?"

"No. They seem to avoid me. I can't get them to return my telephone calls. They came here a year ago. I suppose they're very bitter."

"Have you written to your father about them?"

"Not yet. I thought I would wait until I get home on leave."

"Good. What could he do about it, anyway? He'd probably write to them and cause all sorts of problems for himself and you.''

''And for the consulate?''

''Perhaps.'' The consul general shrugged his shoulders and looked older than he should have. He was dressed in a correct double-breasted navy blue suit. On his lapel he wore the tiny ribbon-bow of the Iron Cross, and on the pinky of his left hand was a gold signet ring with his family's crest. His slim, aloof face, a cross between army officer and bishop, was almost perfect for his métier. He said, ''After all, Hilde, *mein Kind*, let's be clear about one thing: A vast number of good things are being done in Berlin! All in all, there have been few *real* mistakes. Look at Germany's position in the world today! And when the *Führer* felt there were elements which compromised Germany, he took firm steps.''

''You mean about the Jews?''

''No. About Ernst Röhm and his bunch of storm trooper thugs. The *Führer* certainly did not spare those men, although they were once the heart and soul of the party.''

Everyone in Germany was aware of the recent execution of Captain Ernst Röhm, the chief of the S.A. storm troopers, and dozens of other top S.A. leaders. The *Führer* explained that these men were power-mad traitors who wanted to take over the movement and the country. Hilde had seen them all in Nürnberg. They were scum, loud, common, vulgar, the worst. She was happy when she heard of the purge. She hoped the *Führer* had finally seen the light about some of his old cronies. But since then, others just like them had taken over the S.A., and Streicher, the worst of the ''Old Fighters'' became *Gauleiter*, governor, of her beloved Franconia. She was about to say these things to the consul general, but something told her to keep still. He seemed so unsure and worried, and he obviously wanted to avoid the whole subject. So she said no more. For now, she would continue to think her thoughts, and she would help to protect the consul general against the ''new people'' and their innuendos.

So she nodded and said, ''*Na, ja*, I suppose I'll just have to wait and see.''

Then she left his office.

The consul general sat very still, fingered his ring, and repeated to himself what she had just said. He, too, decided to wait and see. He could hear the noise of London traffic outside, muffled by the windows.

Early in 1935 the consul general's dilemma was resolved. He was recalled to Berlin. A new ambassador to the Court of St. James was appointed, a clever businessman and old-time party member called Joachim von Ribbentrop, who felt that senior foreign service executives serving under him had to be party members, the least he could expect from people in sensitive jobs. No one doubted the consul general's expertise, but he would have had to work hand in glove with the new ambassador. Besides, several London consular people, all solid party members, had expressed doubts about the old consul general during a recent confidential review that had begun with the N.S. takeover. No one accused him of anything approaching disaffection or disloyalty, but there now was a cloud over his capacity to function. He was not offered a new assignment, so he took the hint and retired to his villa in Berlin Dahlem.

He was a widower, and his children were not in Berlin. So every morning he rode his favorite saddle horse in the Tiergarten Park and played tennis at the Rot-Weiss Club. He was not bitter. Rather, he was relieved to avoid a test of principles. Certain doubts came to haunt him, to weaken the fiber of lifelong beliefs, and he shut them away. He had done his best, and he would now try to enjoy his leisure. He never joined the party.

Within a week of the consul general's transfer, Hilde asked for the home leave that was due her, and she left London. She did not wish to continue under the new consul general, a Munich lawyer who had spent two years at Rugby School in England and spoke excellent English. He was a *Sturmbann-führer*, a major in the "general" SS, which contained many lawyers, doctors, and other professionals. SS catered to the "better circles." It was much harder to join, than the more plebeian SA, the storm troops. SS standards were stricter, and it had become *de rigueur* for those with ambition. It helped their careers, socially and economically. Usually, they wore their handsome black uniform only for weekly meetings or for special party occasions, but many SS people also liked to wear it at social events like weddings or formal dinner parties. Of course, the new consul general did not wear his SS gear in London. But he was always sure to display his little SS lapel pin, and he also brought along a suit of the New Diplomatic Corps uniform, a navy double-breasted affair with much silver embroidery. He was quite charming, rather handsome, and Hilde had to admit, despite herself, that under different conditions he might have been fun to work for.

Yet she was adrift. No one could have believed more devotedly in Germany. She was genuinely happy that Germany seemed to have recovered financially. So many people had lost everything during the Weimar years. It felt good to be part of a new, vital country. But the racial laws were beyond her comprehension. So much of her recent life had been spent meeting decent Germans forced to leave their homes for reasons that seemed flimsy and false.

Because of Karl-Heinz, she found it unexpectedly easy to leave her job. They wrote to each other, telephoned, and cabled. They had both found something they wanted to keep. When Hilde got home to Nürnberg, Karl-Heinz came to visit and they decided to get married.

First, Karl-Heinz wanted to ask Dr. Antmann for Hilde's hand in the classic German way, which amused her no end. She accused him of being *Teutsch*, not just *Deutsch*, more German than the Germans. Her very worldly father would cringe at this nineteenth-century ritual. *"Na, also,"* she said, "you must be joking! I hinted to Papa we're going to marry, so you don't have to go through all that nonsense. Let's just get my parents to lunch at the Grand Hotel tomorrow, and we'll break the news to them."

"Absolutely not. I'll do it the official way," said Karl-Heinz. "I have to overcome a major handicap."

"What?"

"Being from Berlin. Everyone here thinks we're *Untermenschen*, subhuman and barbaric."

"But my parents aren't stuffy Nürnbergers!"

"I don't want to take a chance. Stop laughing at me. I said stop it!" He grew huffy.

"All right, if that's what you want, you stupid ass!" She threw up her hands and dropped the subject, and she also tried to stop laughing.

The result was that small, rotund, balding Professor Dr. Antmann, one of Europe's most renowned art connoisseurs and a specialist in sixteenth-century lithography and painting,

who had been elbow to elbow with those in power, drank two
very large glasses of brandy, which he hated. He had to
prepare himself for this ordeal with his future son-in-law,
who was being stupidly formal. After Hilde wrote volumes in
her letters about Karl-Heinz Dorn, he had met the boy and
thought him wonderful. That afternoon they went at it.

"*Herr Doktor?*"

"*Jawohl?*"

"May I speak to you about something of great importance
to your daughter and myself?"

"*Ja*. Of course."

"I would like to ask permission . . ."

"*Na, ja*, it's fine with us."

". . . your permission to speak to you . . ."

"I already said it's *in Ordnung*. It's all right."

"What's all right, *Herr Doktor*? To speak to you?"

"No. The thing you wanted to speak about."

"Then it's not all right?"

"*Also, genug jetzt!* Let's get this whole thing straight.
Hilde's mama and I will be delighted to have you in the
family as our son-in-law. *In Ordnung?*"

"*Danke vielmals, Herr Doktor!*"

"Here, my boy, have some Asbach. It's awful. But at least
you can get a little plastered on the stuff, just like I am now.
God, I never knew you Berliners could be such formal idiots!"

So they kept drinking. An hour later, when Hilde and her
lookalike mother got mildly curious about them, the two men
tried their best to look sober. Then, after a long nap to allow
the two future male relatives to recuperate, they all went to a
Bratwurst restaurant near Market Square and enjoyed themselves like the solid *Volksgenossen* and citizens at the other
tables. Nürnberger *Bratwurst* is so good that when Franconians
return from long trips, they have been known to burst into
tears at the sight of their first home-stuffed *Bratwurst*. On the
other hand, this may also be due to the large amount of
Frankenwein they drink waiting for the *Bratwurst*.

The next day Hilde sent her formal resignation to Berlin.
She stated that she wished to enter the "state of marriage."
The Foreign Office put no objections in her way, partly
because her name had appeared in dispatches from London,
describing her as sympathetic to the old consul general.
Certainly, this did not brand her as disloyal, but it signaled

future problems. Easier to accept her resignation! Like all members of the service, she was under routine surveillance, and her liaison with Dorn was known. Dorn seemed *einwand-frei*, acceptable, from the racial and political standpoint. His father was a party member, and although he worked for a Jewish concern, he might soon become useful when KaDeBe was *Judenrein*, cleansed of Jews. The government had made itself quite clear.

It was shameful that several department stores, banks, and manufacturing concerns still had Jewish affiliations. Germany could conduct its business without help from these outsiders. Jews were internationally connected, and would always put their selfish interests ahead of Germany's. Their true aim was to control international commerce and finance.

"Paragraph Five," a section of the new Reichs laws of September 1935, defined once and for all who was a Jew and who was of mixed blood. Jews and certain mixed-bloods could no longer be citizens and thereby could no longer head German enterprises. Unable to participate in the German national process, they had to be removed. It was that simple; these laws were enacted to facilitate the recovery and future of Germany. Despite foreign propaganda, these laws were not malicious any more than one would consider it malicious not to permit a simple saddle horse to stand at stud with an Arabian mare. There were Germans and there were Jews, separate peoples of uncongenial blood. Germany was a country of laws. Anyone could refer to the commentary by Dr. Frick, Reichs Minister of the Interior, dated September 15, 1935, very just and correct:

> The laws regarding citizenship and blood do not have the purpose of putting members of the Jewish people at a disadvantage because of their inability to be full citizens. Instead, the elimination of Jewry from participating in the German governmental process and the prevention of further racial intermixing are totally necessary for the secure future of the German people. Jews shall not be prevented from earning a livelihood in Germany. But from here on, the future of Germany shall be solely in the hands of the German people.

As the *Völkische Beobachter* newspaper had written:

Let no one be deceived by the small number of Jews in our midst! There were only 160,000 in Berlin at the time of the takeover and Berlin is a city of four million people.

In 1932 the total Jews in the Reich represent only about one percent of the population. This very fact is proof of their power, their danger to the future of our people. We must cleanse ourselves of Jewish influence. We must be ruthless!

Karl-Heinz and Hilde had a civil wedding because Hilde was Catholic and Karl-Heinz was not. Fortunately, no one, not even Hilde's sister who taught kindergarten in Munich and was chubby and cheerful, objected to the lack of religious ceremony.

The Dorns moved to Berlin, and they were lucky to find a small apartment on the top floor of a corner building on the newly named Adolf Hitler Platz. The big square, in the west of the city, was flanked by expensive apartment houses. It was the last urban area before the gardens and forests that bordered the city. Hilde's *Mitgift*, her dowry, was used to buy furniture. They had a bedroom, bathroom, small dining room, and a sort of salon-sitting room that ended in a small open balcony facing the square. They could even look across at the new Goebbels apartment.

The neighborhood was a bit too rich for a young couple, but the Antmanns helped out. They even supplied a wedding gift, a sleek little BMW 328 convertible. Also, KaDeBe raised Karl-Heinz's salary at the suggestion of Schmidt.

Herr Kommerzienrath Adalbert Goldner, KaDeBe's tall, dignified chairman of the *Aufsichtsrath*, the board, had to think of the future of the store. He realized that technically he was Jewish because of both his grandparents, though Goldner could not believe that the new anti-Jewish policies could ever apply to him. The Goldner family had built KaDeBe into the showplace of Berlin and one of Europe's great stores. It ranked with Harrod's and Galléries Lafayette, and even American visitors were impressed. Adalbert Goldner was a third-generation Christian, since his Jewish grandfather had converted to the Evangelical church. His family's conversion was not a matter of opportunism. His grandfather felt it was the family's duty to become part of the community.

Typically, therefore, Adalbert Goldner opposed the idea of Zionism, which he considered divisive. How could a man be loyal to two countries, his own and Palestine? In his view, being Jewish was a matter of religion, not of nationality. A man was a German Jew or a French Jew just as others were Catholics or Protestants. Synagogues and churches were different buildings for the service to God, but they had no bearing on a man's nationality.

Kommerzienrath Goldner (the title went back to the Weimar Republic) did not consider himself better than Jews like Schmidt, but, after all, the Goldners were different. Like the Hamburg-America Line Ballins and the Rathenhaus of A.E.G. Electrical Industries, they were vital to Germany, despite the temporary aberrations of this new government. Besides, Hitler was not even German, but Austrian! Certainly Berliners would never harm the Goldners. The Goldners *were* Berlin!

So despite the Nazis, the *Kommerzienrath* continued his life as before. Two of his sons were on the staff of the store. The family villa on Kaiserdamm was staffed with the same aging butler, maids, and cook. Ockert, his chauffeur, still drove the *Kommerzienrath* to work in a venerable 1928 Daimler-Benz limousine. Everyone in Berlin knew the tall, old-fashioned car and its 1A-1234 license plates. Most of the old-time *Schupos*, the Berlin cops, saluted when he passed.

The *Kommerzienrath* was known as *"Der Olle,"* the Old Man, and was considered a bit of a character, which he relished. His apocryphal *bon-mots* became Berlin folklore.

A few years before Hitler, an ambitious hostess had snared the Goldners to a formal dinner party at her home. She gushed, *"Ach, Herr Kommerzienrath,* having you here is one of the great moments of my life!"

He looked down at her benignly, and with the broadest Berlin street accent said, "Well, good lady, then you ain't had much of a life."

When he heard one of his executives bellowing behind closed doors, he asked why the man was shouting. He was told the fellow was talking to London.

"Tell him," said *"Der Olle,"* "to use the damn phone!"

In their forty-year marriage, *Frau Kommerzienrath,* Hannelohre Goldner, had often disagreed with her husband. She did not trust the future. She came from the great Jewish publishing family, the Schorrs. Ever since the day Adolf Hitler became chancellor, the Schorrs found themselves in confrontations with Dr. Joseph Goebbels, who "invited" them to submit all future projects for his ministry's approval or to cancel them at once.

The Schorrs had no doubt about their future in Germany: They would soon be thrown out of their own company and forced to leave after accepting a token payment for their stock in Schorr A.G., so they made all arrangements to wind up their German business and leave the country.

They begged Hannelohre to warn her stubborn husband.

One night after dinner, the butler had served coffee in the library. Then, when they were alone, she opened the subject.

"Bertchen, Ulli asked me to speak to you about something important."

"What," he asked, lighting an Upman corona, "did your distinguished brother Ulli have in mind?"

"Emigration. They're going to wind up the Berlin firm this month and move to Geneva or London. They'll run the rest of the company from there."

He shook his head. "I think they're lunatics."

"Really? Bertchen, now look. I know you're not fond of my family, but you must admit they're not stupid."

"Stupid? By no means. Panicky? Yes."

"*Liebchen*, I don't want to bring back the old squabbles. We know what a fuss they made when I converted to marry you. That's all ancient, dull history. This is different."

"Hanni, I've been waiting for your brothers to get a kick in the behind sooner or later. Until recently, they've published some awful *Scheisse*, if you'll pardon my language. That novel about the homos and all the Communist *Dreck*. You know me. I've got a foul Berlin mouth and I'm not exactly a prude, but sooner or later the boys had it coming. Nothing to do with being Jewish. Just a matter of bad business judgment on their part about what the German public will swallow. Not all of Germany is like Berlin."

"It's their contention," she said, "that no Jew will survive in Germany. They want to warn you in the most earnest and brotherly way."

"I think they're talking rubbish! Anyway, we haven't been Jews since grandfather's time."

"Do you mind," she said, "that the Goldners were once Jews, now that the question has become so acute?"

"Hanni, you know me better than that! We've never pretended to be anything we aren't. Isn't that true? But to my mind, first we've always been Germans."

She shrugged her shoulders and the subject was closed. She had to admit that nothing had changed in their lives since the new government came. Perhaps Adalbert was right.

Ockert had been the *Herr Kommerzienrath*'s chauffeur for nearly twenty years, ever since he was a raw kid from Neukölln, the old part of Berlin. He was an angular man of forty with dusty blond hair, pale eyes, and high Slavic cheekbones, who had grown a small paunch. He had two kids in upper school and a fat, happy wife, Anna, who could cook like an angel and curse like a beer-truck *Kutscher*. Obviously Ockert had no problems.

Even during the terrible inflation and depression, he had nothing to worry about. In Berlin, when you were *Kommerzienrath* Goldner's chauffeur, that really meant something. Everyone knew 1A-1234, and it gave you a lot of pull and prestige among the other drivers. The old man helped him with everything from hospital bills to schools to life insurance. Ockert, in turn, was loyal and hard-working and completely dependable. When things were rough in 1930, Ockert fed his brother, his in-laws, and half his pals. He never hesitated to ask the old man for help for the others, but he didn't ask much for himself.

The Ockerts had a little flat over the garage building about thirty meters from the main house, which they had fixed up to be very *mollig*, cozy.

One evening Ockert had delivered the *"Olle"* to the main house and was putting the limousine to bed. He wiped the windows, checked the tires, and then closed the garage and climbed upstairs to their little foyer.

His wife kissed him and said there was someone waiting, a nice looking, gray-haired fellow in his late forties in a business suit, who was sitting on the couch, drinking some of Anna Ockert's famous coffee. Coffee was so expensive that most working-class wives cooked what Berliners called

"Blümchen" Kaffee, coffee so thin it tasted as if it were brewed from daisies. Not Anna Ockert. Hers tasted like that served in the expensive *Romanische Cafe* on Kurfürstendamm.

The stranger stood up and said, *"Herr* Ockert?"

"Yes."

"I am *Sub Inspektor* Tunnes, *Geheime Staatspolizei."* He held out a small, oval brass tag. Embossed on the front was the swastika eagle and the words *Geheime Staatspolizei.* What could the Gestapo want? Ockert was puzzled but not worried.

Inspector Tunnes quickly came to the point. After asking Anna to excuse them, he said, "You're working for a Jew, as you know."

"Well, I always thought that the *Herr Kommerzienrath* was Evangelical. I take him to church every Sunday with his lady."

"Na, ja, but he falls under the laws for racial protection like everyone else. Both his grandparents were Jews, so he is a Jew. So is his wife." Tunnes said it very calmly, stating a fact.

"I've been with the old man for a long time," said Ockert. "I have a lot to thank him for. He's a very decent gentleman."

Tunnes shrugged and seemed embarrassed. "Possible," he said. "But he's legally still a Jew and related to Jews. We have reasons to believe that in the next few months he will be asked to help certain other Jews to leave Germany illegally."

"Really?" said Ockert, shaking his head. "I can't believe *'Der Olle'* could ever do anything illegal! Why, last month when I made a mistake and did a U-turn where I shouldn't have, he made me stop and confess to the *Schupo* on the corner. Would you believe that? Of course, the cop was nice and laughed and said to forget it, and then he saluted the old man. They all know him."

Tunnes nodded. "Nevertheless, here's what we want. We will check with you every week and you will tell us whom you brought where, day by day and hour by hour."

"How?"

"Write a list every Friday and put it in a sealed envelope. Your wife will leave it in the empty milk bottle in front of your door. Please be very *gründlich*, very thorough. And also, besides yourself and your wife, no one, I repeat *no one*, is to know the reasons for my visits. If the other servants ask, tell them I'm a relative of your wife's from Breslau." Ockert shook his head. How did they know she was from Breslau, which, of course, she was.

Then Tunnes left.

What a mess! He told Anna the whole story and her part about the milk bottle. They wondered if they should ask the old butler or the cook what to do, but they decided against that. Perhaps the others had also been approached by the Gestapo, and then Tunnes would find out they broke their instructions. They talked long into the night. They decided that nothing the old man did could possibly be illegal, so there would be no harm in submitting the lists. And then, police are police and one did not fool around with the *Polente*, with the cops. After all, they had two kids.

But where would it end? Ockert had never worked for anyone else. Now he was working for a man the Gestapo suspected!

Ockert shook his head. *Scheissdreck!*

Subinspector Erwin Tunnes came from Norderney, one of a string of islands that guard the German coast against the fierce North Sea. He went to school in a one-room, thatch-roofed hut with forty other blond Friesian kids. On stormy days, when the raging sea pounded the island and covered the beaches, the kids were glad to be indoors instead of tending cows and sheep. But many kept their eyes on the scudding clouds outside, wondering if their fathers, who were out fishing, would be home that night. Every winter, men were lost and kids wore black armbands. If they were boys over thirteen, they would then leave school and go to work on the trawlers.

Friesians are large, gentle people, who speak their broad *Plattdütsch*, the language that hovers between Danish, German, and Dutch. By blood they are close to the Danes and the Hollanders, and in mind they are stoic and patient like most seafaring people. They took care of their families and of each other and they distrusted mainlanders.

Each summer they were swamped by vacationers from the north of Germany, many of them Berliners, people who loved Norderney Island, but who never knew it in fall and winter when it was cruel and harsh.

At eighteen Erwin Tunnes decided to leave the island. He wrote to the Berlin police, who often recruited men from the island, and he became a Berlin policeman in a tight navy blue uniform, with shiny leather helmet, puttees, and belt, doing street patrol in Charlottenburg. He saved several lives in accidents and handled a stabbing case with calm and skill. He also made several difficult arrests. Then, during the 1919 revolutionary period, his unit got involved in fierce street battles with political rioters, and he once cooled off a dangerous confrontation by walking calmly across an open square as both sides were ready to shoot. As a reward, he was promoted to the *Kriminalpolizei*, the plainclothes force. He learned his investigative skills during the wild Berlin twenties and became one of the best detectives in the city. Homicide, drug smuggling, fraud, embezzlement, blackmail, protection rackets, pimping and prostitution, white slaving, female and male homosexuals, all were part of his schooling, and Berlin gave an advanced course. Among Berlin's criminals he had a reputation for being decent. He did not believe in harsh methods, because it was more efficient to spend time on thorough investigation.

Berlin! How could he describe it to anyone he had ever known up on the island? Berlin's lowlife revolved around the Alexanderplatz just a few meters from police headquarters! Outside, ten-year-old boys hustled for their older sisters. Drug pushers used code to tell where they sold their wares, codes that they drew on street posters and that the police had to break each week. When whores died, their gold fillings were knocked out by their pimps and pawned.

Berlin's criminal gangs had their headquarters in dives around the "Alex," within a pistol shot of police headquarters. On the Kurfürstendamm, homosexual bars attracted these toughs who robbed the fags at closing time.

Political parties provided other problems. They fought pitched street battles with much loss of life.

His private life was secondary. There was a girl he almost married, but she took off with a foreigner and so he had stayed a bachelor. Three or four women, some of them whores, consoled him whenever he was lonely. He was fair with them and took good care of them.

After the N.S. takeover, he was selected for a new elite national criminal police, the *Geheime Staatspolizei*, also known as the Gestapo. It was a great honor. Only top men were picked. The work was much more interesting. Then, two years

later, after the Röhm mess, the Gestapo was assigned to the
SS.

The SS people stayed at headquarters in their black uniforms,
while the Gestapo men in plainclothes did all the field work.
Their new chief was an SS general called Reinhardt Heydrich,
a mysterious man who was surrounded by rumors. They said
he could be very fierce.

Most interrogations were conducted by the SS and, from
what Tunnes saw, not too effectively. Suspects often ended
up badly hurt or even dead. Poor police work!

The SS built new prisons, outdoor labor camps, the first
one at Dachau north of Munich. He heard these were tough
places, but he was not too impressed. Jails were jails, not rest
homes. If someone was fool enough to deserve jail, he had to
take the consequences. Tunnes did not believe in coddling
criminals, and the idea of outdoor labor camps sounded good.
Jails in the cities were overcrowded with convicts from the
wild twenties and thirties.

Things had settled down since the N.S. takeover. All the
rough stuff in Berlin had stopped: The homo bars were closed,
there was no more drug smuggling, and prostitution was on
the decrease. The economy had straightened out, and there
were few unemployed. That's why Tunnes had joined the
party the month Adolf Hitler became *Reichskanzler*, and he
had liked Hitler even before the elections.

The SS boys had their own secret police, the S.D., who
were mostly involved with racial offenses such as intermarriage,
interracial sexual affairs, and the Jewish problem.

The obvious solution was to get Jews out of Germany, and
the laws stated that Jews were free to leave. They could get
emigration permits once they declared all their holdings and
paid a stiff emigration tax. And why not? After all, they had
made their fortunes in Germany! Most Jews did not let this
tax deter them from leaving, but most other countries demanded financial guarantees, and this tempted Jews to break
the law, smuggling valuables across the border during supposed business trips. They stuffed their cheeks, swallowed
jewels, even shoved them up their rectums. Some managed to
bribe Aryan Germans, non-Jews, into making cash deposits
abroad, for which they would be repaid in Germany with fat
bonuses.

Tunnes considered most new laws quite reasonable and

correct, but this new ordinance with which you could hold a
man forever to protect him against harm from the population?
It made police work easier, but, to his mind, if you had a case
against a man, you quickly stuck him in front of a judge
instead of holding him without charge. And the new racial
laws? Supposedly, these laws were meant to preserve the
purity of Aryan blood and all the honesty that goes with such
Aryan blood. That was *Bockmist*, a bunch of horseshit! Ninety
percent of the criminals Tunnes had arrested were of pure
Aryan blood. Besides, Tunnes knew many Jews and liked
them. In fact, the assistant commissioner of Berlin Police in
1931 was a Jew and a very decent fellow. He could understand how these laws would protect Germany against vermin
like those Polish and other Estern Jews who were often
small-time *Schieber*, crooks, around Berlin. But real German
Jews were Berliners like any others, and it was not in Tunnes's
nature to prejudge a man. But he was trained to enforce the
law, and so he did his job, which could sometimes become
unpleasant, like the Goldner case.

To launch the investigation, Heydrich himself had called a
special meeting in his office, where Tunnes had never been.
Present were several Gestapo bigwigs and four SS men,
headed by a young *Sturmbannführer*, a major, who called
everyone to order. He wore the diamond-shaped S.D. patch
on his left sleeve and turned out to be liaison officer with the
Propaganda Ministry, which explained what he had to say.

"Gentlemen, I am here to advise you of an extremely
important matter that has come to our attention." He glanced
at Heydrich, who sat behind him, one booted foot on the edge
of his large desk. Heydrich's arms were folded over his chest,
and he looked bored.

The major continued: "Most of you know the name of
Goldner, the Jew who runs the KaDeBe department store."
The listeners nodded.

"This man is related to the Schorr family, the Jew publishers.
They are intermarried."

A baby-faced lieutenant cut in, "The Goldner woman is
sister of the Schorrs." He smiled, self-satisfied.

"They are in-laws," said the major. "As you may know, I
have been assigned as liaison to the Reich's *Propagandaministerium. Reichsminister* Dr. Goebbels feels that Goldner

will probably help the Schorrs to smuggle their fortune abroad.''
The major turned to Heydrich, who nodded for him to go on.

''Dr. Goebbels is anxious to prevent this. These Schorr
people have made millions publishing the sort of smut that is
now banned. It would be ironic if they could take the booty,
which they looted from Germany, and shove it into foreign
banks.'' The major stepped forward, put his hands on his
hips, planted his spread feet on the thick rug, and said,
''Let's get these pigs! Any suggestions?''

No one had much to say. There were a few mumbles, some
shrugged shoulders. No one wanted to be first.

Heydrich slipped out from behind his desk, and the major
retired discreetly.

''Thanks, *Sturmbannführer!* I appreciate the briefing.''
Heydrich's voice was high-pitched. ''I think I have the perfect man for this job, because he knows the Charlottenburg
and Dahlem scene like no one else—Tunnes.''

Tunnes said nothing. He just nodded.

''How,'' asked Heydrich, looking at the big detective,
''how do you think we ought to tackle this?''

Tunnes said, ''I suppose if we want proof, we have to get
it from good sources. There are probably four or five kinds of
surveillance we can institute. Two at Schorr, two at KaDeBe,
and one inside the Goldner household.''

''Why only one there?''

''Well, sir,'' said Tunnes, ''Goldner is quite a distinguished old fellow.'' He paused. ''Even if he's a Jew.'' He
could feel the critical looks from the SS men in the room, but
he carried on. ''People like that are usually surrounded by
loyalties. We have to find a person who's close to him and
who would act for us, probably someone who doesn't think
he's betraying Goldner.''

''Any idea who?'' asked Heydrich.

''No, sir, but I'll have the name by tomorrow.''

''*Knorke!*'' said Heydrich, using the old North German
term for ''great!'' Then he pointed at Tunnes and said, ''Tunnes
is in complete charge of this case. All of you will coordinate
through him, and he will make all assignments. He will report
to me directly, if that is agreeable?'' And he turned to the
senior Gestapo official present. The Gestapo man, though
senior in rank to Tunnes, was only an administration man and
quickly signaled his approval. He was not a field man. ''Good,''

said Heydrich. "Thank you, gentlemen. Tunnes, can I talk to you?"

Tunnes stayed, alone with the general. They sat at a low table and an SS trooper brought coffee.

No one knew much about Heydrich, a former navy officer. He worked directly for Heinrich Himmler, and they said that he also spoke to the *Führer* daily. He was extremely tall, with a bony face, a long hawk nose, and a military haircut. He moved gracefully, his black uniform emphasizing his slim legs and torso. On his chest, along with his party decorations, he wore the badge issued to Germany's leading athletes, the golden *Sportsabzeichen*, because he had once been a champion fencer. There were many rumors: He was supposedly a concert-quality violinist, a homosexual, a masochist, a sadist. Everyone in the party had another story. Tunnes was sure most of these were nonsense, but one thing was sure: Reinhard Heydrich was the most feared man in Germany. The S.D., the security service of the SS, was the party's secret police, and even the Gestapo were careful around them.

"Tunnes," said Heydrich, "tell me how you feel about this case."

"How do you mean, sir, how do I feel? About the truth of it? Well . . ." He shifted uncomfortably in the big armchair. "I still believe in getting proof before I give an opinion."

"Even when the case comes straight down from the *Propagandaministerium*?"

"Particularly then! I should hate to come up with half-baked facts. I can promise you, sir, that if Goldner does anything illegal, I'll have proof."

"Suppose he only *plans* to do something illegal?" Heydrich was smiling, like a cheerful greyhound.

"If I have proof that he has illegal intentions, I will get you this proof."

"What will you do if you get such proof?"

"Do?" said Tunnes, his big, lined face showing surprise. "I shall do nothing. I shall hand you the evidence for you to decide the disposition. If you then order certain action, I shall take it."

Heydrich finished his demitasse. "Tunnes," he said, "you're a *rara avis*, a unique creature: the professional. You have no axe to grind, do you?"

Tunnes shook his head. "You're wrong, sir. I have one

axe to grind. I hate to see crimes committed. And I try to prevent them."

Heydrich nodded and stood up, dismissing Tunnes, who gave him the raised arm salute. *"Heilitla!"* he said, party style, drawing the words together.

"Heilitla!"

When Tunnes's vast back had left the office, Heydrich returned to his armchair behind the desk. He was smiling broadly. Tunnes was fantastic, a real *Kerl*, a first-class man. Nothing seemed to shake him. When Heydrich was a navy officer, he had known many sailors who were Friesians, like Tunnes, and he had liked them all.

The assignment was flattering, but Tunnes wished someone else was handling this particular case. He knew the old *Kommerzienrath* by reputation because *"Der Olle"* was a famous Berliner. The best point of leverage was probably Ockert, the chauffeur. The butler was too old. The cook was a sentimental old woman. The maids could not know enough about events upstairs. So he picked Ockert. He could have sent one of his people to organize things, but he purposely went himself, to make sure no one in the chauffeur's family got rattled. He also explained some background to Ockert, which one of his subordinates could not have done. This was necessary so that loyal Ockert did not go off half-cocked.

Tunnes only hoped that he would not be the one who had to arrest Goldner.

He was going to ask one of his old *Kameraden* back in the Alexanderplatz police headquarters for advice, but he decided not to. These days everyone played *hart auf hart*, for keeps. In fact, he was not even sure that the Berlin *Kriminalpolizei* had been briefed about the Goldner matter.

The newlywed Dorns settled into their new flat. During her two years in London, Hilde had developed a taste for English decor, so their new place looked like a Sussex Country house: bright floral upholstery prints, graceful wooden furniture, and curtains in light shades. Walls were painted in light blue or light yellow with white contrast moldings. The effect was sunny and light, helped by the fact that they were on the top floor of the apartment building.

The fashionable N.S. party style was quite different: heavy

wooden furniture, wall-to-wall carpeting, and low, massive coffee tables surrounded by huge, square armchairs and couches. Every photo of the *Führer*'s offices and homes showed this look, but few people in Berlin copied it.

Hilde scouted the Kurfürstendamm for English-style furniture, and some charming eighteenth-century paintings arrived from Nürnberg, a gift from the Antmanns.

Berlin had changed under the new regime. There were red swastika banners everywhere, and the swastika eagle was on everything from mailboxes to schools, although the Berlin "bear" still reigned on buses and tramways. The streets were filled with uniforms: S.A., SS, N.S.K.K., army, the new air force blue, and Hitler Youth.

Soon, Berlin would be host to thousands of foreigners for the Olympic games, and so the most blatant anti-Jewish poster had disappeared. But then, sooner or later the anti-Jewish propaganda had to calm down, as everyone knew.

The *Romanische Cafe*, the famous coffeehouse, was still booming. In the old days, everyone from Lubitsch to Dietrich used to sit there and gab.

Now the Jewish film and theater people had left, but many actors, directors, writers, and journalists were still there. Foreign companies still had offices in Berlin, and their executives loved the city. Hotels were full. Restaurants were crowded. Everything seemed to be on the upturn, so Karl-Heinz was aghast when Schmidt told him he was leaving Germany. It was inconceivable!

"Siegfried, you're like a father to me, but I have to tell you frankly: You're *verrückt*, crazy!"

"Not as crazy as you think," said Schmidt.

"This will all blow over."

"What, the N.S.D.A.P.?"

"No. But the whole anti-Jewish business. They don't mean people like you!"

"Whom do they mean then?"

"Oh, you know exactly, Siegfried. Don't play the fool with me!"

"The law is very clear. According to the law, I cannot take part in German life."

"Siegfried, my father, your friend, was a party member. Do you think he would have wanted you to leave?"

"Your father did what he thought was right. And he could not have changed the racial laws, could he?"

Karl-Heinz was irate. "The Goldners," he said. "They're not leaving, are they?"

Schmidt permitted himself an ironic laugh. "According to them, they're not Jewish. They're Christians."

"What's wrong with being Christian?"

"Nothing. Unless you're a converted Jew. Then you stay Jewish."

"You sound just like the party's racial laws," said Karl-Heinz.

"*Na, ja.*" Schmidt laughed. "I knew that sooner or later the party and I would agree on something." He paused and shook his head. "Karlchen, please, don't let it concern you. My future can't be your responsibility." He was about to continue but changed his mind. There was nothing left to say. He put his wide hands on the younger man's shoulders. "I told them to promote you to my job. I hope they take my advice."

"Siegfried, I still think you're absolutely crazy!"

"You mean *Meschugge*," said Schmidt, "the way Berliners have always said it, even though it's a Yiddish word. Anyway, Karlchen, you're a first-class fellow. This is no fault of yours. But they? The others? *Na*, they can all kiss my ass!"

And so, Siegfried Schmidt left KaDeBe and his homeland.

Karl-Heinz took over much of Schmidt's work, but he was not promoted. Although he was silently annoyed, he was also somehow relieved, because he really did not wish to benefit from Siegfried Schmidt's bad luck or bad judgment, whichever would turn out to be correct.

Hilde understood completely and threw her arms around him. "Karlchen," she said, "how could I have married such a heartless fellow?"

Yet, although they grew closer and closer, Hilde had still never spoken to him about the doubts that began in London.

One spring evening they drove the BMW, top down, west from the square, down the wide Heerstrasse, the old Army Road, toward the bridge over the Mueggelsee Lake and then down to the docks. It was a warm and gentle night, clear and quiet. Dozens of little sloops hung on their moorings a few yards from shore. They parked the car and took a slow walk to a small dockside restaurant, where they ordered coldcuts, the usual Berlin evening fare. Berliners ate heavily at lunch but had light suppers. It was too early in the year for the pest of the Berlin Lakes, *Mücken*, the tiny mosquitoes that were historically the subject of much humor. Supposedly the newest protection against them was to play the *"Horst Wessel"* song, the Nazi anthem. Then, when the *Mücken* raised their right front feet to salute, one could swat them.

The place was quite empty. There were only two other couples sitting on the other side of the open terrace near the water.

Hilde said, "When Siegfried left, it brought back a lot of things to me, Karle, things I haven't thought about since London."

"Like what? By the way, you're turning into a Berliner."

"God forbid. Why?"

"Because you're calling me Karle."

"I was infected by a Berliner I slept with!"

"Mensch." Karl-Heinz was laughing. "Some tough broad I married. *'Ne wilde Pflanze!'* "

"Back to Siegfried. In London, where the Schmidts are going, I met many emigrants, first-class people, real Germans. I can't believe we should shove people like that out of our country!"

"Hilde, first of all, no one has shoved them out. They left of their own will."

"Wouldn't you leave if the new racial laws applied to you?"

"Liebling, I have a confession."

"What?"

"I haven't read all the new laws. I know that if both grandparents were Jewish they consider you a Jew. What's wrong with that? Of course, Jews can't belong to the N.S.D.A.P. and they can't marry Christians. But hardly any of them marry Christians anyway. They have always married each other. Siegfried's wife is Jewish, isn't she?" Karl-Heinz paused. "What else? Oh, they will soon have a 'J' in front of their car license plate. I read that today. But it will take years until all the plates are renewed. Also, Jews can't be appointed to government jobs."

"Isn't all that enough?"

"Well, I have to admit things like that can't make Jews

very happy. But there have been times in history when Protestants were treated just that way in your southern part of Germany. And, if I remember my history, the Boers in South Africa were really kicked around by the English, but they stayed. And in America, the Negroes live like swine. I read they can't even use the same public lavatories, but they don't pack up and leave America."

"Karle, stop it. You're using some lousy examples. I've read the newest laws, and listen to this." She counted on the fingers of her hand, trying to remember. "Heine, Mendelssohn, Bruno Walter, Klemperer, Max Reinhardt, Einstein—these are just *some* of the people the party calls 'undesirable,' the great artists and scientists whom foreigners always mention when they admire Germany."

"Then, Hildelein, tell me honestly." He looked around to see if someone could hear. "You don't believe in National Socialism?"

Hilde shook her head. "I didn't say that. I absolutely agree with certain things. I think the Versailles Treaty was an abomination. We must have our industrial areas if we are to survive. We deserve the right to defend ourselves and to have an army and navy. After all, we're a first-class people. Without our artists, our scientists, our writers, the world would be a poorer place. If you compare us with other nations in Europe, we're head and shoulders above most of them."

"Then what are your complaints? Just this ridiculous Jewish business, which the party will soon get over, as we all know. That's why I think Siegfried was panicking."

"No, he wasn't." Hilde was adamant. "He was quite right. This is *not* a temporary thing! You never worked for the government. I did. The anti-Jewish laws, the so-called Nürnberg Laws—and I shudder that they are named after my home town—they are the basis for the whole miserable theory of racial superiority. For that, they need the Jews! Who else is nearby, and defenseless? The Jews are supposed to be such a worldwide power! Then why can't they defend themselves? Anyway, the whole Nordic business is a joke. Look at Berlin: full of Slavic people from the Polish border and Celts from the Spreewald forest and heaven knows what. Whenever someone is light blond and blue-eyed, they turn out not to be Berliners, but from the Baltic or from Friesland up north. It's all a lot of *Scheisse*, the whole Aryan nonsense. Do you know in Bavaria many of our Tyroleans look so Jewish that they call anyone Jewish 'Tyrolean' behind his back?"

"*Na, ja,* Hildelein. In the meantime, suppose you are right and this is all very rotten. What can we do about it? Let's assume the anti-Jewish business is just a cynical device, and that sooner or later they'll give it up."

"No," she said. "Even worse. I think the *Führer* really hates Jews. The others may be cynical, but he really believes he's right!" She shrugged. "We're helpless. But I feel that someone has robbed me."

"How?"

"Because I hate to see all the good things they are doing get messed up, *versaut,* by something so shameful."

They drove home to Adolf Hitler Platz in silence.

The Olympic Games came to Berlin that summer, and the Dorns spent as much time as they could at the new Stadium. Hilde became a guide-interpreter, a stroke of luck, because they got scarce tickets. The games were superbly organized and staged, and everyone was proud. Also, German athletes won most of the gold medals. During the day, Hilde worked in the Olympic Village, and each night she was full of stories about the athletes. The Americans were the nicest and very proud of their Negro stars, Owens and Metcalfe. She told Karl-Heinz, "I met Owens. He was charming! Oh, and a very pretty American girl diver made a sexual pass at me! Who says these things only happened in Berlin? Our German athletes are very helpful to the foreigners, very brotherly, and everyone in Olympic Village is full of compliments for the way Berlin has organized the games! And listen to this: Our top fencer is a blond girl with classic League-of-German-Girls Aryan features, and it turns out she's Jewish! So when someone from the party questioned her right to compete, Göring supposedly told the team managers to let her. 'But,' they said, 'she's a Jewess!' So Göring shook his fat fist and said: 'I decide who's Jewish!' The girl fenced very well, but no one told the *Führer* she was Jewish."

Karl-Heinz loved the gossip.

The surface of life began to change. For instance, one heard more "*Heil Hitler*" than "*Guten Morgen*" or "*Guten Tag.*"

Originally, people did it to "kiss ass." Then it just became reflex. One raised one's hand and slurred *"Heilitla!"* Then most business letters adopted a new closing: *"With German Salute, Yours Very Cordially,* etc., etc.'' The German Salute meant *"Heil Hitler."* That, too, became a fad. Only superficial things, these, but they became part of one.

When Siegfried and Ruth Schmidt left Germany, they found out their German passports had a new addition. A large ''J'' had been stamped onto the page near their pictures. After they arrived in London, the German consulate general called in their passports to add even more:

He became Siegfried *"Israel"* Schmidt and she became Ruth *"Sarah"* Schmidt, another new regulation because often you could not tell Jews by their name alone. On Goebbels's staff, they always joked about Alfred Rosenberg, who was the chief race theorist of the party. Behind his back, Goebbels's people called him Alfred *"Israel"* Rosenberg. Then there was a game in the corner *Kneipen*, the beer pubs: How do you turn a top Nazi into a Jew? Easy. They took nine matches and arranged them into the name of the minister of the interior, L E Y. Then they moved one match to make it L E V I.

Göring, the fat one, *Der Dicke*, had just married Emmy Sonnemann, the actress, also fat. There was a lottery on which sexual positions they had to assume to reach each other in bed. They also said that he now wore makeup. Supposedly the reason stage producer Max Reinhardt left Germany was not that he was a Jew. He got fed up with Göring requisitioning his stage costumes.

The definition of an Aryan? "Tall like Goebbels, slim like Göring, and blond like Hitler."

Another story going the rounds of Berlin: Himmler had recently ordered nutritional studies for the elite SS so that they would get a perfect diet. Everything in this experimental diet had to be administered by enema. The first SS volunteer was told they would feed him some tea rectally and that he should yell if it became painful. So they started gently pouring some tea into his rear. After a few seconds, the SS man yelled: *"Stop!"* They stopped at once. "What's wrong? Too hot?" "No," said the SS man. "Too sweet!"

Berliners were proud that they did not treat the movement with the abject respect shown by the rest of Germany. On the other hand, they admitted that, all in all, the new government was doing a fine job.

By 1936 forty thousand Jewish Berliners had emigrated. It was a minuscule part of the population, and it happened very discreetly. One day people were in their apartment. The next day they were gone, but their departure cast no pall over the good mood of that summer. The nearby lakes and rivers were filled with young sailors who finally had the *Zaster*, the dough, to own a car and a boat.

As a reward for good production, working-class people from the Neukölln and Moabit districts were going to the Mediterranean on cruises arranged by *KdF*, a party organization called "Strength through Joy."

They were making films full blast in the Neubabelsberg studios. Gustav Fröhlich, who was Germany's greatest screen idol, was rumored to have beaten up Goebbels for making advances to Fröhlich's wife, a movie star. Goebbels was a horny little bastard. He had laid many leading movie actresses and had a lot of little *Pipimädchen* on the side.

Berlin was always *kess*, sassy, and its big *Schnauze*, the famous Berlin yap, was bigger than ever. That year, with a few exceptions, Berliners lived like *"Gott in Frankreich,"* the German term for total bliss: "The way God would live in France."

Each morning Karl-Heinz took the slow self-service elevator to the street floor of his apartment house, then the bus from the square to KaDeBe. Berlin apartments ranked according to floor. Ground floor or *parterre* was poor. The next two flights up, excellent. The top two were mediocre.

The house on Adolf Hitler Platz was a luxury building. Karl-Heinz took the bus, but most other tenants got into their chauffeured Mercedes, Maybach, Horch, or Brunzig. One car especially raised Karl-Heinz's blood pressure: a new dark blue, supercharged eight-cylinder Brunzig 900K convertible with red spoke-wire wheels, red leather upholstery, and a tan roof. It had a five-seater, two-door body with a three-meter-long hood and twin spares on the rear. A chrome bar between the headlights displayed a lineup of enameled badges from the world's finest motor clubs. The whole machine exuded power, speed, and style, and it belonged to Armin Zoss, director of worldwide sales for Brunzig A.G., the automobile firm.

Karl-Heinz saw Zoss one morning when the old, trim roué with the small gray mustache got into the elevator on the second floor. They exchanged nods while his butler held the door. Downstairs Zoss's chauffeur, in blue uniform to match the car, opened the door on the driver's side and Zoss drove himself off while the chauffeur sat beside him. Many years later, when someone asked Karl-Heinz Dorn what he considered really stylish he said, "A 1936 900K Brunzig convertible with the roof down, the owner driving, and the chauffeur *sitting next to him*."

He could hardly concentrate on his newspaper on the way to work. He was dreaming of glory and large Brunzigs.

Like all Nürnbergers, Hilde loved skating, so they joined the Berlin Skating Club around the corner, which had an open-air rink. The B.S.C. ice hockey team, all amateurs, played at the level of an Olympic squad. Ice hockey was one of Berlin society's favorite sports, along with riding and tennis. B.S.C. gave many parties, and the Dorns went to all of them, where they saw movie stars and playboys and race drivers and business chiefs. In summer, B.S.C. became a tennis center. Tilden had played there against von Cramm, preceded by rumors of their homosexual adventures. Even under the new regime, Berlin had not discarded all of its dissolute ways. They said that at a huge party hosted by Goebbels on the Pfaueninsel, a charming little island nearby, all hell broke loose: Goebbels had invited the movie and theater crowd and a lot of leading party *Bonzen*. Someone thought it would be a good gag to convince some SS fellows and some young homo actors to crash the party as pairs with the homos in drag. So a lot of handsome SS men turned up with unusually pretty girls. These girls then lured some party bigwigs into the bushes, where the pretty girls turned out to be pretty boys. Goebbels had fits, but he had to hush things up. Everyone hoped the *Führer* would not hear about the whole mess.

The Dorns were an attractive new addition to the B.S.C. Soon, they were invited for weekends to country houses in Wannsee and to dinner parties at great restaurants like Horcher. Objective as ever, Hilde told Karl-Heinz that the "Dorns are a nice young couple, but beginning to suffer from delusions of grandeur, from *Grössenwahn*." Karl-Heinz agreed completely, and they kept right on having a good time.

Young Berliners had many enthusiasms, but cars came first, and of all the car maniacs in a car-crazy city, Karl-

Heinz was the most maniacal. Fortunately, Hilde was also a good driver, and Karl-Heinz had always liked women who drove with élan. She looked very *schneidig*, very snappy, driving their BMW. Berlin's old cab drivers gave her many roughneck compliments, and at the taxi stands they talked about "the wild brunette," *"Die Tolle Brünette im BMW."*

One day when she drove to KaDeBe to pick up Karl-Heinz, an old cabbie leaned over at an intersection and winked at him. *"Mensch,"* he said, "what's an old fart like you doing with a young girl like her? *Die hat woll'n Knall*? She must be off her rocker!"

Berlin was a city with two souls. World capital and provincial town. They would drive to Wannsee Lake for a Sunday *thé-dansant* at someone's country house. Lots of handsome people, lots of tango dancing, all the new international hits, played by a small dance band. But on the way there, they might stop at a noisy roadside *Gaststätten* inn for huge round schooners of weak, cold, Berlin summer beer called *"Ne Weisse"* which was sweetened with a shot of raspberry juice. At the open-air tables all around, there were laboring-class families singing and shouting. They were in the outdoors, the affliction of the Berlin lower classes, who considered Sunday lost without their family outing. Everyone had to get involved in their celebrating, even the Dorns with their English-style clothes and their racy little BMW parked outside among the three-wheeled mini-trucks, ten-year-old Opel sedans, the tiny, green froglike vehicles called *Hanomags*, and lots of motorcycles with sidecars, all bought *auf Stottern*, "stammering," the highly descriptive way of saying on the installment plan.

One Sunday morning between sets of tennis at B.S.C., Armin Zoss, who was with a blonde, came over to them. Hilde knew the girl from Nürnberg, and the two women kissed.

Zoss said, "We've seen each other in the elevator and, of course, I've spotted your great little car. Anyway, are you two free tonight? Buffet at my apartment? Nothing formal, just a few friends."

Karl-Heinz said, "Of course. But we may be a little late. You know how slow the elevator is."

Good. He had wanted to meet Zoss. (If only to ride in that Brunzig!)

The Zoss apartment was vast. Salon, library, smoking room, dining room, music room, billiard room, master and guest bedroom suites with dressing rooms and servants' quarters. He had the whole floor. Karl-Heinz, prowling, found a "Brunzig" room, just off the dining room, ringed with framed and autographed photographs of every major race driver in the world as well as movie stars, singers, producers, business heads from Monte Carlo to Rio, besides emirs, maharajas, and various heads of state. On a separate pedestal stood a photo of the *Führer*.

Adolf Hitler posed stiffly in his black eight-seater convertible Brunzig, his arm outstretched in the salute. The photo was framed in heavy bronze with a sculptured swastika eagle at the top. The inscription read: "To Armin Zoss, who serves Germany with honor," and it was signed in the familiar scrawl.

"Na, ja," said Zoss, who had come into the room where Karl-Heinz stood alone. "I guess we have the most important client in Germany. Makes an old sales fellow like me feel good!"

"How many Brunzigs does the government have?"

"None," said Zoss.

"You're joking." Karl-Heinz was incredulous. He had seen hundreds of them.

"None," Zoss repeated. "We keep a whole fleet at their disposal. They prefer it that way, and so do we. They're all 900K models just like the *Führer's*, but his is a little bit different."

"In what way?"

"That I can't tell you. But, my dear Dorn, there's a way you could find out for yourself."

"How do you mean?"

"You could find out by coming to work for Brunzig A.G."

"Are you offering me a job?"

"Right. *Genau.*"

"Na, ja," said Karl-Heinz. "That's very flattering indeed. And of course I am crazy about cars. But I don't know a thing about your industry. I would have to start all over again as a *Lehrling*, as an apprentice."

The butler appeared, carrying two trays of langouste rémoulade, caviar, smoked trout, and two glasses of champagne. Happy days, thought Karl-Heinz. Hope Hilde doesn't expect this tomorrow night! The man served them on two small tables and left. They were alone in the room, obviously intentionally.

Zoss raised his champagne glass. *"Prost!"* he said, and they drank. Then he continued. "I hope you don't mind, but I made it my business to find out about you when you moved into the building. I like to know about my neighbors. Friends at KaDeBe told me what I wanted to know. They think you're one of their top young people. You speak languages, you've traveled for them, and your wife is adorable and also very international."

Karl-Heinz was not sure whether to be annoyed or flattered by this investigation.

Zoss explained, "It was more than idle curiosity. Actually, I could have asked our landlord to tell me all about you because he's a friend of mine. Anyway, I think you are absolutely qualified for the job I have in mind. We need someone who can handle certain sensitive assignments, who can travel abroad, who can deal with foreigners, and who can be very diplomatic."

"What sort of job are you talking about?" asked Karl-Heinz. "Without wanting to sound pedantic, does it have a description?"

"Yes. Let's call it 'press attaché' although it won't really involve the press."

"That's good. I don't know them."

"Keine Sorge! Don't worry about it," said Zoss. "Anyway, if you trust me, and some people do"—he waved in the direction of the photos—"you will not regret switching employers." He pointed at the food, and they ate and chatted, mainly about the people in the photos. Finally, Zoss said, "Oh, I must withdraw one compliment."

"Which one?" said Karl-Heinz.

"The one about the BMW. I *hate* BMWs."

"I can't," said Karl-Heinz, "afford a Brunzig like yours," and Zoss laughed.

When they finished, they rejoined the others in the dining area.

There was a young SS major who had obviously arrived late while Zoss and Karl-Heinz were still having their tête-à-tête. Zoss greeted him warmly and then introduced him to Karl-Heinz as *Sturmbannführer* von Bernsdorfer.

"Bernsdorfer is on the *Führer*'s staff."

The SS man was slim, slight, and light blond. He shrugged his shoulders in a deprecating way and said, "*Na, ja*, if you call running a travel service staff work." Then he explained to Karl-Heinz, "Actually, I'm in charge of all transportation for the *Führer* and his staff." He pointed at the embroidered "L.A.H." on his left sleeve and said, "You know that we in the Adolf Hitler Bodyguard have to move around a lot, because the *Führer* never stays put very long. He has the Brunzigs and the *Führertrain* and the *Führerplane*, and they all have to be in the same place at the same time, no matter where. Of course, the *Führer* prefers the Brunzigs!" And Zoss smiled.

"God, what a job," said Karl-Heinz, "to get everything organized. I don't envy you. Do you have to worry about every one of the top people?"

"No," said von Bernsdorfer, "not the *Reichsmarschall*. Göring's own people take care of his needs. Good thing, too. You know how fussy *Der Dicke* is." Karl-Heinz smiled that someone on the *Führer*'s staff poked fun at the fat *Reichsmarschall*. Von Bernsdorfer's boots were of thin leather and beautifully cut. Also, his breeches were perfect, real riding ones, instead of the big-winged pants affected by most SS people.

So Karl-Heinz said, "Obviously you like to ride. . . ." and the moment he had said it, he was ready to kick himself. Von Bernsdorfer! Of course! He was the number-two or -three man on the German equestrian team that had done so well in the Olympics and in all the international horse shows.

Before von Bernsdorfer could complete his modest "Yes, I do some riding," Karl-Heinz said, "I'm an idiot! Of course, I know who you are. In fact, we met at a party at B.S.C. last winter. But you were not in uniform. That's my only excuse for not recognizing you."

Von Bernsdorfer shrugged. "Why should you recognize me? Anyway, the reason I'm in these"—he pointed to the uniform—"is that they called a last-second staff meeting. Many of us don't wear uniforms on weekends. But for staff meetings the bigshots like to have us all shiny and pressed so they can pull rank on us. I have been talking to your wife, and she tells me you live here in the building?"

"Right."

"My compliments. This is quite an address."

"It's easy, *Sturmbannführer:* I have a rich wife."

"In that case, even more compliments."

Later, back in their apartment, he told Hilde of Zoss's offer. "That," she said, "is why he had von Bernsdorfer there."

"What has the SS to do with it?"

"If you were to go to work for Brunzig in a sensitive job, he wants to make sure the party people approve. Von Bernsdorfer is his link between Brunzig and the *Führer*'s headquarters. It would bypass a lot of lengthy investigations."

"Clever girl," he said.

"Very clever girl," she said.

"Only one thing," said Karl-Heinz. "He talked to me about press liaison. That doesn't sound too earthshakingly important, even if it's well paid."

"Well, maybe there are some things he hasn't yet told you about."

"Hilde, you're a born intriguer."

"Karle, don't forget I was once head of the Gestapo in London." He laughed and threw a pillow at her.

"Von Bernsdorfer is nice," he said.

"Why not?" she said. "The SS are not *Übermenschen*, supermen. They're just like everyone else. He's a well-known horseman, and he has a title. That's probably why they brought him to headquarters. You know what snobs they are in the SS. And then they assigned him some dull, logistical stuff. In the diplomatic service, we also had types like that, very chic, who were assigned routine jobs just so they could be around the embassy for entertainment purposes."

"That's why you keep me around," he said.

"Oh?"

"For entertainment purposes." And they proceeded to have a party.

The chief rabbi of Berlin was a tall, slightly stooped man in his middle sixties with a small, well-tended mustache and beard, like an English Edwardian. He had dark blue, almost violet-colored eyes under beetled gray brows, giving him the air of an angry Chinese Mandarin. But he was never angry. During the 1934 Yom Kippur services in the great synagogue in the Fasanenstrasse, there were gangs of storm troopers, S.A., outside, shouting anti-Semitic threats. "*Juda, verrecke! Jews, croak!*" Their local commander probably thought they were performing important duties for the party. Their shouting and ranting could be clearly heard by the worshippers. So the chief rabbi left the pulpit and walked outside to face the thugs. Then, they say, he raised his robed arms toward heaven and prayed, "*O Lord, Thou hast made us Thy Chosen People. Now, Lord, do me a favor: Choose someone else!*" After all, the chief rabbi was a Berliner.

He did not come from a religious family. His people had been small merchants since Frederick the Great's time. The chief rabbi first felt his calling when he was a law student at Heidelberg. He then went to seminaries in Vienna and Jerusalem, and in 1901 the handsome young man was ordained a rabbi in Berlin, presiding over a wealthy new congregation in Charlottenberg. Its members were successful and secure. They were mostly Berlin-born or from Breslau and West Prussia. He became acquainted with Theodore Herzl, the Viennese journalist who was the founder of Zionism, but he disagreed with Herzl's ideas. He understood the Austrian Herzl's dedication to a Jewish home state. But Zionism was not for German Jews, who had Germany. This was their homeland.

During the war, the chief rabbi became a decorated army chaplain, the first Jewish clergyman in the kaiser's forces, and when he came home, he tried hard to keep his flock clear of Berlin's debauch. Most Berlin Jews managed to survive depression, inflation, and all the other dangers of the twenties. Many became distinguished scientists, artists, business leaders, doctors, and lawyers. The end of the war also brought Jewish refugees from Poland, Lithuania, Hungary, Roumania, and Russia, and the chief rabbi had to help them to blend into Berlin's civilized Jewish community. At times, the refugees were an embarrassment because of their Yiddish language and their strange ghetto clothes. Still, they were Jews. Even if there were crooks among them, after their decades of suppression, that, too, had to be borne.

Then came the Nazi takeover, and now the chief rabbi was spiritual guide to a group of loyal German Jews, who were being robbed of their homeland. He saw himself with an alternative he had long ago dismissed: Zionism.

Only recently, he had had a meeting that had made his scalp crawl. He was called to the office of a senior SS functionary and told that the authorities were "quite willing to help Zionist organizations funnel Jews into Palestine." Of course, there were many Zionist training groups throughout Germany, but the British made it impossible to enter Palestine. Many Jewish refugees became internees in Mediterranean and Adriatic ports after they tried to land in Palestine illegally.

The British chief rabbi had just sent an urgent confidential message, asking him to stop these landing attempts. How could he stop German Jews from trying? Where else could they go? The British, the French, the Americans, even the Central and South Americans were beginning to slam their gates shut.

For himself, the chief rabbi felt he was too old and too German to involve himself in Zionism, but he could act as a buffer between the Nazi authorities and Berlin's Zionists.

By helping Zionism, the SS were simply trying to get rid of Jews. They certainly had no kindness in mind. At the same time, they could irritate the British government.

The chief rabbi had much greater worries. A few lucky men had recently been released from the concentration camps at Dachau and Sachsenhausen, upon promising to emigrate at once. These people told him there were things ahead much worse than the fiercest pogrom ever committed by Russian cossacks. Men of intellect, renown, and courage sat in his study, crying like children. Days of terror lay ahead, and they needed all the help he could get. Their survival was at stake.

The chief rabbi finally did what he had resisted for weeks: He picked up the phone and asked his secretary to connect him with *Kommerzienrath* Goldner.

The *Kommerzienrath* showed the chief rabbi to a leather armchair and offered him a cigar, which the chief rabbi declined.

Fall had come early, and the oak trees outside in the garden of the Goldner villa were almost bare. The chief rabbi had arrived after dinner.

The *Kommerzienrath* lighted his cigar, waiting for his guest to speak. The chief rabbi tapped his fingertips onto the arms of the chair and said, "*Herr* Goldner, as you know, we have not had much contact with each other."

Adalbert Goldner nodded but made no comment.

The chief rabbi continued, "The affairs of the Jewish *Gemeinde*, the congregation, are mainly in the hands of those of the Jewish faith. But now, more and more, whatever we do is influenced by new . . . conditions."

"You mean the new laws?"

"Yes. And they get more difficult every month. For example, did you know that beginning next month all automobiles owned by Jews must have a 'J' in front of the license numbers?"

"No. I did not."

"It is a small thing, but it will deter many Jewish businessmen, doctors, lawyers, and others from owning a car. They would rather not expose themselves to any potential trouble by having a 'Jew' license number."

"I can't blame them," said Adalbert Goldner. He wondered why he had not heard about this new regulation, but it probably did not apply to him. A Goldner with a "J" license plate? Laughable!

"To continue," said the chief rabbi, "I now need your help."

"How?"

"You are a possible link with the authorities. We need representation by someone as distinguished as you."

"*Na, ja, Herr Hauptrabbiner*, surely you yourself are sufficiently respected to function as a spokesman."

"I?" said the chief rabbi. "To them I am a . . . rabbi. They see in me everything they hate. Even wearing my Iron Cross or my old army uniform, I would still be a *Rabbiner*."

"How about others of your faith? Surely there arc bankers, physicians, lawyers, people in the academic world?"

"Perhaps. But many have left, and few of those still here have your standing in Berlin."

"And perhaps," said Adalbert Goldner ironically, "it's also because I'm Christian."

"Yes. Perhaps." The chief rabbi nodded and smiled sadly.

"And so you come to me?"

"Yes, *Kommerzienrath*."

Anger was building in the old merchant, anger he had stored for years. Certain Jews had always shunned the Goldners because they were Christian converts. His very in-laws, the Schorrs, had refused to attend his wedding because it was a church wedding. There were decades of slurs and innuendo from the Jewish community. He had kept calm and swallowed it all. And now this old idiot sat there and asked for help from him, Adalbert Goldner, the convert, the traitor!

"You know," he said, "until now, the Jewish congregation did not see fit to have any contact with my family. I suppose you thought we were terrible people?"

"Terrible? No," said the chief rabbi. "But surely you can understand how I, personally, had certain reservations?"

"At least," said Adalbert Goldner, chuckling, "at least you're being open with me. You're right. I can't blame you personally for feeling as you do. But the others, those snide *Schneisskerle* who called us names because we *believe* in Christianity."

The chief rabbi leaned forward, fascinated despite himself. He said, "You *really* do, don't you?"

"Absolutely. And I also believe with all my heart that the whole catastrophe could have been avoided, *years* ago, if Jews had joined the other Germans instead of being stubborn and staying different. After all, it's the same God. You can't blame the simple German *Bürger* for being suspicious of people who wish to remain strangers. Hitler could not have attacked the Jews if the Jews had long ago become part of Germany!"

The chief rabbi shook his head. "Why not stay different?" he said. "What's wrong with our tradition? Why should we be punished for loyalty to our own faith? We've stayed Jews in other countries like England, France, and America. . . ."

"A grave error," Goldner interrupted. "And it will cost much pain, that error."

"Let me ask you," said the chief rabbi, "do you feel safe?"

"So far, yes. We've been Christians since my grandfather's time, long before the last kaiser."

"What about the Nürnberg laws, the racial definitions?"

"*Na, ja*, all sane people I know think that the government will have to change its tune. Otherwise, it would cost Germany too heavily, even internationally."

"So you really think other countries will help us Jews?" said the chief rabbi. He shook his head. "I can assure you, no one will help. But I hope you are right and that the German laws change."

"I am sure they must. Hitler is an Austrian who does not

understand that Germans are *gerecht*, are just people. And also, I still believe that part of this mess is the fault of those who insist on being different . . . special."

"The fault of the Jews?"

"Yes, the Jews. Look, to get back to what you requested, I shall try my best to help. But don't ask me to patch up things that your precious congregation helped to tear up."

They parted courteously, but the atmosphere was cool.

The butler helped the chief rabbi into a taxi, and Adalbert Goldner returned to his library.

And the biggest crime of all, he thought, is that you Jewish *Arschlöcher* have even made me doubt my own future! Thank God Hanni had not heard this whole conversation.

The young SS *Hauptsturmführer* captain leaned forward, arms folded over his chest. He wore his daily *Dienstanzug*, black uniform jacket with single epaulet and rank insignia on the lapel, leather belt with round officer's buckle, shoulder strap, swastika armband. His shirt was tan, his black necktie was pinned with the enameled party badge. His boots were slim, worn over black breeches with the oversized "wings" favored by many young SS officers. On his left sleeve was the diamond-shaped embroidered patch of the S.D. The sides of the captain's head and his neck were clean-shaven, leaving a small island of hair on the top. Despite his trim, well-muscled frame he looked like a schoolboy, although he was twenty-nine.

He was Tunnes's opposite number in the S.D., and Tunnes rather liked him. This was one of the few SS people anxious to listen and to learn police work.

The two men were in Tunnes's office at Gestapo headquarters, a small corner room with tan walls, dominated by the standard portrait of the *Führer*. The desk faced the far wall under the picture. The other walls were covered with gray file cabinets, and over the cabinets on shelves were long rows of three-ring binders with flat, labeled backs.

All Gestapo offices were drab and workmanlike, in contrast to the SS offices, which were dressed up with party insignia, photographs of parades and units, honor daggers and mounted flags.

Tunnes stretched out in his scuffed leather armchair, his hands clenched behind his head. He wore a rumpled tan tweed suit and a knitted wool tie, and the tips of his shirt collar curled upward over his lapels. He looked like a North Sea captain, ashore for the day, uncomfortable without his sweater, pea jacket, and deck pants.

"Tunnes," said the SS officer, "you're right. I think it would be damn foolish, *Quatsch*, to enforce the regulation while the man is under surveillance. It might foul things up."

"Good," said Tunnes. "Glad you agree."

The young captain smiled apologetically. "Look," he said, "you know the police better than I do. No insult meant, but they're sometimes inclined to be a bit, oh, rigid, don't you agree? So, could you please . . . ?"

"Yes," said Tunnes. "I'll take care of things. I have some old pals down at Alex." He called Berlin police headquarters by the same nickname everyone used. He would talk to friends in the Traffic Police, the *Verkehrspolizei*, to tell them that Gestapo and S.D. had decided to postpone enforcement of a "J" plate for *Kommerzienrath* Goldner's limousine.

Goldner was technically a Jew, but an exception had to be made. If "*Der Olle*" gave up his car, that would put Ockert out of action. Tunnes had almost forgotten about those "J" license plates, but Ockert had attached a note to his weekly milk-bottle list, asking about it. He was probably worried about his own ass and his standing among the other Berlin chauffeurs, although he seemed like a decent enough fellow. *Na, ja*, one couldn't blame him! When you're an Aryan, it's tough to drive around with a "J" plate.

And so *Kommerzienrath* Adalbert Goldner's personal Daimler-Benz limousine got no "J" plate, to the relief of his chauffeur and also of several senior executives at KaDeBe.

To the *Kommerzienrath*, it was self-understood and proof of his secure position. He could have kicked himself for ever questioning it, and because of that he did not remember the chief rabbi's visit with the satisfaction it should have given him.

The Dorns' bedroom was pitch dark because Hilde had finally won a long battle: She could sleep only when the roll-down jalousie shutters were closed, while Karl-Heinz preferred them open. But this night Hilde was still awake. She nudged him and brought him back from a half-dream. He reached for her and began kissing her breasts and her flat stomach. Her small body was in perfect proportion, rounded thighs to soft, muscled buttocks, tiny navel and slim waistline, wide shoulders and firm little breasts. She was dark-complexioned like many Franconians, and her forearms and thighs were covered with soft blond fuzz.

She began to respond, but then she gently pushed him away. She said, "That's not why I woke you."

They had made much love earlier that night.

"Oh? Then why?"

She said, "I want to hear again about the Brunzig offer."

"*Zu Befehl!*" he said. "Yes, ma'am!"

And he repeated the whole thing: Zoss had taken him to Horcher, Berlin's leading restaurant. Willy Horcher himself greeted and seated them near a table of senior SS and *Luftwaffe* officers and their ladies. Almost hidden at the other end of that table was Hermann Göring, surprisingly not in uniform but in white tie and tails, and without his usual gallery of decorations. He wore only the *Pour le Mérite*, the First World War "Blue Max," under his white bow tie, and the golden party badge on his jacket. When he spotted Zoss, Göring waved: "Zoss! *Wie geht's?*"

Zoss raised his hand—"*Heilitla!*"—and smiled. Then he and Karl-Heinz sat down at their table, and Zoss ordered dry vermouth as aperitifs.

"*Der Dicke*," he said, meaning Göring, "just came from a reception at the Italian embassy; that's why he's not in uniform."

"Why not?" asked Karl-Heinz.

"He's clever, although sometimes he doesn't seem it, compared with, say, the 'Little *Doktor*.' "

Karl-Heinz knew he meant Goebbels.

"So," Zoss continued, "because he can't outshine the *Fascisti* with their magnificent gear and their splendid slim figures, he obviously decided to wear plain *Frack*, white tie and tails. I've seen him do it before. He refuses to be second to anyone except the *Führer*. We just finished the most superb 900K for him, *Luftwaffe* blue, and with chrome wheels, tan leather, and tan top. It's *unwahrscheinlich schön!* Unbelievably beautiful!"

"Did he buy it?"

"*Na, ja*." Zoss shrugged. "Not really. It's a *Luftwaffe*

command car, so it will have 'WL' license plates like all
other air force cars.''

They ordered dinner; Zoss had his favorite lobster rémoulade
and Karl-Heinz ordered *Schlemmerschnitten*, open tartar sand-
wiches with caviar trim, with a piccolo of champagne for
Zoss and a bottle of *Pilsner Urquell* beer for Karl-Heinz.

''It's all fixed,'' said Zoss.

''What?''

''The position with us.''

''*Herr* Zoss,'' said Karl-Heinz. ''I am flattered and grateful,
but so far I have not made up my mind. Besides, the KaDeBe
people have been very kind to me.''

''Yes, I know,'' said Zoss. ''But that's all going to change.''

''I don't understand.''

''This Jewish fellow, Schmidt, whom you worked under,
he's gone, right?''

''Yes.''

''He recommended that they promote you to his job. But
that won't happen.''

Karl-Heinz was amazed. How could Zoss know?

The Brunzig man grinned. ''Don't be too shocked. I told
you I have friends at KaDeBe.''

''Yes, but I had no idea they would discuss internal matters
like this.''

''They don't usually. They did in this case. Let it go at
that. All right?''

''All right, I'll have to accept that. What else did they tell
you?''

''My dear Dorn, I'll repeat part of it, but only for selfish
reasons and because I trust you.''

''I'll keep it to myself, except for my wife. We always
share things.''

''Good decision. She's a bright woman. I learned a lot
about her, all first-class.'' Then he saw a small wave of
annoyance on Karl-Heinz's face, and he quickly continued,
''First of all, you won't get the promotion. Nothing to do
with your ability. Everyone at KaDeBe thinks you deserve the
job, but now there are other considerations.'' He leaned
forward, not wishing to be overheard. ''KaDeBe will be
made *Judenrein*, will be cleared of Jews within six months,
and a lot of outsiders will be brought into the store, people
with solid party affiliation and good commercial background,

who need retailing experience. The man taking Schmidt's job will be one of these."

Zoss leaned back into his chair. "Some cruel things have to be done when the firm gets restaffed for political reasons. Can't be helped. Anyway, I think you might be well out of it."

Karl-Heinz was sad and disappointed that Siegfried Schmidt had turned out to be right after all. Then he looked Zoss straight in the eyes and after a moment he said, "And what about the *Herr Kommerzienrath?*"

"Goldner?"

"Yes."

"You know the answer as well as I do. It's quite clear what will happen. He's a Jew. He will have to be replaced. The government wants to prove that any German enterprise can be run by Aryans, and that Jews have no monopoly on brains."

"That's not what I mean," said Karl-Heinz. "My father was a party member, and I certainly am all for the things being achieved by the movement. But the Goldners? They've always been Protestant."

"That's not what the law says. You know it as well as I do."

"*Na, ja,*" said Karl-Heinz, "I'd better quit before I get accused of being a Commie from the old K.P.D."

"Don't upset yourself," said Zoss. "I just think you're a normal, decent *anständig* fellow. But it's a new world, and you'd better harden yourself."

"Yes," said Karl-Heinz, thinking of Schmidt, "an old friend told me that a while back."

There was a pause while the waiter served their dinners. Finally Zoss, who was ready to start eating, put down his fork and knife, reached for Karl-Heinz's arm and said, "Yes, I know! Sometimes these things are not very palatable."

"True," said Karl-Heinz. Even Schmidt had told him that he must not feel responsible. For a while they ate in silence.

The Göring table was like a magnet, drawing people from all over the restaurant, who came to pay homage. To Karl-Heinz's surprise, Göring was not an ebullient man. He listened, smiled, and said a few cordial words, but he seemed quite cool and detached.

Zoss said, "He's not at all like the public image, is he?"

"You're reading my mind. I've been watching him, and he's not the jolly innkeeper they picture in the *Berliner Illustrierte*."

Zoss smiled. "Maybe soon you'll be able to judge for yourself." He signaled for coffee and cognac. Then he tapped the table with his knuckles and said, "Here's the job we have for you. I told you that we put many of our cars at the disposal of the party and the government. We need someone to be our liaison in that whole operation. It could sometimes be like walking a tightrope, because there are many prima donnas up there, who will need careful handling, but it's a fantastic job."

Karl-Heinz asked, "Is it like von Bernsdorfer's assignment?"

"Not at all," Zoss said. "Von Bernsdorfer is nothing but a transportation clerk. You would actually be an emissary for Brunzig."

"I still don't get the *Kern*, the 'gut' of the job."

"The job is to sell Brunzig A.G. to the bigshots, to make us look good!" Zoss spoke slowly, as if he were instructing a ten-year-old. "You'll also deal with certain foreigners. They all know Brunzig from racing, but now they must learn that we also do other things. Most of all, Brunzig A.G. is the automobile company closest to the party, to the government, even to the *Führer* himself. We have competitors who are anxious to elbow us out of the way. We want to be sure that we always give the finest impression and show our best side. The big stuff will be done back in Stuttgart by Gerhardt Brunzig and a few of us around him. But we need someone like you and a few other young men right on the firing line. Do you think you can do it?"

Karl-Heinz had no doubts. He said, "Of course!"

Zoss nodded. "*Prima!*" he said. He was delighted.

This was the story of the previous evening as Karl-Heinz once more told it to Hilde. The next morning, early, she was anxious to get back to the subject. While he had his breakfast coffee and buttered *Knüppel* roll, she asked, "Karle, is there any reason why you feel reluctant? Any reason why you don't want to take this job?"

"None."

"Then do it! KaDeBe seems to be a lost cause anyway."

Karl-Heinz phoned Zoss later that morning and told him he was accepting.

• • •

Villa Ritterschwert, the Brunzig family home, was named after the *Ritterschwert*, the company's Knight's Sword emblem. Old Hubertus Brunzig bought the mansion in 1909 from a bankrupt steel manufacturer. It was perched high in the hills, and it overlooked Stuttgart's kettle-shaped center, including the Brunzig factories. Hubertus Brunzig was buried in a vault on the estate.

Ritterschwert was now the home of Gerhardt Brunzig, the founder's only son and *Generaldirektor* of Brunzig A.G. Old Hubertus was a bull-necked man who began his career as a machinist in a railroad factory, but his son Gerhardt betrayed none of his plebeian ancestry. A tall man in his forties, he had the natural grace of a landed aristocrat. Perhaps he was the finest example of old Hubertus's designs. It was astonishing how many graceful objects had emerged from the founder's talented brain, even the Knight's Sword symbol, which was copied by many manufacturers. The only ugly thing about Brunzig was the villa, a pompous mummy of Germany's industrial revolution. Gerhardt, who had grown up there with his two sisters, was in the habit of apologizing for it. He would wave a slim hand in the direction of the armor- and antler-bedecked walls, and say, "People in my father's day had odd ideas about decor."

Yet he refused to change a thing because his instinct told him that to change the villa was to destroy the sense of longevity valued by automobile manufacturers. A young industry clutched onto its short history.

Karl-Heinz was met at the Stuttgart railroad station by a gray-liveried chauffeur with one of the legendary black, eight-seater-convertible "Himmler *Panzers*," as they were irreverently called. He was about to step into the back of the car but instead he decided to sit up front with the driver. When they pulled into the villa's cobbled courtyard, the servant who was waiting automatically opened the back door until he spotted the passenger in the front.

Karl-Heinz was shown into a small salon, where he waited, surrounded by mounted stag heads on the walls. There was also the massive head of a fierce boar, lips drawn up in hatred, tusks ready to rip. Gerhardt Brunzig stepped through a door, pointed at the boar's head, and drawled, "That's what you get for accelerating too hard when you have poor brakes."

Karl-Heniz tried to be polite. "A wonderful trophy," he said.

"My dear Dorn," said Gerhardt Brunzig, "to this day I cannot understand what's so marvelous about shooting creatures that can't shoot back. They ought to teach the use of firearms to wild game. It would even things up, don't you agree?"

"True," said Karl-Heinz, "but it would limit the size of hunting parties."

Brunzig was startled. "A man with a sense of humor? What a rare find! Most of our new executives are very, er, serious."

Brunzig was dressed in the English manner: gray, double-breasted chalk-stripe suit, brown suede shoes, white cutaway-collared shirt, and navy and white polka-dot tie. His longish blond hair was pomaded and parted low. He had a startling resemblance to the Prince of Wales, and he obviously fostered that impression. His ambitious father sent Gerhardt to an old English school, which had left its mark. Somehow, he seemed slightly foreign to the German eye.

They sat down in facing high-backed church chairs. Brunzig brought up Zoss. "Very clever fellow that! My father originally hired him for the old Berlin showroom, and today Zoss runs all passenger car sales. I find myself involved in other parts of the firm right now." Then, answering Karl-Heinz's unspoken question, he said, "We make everything from tractors to aircraft engines and, of course, a lot of military hardware. We're about to demonstrate a new command vehicle. Why don't you come out to the test grounds tomorrow? You'll see that Brunzigs can really perform."

"I'd like that."

"Good." Brunzig shook his head and smiled. "Poor Dorn! What a nuisance to come here to smoky Stuttgart! But everyone felt it would be good if we got acquainted. Zoss picked you for some very interesting work, and I suppose it's important to know as much as possible about the company, even about your host!"

"*Herr Generaldirektor*, I certainly am the one who's a nuisance. They could have put me up at a hotel."

"Oh, I usually prefer that our management people stay here with me. It's no trouble. We have plenty of room, as you'll see."

Karl-Heinz soon knew what Gerhardt Brunzig meant. There were corridors of guest bedrooms and bathrooms, almost like a hotel. The servants had unpacked his clothes and had laid out his *smoking*, dinner suit, shirt, and black tie. Zoss had prepared him that one dressed for dinner at Ritterschwert, so he borrowed a dinner suit at KaDeBe. Now he struggled with the unaccustomed torture of stiff separate collar and black bow tie. If Hilde were only there to help! Promptly at seven, he went downstairs, where the butler showed him into a small music room. His host and some others were drinking aperitifs. A footman offered him a glass of vermouth.

Gerhardt Brunzig, dressed in a Saville Row dinner suit, said, "Ah, there's our newest Brunziger, *Herr* Dorn from Berlin. Come and meet some old friends." He introduced him. "*Herr Doktor* Maut, Major and *Frau* von Totten, and Anneliese von Konsky." The men exchanged small nods. Only the major brought his heels together. Karl-Heinz shook hands with the ladies. Hand kissing was not his style, too Austrian.

Dr. Maut said, "You're a Berliner? I miss Berlin. Did my studying there."

Major von Totten, a square-faced, balding man, joined Dr. Maut. He smiled at Karl-Heinz. "I hear you'll be working with us."

"I wish," said Karl-Heinz, "I could give you an answer to that. My duties have not yet been clarified, at least to me."

"*Ja*," said the major, "I don't want to be *indiskret*, but I think tomorrow you'll see some new stuff we've all been waiting for and which will be tried by our top staff people."

"Good," said Karl-Heinz.

Dr. Maut said, "Why don't you tell Dorn that tomorrow he'll meet the newest of my children."

The major smiled. "He's right. We'll soon see what he came up with this time." Everyone knows about the famous Dr. Maut, who had designed everything from race cars to tanks.

At dinner, which was served in one corner of the immense neo-Gothic dining hall, Karl-Heinz was seated next to *Frau* von Konsky, an angularly stylish woman in her late thirties who wore a low-cut black evening gown. He complimented her on it and she said, "Berlin. It's from my dressmaker there. These days Berlin has such good *couturiers* that I hardly buy anything in Paris." She spoke with a Hungarian accent. "Now that I live in Berlin most of the year, I really adore it. My ex-husband used to prefer Paris. It was one of our constant battles."

"You must be a good friend of *Herr* Brunzig?"

"Friend and business associate. I represent various international companies. Basically, I'm a sales agent. That's why I'm here today, to see Maut's new *Kind.*"

"Does he always call them children?"

"For as long as I've known him. I think he'll do anything for anyone who'll finance his new ideas. Thank God he's with Brunzig. I'd hate to think of him with the Russians."

Anneliese von Konsky and Karl-Heinz got along well, which was not lost on Gerhardt Brunzig. He had to admit that Zoss really knew his business! This young Dorn fellow would work out just fine.

Frau von Konsky had talked to Dr. Maut on her other side, then turned back to Karl-Heinz. "I was telling Maut," she said, "that I was at the Berghof last week and the *Führer* is looking forward to Maut's new Brunzig. The *Führer* is a fanatic about Brunzigs, you know. It's the only car he will ride in."

"I didn't know," said Karl-Heinz. "Why?"

"He was once in an accident, and he was in a Brunzig. The other car, not a Brunzig, was destroyed, but the Brunzig was almost untouched. You know he is very superstitious. He often does things on sheer instinct."

"Have you known him long?"

"I met him a few years ago through Jan Telesty."

"Telesty?"

"A fascinating character, an Austrian in the SS. He's absolutely immense, maybe a head taller than you, and I'm told that he trains SS troops for all sorts of special combat and parachute work. Anyway, Telesty was a friend of my former husband. The *Führer* absolutely adores Telesty, calls him his super soldier. The *Führer* likes flamboyant people."

"You obviously understand him."

"He's been very kind to me. He found out I was in the armaments business, so he instructed his people to let me handle certain deals with the Italians and the Spaniards."

"What does von Totten do?"

"He's a great ordnance expert, an absolute genius. The

von Tottens are an old military family, always army people, and the major has graduated from every staff school and engineering college. He must hold five doctorates in military science. They're fine people, *Erstklassig*. . . ."

The dinner broke up early.

The next morning came up gray and windy. After breakfast, which was served in the bedrooms, they assembled in the main hall and were driven into the nearby hill country until they arrived at the fenced-in Brunzig test grounds, where guards with the Knight's Sword on their caps and tunics waved them through the gate.

The test grounds incorporated everything from a high-banked oval racetrack to tank traps. They stopped in front of a low building, half hangar, half offices. One of the large doors slid open, and out rolled an army-gray vehicle about the size of an open eight-seater. It was quite low, but instead of rear wheels it had tanklike tracks. The visitors walked around this strange hybrid, while Dr. Maut explained.

"This is G.F.W. twelve, a new command car. It can handle the same terrain as a tank, but it has a paved-road speed of up to one hundred and thirty kilometers an hour. For sustained road travel we use a mechanism to shed the rear tracks and then G.F.W. twelve runs on its tall bogey-wheels. The tracks can be remounted in seconds for cross-country terrain work. On open, flat cross-country runs, it can do nearly a hundred. G.F.W. twelve has built-in hydraulic jacks with swamp feet so it can free itself from most obstacles. It also has self-winches and can lift itself out of a ditch or up the side of a cliff almost vertically."

"Fantastic," said the major. "This will change armored warfare." Then he explained to the group, "Until now an armored commander was tied to a slow tank, a fast car, or a light plane, which all have their obvious drawbacks. With this vehicle, a *Panzer* commander can move like lightning and still handle the same terrain as his *Panzers*."

The chief test drive of Brunzig then gave a virtuoso performance: G.F.W. 12 climbed up impassable slopes and then ran at high speeds on an oval racetrack.

Dr. Maut, in green loden coat and green velour hunting hat with a trim of badger brush, asked Karl-Heinz, "*Na*, Dorn, what do you think? Any questions?"

"Only one question, *Herr Doktor*."

"About the performance?"

"No. That's fantastic. What does 'G.F.W. twelve' stand for?"

"*Gelände*—terrain, *Führer*—command, *Wagen*—car. Number twelve."

"Why number twelve?"

"Because I'm a stupid ass. It took me twelve versions to reach this final prototype." Dr. Maut was doubled over with laughter at his own expense.

"*Danke, Herr Doktor.*"

"*Bitte, Herr* Dorn."

Gerhardt Brunzig strolled over. In his Burberry trenchcoat, plaid wool scarf, and British hunting cap he might have been watching a field trial on the Scottish moors. Karl-Heinz was reading a red brochure marked "*Geheim*"—Secret—which had just been handed to him. It gave the details of G.F.W. 12. Brunzig asked: "*In Ordnung?* Do you like our new beast?"

"Fantastic," said Karl-Heinz, raising the brochure.

"Zoss asked that you accompany Dr. Maut and him on a special demonstration next week."

"Where, may I ask?"

"Near Berlin. But you'll soon find out about it. I've got to stay here because we've got all sorts of things brewing. Besides, our racing team has to test a new engine because the *Scheiss*-Italians just switched the formula on us. We were beginning to win all their races, so they changed the rules. Papa Hoegel, our racing manager, is ready to wet his pants, he's so furious. So I shan't see you for a while. Zoss will fill you in on your duties. I was only supposed to check your teeth, *auf den Zahn fühlen. Hals und Beinbruch!*" It was the curious way race drivers wish each other luck. "Hope you'll break your neck and leg!" Then he joined Anneliese von Konsky in a 900K and they drove off. She turned and waved to Karl-Heinz.

Karl-Heinz and Zoss stood in front of the G.F.W. 12 in an open field on the military reservation at Döberitz near Berlin. Alongside the G.F.W. 12, a company of infantry was lined up in formation, rifles ordered, while their impeccable young lieutenant checked and rechecked his men. The weather was brilliant, bright blue sky, no cloud in view, and a gentle breeze from the west, and it was warm for the time of the year.

Then a black, open Brunzig, driven by an SS officer, pulled up in a cloud of dust. In back sat Dr. Maut and Major von Totten in uniform and in front, next to the driver, was Adolf Hitler.

Karl-Heinz had seen the *Führer* at the Olympics, far away in his special box, but he had never expected to stand this close to him.

The infantry company came to attention and brought their rifles to a crashing "present." Adolf Hitler got out of the car and raised his hand with bent arm to acknowledge the young officer's sweeping sword-salute. His eyes quickly looked up and down the gray line of soldiers, but he waved off the lieutenant's offer to inspect. The *Führer*, dressed in trenchcoat and wearing a tan party cap with maroon trim, looked like a busy man who had been pulled away from his desk and promised a special treat. He briskly walked over to the G.F.W. 12, his brown boots gleaming. Dr. Maut and Major von Totten followed.

"*Mein Führer*, you remember *Herr Direktor* Zoss of Brunzig?"

Zoss raised his right arm in a stiff salute. He snapped, "*Heilitla!*"

"Yes, of course, Zoss. *Wie geht's Ihnen, mein Guter?* It's been a while, hasn't it?" Adolf Hitler's voice was deep and a bit hoarse. He spoke with a melodious Austro-Bavarian accent, which was much more apparent in conversation than in his speeches. He shook hands with Zoss, who then said, "*Mein Führer*, allow me to introduce our newest young staff member, Karl-Heinz Dorn."

Adolf Hitler's gray eyes swung toward Karl-Heinz and looked straight into his. They were friendly, and he was smiling. Karl-Heinz imitated Zoss: He pulled his heels together in a military manner, raised his straight right arm to shoulder height and slightly to the side to avoid hitting the *Führer*. "*Heilitla!*"

The *Führer* swept up his hand in response and then extended it for a handshake. "Dorn," he said, "where is your home?"

"Berlin, *mein Führer*."

"*Na, ja,*" said Adolf Hitler, grinning. "There *are* a few

good Berliners. After all, you have a brilliant *Gau*leader.''
He meant Dr. Goebbels, who was the Berlin party head. Then
Hitler continued, ''*Viel Glück bei Brunzig*, much luck. Fantastic cars. Absolutely fantastic!'' An army photographer and
one from the SS had been snapping pictures since Hitler had
arrived.

Karl-Heinz stepped back, and the *Führer* turned to Dr.
Maut while the cameras clicked. Then the *Führer* waved to
Zoss and von Totten, who joined him to pose for more
photographs. Finally, a test driver started some of the same
driving demonstrations Karl-Heinz had seen at the Brunzig
test grounds.

Twenty minutes later it was over, and a stunned Karl-Heinz
sat in Zoss's blue 900K on the way back to Berlin. No one
had told him he would meet the *Führer*. He could feel the
man's grip: dry, warm skin, a quick pressure, and then the
hand was quickly withdrawn, like a privilege given and then
taken away.

They were on their way back to Berlin. Zoss, who was
driving, chatted, but Karl-Heinz was not listening. Then,
finally, he heard Zoss mention von Bernsdorfer.

''Sorry, *Herr Direktor*,'' said Karl-Heinz. ''I was day-
dreaming. What about von Bernsdorfer?''

Zoss nodded. ''I know what you mean. The first time the
Führer spoke to me, I was in a fog, too. I was saying that
von Bernsdorfer still hasn't seen the G.F.W. twelve, so we
left it out in Döberitz and you can do the honors tomorrow.
Most of the technical stuff is in the red brochure and it's quite
simple. But I doubt if von Bernsdorfer will care much about
the technical side. Horses? Yes! Machines? No! The SS will
get four G.F.W.s: two for the Berghof, and two for Sepp
Dietrich. He's the SS general who commands the *Leibstandarte
Adolf Hitler*, the bodyguard. He's also von Bernsdorfer's
chief. In case he turns up, he's a tough little bastard, a real
street brawler, so don't let him scare you. We stole another
test driver from Papa Hoegel, who yelled and complained
because he's got weeks of testing ahead for the new race
cars.''

''Yes, I know. *Herr Generaldirektor* Brunzig told me about
it.''

''Poor Papa has been at the Nürburgring track for a week,
working on fuel mixtures and cylinder-head temperatures and

valve settings and all that junk. He hates to use the race drivers for testing because they get bored and start fooling around. That's why he needs his test drivers. They do what they're told. Oh, by the way, don't lose that brochure. It's classified secret.''

"I won't.''

"Poor von Bernsdorfer!'' said Zoss as an afterthought. "He's really got a stupid job. Those snobs at the SS keep him around because he's society, *salonfähig*. He's also a pet of the *Führer*. Adolf Hitler admires athletes, and he likes to be surrounded by good-looking young people. All his aides are that same type. I figure he also took to you. That little joke about Berlin! He's usually uncomfortable around Berliners, so he must have thought that you're *in Ordnung*, all right!''

"I'm glad, *Herr Direktor*.''

"Oh, one more thing: Cut out the '*Herr Direktor*.' It's not our style at Brunzig. We're a young company, not like the Krupps and the other heavy industry boys. We like to think we haven't yet got hardening of the arteries.''

"*Gemacht, Herr* Zoss.''

"I can't believe it,'' said Hilde.

"It's true,'' he said. "I actually spoke with the *Reichskanzler und Führer*, Adolf Hitler!''

She shook her head. "What was he like?''

"I knew you'd ask that, and I can't remember now. Honestly. It's all a haze.''

"Oh, come on, Karle. . . . Was he tall? Was he pale or tanned? Did he smile? What about his voice?''

"Tall? No. Shorter than I, now that I think of it. He was sort of pale. His voice? Quite deep and a bit hoarse. Oh, by the way, *very* Austrian. The cameras were there, so he smiled a lot. And he joked with me.''

"What kind of joke?''

"He asked where I was from. I said Berlin. So he said there are *some* good Berliners, and, after all, we have clever Dr. Goebbels as *Gauleiter* or something like that.''

"Some joke! Not much of a compliment for Berliners.''

"We're used to it, don't forget. Everyone in Germany hates Berliners. Why not? We're clever and charming and modest, and we have brilliant taste.''

"Only in wives."

"Right!" said Karl-Heinz.

How proud it would have made his father that he had
spoken to the *Führer!* How his father had worshipped this
man! That one night listening to a Hitler speech had changed
his whole life and had brightened what remained of his days.

And Siegfried Schmidt? asked a nagging inside voice.
Schmidt had not panicked. He had been right. New anti-
Jewish laws were added each day. Zoss had been offered
dozens of excellent Brunzigs that Jews were anxious to sell
back to the company at a great loss. The "J" license plates
had done that.

For now, Hilde and Karl-Heinz avoided the entire subject
by unspoken agreement. They had not raised it since that
night in the restaurant at Müggelsee. But one thing was now
clear: The party's view of Jews would never change. They
had not heard from Schmidt, and Karl-Heinz guiltily admitted
that he did not mind.

Now the Schmidts were added to the subjects they no
longer discussed.

SS *Gruppenführer*-General Sepp Dietrich had the squashed
face, bull neck and chunky, short body of an old middle-
weight prizefighter, a fair comparison because Dietrich had
survived years of street fights and indoor brawls before the
N.S.D.A.P. takeover. He had headed the *Führer's* SS bodyguard for years.

He was an *Alter Kämpfer*, an Old Fighter, an honor society
within the party. Dietrich himself was said to have fired the
shot that executed Ernst Röhm, the S.A. chief who plotted
against the *Führer*, but that was only rumor.

Dietrich, trailed by von Bernsdorfer and two other SS
aides, stopped in front of the G.F.W. 12, planted his feet, put
his fists on his uniformed hips, and stared at the new vehicle.
"*Scheissdreck!* This thing is just a pile of turds until I see
what it can do!"

Von Bernsdorfer, who stood behind his chief, smiled
apologetically, but Karl-Heinz was not rattled.

"*Herr Gruppenführer*," he said. "You're right." Then
they began the demonstration.

Twenty minutes later, Dietrich was all smiles, as were his

three black-uniformed SS aides. The general tapped Karl-Heinz on the chest with his black-gloved, clenched fist and said, "*Erstklassig!* Absolutely first-class. Frankly, I was goddamn angry that Maut didn't take the time to be here."

"Dr. Maut," said Karl-Heinz, "is at the Nürburgring with our new race cars. I realize I'm not a big wheel, but I hope I can answer any questions, although I am quite new with Brunzig."

Von Bernsdorfer interrupted with a conciliatory smile. He told Dietrich, "Brunzig thought you ought to meet Dorn because I shall be working with him closely. He will be Brunzig's liaison with us."

"*Na, schön*, all right then," said Dietrich, mollified, pointing his thumb at the G.F.W. 12, "but one question: What about bottom armament on that sled? Doesn't matter how fast you go if you get your balls torn off by a landmine."

Karl-Heinz had studied the manual. "Sixteen-millimeter bottom armament. That's as much as the car will take. With its flank armor and front and back plating, it already weighs four thousand kilos."

Dietrich was impressed. "Good," he said. "You're not just a pretty boy. You also know your stuff." Then he asked, "How did the *Führer* like this crate?"

"He seemed very impressed."

Dietrich nodded, raised his arm in a quick salute, and stomped off, followed by two aides. Von Bernsdorfer stayed for a moment to say, "Dorn, you did just fine! *Prima!*" Then he followed the tough little SS general.

Zoss was delighted. His protégé had passed two important tests: The *Führer* had liked him and he had already heard from von Bernsdorfer how well Dorn had handled the prickly Sepp Dietrich. Only one thing remained to be done. "It's time," he told Karl-Heinz, "for you to join the party. I will arrange everything. Also, the N.S.K.K. You need some sort of uniform. I can get away with my civvies because of my international work, but you will have many reasons to wear uniform. Anyway, you will look very snazzy."

Most people in the automobile industry joined N.S.K.K., the National Socialist Motor Corps. N.S.K.K. ran everything from driving schools to traffic clinics. It also licensed racing and was the German affiliate of most international automobile associations. It even issued international driving licenses. One could spot N.S.K.K. members at most German automobile events, because they wore black breeches and boots, tan shirts, and black caps almost like the SS, but their insignia were different. Although N.S.K.K. supposedly were to "provide the motorized nucleus for the nation's defense," nobody took that part too seriously. Mostly, members liked their special privileges, like sitting in the pits at races or getting through when roads were blocked for parades, but they all tried to dodge weekly meetings and other dull duties.

The idea of party membership did not shock Karl-Heinz. It was no longer like the early days when his father had joined and when party membership was a major commitment. Now it was almost a pro forma gesture. Besides, one had to admit that it became increasingly more difficult to maintain the momentum of a career without being a party member. Almost everyone he knew had joined or was about to.

Everyone except Hilde, but then Hilde no longer wanted a career. Had she stayed with the foreign service, she certainly would have had to join. Nevertheless, his instincts told him not to tell her about joining the party . . . yet. Hilde had to be handled with discretion, and he was not sure how she would receive the news, with her increasing reservations about the party.

It irritated him that Hilde might object to his joining. She was a loyal German and she had never really said a word against the *Führer*, but because of her time in London she had this peculiar spleen about the Jews. She was probably right, but what could they do about it? They could not change the whole structure of the movement. So long as the two of them, Hilde and Karl-Heinz Dorn, behaved decently and did no Jew any harm, that ought to be enough. That ought to satisfy Hilde's precious sense of integrity!

At three in the afternoon on the fifteenth of January nineteen hundred and thirty-eight, *Kommerzienrath* Adalbert Goldner, head of the board of KaDeBe Stores A.G., sat for the last time in his accustomed chair at the head of the boardroom table. At five minutes past three, the vice-chairman, who had been with KaDeBe twenty years, asked for attention.

"I have here a letter from *Reichs Innenminister* Wilhelm Frick which forces this board to take certain actions. The most important one of these is to demand the resignation of the head of our board. I must say that I deeply regret having to convey this order, but we all know that it cannot be altered and must be carried out promptly.''

All eleven men on the board rose to their feet. The only one who remained seated was *"Der Olle,"* *Kommerzienrath* Goldner. There was total silence, but somewhere outside, in one of the other offices, one could hear a phone ring, muffled, far away. One of the directors, a short fat fellow at the end of the table, was breathing heavily. He began to cough, but stifled the disturbance. For a while the *Kommerzienrath*'s fingers drummed on the polished oaken table top. Then he looked up at the men, each one of whom he had brought onto this board during the last twenty years to help him run KaDeBe.

"Na, meine Herren!" he said, arms extended, fingers still drumming their soft rhythm. He spoke in the thickest, broadest Berlinese, *"Der Mensch denkt, und Jott lenkt. Rejen Se sich nich auf! Machen Se sich kehnen Fleck! Ick jeh ja schon!"* They heard him: "Well, gentlemen, man proposes and God disposes. Don't get upset! Don't get your bowels in an uproar! I'm getting out!"

Then he rose, a tall man drawing himself to his full height, jacket open, thumbs hooked into his vest pockets, and left the boardroom of his ancestral business without a word of good-bye or even a look back.

Ockert had already been alerted. After a male secretary helped the *Kommerzienrath* into his fur-trimmed *Paletot* coat and handed him his bowler hat and cane, the old man went straight to the garage under the store via private elevator. Ockert, wordless for once, drove him to the villa on Kaiserdamm, where *Frau* Goldner was waiting. Earlier, she had received a confidential warning from an old woman secretary at KaDeBe. So Hannelohre Goldner knew what to expect. But when her husband arrived, she could not believe her eyes. *"Der Olle"* was in excellent spirits. They had tea, and she waited for a crack in that façade, but she waited in vain. He stayed as he was when he came home. Incredible! He had come to terms with this disaster.

Their sons arrived shortly after dinner. They, too, had been forced to quit. The two younger Goldners were completely bewildered. They were fourth-generation Protestants and mar-

ried to Christian women. Their children had been baptized in
the Kaiser Wilhelm Memorial Church. The *Kommerzienrath*
calmed them, cheered them up, and advised them to emigrate
at once. They went home to their wives and children to take
charge of their lives. They left by taxi, because their cars had
been "J"-tagged.

The Goldners' dinner was almost cozy. They had not been
this close since they were a young couple. Afterward, in the
library, he said, "Hanni, we have a lot of work to do. You
must help me."

He wrote several longhand letters to his attorneys. All
property was to be disposed of as quickly as possible. The
servants were to be discharged after receiving a year of salary
in advance. All tangible assets were to be declared to the
government for emigration proceedings, which were to be
initiated at once.

He also wrote to all the servants, explaining the reason for
their dismissal and that they would receive salaries for one
year ahead. He asked Hanni to help remind him of any loose
ends.

"Ockert," she said.

"What about him?"

"He has kids. If the garage house gets sold, what's going
to happen to him? He'll need a place for his family. The
others have no children."

"You're right, Hanni. Why don't we give him the garage
and the car?" So he added a letter that transferred ownership
of the garage house and the 1928 Daimler-Benz limousine,
license plate 1A-1234, to the chauffeur and his family.

Before going to bed, "*Der Olle*" said, "England won't be
so bad. We have many friends there, don't we? And your
family." He slept soundly, although Hannelohre Goldner
stayed awake through most of the night. She knew there was
no choice, but it hurt deeply to leave everything.

At six in the morning she finally fell into a fitful sleep.
Kommerzienrath Goldner shot himself to death about seven
that morning, the sixteenth of January 1938. He was alone in
his library, and he used a small-caliber pistol he had always
kept in his desk. He left a letter for his wife, a letter for the
mayor of Berlin, and a letter for the chief rabbi of Berlin.

The *Stürmer* printed this story, underlined in garish red:

JEW ADMITS GUILT!

The Jew Adalbert Goldner was dismissed summarily from his position at KaDeBe. In an open admission of guilt, he then killed himself. We say: Good riddance to one more example of Jewish vermin!

Of course, decent people never read the *Stürmer*. Neither Zoss nor von Bernsdorfer or Gerhardt Brunzig or the Dorns read the *Stürmer*. So they could not know the viciousness of this lie. If they had, there was not much they could have done to correct it. But they did read the actual facts in the *Völkische Beobachter*, the offical party newspaper, and in the morning *Berliner Tageblatt*. Each of these papers noted in a small paragraph that the Jewish merchant Adalbert Goldner, formerly head of the KaDeBe store, had taken his own life.

Hilde was first to see it in her paper at breakfast, and Karl-Heinz was very shocked. "*Der Olle*" had been quite a character!

Armin Zoss said nothing. It would have sounded as if he was bragging for having predicted that the Goldners were through.

The next Sunday, Karl-Heinz said he had to go to the Brunzig office to get some important papers, and that he would be back home by noon. Actually, he had a surprise for Hilde.

She tried to stay in bed but she could not go back to sleep, so she dressed and found herself with the wish to go to church. She had not attended service for a long time. Karl-Heinz and she had never joined a Berlin congregation.

She walked to the Catholic church a few blocks from the square. The sidewalks were clear of snow and the air was cold and dry, a typical sunny winter day. The church stood on a small square among gardens and villas. It looked like a cheerful English country abbey. Even its cemetery, which nestled next to the rectory, was like a garden in winter, covered with snow from the week before.

She sat down in a back pew and did not take part in the actual ritual, but the organ music, the sound of Latin, and the hymns calmed her and warmed her. After the service she walked slowly back to the apartment, detouring to watch the skaters at B.S.C. The hockey team was practicing, and she could hear the slap of stick against puck and the crunch of skates. When she got to the apartment, she brewed herself coffee and listened to Mozart on *Deutscher Rundfunk* radio. She hoped Karl-Heinz would get home soon.

She could not know that to surprise her, he had dressed in his new N.S.K.K. uniform. Now he looked at himself in the mirror, the first time he had seen himself in a party uniform. He had to admit that he cut rather a *schneidig* figure as *Hauptsturmführer*-Captain Dorn, N.S.K.K., although he was stiff-legged in his tight black breeches and slim black boots. He wore the brown party shirt with N.S.K.K. captain's insignia, black tie pinned down with his party badge, leather belt and chest strap, and black service cap. On his left arm was a red swastika armband.

When he got to the front door of their flat, he fumbled the key out of the deep pockets of the breeches.

"Is that you, Karle?" She was in the kitchen.

"No. It's Wolfgang Amadeus Mozart from downstairs. I came to complain about the music. Much too loud. And such junk!"

Still from the kitchen: "Want some coffee, *Herr* Mozart? My husband isn't home, so maybe . . . Oh, my God!" She had caught sight of him in his uniform. "Karle!" she was shaking her head, distressed, "Why did you do it?"

"Do what?"

"*Join the SS!*"

"Not the SS, *Doovkopp!* Nothing as fierce as the SS. Only the poor old N.S.K.K., the Motor Corps. Look . . ." He showed her his N.S.K.K. insignia. "*Hauptsturmführer*," he said. "Captain, right from scratch! What do you think of that?"

She pointed at his new party badge. "Then you joined the party?"

"Of course. It's the only way I could join N.S.K.K."

Silence.

"Zoss insisted I join N.S.K.K. It's absolutely necessary."

Silence.

He took off his black uniform cap, threw it on a table, and sat down on the couch. "May I have that coffee you offered?"

"Yes." She brought the coffee, with milk and no sugar, the way she liked it.

"All right," he said, "what's wrong?"

"Don't you know?"

"I guess I do. Why did I join the party?"

"No. Why did you join it behind my back?"

"Because I knew you would make a fuss, just as you're doing now. Anyway, I had to. I had no choice."

"Karle, so far as I am concerned, there's still no excuse. After all, I was the one who wanted you to join Brunzig. I certainly encouraged you to get ahead. *Stimmts?* True?"

"*Stimmt.*"

"And I can understand there are some things one just has to do. I'm not a fool. But joining the party is not having to attend a dull business banquet or being nice to some idiot client. Joining the party is a big commitment, and you had no right to make it without consulting me."

Karl-Heinz took off his uniform and put his party badge into the case with his cufflinks. The Sunday was ruined.

Inspektor Erwin Tunnes first caught sight of Dachau Labor Camp on a chill and blustery February morning. He arrived in Munich on the overnight train from Berlin, and a Gestapo sedan drove him through the nearby town of Dachau and then over open country alongside a railroad track. Both the road and the rails dead-ended in the camp.

The camp's main gate was surmounted by a semicircular sign: "*Arbeit macht Frei*," "Work sets you free." The driver and Tunnes identified themselves to two "Death's Head" SS guards, and they passed through the first of several high, electrically charged (he could see the porcelain insulators) barbed-wire fences. There were machine guns on the guard towers and spotlights every fifty meters, both inside and outside the camp perimeter. The place seemed absolutely escape-proof.

Tunnes, born on an island, had never overcome the claustrophobia he got each time he visited a prison. This one was no different. They drove into a courtyard and pulled up in front of the administration building. Two more SS guards with rifles came to attention, and inside the door another SS man checked his papers. He walked down a long hallway to the sounds of steel-heeled SS boots cracking on the cement floors, and then he saw a familiar sign: "S.D. Liaison Offices."

The camp S.D. officer was an effete, blond young SS *Obersturmführer* lieutenant, happy to see an outsider.

"*Na, also*," he said after coffee was brought by a corporal, "how good to see a face from Berlin! This place is really *scheisslangweilig*, dull as hell." He spoke like a Berliner. "Later we can drive over to Dachau for lunch. I found a good little place."

They got down to business: the case of Herta Jakobson. The investigation involving the Goldners and the Schorrs had produced no evidence of fraudulent acts on the part of either family. Besides, old Goldner's suicide stopped that phase of the case. The Schorrs were eventually given their exit permits, and after paying a large emigration tax, they had left for England, where they owned a small publishing firm. *Frau* Goldner also went to England.

However, because the Goldner's phone was tapped, Tunnes knew of a call made at ten on the morning of the fifteenth of January from someone at KaDeBe to the Goldner woman, warning her that her husband would be dismissed later that day. The caller turned out to be an old KaDeBe secretary, Herta Jakobson, with the store for nearly thirty years. Hers was an understandable act of personal loyalty and of no real importance from a criminal standpoint. Jakobson, an old maid, seemed harmless enough, but her name was put up for a routine investigation. They soon struck gold. Herta Jakobson turned out to be the key person in a smuggling ring for emigrating Jews. It worked quite simply: Whenever KaDeBe buyers went abroad, they were asked "as a favor" to take along some extra pieces of luggage. This baggage supposedly contained personal purchases for KaDeBe's foreign commissionaires. The contents—cigars, brandy, gloves, towels, and foodstuffs—were always declared to foreign customs.

Undeclared were jewels, currency, and even gold bullion concealed in false double bottoms, or sewn into the linings of the luggage. British and Swiss customs had discovered some of this contraband but had been persuaded by powerful emigrant organizations to keep silent. All penalties were happily paid. Gestapo finally learned about the whole mess through their paid informants. One of these, a Jewish refugee in London, was trying to protect his family, which was still in Germany, waiting to join him.

Surprisingly, Herta Jakobson seemed to have made absolutely no money out of the smuggled assets. She readily confessed, but said she was a Christian helping innocent people. This idiotic attitude seemed her only motivation, but Tunnes was sure that others in the ring were getting rich. He interrogated Jakobson for other names, but she was extremely stubborn, and he decided that a few weeks of confinement might make her change her tune. The S.D. sent her to Dachau.

Cases like this always made Tunnes uncomfortable, since he preferred to deal with straightforward, criminally motivated acts: murder, larceny, blackmail, or assault. Like many older Gestapo officers, he was basically still a policeman. The S.D.-SS boys and the younger Gestapo men were more at home with the new crimes, committed against the new laws. He wished Heydrich had assigned another Gestapo officer, because from the beginning, the Goldner-Schorr-Ockert-Jakobson case was distasteful. He suspected it was not over yet and would one day return to haunt him.

"*Die Jakobson*" said the Dachau S.D. lieutenant, "is now number three-eight-four-nine-two." He handed her case-folder to Tunnes. It was always startling to see the immediate change from civilian to prisoner. Herta Jakobson, when arrested, was a tiny, plump fussy woman with ice-blue eyes and carefully waved, bleached-blond hair. Now he saw the side and front prison photographs: Her face was haggard, devoid of lipstick or makeup, hair trimmed short, throat wrinkled and dewlapped like that of an old fowl. She wore a striped prison uniform. He remembered her tiny apartment in the garden area of Zehlendorf. Her little DKW convertible, obviously her pride and joy, was parked in front of the building. When she got arrested, she kept asking him to make sure "the car was safe." Actually, it was requisitioned as soon as she was shipped off, because the state took custody of a convict's assets.

"Of course," said the S.D. lieutenant, "we don't know any of the details. To us, she is here as a currency smuggler." He was obviously miffed that he had not been fully briefed.

He offered Tunnes a gold-tipped Muratti cigarette, which Tunnes declined. The SS man then lighted his own with a Death's Head–decorated *Tausendzünder* lighter. He pursed his lips and blew a stream of smoke toward the ceiling. "*Na, also.*" He shrugged. "I am sure you have good reason for wanting to see her. Would you prefer it here or nearer to her cellblock?"

Tunnes said, "First, I want to go into the camp to see

where she is housed. It will give me a better perspective.
Then I can interrogate her here at headquarters.''

The lieutenant rolled his eyes in disgust. ''It's such a
damned *bore* to walk miles into the camp. But, if you insist,
let's go.''

Accompanied by two SS guards, they walked toward the
low barracks of the main camp. After passing yet another
barbed-wire fence, they were in the actual prison blocks.
Jakobson, Number 38492, was in the women's area, a kilometer away. Now he saw the first prisoners, Jews, according to
the yellow cloth star sewn onto their striped canvas jackets.
They were carrying heavy cases of supplies into a warehouse.
The prisoners, who did not raise their heads, were commanded by a *kapo*, a trusty without a star, a tall, fat fellow,
whom Tunnes knew. It was Mertze, a violent man with a
long record of prison terms. Tunnes had seen Mertze's shaven
skull in many other prisons, and he recognized him at once.
In fact, he had once sent him to jail. The lumbering trusty
screamed at the Jews to show off in front of Tunnes and the
SS.

Tunnes said, ''That's some shit they picked as a trusty! I
know his record. He's the worst kind of swine.''

''Oh, come on,'' said the S.D. lieutenant. ''The Death's
Head boys know what they're doing. And besides, he's only
got Jews.''

''I know what kind of stuff he's capable of,'' said Tunnes.
''I hope these Jews are as criminal as he is and that they have
thick skins.''

''They're Jews.'' The lieutenant shrugged disdainfully, dismissing the subject.

The camp was gray, clammy, bathed in the coal smoke of
the mess halls. In the distance, they could hear a voice yelling
commands and the groan of a truck wallowing through mud
where new barracks were being constructed. Tunnes saw only
one SS guard on foot, a sergeant. The others were in the
guard towers, manning machine guns. Prisoner trusties seemed
in charge of everything. At a hospital, there stood long lines
of almost-nude prisoners, thin towels around their blue-frosted
shanks, waiting for treatment. The SS lieutenant wrinkled his
nose in disgust. ''These swine are so filthy they have to
recheck them over and over. Lice, fleas, everything.''

The women's barracks were low, single-story buildings,

part wood, part cement. The inmates were at work from six in the morning to six each night, so the barrack where Jakobson was housed was empty.

Three tiers of wooden bunks lined the walls and almost reached to the low ceiling. These bunks were padded with coarse straw mattresses. In the center passage, under bare electric bulbs, stood some rough wooden tables and chairs. Everything smelled of carbolic.

Tunnes did not like it. Prisoners should be in cells, two by two, else they developed mass attitudes. These women prisoners could infect each other with ideas; so they probably got disciplined with exceptional severity. Besides, they were commanded by trusties and he hated trusties, who were usually ass-kissing swine. Prisoners could never get just treatment from trusties, and even the foulest bastard prisoner was entitled to rudimentary justice. So far as Tunnes was concerned, prisoners deserved harsh discipline, but it had to be administered by trained guards, professionals. This whole camp looked like a typical SS venture, incompetent and patchwork.

As they walked back to the administration building, Tunnes's trained eye spotted two faces he knew. One was Rosenberg, a lawyer from Berlin, who was pushing a wheelbarrow with buckets full of dung from some latrine. The other convict was Erdmann, also from Berlin, a dentist. The two prisoners did not see him. They took turns with their heavy load, and kept their faces down. The wind brought the stench of their cargo, and the SS lieutenant turned his face in disgust. At a crossroad, the two convicts passed an SS guard. To speed their pace each one took one arm of the barrow. But the SS men paid no attention to them. He aimed for Tunnes, stopped, saluted, and yelled, "*Herr Inspektor*, the woman three-eight-four-nine-two is ready for you." He pronounced it with great care, like a telephone operator repeating a long-distance number. Another crashing straight-arm salute and he marched away.

On the way back to the administration building, the wind hit them head-on. The lieutenant turned up his collar, stuck his hands deep into his greatcoat pockets, and cursed when an SS guard saluted him, so that he had to brace up and respond.

"Before I get to work on Jakobson," said Tunnes, "I would like to see the files of two prisoners: a Berlin lawyer named Rosenberg and a Berlin dentist called Erdmann."

"Rosenberg?"

"Yes." Tunnes thought a bit of acid was indicated. Did the SS good! "Like the *Reichsleiter*. But probably not the same first name."

"That's one. And Erdmann? Dentist? E-R-D-M-A-N-N?"

"Correct."

The SS lieutenant was annoyed by Tunnes's reference to Alfred Rosenberg, the party's chief race theoretician, but so far as Tunnes was concerned why not nettle these incompetent SS *Arschlöcher?*

The files soon arrived. He found out that Rosenberg and Erdmann were both there for the crime of *Rassenschande*, "racial bespoilment."

Tunnes remembered that Rosenberg, a bachelor, lived with an actress who was Christian. Reading further into the file, he saw it was this relationship that had brought his conviction. Rosenberg had chosen to ignore the law prohibiting this situation, so he was sent to Dachau and she was sentenced to serve a shorter term in Plötzensee jail. Tunnes knew her. She had once been the toast of Berlin's cabaret set, but she was no longer young and pretty. Of course, the law was specific, but it seemed harsh punishment.

In the case of Dr. Erdmann, a married man with children, he had employed a Christian housemaid under the age of forty-five when this, too, was specifically prohibited. Young Aryan girls were not allowed to work in households with male Jews. According to the official explanation, the danger of sexual contact with Jews was ever-present, since they were well known for their lechery. Dr. Erdmann was denounced and sentenced to hard labor. *Na, ja.* Erdmann also knew the law!

Still, Tunnes remembered the hundreds of criminals he had sent to hard labor. They were quite a different sort. . . .

Jews were stupid not to leave Germany. If he were Jewish he would "advance to the rear" and get the hell out! Those two, poor, stupid bastards. Too bad. He couldn't help them. No one could. And why the hell should he?

They moved to the interrogation chamber, which was in total darkness. When he stepped inside, they turned on a harsh blue spotlight that focused on a woman. If this was Herta Jakobson, she was almost unrecognizable. This shriveled thing that sat on a wooden stool, shaking, head down, gray hair at stubble length, scrawny forearms side by side on shivering thin thighs could not be the woman Jakobson. He was about to say so when the creature looked up, and it was she. There was no mistaking those blue eyes. They were loose in their red sockets until they found him. Then she tried to compose herself and focus because she seemed to recognize a link to her long-ago past, although she had only been in Dachau a few weeks. But she said nothing. Her lips were folded between her teeth, bitten closed to stop their quivering.

Tunnes took the S.D. officer outside. "What happened?"

"You mean to her?"

"Of course!"

"How should I know? You'll have to ask the Death's Head people."

So, they called out a guard *Hauptscharführer*, a sergeant major, who stood at stiff attention until the S.D. lieutenant told him to stand at ease. Tunnes again demanded to know how she had been treated.

The sergeant major said, "She was difficult."

"How?"

"She wanted to wear the Jew star, but she's no Jew. She wanted to be in a Jew barracks, but she belonged with the Aryan criminals. She tried to run over to the Jews. She had to be taught."

"How?"

"Withdrawal of privileges."

"Like what?"

"Sleep. Rations. Mattress."

"What else?"

"Disciplinary instructions."

"What the hell is that?"

"Look, *Herr Inspektor*," said the sergeant major, "we try to run things efficiently." Then he turned to the S.D. lieutenant. "*Herr Obersturmführer*, if the *Herr Inspektor* has any complaints, may I ask him to register them in Berlin?"

Tunnes's rare temper rose. He was absolutely furious. "Yes, goddammit," he roared at the SS sergeant major. "I certainly have a complaint! You lousy bastards have made that woman inside *useless*. I need an intelligent suspect, not a babbling wreck! This is arch sloppiness! The commandant of this camp will hear about this! You are dismissed, sergeant major."

"*Zu Befehl, Herr Inspektor*," yelled the sergeant major,

responding like a marionette to Tunnes's roaring command. He saluted and withdrew.

The S.D. lieutenant lifted a cynical eyebrow. "Come, now, *Inspektor*, do you really think that they'll change anything here? You're talking about one of *Reichsführer* Himmler's pet projects. The way they do things here is the way *he* wants it done."

"That doesn't excuse inferior police work."

"Oh, have it your way." The S.D. officer shrugged.

They went back into the interrogation chamber, but Herta Jakobson could only mumble. She kept pointing to her tattoo on the inside of the left forearm, repeating over and over "Three-eight-four-nine-two, three-eight-four-nine-two . . ."

Tunnes asked one of the guards, a corporal, "Does she ever say anything else?"

The guard said, "I really can't tell, *Herr Inspektor*. That's all I heard her say since I brought her here. I think"—he pointed at his own forehead—"that she has a *Knall*, that she's nuts." Then he took a notepad from the side pocket of his black tunic, pulled a pencil from his inside pocket, licked the point of the pencil, and asked, "What do you want to do with her? What's the disposition, *Herr Inspektor?*"

"Let her rejoin her barracks and have a doctor look her over."

"In connection with your investigation, sir?"

"No, corporal, because she's sick."

"Well, *Herr Inspektor*, the *Kommandatur* will decide that, I suppose. The prisoner in charge of her barracks tells me this woman is not much use the way she is now. She still runs over to the Jew women when the trusty doesn't watch her. Stupid bitch!"

Tunnes had had enough. He left the room. The S.D. lieutenant mentioned lunch, but Tunnes excused himself and was driven back to Munich, where he boarded the afternoon *D Zug* Express to Berlin. He sat in his compartment working on his report until seven, when he went to the dining car, but he was not really hungry. So he had some Friesian Schnaps and kept drinking for the rest of the trip.

SS *Brigadeführer* Reinhard Heydrich, chief of the S.D. and the Gestapo, leaned forward. In a soft, high, womanish voice that was barely audible he said, "Who the hell do you think you are to criticize the SS, its institutions, and *Reichsführer* Himmler?'' His face was contorted with fury, and with his long, bill-like nose, hovering over his desk, his arms like wings and his hands like claws, he looked like a vulture atop a carcass. This was the Heydrich everyone feared, but few men ever had the bad fortune to see.

Tunnes was unshaken. ''You charged me with the Goldner-Schorr case. This smuggling ring came out of it. Now, those people in Dachau have robbed us of our main witness through their gross negligence.''

Heydrich could not believe his ears. He held Tunnes's written report in his hands and shook with anger, rare for someone as coldly objective. To hear this Friesian ox, this dull peasant *Spiesser* asshole, talk back to him!

''Tunnes,'' he said, getting himself back under control, once more remote, ''the only reason you were allowed to deal directly with me instead of through your superiors is that this case came from *Reichsminister* Goebbels and landed in my lap. I told them to send me a good Berlin *Kriminal* man, that's why you were picked. I think they made a mistake. You are now relieved of this case, which will become an S.D. matter. You are to wait reassignment. You may go. *Heilitla!*''

At his secret signal, the door opened, admitting an SS *Obersturmführer*. Heydrich swiveled his chair until the back was to Tunnes, while the other SS officer escorted the Gestapo man out. Erwin Tunnes, who had done his best since he was a blundering Friesian recruit in the Berlin Police, knew that his career was over.

Zoss and Karl-Heinz were on their way to Rome on the night express, which also had a special freight car for the G.F.W. 12 they were bringing to Benito Mussolini, the *Duce*, a gift from Brunzig A.G., although the suggestion came from the *Führer*. As the train puffed its way up into the Alps toward the Brenner Pass, Karl-Heinz sat in the dining car listening to Zoss, while the magnificent snow-capped mountains passed outside, blue in the moonlight.

''Quite a change,'' said Zoss. ''When the *Führer* first came to visit the *Duce* in thirty-four, Mussolini was in all his glory and Adolf Hitler was in a simple civilian raincoat, being outtrumped by the *Fascisti*. Later, when the *Duce* came to

Munich, things were quite different. You could soon tell who
the new boss was. Mussolini's mouth certainly hung open.
He couldn't believe what we've done in Germany and what
the *Führer* has achieved. I think Mussolini must have kicked
a few Roman rearsides when he got back to Rome, because I
was with him in Munich for a few days and you could see his
mood going downhill by the minute."

"Are we rubbing it in by bringing the G.F.W. twelve?"

"*Na, ja*, maybe a little bit. But by now the *Führer* and
Mussolini have become *Kameraden*. He mentioned this whole
idea to Dr. Maut that day at Döberitz. Maut then told me, and
I told Gerhardt Brunzig! So, here we are on our way to the
Palazzo Venezia. I also have a hunch that you'll see the good
Frau von Konsky there."

"Really?"

"Whenever there's a deal to be made, she's there. I imagine Gerhardt Brunzig wants to sell a few of these cars to the
Ravioli Warriors—excuse me, to our heroic Fascist allies,
and von Konsky is his sales agent. Also, von Konsky will
guarantee that there's no stink in Berlin about Brunzig doing
a little business on the side."

"She told me that the *Führer* has been very kind to her."

"Very kind," said Zoss.

"Do you mean there's anything between them?"

"No, not that. But the *Führer* likes society women. He's
always, well, *awed* by them. I've seen him get quite gaga
over certain ladies."

"How?"

"Not affairs. Not that sort of thing, but lots of hand kissing
and bowing. Anyway, I know there is someone at the Berghof
who is his mistress."

"Do you know her name?"

"Braun. Nice girl. I've seen her with him, although everyone tries to screen them from outsiders. She always arrives at
the Berghof in a separate car. One of the Italians, Count
Ciano, the *Duce*'s son-in-law, has seen them together often.
They're just like any other couple. Ciano told me about her
last year when I was in Rome. I think Braun's sister is now
married to Fegelein, the SS general who's Himmler's liaison
man to the *Führer*."

Zoss was drinking dry martinis, a habit he had picked up in
America in the twenties when he went on a promotion tour

to New York and Hollywood. Explaining the correct mixture to the German barman on the *Mitropa* diner had not been simple: three parts gin to one part dry vermouth and then lots of stirring and an olive on a toothpick. The barman was unfazed. The Munich-Innsbruck-Milano portion of this trip was always full of eccentrics and foreigners. So long as they tipped well . . .

"Wait until you see Ciano," said Zoss. "I mean *Count* Ciano. He's married to Edda Mussolini, and it's hard to tell which one of the two has more affairs. They both fuck themselves half to death and no one dares to tell the *Duce*. He thinks his daughter is a vestal virgin and that Ciano is Mark Antony. Not a word penetrates to his Villa Torlonia. By the way, did you know Mussolini rents it for one lira a year? Excellent bargain!

"Edda Ciano even tackled me once, when they were vacationing at the Villa d'Este in Como. We were all there just before the Mille Miglia. I had asked her to dance out of sheer courtesy. Anyway, the next thing I knew she had unbuttoned my fly and was holding me by the tail. Very unorthodox for the tango! I was lucky to get my *Schwanz* back at the end of that number. She had a grip like a mountaineer." The martinis were having their effect, and Zoss looked around to make sure other passengers had not overheard him, but they were all alone at their end of the diner.

"Anyway," he continued, "the *Duce* is not without his own little *Techtel-Mächtel*, as the Viennese call it, a little hanky-panky. He's got an actress called Petacci, Claretta Petacci. Quite a piece of work! The only one who doesn't know about her is his wife, old Dona Rachelle Mussolini. In fact, the *Duce* has masses of women. One French girl had to be barred from the Palazzo Venezia by the French ambassador, Chambrun. She was so angry she shot him in the ass later. Not the *Duce* . . . the ambassador!"

At Innsbruck they climbed down to the platform and the thin cool mountain air turned their *Schwips*, tipsiness, into instant sledgehammer fatigue. While the train waited, huffing and puffing steam, until passengers boarded for the final leg into Italy, the long, maroon *Mitropa* sleeper with its windows screened from the platform beckoned invitingly. It was strange to be in Austria without having gone through

customs, but it was now part of Germany and seemed as if it
had never been a foreign country.

Karl-Heinz excused himself, boarded the train, and was
soon fast asleep in his compartment. He woke up once, when
they stopped at the outskirts of Milano, probably to change
engines, and he opened the shade. Outside was a dismal
industrial suburb, so he went back to sleep. They breakfasted
as they passed through the Tuscan hill country toward Florence.

On arriving in Rome the Italian army-colored G.F.W. 12
was unloaded by two Brunzig mechanics who had spent the
trip at the other end of the train in a second-class compartment.
Then a Lancia staff car ferried Zoss and Karl-Heinz to the
Grand Hotel, a relic of the Napoleonic style. Karl-Heinz
checked into his satin-walled room to dress in his N.S.K.K.
uniform, since they were to present themselves to the *Duce*
shortly after lunch. The G.F.W. 12 was taken ahead to Villa
Torlonia, the *Duce*'s residence, where the ceremony was to
take place.

Now they were in the velvet-bedecked bar of the hotel,
drinking Camparis until Anneliese von Konsky joined them.
Frau von Konsky had arrived the day before and was also
staying at the Grand. She wore a very simple gray flannel
jacket and skirt with a bright yellow cashmere turtleneck
sweater. She had on flat-heeled, crepe-soled suede country
shoes, string-colored driving gloves with leather palms, and a
canvas and leather sports bag slung over her shoulder. On the
lapel of her jacket was her only jewelry, a diamond-ringed
N.S.D.A.P. badge. Zoss raised an appreciative glass. "Anneliese, you always look wonderfully chic. I wish you could
give lessons."

"Armin, you old salon lizard, you lie like a professional.
And when it comes to women you're an absolute disaster. But
I love to hear you lie!"

Then she shook hands with Karl-Heinz. "Dorn," she said,
"the uniform becomes you. *Donnerwetter*, you're a good-
looking creature!"

Karl-Heinz smiled and kept still. This was swift company,
and he did not feel up to joining in the game, not yet.

The final member of the party came up the steps into the
lobby and then aimed for the group of foreigners; a splendidly
uniformed, pressed, and polished young captain of *Bersaglieri*
whom Anneliese von Konsky introduced as the Marchese di

Navone. They went to the open terrace for lunch. The marchese was extremely nervous and jumpy, obviously frightened of the upcoming meeting with his chief of state and supreme commander. Zoss and Anneliese von Konsky seemed to take things in their stride and ordered a sizable lunch, so Karl-Heinz decided to follow suit, but the marchese did not order. He said he was not hungry.

Anneliese von Konsky said, "What's the matter with you, marchese? Surely you've met the *Duce* many times? Aren't you one of his aides?"

"Yes, of course! I see him every day, but today he will be in an extra-foul mood. Something has happened."

"Oh?"

"*Ecco.* You know Marshall Balbo?"

She nodded. Everyone knew Balbo, the famous pilot who had flown across the Atlantic with a whole squadron of Italian planes. The marshall was one of Mussolini's closest friends and one of Italy's great heroes.

"Now this is confidential: They say Balbo was so angry that the *Duce* accepted your new German racial laws for Italy that he flew all the way from Tripoli to Ferrara, his home town. The mayor of Ferrara, Renzo Ravenna, is a Jew, so first Balbo made a courtesy visit to every prominent Jew in Ferrara; then he took the mayor to the most exclusive restaurant in town and hosted him at dinner. Balbo is a hero and governor of Tripoli, and he has much prestige! The *Duce* must be furious. As it is, recently Balbo has been most disrespectful. He only speaks of the *Duce* as the 'founder of the empire,' and he does not quite mean it in a flattering way. He says things like 'Can the founder of the empire see me, or is he in the bathroom?' As it is, now we in the Italian army have to do the *Passo Romano*, your German Parade steps that the English call the goose step. And the army is furious! Our chief of staff, Marshall de Bono, said our soldiers are so short that we'll be an army of stiff-necked midgets." Navone had to grin at the picture. Then he continued, "These new anti-Jewish laws are not so easy in Italy. Our Jews have been here since Roman days. For example, General Pugliese, Italy's most decorated soldier, is a Jew."

The Germans had no comment, and the marchese fell into morose silence, nibbling on a roll and thinking his private thoughts. Karl-Heinz thought of his father's friend Simon and

of Siegfried Schmidt. Good thing that Hilde had stayed in
Berlin. She would have thrown a few bombshells into this
conversation.

Promptly at three-thirty in the afternoon they lined up on
the sun-flooded lawn in front of Mussolini's immense residence under the Acropolis-style façade. Anneliese von Konsky,
Zoss, Karl-Heinz, the marchese, a platoon of plume-hatted
Bersaglieri Mountain Infantry, their officers, and the mechanics from Brunzig all expectantly fixed their eyes on the large
door on the left of the house, under a circular portico, but
they looked in the wrong direction. The *Duce* had stepped
onto the large balcony about ten meters above them. He stood
there between two Doric pillars, looking down at them. Not until
they heard the *Bersaglieri* come to attention as their officer
waved his curved sword in the direction of the balcony did
they spot the *Duce*. He raised his right arm, thrust out his
famous chin, and nodded at the group below. Then he disappeared and shortly thereafter came through the door everyone
had been staring at originally.

Benito Mussolini walked bolt upright with a rolling athletic
gait, his left fist on his waist, his head held high. He wore
riding breeches and boots, topped by a knitted short-sleeved
shirt. Out of the corner of his eye, Karl-Heinz spotted a
groom leading a white Arabian horse toward the lawn in back
of the *Bersaglieri*.

The *Duce* walked up to Zoss, who saluted, bowed, and
then introduced Anneliese von Konsky and Karl-Heinz. He
was also about to present the marchese, but fortunately realized this would have been a *faux pas*. The *Duce* accepted
each introduction with a curt nod of his shaven head. For
another man, the stance, manner, and walk would have seemed
those of a *poseur*, but they suited Mussolini.

The *Duce* spoke good German. "So, this is the vehicle my
friend Adolf Hitler has sent to me? It looks interesting. I shall
have our people from Alfa Romeo and Fiat study it next
week. Also, Navone, see to it that the car is brought out to
where I shall be exercising Fru Fru. I want to drive it myself
through some real terrain. *Capisce?*"

"*Si, Duce!*" said the marchese, snapping to attention.

Mussolini made one circuit of the car, then posed for
several photographers who came from the house and took
dozens of shots of the event and everyone there.

"I am very grateful to you, *Dottore* Zoss, and to your associates. Thank you, too, Contessa von Konsky. I had a letter about you from Galeazzo Ciano. He said he would meet with you later today. Signori . . ." He saluted and left, walking toward his horse.

Zoss and the others turned toward his departing back. The *Bersaglieri* presented arms. The *Duce* mounted and rode off at a canter. Everyone stayed at attention until he was out of sight.

"Short shrift, don't you think, Marchese?" said Zoss.

The captain shrugged. "That's the way he is. Very changeable. But all in all, the *Duce* is *stupendo*. I think when you get back to the hotel, you will have a surprise waiting. So will *Capitano* Dorn." Karl-Heinz was a little startled by the title until he realized that his *Hauptsturmführer* N.S.K.K. insignia became "*capitano*" in title-conscious Italy.

His surprise came in the form of a package on the table in his room, tied up with red, white and green ribbon and sealed with green wax. He opened it with great care, to find a red velvet jewel case and a leather tube containing a parchment scroll. Inside the jewel case was a lavish enameled white cross, a decoration, attached to a red and white striped ribbon. The accompanying rolled-up, hand-scripted certificate stated that he had been created a *cavaliere* of the order of the crown. Also in the box was a small red and white ribbon of the kind one pinned onto a uniform. Karl-Heinz could not resist. He took off his tunic and pinned the ribbon over the top left pocket. Then he put it back on and admired himself in the mirror, *Hauptsturmführer Cavaliere* Karl-Heinz Dorn! He then changed into a double-breasted navy civilian suit before meeting the others for dinner. *Cavaliere* Dorn? He liked the sound of it. Hilde would laugh, of course, and she was right. To get a decoration for accompanying an automobile on the train. Ridiculous! But still. *Cavaliere* Dorn? *Nicht schlecht*. Not bad. Not bad at all.

Downstairs in the bar, he joined Zoss, Anneliese von Konsky, and the marchese. The Italian was in beautifully cut civvies.

"Did you like your surprises?" he asked.

Zoss said, "Please call me *commendatore*, and my young friend here is now *Cavaliere* Dorn. That was really *reizend*, delightful, of the *Duce*. I had met him a while back, you know.''

"Yes," said the marchese, "he remembered you. Actually, he is not too enchanted with the Brunzig company because of the way you've been beating our Maseratis and Alfas. You may not have it so easy this season.''

"The new formula?''

"The new formula. *Vero*.''

"Papa Hoegel, do you know him? He is cursing so loud you can probably hear him right across the Alps.''

"That's bad. We all know Hoegel. When that man curses, we're in trouble. The only manager we've got who's as good as Hoegel is the team director for Alfa-Romeo, Enzo Ferrari. But we don't have your engineers because the *Duce* still won't allot government subsidies for race cars, the way your *Führer* does.''

"Who says the *Führer* does?''

"We all assume so.''

"You assume wrong. The subsidies are not for racing. The subsidies are for military research!''

"*Bene*.'' The Italian shrugged, raised his eyebrows, bobbed his head, like a man arguing with a child. "All right, so it's for the military stuff. It all amounts to the same thing. It's money. That's what our manufacturers need. The *Duce* is furious when our cars get beaten, but he won't help. Worse still, some of our best drivers, like Nuvolari, are switching to German cars!''

Zoss wanted to drop this disagreeable subject. He said, "Let's go to dinner.''

A small orchestra played dance music in the dining room, and they were shown to a table overlooking the dance floor, which was crowded. Roman society loved dancing to American jazz. Karl-Heinz realized how little dance music they played in Berlin, where they once had the best jazz bands in Europe; now one never heard it on the radio, and at the hotels they played waltzes and tangos. Amazing how life could change in small ways and one had not noticed. Even B.S.C. had changed because there were few foreigners since the Olympics. The parties were more like old German "*Feste*,'' and less like the cocktail dances of 1936.

Anneliese von Konsky sat next to him, drinking champagne.

Her simple black dress was cut very low in back, and she had suntanned skin.

"Where did you get your tan?" he asked.

"I was on Elba with some friends. It's extraordinary over there, very simple, like a large fishing village, and they own a lovely villa. We sailed a lot and swam."

He asked her to dance and realized that he had not held a tall girl since he married tiny Hilde. Anneliese von Konsky's face was almost next to his, and he could smell her hair and her powder. His right hand was on her bare back. He could even sense the small muscles right under the skin as she followed his lead. He was a good dancer, something his school pals used to joke about. "Karle will make a bit of *Zaster*, of dough, this weekend as an *Eintänzer*, a gigolo!" In those days, many Berlin dance halls had male taxi dancers, all with slick black hair like Rudolph Valentino. Ladies bought tickets to dance with them, and sometimes the *Eintänzer* were paid escorts for ladies out "on the town." Before he got the job at KaDeBe, he was seriously tempted to try it. But if his dad had ever found out, it would have hurt him, although they could have used the money that grim winter of 1932.

Anneliese von Konsky was beginning to enjoy herself. She had managed to avoid the marchese, who was doing his Roman best to leave no opportunity untried, and had flirted with her every free second since she arrived in Rome, despite his obvious worries about the *Duce*'s mood. *Gott*, he was boring! An empty-headed fool who was lucky to have some family money so he could be a flunky to the *Duce*, one of two dozen little aides. She'd kill Ciano for assigning this little idiot to her! Maybe Ciano thought she couldn't find her own bedmates!

Now, this boy Dorn was another matter entirely. She had liked him ever since Villa Ritterschwert in Stuttgart. The only thing then was to find out if the boy belonged to Gerhardt Brunzig. But Gerhardt had only just met Dorn an hour before she did, and he did not seem interested, which was his bad luck, because she was now happy to take over!

Karl-Heinz woke up suddenly, startled, although there had been no noise. For a second, he did not know where he was until he saw her lying on the other bed. The room was dark except for a shaft of blue moonlight reflected from a marble-

topped table. He spotted light from the crack under the door
to the sitting room. Anneliese was sleeping heavily, anesthe-
tized by wine and cognac. Karl-Heinz was amazed that he
had no hangover. His head was clear and he was almost too
wide awake. Perhaps it was the marijuana cigarette he had
smoked. Anneliese got them from some American musicians
in Paris, who called them reefers. It looked like any other
cigarette and smelled like burning leaves on a fall day.

This was the first affair he had since he married, and he
knew he would feel guilty. It was inevitable. His clothes were
neatly stacked on the armchair at the foot of the bed. He
remembered how she stared while he systematically folded
his shirt, pants, jacket, underpants, and how she finally burst
out laughing when he stuffed his socks into his shoes. It was
an obscure discipline he imposed on himself, although his
head seemed to float free and his arms and legs had a life of
their own. He experienced what followed quite objectively,
her lovemaking that began by manipulating him, until she
herself got lost in the sex dance she had choreographed.
Something within him stayed sober, ice cold, like a voyeur.
Her lovemaking was experienced, inventive, exotic, and yet
strangely routine, like an actress who tries each evening to
give fresh meaning to the same old dialogue. He could not
lose himself completely, and it was he who stopped first and
fell asleep. Now, he wanted nothing more than to get back to
his room, so he carried his clothes into the sitting room and
got dressed among the shambles of their drinking and smoking,
the buckets with empty champagne bottles, half-filled glasses
on the floor, an ashtray with reefer stubs smoked down to the
last centimeter. The room stank of stale smoke and perfume.

He peeked into the bedroom, and she was still sleeping in
the same position. He thought of leaving a note, but he did
not. She had gone about the seduction so systematically and
humorlessly, *quid pro quo*. They had fucked each other thoroughly and therapeutically.

He walked down the stairs to his room instead of using the
lift with its weary night operator. There was no need for
witnesses. He was sure that Zoss and the marchese knew
nothing. They had all finished dinner at midnight, and he
went back to her suite much later.

Back in his room, he took a bath and went to sleep. The
hotel operator woke him at nine. Zoss and he were to leave

on the afternoon train to Berlin, so he had time to visit the Colosseum, the Forum, St. Peter's Square, and the Pantheon, all within two hours, made possible by the reckless and talented driving of an Italian army chauffeur whom the marchese loaned him. Zoss did not join him because he had a meeting with Count Galeazzo Ciano and Anneliese.

Later, on the train, over one of his favorite martinis, Zoss confided that "when it comes to a little bribery, give me a senior Italian official any day."

"You mean Ciano?"

"Did I say Ciano?"

"*Nein*, but I think you meant Ciano, right?"

"*Na, ja*, let's say that the count will now be able to complete the new wing on his seaside villa."

"Oh?"

"Yes. It's beautiful. His wife Edda loves it. This year they may even go there together."

"A fine example of Fascist family life, don't you think?"

"*Erstklassig! Prima!*" said Zoss. "Not the family life. The martini!"

At Milan, their porter brought a telegram and Zoss said, "When you get back to Berlin, pack up your wife and get down to Munich. You have some interesting days ahead. And by the way"—he pointed at the cigarette Karl-Heinz was smoking—"where you're going, you'd better cut that out. Your host doesn't like it."

Karl-Heinz, who smoked very little, was just trying to get the taste of the marijuana and of Anneliese von Konsky out of his mouth.

A letter had arrived from Siegfried Schmidt, in his familiar, old-fashioned German script:

Lieber Karl-Heinz, *Liebes* Hildelein!

I think of you two so often and now I found an opportunity to transmit this letter to you privately without embarrassing you through the mail and the censors. No, dear Karl-Heinz, don't protest! I know what a decent man you are, and I can hear you saying, "I don't care who knows if I get a letter from an old friend!" But there's no use taking any unnecessary chances.

My duties here are varied and interesting. I travel all

over the world for my store (except to Germany and Austria, of course). I thought I knew the English language, but I've had to learn it all over again. Hilde would be proud of me. By the way, people at the consulate, some of your old collaborators, still miss you, Hilde! (Don't ask me how I know.) We have applied for British citizenship; so, we hope, in a few years we shall no longer have to visit our consulate. I know it is ridiculous, but I still feel almost at home in a place where everyone speaks German.

We saw *Frau Kommerzienrath* Goldner last week. We visit with her as often as we can. Her relatives have a large house in Hampstead and she is well and comfortable, but she misses ''*Der Olle*'' very much and his Berlin humor, and she gets homesick for Berlin, as I do.

I understand that you, dear Karl-Heinz, are doing extremely well at Brunzig. They can provide you with much better opportunities than KaDeBe. By the way, do you still think I was panicking?

All my warmest wishes and regards to both of you from Ruth and your old friend and ''Papa,''

Siegfried

By the way: Should you be in England, Karl-Heinz, I think it is better if you do not take a chance on looking me up. You know how much I should like to see you, but you must take no risks and you must think of Hilde. After all, I brought you two together! So I have some rights.

The letter was on plain paper, without a sender's address or any other identification. He had obviously gone to a lot of trouble to protect the Dorns.

"How did you get it?" asked Karl-Heinz.

"It came to the house while you were in Rome. Someone left it for us with the *Portier*."

"God," he said. "That was risky."

"Oh, come on! No one knows how it got here. Aren't you glad to hear from him?"

"Yes, yes, of course, but it could have caused a lot of trouble!"

"But, Karle, it didn't. Anyway, we should be happy he still cares."

"Why shouldn't he? We didn't do anything to him, you and I."

"That's not the point. Many Jewish emigrants hate all German Aryans."

"Well that doesn't apply to us. We've been decent."

"Decent?"

"*Na*, we've never done any harm to Jews."

"Is that enough?"

"It's enough for me."

"*Na, ja*, enough for you. But I'm not sure it's enough for me. I've done a lot of thinking recently. You've been away from Berlin and you don't realize what's been happening here."

"What?"

"People are disappearing. The priest at the church I go to? He's gone."

"Since when do you go to church?"

"I've been attending services at the little Catholic church near here."

"The one behind B.S.C.?"

"Yes."

"What happened to the priest?"

"He delivered a sermon two Sundays ago when you were in Stuttgart, and I guess someone in the congregation took offense and denounced him. All he said was that several parishioners had joined the SS and now they no longer came to services. He wondered why. Didn't the SS believe in Christ? Or had they found a new God?"

"*Natürlich!* Of course, that's a damn fool sermon! No wonder he got in trouble!"

"I don't think he was foolish at all. He had a perfect right to ask the question. They were his parishioners. Anyway, some SS people came to arrest him. Now we have a new priest, an old man, very meek. Also, have you heard about Dachau and Sachsenhausen?"

"Something. They're SS prisons?"

"They're concentration camps."

"Prison camps?"

"Call it what you will, they're political prisons. I hear that they are barbaric and that thousands of people are held there without trial, often because they were falsely denounced, and many just because they're Jews! People who get sent there are treated like animals even though they're not really criminals.''

"Who tells you all this nonsense?''

''I meet people at the church and quite a few others who are 'up to here' ''—she made the gesture of holding her throat—''and who think the party has gone berserk. I also spoke to some old friends from the foreign service. They think Hitler will bring war. He's certainly talking like a man who wants it. First we took back the Saar. That was good, because it was really German. Then Austria. Well, maybe the Austrians wanted to be part of the Reich. Now the Sudetenland. But that's part of Czechoslovakia. They also told me he's about to try for Danzig and the Polish Corridor. Sooner or later the English and the French will call a halt. Meanwhile, some of our best people are leaving Germany!''

"Jews?''

''Not only Jews. Many others, like Thomas Mann and Gropius and Mies van der Rohe and theater people like Conrad Veidt and Marlene Dietrich. And what if the others are Jews? Can we afford to lose Einstein or Bruno Walter or Max Reinhardt and Kandinsky?''

Karl-Heinz was horrified. She was obviously off in dangerous territory, his own fault for being away so much. ''Darling, suppose I were to agree with you, what can we two do about it?''

"There must be something!''

''*Na, ohne mich!* Without me! Leave me out of it! I don't intend to ruin our lives for some misguided idealism of yours. You were a fool to keep Siegfried's letter. You should have burned it and told me what it said.''

"Burned it? Why? Is it a crime to get a lovely, warm letter from a dear old friend?'' Hilde laughed ironically. ''And someone to whom you owe a great deal?''

''I am fully aware that Siegfried was very kind to me.'' Karl-Heinz was beginning to lose his temper. ''And I don't forget it. Dammit, he was the one who told me not to contact him, not to bother with him, not to feel responsible for him. I won't allow you to make me feel like a *Schuft*, like a heel, just because I've got a level head on my shoulders, and I'll be damned if I'll let you throw away everything!''

''As you wish, *cavaliere!* Just as you say, *Herr Haupt-*

sturmführer!'' Her heavy-handed sarcasm finally sent him into a rage, and he left the apartment, slamming the front door. For the first time since he was a bachelor, he went to a *Kneipe* and swilled Asbach brandy until he was drunk. When he finally weaved his way back to the apartment, the lights were out and Hilde was asleep.

Hilde Dorn knew they had to talk about it, that keeping silent would flaw their marriage and she prayed that it had not happened already. She would not, and could not, compromise. She fully understood why he wanted to protect what they had. After all, he had once been very poor, while she never wanted for anything, but she had to make him see that something evil was growing all around them and that her early London suspicions had become sad realities. The price of National Socialism was too high, if the reward for economic recovery and international prestige was indecency, fear, suspicion, and cruelty.

The morning after their argument he was abjectly sorry. Although his head was splitting and throbbing, he cooked breakfast and brought it to Hilde on a tray. He kissed her. ''Sorry I lost my temper.''

She, too, was contrite. ''I was disagreeable.''

''Let's not talk about it anymore. . . .''

But she would not let him postpone for long what had to be said, sooner or later. That night they went to a small neighborhood restaurant in Charlottenburg, near Karl-Heinz's old home. The place was little more than a simple *Bierstube*, and they ordered Berlin *Brathering*, cold, fried marinated fish with sliced potatoes and two bottles of *Pilsner Urquell*. Hilde looked around to see if anyone was close, which underscored what she was about to say.

''Karle,'' she said, ''we have to do something, or else we will all lose our Germany.''

Even in the dim light she saw him grow pale. His head swiveled as his eyes swept the room. ''Are you completely mad?'' he whispered. ''You can't talk about that sort of thing in a public place.''

''What's happened to you, Karle? You act as if you're scared of your own shadow. If you don't want to talk here, we'll go home and talk there.''

So they ate in silence, paid the bill, and took a taxi back to the apartment.

"Now," he said, when they had settled, "what was that all about?"

Hilde looked straight into his eyes. "I think it is time for Germans to protest many terrible things being done in the name of the party. Just look at the two of us whispering in a restaurant, scared to speak openly! Siegfried and his wife having to leave the country because he committed the crime of being born a Jew. By the way, Jesus committed the same crime. Tell me what Siegfried Schmidt ever did against Germany?" She continued, "Thousands are being maltreated. I knew many in Nürnberg and England. Wonderful people. Your old chief, one of Germany's great men, killed himself because they took away his life's work for being a Jew."

Karl-Heinz protested, "He did not have to kill himself! He could have left the country like the others. . . ."

"Why should he have left his country? Wasn't he part of Germany?"

No answer.

"You," she said, "my own Karle, are petrified because an old dear friend sends us a letter. You are frightened when your own wife says certain things in public that you think could get us into trouble. But what did I say? Did I say, 'Let's assassinate Hitler'? No! All I said was that I love Germany and I don't want us to lose it. I could have gone on to say, 'We must kill all Jews to save Germany.' But you took it for granted that anyone listening might have us arrested. Paranoia, that's what they brought us!" Still no comment from Karl-Heinz.

"Now," she said, "here are the things I have seen: My old boss, the consul general, was hounded from office because he seemed to disagree with certain things *even though he never said so!* There is now no more room for disagreement in Germany. Obviously, the Nazi system is too fragile for opposition. My priest was arrested because he questioned the behavior of some of his own parishioners. I can no longer buy Heinrich Heine's poems, because Germany's great poet was a Jew. I can no longer see Shakespeare staged by Max Reinhardt, or watch Elisabeth Bergner act, or enjoy paintings by Max Liebermann. Am I a child who must be taught artistic manners?

Karle, it's turning us all into spineless, cowardly, prejudiced fools!''

She waited for his response, but none was forthcoming. He was still unwilling to accept the fact that this girl was now a strong, strange woman, principled and stubborn. Perhaps it had always been there and he had ignored it. Now she had become a threat.

Like a man with a spooky horse he now tried to assuage, calm, pacify. ''Look, Hilde, I have to go on a special assignment. They wanted you to come along, but perhaps it might be better if, instead, you visit your parents in Nürnberg for a few days. I'll say you had family business and Zoss will understand. I'll join you as soon as I'm through. Then we can get this all straightened out.''

''Where will you be?''

''Near Salzburg.''

''How near Salzburg?''

''Berchtesgaden.''

''You mean the Berghof? Adolf Hitler's Berghof?''

''Yes.''

''Jesus and Mary!'' Hilde was aghast. ''Do you mean they wanted me to go to the Berghof with you?''

''Yes. Seems the *Führer* likes to have young couples around, so Zoss asked if you would go. But not now. The way you feel it would upset you too much.''

''You're afraid of what I'd say or do.''

''Perhaps.''

''Karle, would I ever do anything to harm you?''

''I don't think so, not willingly, but I'm not sure. . . .''

''Aren't you?''

''No, Hilde. You've changed a lot.''

''I haven't changed. You just haven't been with me to see things as I've seen them. Maybe you're right. I'll go home to Nürnberg.''

The convoy to the Berghof assembled very early on an abnormally warm October morning in Munich's Englischer Garten Park. It was led by three black Brunzig ''Himmler *Panzers*,'' each filled with SS personnel. Then came the Brunzig group—Gerhardt Brunzig, Zoss, Dr. Maut, Karl-Heinz, and Anneliese von Konsky—who rode in two identical pearl-gray 900K five-seater convertibles. Finally came two, field-gray G.F.W. 12s with the SS insignia of the L.A.H., the *Führer*'s bodyguard. These were the cars that would be presented to the Berghof.

The column was ready to leave for Rosenheim, the first stop about fifty kilometers from Munich, when they heard the deep, massive exhaust of an old, white, open, two-seater twelve-cylinder 500C driven by Hannes Morgenroth. If you wanted to get the undivided attention of any hundred German schoolboys, all you had to say was "Hannes Morgenroth." He was Germany's legendary automobile racing champion, the winner of every major grand prix since the late twenties and Brunzig's number one.

Morgenroth pulled up alongside and yelled over his rumbling engine, "I'll drive up with you. They're expecting me. I'll meet you at Rosenheim at the Goldener Hirsch Inn. We can breakfast there!" Then he revved up his engine, banged in the clutch, and shot off, supercharger screaming, huge, old-fashioned tires throwing up gravel and dust. Within seconds his car was out of sight.

After fifty kilometers of fast driving, they found his 500C peacefully parked in the courtyard of the Goldener Hirsch in Rosenheim.

Morgenroth was in the lobby, reading a Munich paper, drinking coffee, and smoking English Player cigarettes.

"Did you," he asked, "get lost? Or what is your excuse for this unseemly dawdling? I'm starved!" Then he jumped up, made a deep bow, swept his right hand like an ancient cavalier, and said, "Oh, my God, oh, saints protect me . . . I have been careless and impertinent in front of my employer, the master of Villa Ritterschwert, his Excellency *Herr Generaldirektor* Gerhardt Brunzig! Oh, woe is me . . ." and he fell to one knee.

Gerhardt Brunzig grinned. "Stand up, you asshole," he said. "You're a genius driver. You're a lousy actor." They embraced, an Italian custom everyone in the racing world had picked up.

Karl-Heinz was introduced and babbled something about "having seen you race since I was a child." Zoss winced. "Come on, Dornchen, stop making all of us feel like old men!" Karl-Heinz realized his *faux pas*, but Morgenroth grinned at him. "I've been driving races since I was six. So you're probably right!" He kissed Anneliese von Konsky on both cheeks *à la française*, smilingly ignored an SS major's "*Heilitla*" salute, and made a short bow to Dr. Maut. He was definitely the center of attention, the star. Waiters came to stare, the concierge asked for an autograph, and heads swiveled among the guests in the lobby. Like Max Schmeling, Morgenroth had been a national hero long before the Hitler takeover, although he would have disliked being compared with a boxer. He considered himself somewhat of a *flâneur* and international bon vivant, far above a mere prizefighter.

Morgenroth had never joined the party or the N.S.K.K., much to Zoss's chagrin and Papa Hoegel's amusement. According to the rumor at Brunzig, Morgenroth said he did not *need* to join the N.S.K.K. It was their place to join *him*. Everyone wrote it down to vanity and left him alone to win races, which he did regularly, even though there were many new, young race drivers.

Morgenroth, Dr. Maut, and Gerhardt Brunzig excused themselves. They sat down at an isolated corner table and instantly fell into deep discussion. Zoss, Anneliese von Konsky, and Karl-Heinz, at another table, confronted a heavy Bavarian breakfast of smoked ham, eggs, sausages, preserves, and smoked trout, but Anneliese von Konsky had only coffee. She treated Karl-Heinz like a recent acquaintance, and Rome seemed long forgotten.

Pointing his thumb at Gerhardt Brunzig's table, Zoss said, "They're talking about the new formula. Papa Hoegel is having troubles, and they want Morgenroth to help them solve things, but he hates testing. Can't blame him. It's dangerous and boring. Also"—he leaned forward, conspiratorially—"he won't let them paint the swastika ensign on his car. Dr. Goebbels instructed the chief of N.S.K.K. that all German race machines were to carry the national emblem. Morgenroth insists that the regulation international racing car color for Germany is white or silver, which should be enough. It always has been. The Italians have red; the Belgians, yellow; the British, green; and the French, blue. They don't use flags."

"Is he against National Socialism?" asked Karl-Heinz under his breath with a sideways glance at the SS group at the next table.

"No. Not really! He just hates letting anyone tell him what to do, so he won't let them paint things on 'his' car. Besides, he has many old friends among the foreign drivers, and he's afraid he'll get kidded by them. He has a very thin skin.''

Karl-Heinz shook his head. "He seems to get away with it.''

"*Na, ja,* so long as he wins races.''

Anneliese von Konsky, monosyllabic since they started the trip, said, "Hannes is a wonderful fellow, a first-class gentleman.''

"You were once great chums, weren't you?'' said Zoss.

"So we were. Twenty years ago, when we were both youngsters and he was still driving his own race cars. I begged and borrowed to get him some sponsorship. Sometimes Hannes couldn't even afford the gasoline to drive to the races.''

Karl-Heinz thought their greeting had been quite offhanded, considering they obviously had been lovers, but he said nothing. Zoss felt no such reluctance. He tweaked her, "You two didn't exactly fall around each other's necks?''

She shrugged and smiled. "*Tempus fugit. . . .*''

But when they resumed their trip, Anneliese von Konsky was in Hannes Morgenroth's 500C, and they soon disappeared in the direction of the Chiemsee lake, once more leaving the others far behind. Karl-Heinz was relieved, free of any obligation to her.

They passed through Prien, where, as Zoss told him, the *Führer* always stopped for pastries and the superb view of the lake. Then they crossed the old Austrian border to Salzburg and finally south to Berchtesgaden, back into Germany. Visitors to the Berghof, particularly foreign ones, were often taken via this route on principle, to make it clear that there was no longer a separate Austria. Zoss said it had made a forceful impression on some English industrialists he had accompanied recently. "The English were startled, but they made no mention of it. As Berliners say, 'When you stick your nose into certain things, you can wind up breathing through your ears.' ''

They entered the *Berchtesgadener Land*, the beautiful Bavarian Alps all around and above them, and then they aimed for *the* mountain, the Obersalzberg, which housed the Berghof complex. After they passed the main gate, they entered a sizable town, built up around the base of the mountain. Zoss, who was an expert, pointed out the hotel, kindergarten, barracks, drill hall, post office, plant nursery, and garages. At one end of the settlement, below most other buildings, was the *Führer*'s own retreat, the real Berghof, a very large Bavarian chalet.

The weather had changed. A chill wind blew low clouds through the mountain passes, blanking out the valleys below.

The two G.F.W. 12s were driven to the garage next to the SS administration building. The houses resembled local Bavarian farm cottages with pitched and mansarded roofs and stucco walls in cream or gray trimmed with white window frames. SS guards of the L.A.H. were everywhere, standing at their characteristic attention, legs spread, rifles shouldered, a monumentlike military posture invented by the SS.

They checked into the Platterhof Hotel at the center of the complex, which housed only guests of the Berghof. The Platterhof smelled of soap, flowers, washed wood, starched laundry, and Bavarian cooking. Karl-Heinz's room, a small bedroom next to Zoss's large double room, was upholstered with Bavarian flower prints and had plain wooden farm furniture. A portrait of the *Führer* hung in each room, placed over the head of the bed, where Bavarian farmers usually put the crucifix.

On the table of Karl-Heinz's room he found an entire folder of instructions that were to be followed punctiliously.

• When in the presence of the *Führer*, smoking is strictly prohibited.

• Lunch at the Berghof will be served promptly at noon. At 1100 hours guests will assemble on the terrace or in the main hall, depending on weather conditions, to greet the *Führer*. Should he so wish to honor guests, the *Führer* will be present at approximately that time.

• The *Führer* will select certain guests to accompany him on his afternoon walk to the teahouse. The choice of these guests will be announced through a memorandum from *Reichsführer* Bormann.

• After dinner, it is suggested that guests retire to the hotel, unless they are invited to remain in the company of the *Führer*. Those so honored should remain with the *Führer* until he retires.

The memorandum continued into minutiae such as the correct form of address and greeting, suggested apparel, and the wearing of decorations and uniforms. There was also a telephone directory, a map, and special instructions regarding medical emergencies, transportation, and postvisit statements. Naturally, cameras were prohibited without special permission. All this printed material was to be returned before leaving the hotel.

Karl-Heinz hung his uniform and other clothes in a big armoire and answered a knock on the door. It was the likeable SS Major von Bernsdorfer.

The major pointed at the open armoire.

"Dorn! Do I see one of our uniforms . . . ?"

"No, *mein Guter*, it's only the meek old N.S.K.K."

Von Bernsdorfer held up the tunic and raised his hand. "Instant *Hauptsturmführer*. Congratulations, captain! And what's that ribbon I see, lurking on the left chest?"

"The lowest rank of the Italian Order of the Crown. They give it to anyone who knows how to type."

"Very modest, but I heard that you saved the *Duce*'s life singlehandedly. On the other hand, if you had let him die, the old king would have given you Italy's highest decoration!"

"*Na*, they tell me the only way the *Duce* is going to die is from fucking too much or falling off his horse."

"Well, that's my territory. Maybe I can give him some jumping lessons."

"Doesn't need them. Jumps on every woman under fifty."

Suddenly the SS officer put his finger over his lips. He went to the washbasin, turned on the taps, and then whispered in Karl-Heinz's ear, "Holy mother of God, I forgot that some of these rooms may be wired to the S.D. office on the other side of the Berghof. But I'm pretty sure they only do it to the big shots, not to you and me."

"Like Zoss?"

"Yes, maybe. He's got a good mouth for gossip, and he loves to spread *Dreck*. The S.D. are happy when someone dishes out dirt. They're not bad fellows, really, but they're snoops, no question about that. Let's go downstairs."

"Is Sepp Dietrich here?"

"Of course he is. What would the Berghof be without him?" He turned off the water.

The moment they left the privacy of Karl-Heinz's room,

von Bernsdorfer became *Sturmbannführer* von Bernsdorfer, major of the SS, member of the *Leibstandarte Adolf Hitler*.

Under the influence of the Berghof, the distillate of all National Socialism, he changed from an amusing man into a braced-back saluting machine. Now he was on display, both to superiors and subordinates. SS officers had the constant stimulus of salutes from their men, but even more intimidating was the frequent presence of some of the Reich's most famous faces: Goebbels, Speer, Streicher, Ley, Ribbentrop, and their own supreme SS chief, Heinrich Himmler, besides the supreme second rank like Heydrich and Bormann. At the Berghof, von Bernsdorfer was like a mortal always walking among the gods, afraid that one slip would send him to Hades. Karl-Heinz, who had formed his impression of the man through one late party at the Zoss apartment, the Sepp Dietrich demonstration, and the few minutes of lighthearted chatter in the hotel room, was amazed by the change, although the whispering episode in the bedroom should have been a hint. Life was not easy at the Berghof. Yet von Bernsdorfer had preserved his private sense of humor, as he had proved earlier. Karl-Heinz decided that all was not lost.

They met with Zoss in the lobby and then drove to the barracks square in front of an SS drill hall. Many salutes, "*Heilitla,*" and introductions. Then an SS *Obersturmbannführer* colonel of the L.A.H. Guard, an enormously tall, broad, and well-muscled man in his early fifties, outlined the upcoming presentation ceremonial. He used sharp-edged hand gestures to describe the formations of honor guard, color guard, band, SS officers. *Führer*, guests, press, and staff. Everything was as carefully choreographed as a ballet, and the people from Brunzig could not be expected to learn it by heart. Instead, von Bernsdorfer was ordered to become their guide and prompter. At ramrod attention, he yelled, "*Zu Befehl, Herr Obersturmbannführer,*" more like a sergeant than a major, but one look at the tall colonel's iron face explained his response.

Anneliese von Konsky arrived with Hannes Morgenroth in the old 500C. Perched sideways on the white car's cut-out door was the biggest SS colonel Karl-Heinz had ever seen. His face was deeply marked by the *Schmisse* dueling scars affected by university students, which gave him a savage look. He greeted the guard colonel and Zoss with easy familiarity and was then introduced to Karl-Heinz as SS *Obersturmbannführer* Jan Telesty. "Can I go look at your mountain goat?" Telesty asked Zoss.

"Of course," said Zoss. "You'll like G.F.W. twelve. It's Dr. Maut's most recent masterpiece. Over there, in the L.A.H. garage."

"See you later. *Heilitla!*" said Telesty and marched off to look at the new Brunzig.

They lunched at the hotel. Zoss told Karl-Heinz about Telesty, an Austrian rich boy who had joined the SS straight from Heidelberg, where he had studied little but fought dozens of duels in the ancient fraternity manner. Before the N.S. takeover few men fought these duels, because they were illegal, and scars had gone out of fashion. But now the scarred face had returned to favor, and once again, students slashed at each other, protected by shoulder, throat, arm, hand, and eye guards. The idea was to hit only the cheeks with a razor-sharp saber and then to get instant treatment for the bloody but undangerous cuts. Duels were always stopped once first blood was drawn, and no one ever died or even got hospitalized.

It was strictly and literally a "show" of courage, not proof of it. "And don't forget," said Zoss, "that the damn doctors were honor-bound not to patch the cuts perfectly. The idea was to leave a *scar!* Thank heaven I never got involved during my student days! People in other countries still think of us as masochistic barbarians when they see dueling *Schmisse* on a German man's face. I spend so much time with foreigners, it could really have done Brunzig some harm, not to speak of my own immortal career and the many women lucky enough to share its bounty. Anyway," he continued, "the bescarred Telesty is now in charge of special SS shock troops. If war ever came, they would fight from parachutes and small planes and gliders. Also, they would land in seaborne operations as frogmen. He is teaching them all the Japanese martial arts like judo, kendo, ninja tricks, karate, everything to gladden the heart of your average happy-go-lucky sadist."

"I must admit, he looks the type," said Karl-Heinz.

"He *is* the type!" said Anneliese von Konsky, who had joined them and who seemed to know whereof she spoke.

Brunzig, Morgenroth, and Maut were at another table back in deep discussion. At one point, Morgenroth raised his voice.

"That's a lot of shit!" he said. "I hate sitting so close to the wheel. I always think if I could sit further away . . ." His voice trailed off, but his arms demonstrated the new driving position he wanted, with extended arms.

A group of army staff officers with wide red stripes on their field-gray breeches settled at a nearby table. One of them was Major von Totten, who came over. He asked, "How did it go in Rome?"

"*Fantastisch!*" said Zoss. "The *Duce* spent a full twenty seconds looking at his gift. He would probably have preferred G.F.W. twelve if Maut had designed some tits onto the front." He could talk like this in front of Anneliese von Konsky, and she confirmed that he was on safe ground by grinning widely, but the major was taken aback.

He blushed like a schoolboy, cleared his throat, and said, "Very interesting," without seeming to mean it. Karl-Heinz smirked behind his hand. The major excused himself and walked over to Gerhardt Brunzig's table.

"Von Totten is a wonderful man," said Zoss, "but of the old school. I shocked him!"

Karl-Heinz wanted to phone Hilde. He asked von Bernsdorfer, "Can I make a call to my wife in Nürnberg?"

"*Na, ja*, you can. But it's rather complicated, and the phone will be completely monitored, so it's no good for romantic talk."

Karl-Heinz decided it might be better if he passed, considering everything. He could not prewarn Hilde to "be discreet," and anyway, he was not at all sure she would have paid attention. For that matter, the things she might have considered innocent could have been grossly misunderstood. Everyone at the Berghof seemed sensitive to the point of mania about anything that might be interpreted as dangerous, insulting, or simply discourteous to the unseen host whose presence was felt concretely, although few people in the large Berghof compound ever saw him. Still, the face, body, voice, and mind of Adolf Hitler were everywhere, almost touchable. The Berghof was Germany, condensed and microscopic. Outside, the *Führer*'s image was somehow diluted, but the Berghof served it unwatered, full strength, and concentrated.

And, so far, neither Brunzig nor Zoss nor Karl-Heinz had even seen the *Führer!*

But Anneliese von Konsky and Hannes Morgenroth had.

She let slip that they had attended the *Führer*'s eleven-o'clock *Levee* at the Berghof and then had joined the others at the hotel because that day there were no luncheon provisions for them at the *Führer*'s table. Nevertheless, it was considered an honor to meet with him so soon after their arrival, probably because the *Führer* admired Morgenroth, and was always most courteous to Anneliese von Konsky. Morgenroth was polite but not awed. He was a famous German face long before Hitler, and Anneliese von Konsky knew how to count her opportunities. She was delighted to accept the *Führer*'s admiration, knowing that it would remain just that. She was quite aware of the Braun woman.

After lunch, Zoss, von Bernsdorfer, and Karl-Heinz drove to the main garage to check on the two G.F.W. 12s. They wanted to be sure of everything, although it was most unlikely that anything could go wrong.

There were masses of vehicles in the SS motor pool, black "Himmler *Panzers*," small convertible Mercedeses, dozens of field-gray BMW "*Krad*" motorcycles with and without sidecars, armored cars, like PKW Mark II tanks, six-wheeled trucks. The Berghof was obviously armed and motorized to the teeth. The two G.F.W. 12s were spotless and being fussed over by some SS mechanics, under the critical eye of Brunzig's *Herr* Zummer. One of the SS *Scharführer* corporals cursed, "I can't get this *verdammte* thing started!" and Zummer looked at him and said, "Asshole! Turn on the ignition. It helps." He then spit a juicy "oyster" onto the spotless garage floor. An SS sergeant came over, red-faced, about to let fly at Zummer, who fixed him and said, "Son, don't start up with me, or next thing you'll be staring out of your own rib cage like a monkey in the zoo!" a classic Berlin warning.

The sergeant spotted von Bernsdorfer, snapped to attention, saluted, and then, still red-faced, turned away. Zoss took Zummer aside. "Come on, you old fart. Don't make any trouble here, or we'll all get hung by the balls."

"Oh, all right," Zummer grumbled. "Shouldn't let these young shits handle our expensive new equipment."

Then Zoss found what he had been looking for: a tiny car, curved like a beetle, field gray with a sliding convertible roof. "There it is," he said, "The KdF car."

"The what?" said Karl-Heinz.

"The KdF car. The car that the KdF, the 'Strength through Joy' labor organization is supposed to provide every family in Germany for a small investment. In May, they laid the cornerstone for a huge factory at Wolfsburg, bigger than the American factories, where they'll build these things. Sort of a *Volkswagen*, a people's car."

"Who designed it?"

"I'm told the *Führer* had the idea in 1934. He called four experts, including Dr. Porsche, to the Kaiserhof Hotel in Berlin, and outlined the project in fifteen minutes. He even sketched the car. It's taken forever to get going. They're now selling purchase tickets to people who'll get their car by 1940."

"Looks like a Czechoslovak *Tatra*."

"You're absolutely right. The rear engine and the shape came from the Czechs. They're brilliant."

"Really?"

"Well, after the *Führer*'s meeting last September"—Zoss looked around, but only von Bernsdorfer was listening—"we may get a few more!"

"You mean when we got the Sudetenland?"

"Yes. Courtesy of the *Herren* Chamberlain, Daladier, and Mussolini."

They drove back to the hotel.

Karl-Heinz invited von Bernsdorfer to his room. He wanted to know more about the September meetings. "Were you there for the last conference?" he asked von Bernsdorfer.

"Yes. It was in Munich at the new party building. Daladier and Chamberlain came by plane, and we took them to their hotels in 900Ks."

"What was old Chamberlain like?"

"*Na, ja,* he seemed like a sort of grandpa schoolteacher. He was a bit shaken by the flight to Germany. He told us it was his first flight. Daladier, the Frenchman, looked like our family blacksmith."

There was a lot of time until eight that evening when they were all to be at the Berghof for dinner with the *Führer*, the summons according to a letter from the *Führer-Secretary* Martin Bormann, handed to them as they entered the hotel. Von Bernsdorfer was not included, but he did not seem to mind.

"Fortunately, tonight is Günsche's turn." He explained

that they rotated aides. Günsche was the SS aide, a young captain. There were also army, navy, and Luftwaffe aides. Their job was to stand by while the *Führer* dined with his guests and then to sit through the invariable film and the interminable, one-way discussions that followed. The *Führer* spoke, and his guests listened. Von Bernsdorfer sounded like a nephew mentioning a favorite uncle's awful habits. He took off his belt, chest strap, and tunic, kicked off his boots, and stretched out in a chair.

"How," Karl-Heinz asked, "if you don't mind telling me, did you get into this SS job?"

"Don't mind at all. Very simple, really. My father, the old count, is a typical country gentleman who takes care of his estates and minds his own buiness. Our estate is near Wiesbaden and our branch of the family is called von Bernsdorfer zu Kehlsbach. We've had *Schloss* Kehlsbach since the thirteenth century. We were house mercenaries to the Hessian dukes, and they gave up Kehlsbach. It's quite a pretty place. You'd like it. You'll have to come there. My sister is nineteen and rides better than I do. In fact, that's all we know: how to ride horses. Poor father! He sent me to the best *Internat*, the best boarding school, and even got me into a university for three months, and that was that. I'm hopeless. All I can do is make horses jump over fences. In fact, sometimes I'm sure I can speak to horses. They're like relatives, and I miss them. You were talking about Mussolini's horse? That's Fru Fru, a beauty. Came from Tripoli. I know the whole stud, all superb— tiny red nostrils, short back, good-natured—real Arabs, the most extraordinary horses. I wish I could breed them, but they need a lot of love and attention, and one has to be there."

He dug a box of cigarettes out of his pocket and lighted one. "I can get away with smoking here in the hotel, but over in my quarters with the SS bachelor officers, I'd get chewed out. Anyway, father was approached by our Hessian *Gauleiter* to join the party. That would have brought great credit to the *Gauleiter*, but Papa is stubborn. He spoke to some old regimental mates of his, and not one of them had joined the party yet. I don't think they have much against the movement, but they're all stiff-necked. They don't like being pushed, and they suspect the party big shots, the *Bonzen*, are pushy. The *Gauleiter* of Hessia is a complete *parvenu*, no one father would ever meet socially. It goes against my old man's snob instincts. He'll gladly dine with his gardener, but he won't even have a cup of coffee with a bourgeois social climber. So eventually things got rather tense.''

Karl-Heinz nodded. He phoned downstairs for some coffee. ''Sorry I interrupted.''

''I must be a bore. Good idea, coffee.''

''No, go on!''

''*Na, ja*, I was riding on the show circuit. I had just competed in Italy and England, and I was back in Berlin for the horse show. This was about two years ago, when I bumped into Armin Zoss at a party. I told Zoss about my father's *contretemps* with the *Gauleiter*. Zoss knows father very well. Somehow, we kept our money during the bad times, and father bought several big Brunzigs when things were tough, which Zoss has never forgotten. So Zoss suggested that he could get me a job in the party to take the pressure off *Schloss* Kehlsbach and my stubborn old father. Then Zoss fixed things with Bormann, who was the *Führer*'s secretary and still is, although he's now a real bigwig.

''Bormann presented me to the *Führer*, who had seen me ride in competition, and I got my SS commission. So here I am, a horseman who has to deal with motorcars, trains, and airplanes. Oh, and I forgot, sometimes even with motorboats!'' His face showed utter disgust.

There was a knock on the door. Karl-Heinz, thinking it was the coffee, yelled, ''Come in. Door's open!'' But it wasn't the waiter; it was Gerhardt Brunzig dressed in a tweed suit. The two younger men jumped to their feet, but Brunzig laughed and said, ''*Meine Herren*, back on your asses, please.''

They invited him in, and he sat down and produced a hip flask of brandy. ''Anyone got glasses?'' They found two, so Brunzig poured drinks for them, lifted the flask in a toast, and then drank straight from it. ''Booze and cigarettes,'' he said. ''Let's abolish them. But not yet.'' He took another swig. Finally a waiter arrived with coffee and they ordered another one for Brunzig. ''Please,'' said the automobile magnate to the waiter, a young, blond farmboy, ''no Turkish coffee. No Brazilian coffee. Just plain, bad German coffee, *gemacht?*''

''*Jawohl, Herr* von Brunzig,'' and he left.

''I like that,'' said Brunzig. ''Now the kind hangs a title on me. Why, I'm the son of a mechanic, can't you tell?'' He

lifted his perfectly manicured, slim hands for their inspection.
Then he said, "Listen, von Bernsdorfer, why don't you give
up all this nonsense and come to work for Brunzig? Between
you and Dorn here, we could ruin the competition and also
win a male beauty contest." He broke into laughter. He was
getting high.

"Very flattering," said von Bernsdorfer.

"Nonsense. Not flattering at all. Quite true. You'd do fine,
working for us, but Zoss would kill me."

"Why, *Herr Generaldirektor*?"

"Zoss would kill me, his *Herr Generaldirektor*, because he
prefers to have you as our friendly agent in the land of the
Bormann boys. We all love our *Führer*, but do we all love
our *Führer*'s flunky?" He saw the look of panic in the young
SS major's eyes. "Come on now, *Sturmbannführer*, don't
pee in your pants. You're safe. This room isn't wired. Mine
is. I have my sources!" and he wagged his finger. "Even
here, in the lion's den, I have my sources. You don't run a
great, big company like mine without a bit of sly, slimy
guile." He stood up from the chair on which he had perched.
"When this is over tomorrow, why don't you two come to
Ritterschwert with me? I'm organizing a *Fest*, a big party this
weekend, and people are coming from Monte Carlo and St.
Moritz and Paris and London. It'll be fun." When the two
didn't say anything, he continued, "Oh, good. Then you'll be
there! Dorn, I'll tell Zoss. He'll loan you to me for a day or
two. And I'm sure he can also make excuses for you, major."
He left the room with a wave, not at all sober.

That evening, they drove to the *Führer*'s residence.

It was gray and foggy, and a cold wind whistled down
from the mountains. The cars stopped in front of a wide flight
of stairs that led to the terrace in front of the *Führerhaus*.
When they reached the top, two SS guards came to attention
and presented arms. Then they entered Hitler's home and
handed their coats and hats to SS servants in short white
uniform jackets.

Martin Bormann, his squat body dressed in a party leader's
tan uniform, showed them into a reception room, where
Major von Totten and his wife had been waiting. Anneliese
von Konsky, Gerhardt Brunzig, Armin Zoss, Dr. Maut, Hannes
Morgenroth, SS Colonel Telesty, and Karl-Heinz made up the

rest of the party, and it was obvious that Gerhardt Brunzig, as head of Germany's most prestigious automobile company, was to be the guest of honor. Amazingly, Brunzig was sober, pink-cheeked and cheerful. Von Totten, Telesty, and Bormann were the only ones in uniform. Von Bernsdorfer had told Karl-Heinz that his N.S.K.K. uniform could wait until the following day's presentation ceremonial. Gerhardt Brunzig looked ready for Claridge's or the Savoy. He wore a small party badge, as did the other civilians, with the exception of Morgenroth who had the Brunzig sword insignia on his lapel. They all made an embarrassed attempt at conversation about the paintings around the room and the view through the windows, although there was little to see since it was dark outside. Then an SS waiter passed a tray with fruit juices. Gerhardt Brunzig lifted his glass, winked at Karl-Heinz, and said, "You really ought to try this. I drink it all the time." He then poured it down, like a man dousing *Schnaps*. Bormann said, "The *Führer* will be here soon. Perhaps we can take our places," and he lined them up, Gerhardt Brunzig first in the row.

Time passed. Hannes Morgenroth was clearly impatient and fidgety. He stuck his hands in his pockets, pulled them out, stepped away from his assigned spot to look at a vase on a pedestal, and then returned to the group. He took out his cigarette case, but remembered the rules of the house and stuffed it back into his pocket. Finally, he said, "*Na, Herr* Bormann, will the *Führer* ever come to the Nürburgring for the races? I can promise him it's even more exciting than the Olympics."

Bormann stepped aside and said, "Why not ask him yourself?" because Adolf Hitler had entered the room, dressed in a baggy tweed suit.

"Ask me what?" said the *Führer*.

"*Herr* Morgenroth will tell you later. Meantime, *mein Führer*, may I present to you *Generaldirektor* Gerhardt Brunzig of the Brunzig *Werke?*"

"*Heil!*" said Brunzig, raising his arm.

"*Grüss Gott, Herr* Brunzig." Hitler reached out to shake hands. "We've met before when your *Herr* Papa was still alive. And you know, I trust myself to your products every day. Really the finest, much the finest!"

Gerhardt Brunzig acknowledged the compliment by nodding his head.

Then Hitler got to Anneliese von Konsky. He bowed and kissed her hand, speaking with ingratiating courtesy. "*Ja, Gnädige Frau*, what a joy to see you again! I am always so happy when you come to the Berghof, so very happy." He smiled, rubbed his hands, very much the petty bourgeois displaying old-fashioned, middle-class gallantry.

He used the same style with the tall, blond *Frau* von Totten, but he almost ignored her husband. His greetings to Dr. Maut and Telesty were curt and correct, but when he got to Morgenroth, he smiled, shook hands, and said, "I thought about what you told me this morning. I don't think it would work."

Finally, it was Karl-Heinz's turn. "Dorn?" said the *Führer*, "You're from Berlin, *stimmts?* When they showed me the new command car? Right? I rarely forget a Berliner. They don't forget me, either, the good Berliners! But I'm told you're nearly human . . . almost Bavarian!"

Everyone snickered, and the *Führer* continued, "There is no bigger pain in the neck than that Berlin attitude that makes them think they know everything better! Not young Dorn here, of course. Do you have a wife, Dorn?"

"Yes, sir."

"Berliner?"

"No, sir. Nürnberger."

"There you are! I knew it!" The *Führer* slapped his thigh. "His Franconian wife has humanized him! Bormann, we should issue instructions that all Berliners must marry people from south of Stuttgart!" He was obviously venting his spleen about some problem connected with Berlin while poking fun at his youngest guest. Everyone laughed politely.

Then the *Führer* offered his arm to Anneliese von Konsky and led the way to the dining room. Bormann followed, escorting *Frau* von Totten, who towered over him. The rest found their assigned seats through place cards. Instead of being at the head of the table, the *Führer* sat at the center of one side, so that he could speak to all his guests.

More white-jacketed SS waiters brought the first course, lentil soup, but the *Führer* was served salad. His menu was different from theirs. The *Führer* quickly took charge. "I always choose my own dishes. Bormann chose yours. You'll probably get stew. I don't like meat. I have eaten it, but I certainly don't enjoy it. Cadaverous. Can't even understand the so-called blood sports. Göring likes to shoot game. Spends a fortune on hunting those poor animals near his estate. Damnedest thing, that a fat fellow with a rifle can do away with a tall, beautiful stag. Not much of a contest.''

Gerhardt Brunzig looked over at Karl-Heinz, grinning. He remembered saying something similar at Ritterschwert.

"Anyway,'' Adolf Hitler continued without pause, "I grow more and more fond of animals as time goes by. I am certain my dog Blondi will always stay my friend. I am not so certain about most people around me. Except for Bormann, here.'' He pointed his thumb at his secretary.

Then he said, "Morgenroth, that proposal you made earlier?''

Everyone waited to hear what the race driver had suggested to the head of the Third Reich. "The one about using foreign drivers? We've already got one. There's that Englishman, what's his name?''

"Barry.'' Bormann produced the name.

"I realize you want Brunzig to win every race, but it would not be wise,'' said Adolf Hitler, "to have Frenchmen and Dutchmen, Italians and heaven knows what driving our Silver Arrows. After all, Brunzigs are German machines, and it would be sad to think that we don't have enough German men able to win with German cars.''

"*Aber*,'' said Morgenroth, "but . . .''

"No buts. We'll just have to train enough men. I think we ought to start race-driving schools.'' Bormann made notes on a pad near his plate. "Not that I really approve of the sport itself, no insult intended, dear Morgenroth. To me, it's a childish self-indulgence, very juvenile, with the exception of a man like you who is really driving for Germany. Every time you win for us, every time Brunzig cars carry the German emblem to the first place, the world knows where we stand! They know that we do what we set out to do and that we will not be toyed with.'' Almost resentfully, he forked some vegetable pancake into his mouth as if it might stem the flow of his thoughts. The others ate beef stew with vegetables.

Bormann said, "What about the N.S.K.K.? Can't they start a school?''

"Right. Good idea. Instruct Hühnlein!'' Hühnlein was the *Korpsführer* of N.S.K.K.

"And most of all," Hitler continued, "we need your expert help, Hannes Morgenroth. Without you, this thing could not work. That is"—and the *Führer* arched his eyebrows—"as soon as we can persuade you, the *Herr Rennmeister*, our great champion, to honor the N.S.D.A.P. with your membership. You are already a member of the organization that is"—he turned toward Gerhardt Brunzig and his voice became ironical—"that is almost as vital to Germany as the N.S.D.A.P. I'm speaking of the great Brunzig company."

Gerhardt Brunzig sensed the steel under the velvet. In a very soft voice he said, "We are highly honored to have Hannes Morgenroth as number-one driver for our little company. The rest is up to him."

Hannes Morgenroth said nothing. He looked down at his hands, his usual bravado for once in check. Anneliese von Konsky came to the rescue. "*Mein Führer*, we are all looking forward to seeing you in the new car tomorrow. I hope Kempka will drive you around a bit." Kempka was the *Führer*'s chauffeur since the earliest days of the party.

"Yes. If Kempka likes it, it'll be perfect." Hitler said these things without caring who listened. After all, two very senior Brunzig executives were present as well as the designer of the G.F.W. 12. Hitler seemed oblivious to their feelings. He implied that if the *Führer*'s chauffeur said it was good, it was good, no matter who else thought so. It was Adolf Hitler's way.

He got up abruptly, his entrée eaten, and said, "Let's have coffee and cakes in the salon. Also, we have a film tonight."

Finished or not, they stood up, folded their napkins, and followed him. The salon was very large, hung with wall tapestries and furnished with oversized couches and armchairs too far apart for normal conversation. When the *Führer* had led the ladies to their armchairs and had found his own, the others sorted themselves onto the vast couches, frequently quite far from the host. Nevertheless, everything focused on the man in the rumpled tweed suit.

A very tall SS man, probably Günsche, the aide von Bernsdorfer had mentioned, came in and whispered into the *Führer*'s ear. Hitler stood up at once and said, "I have to meet with some people. The conference won't be long. Please excuse me," and he quickly left the room, followed by

Günsche. Bormann also excused himself. Karl-Heinz had settled next to Telesty, who looked bored. "Can't even smoke," said the tall SS colonel. "*Scheisse!*"

"Can't you excuse yourself?"

"Good idea. For just a moment. Come with me."

When they passed Gerhardt Brunzig, Zoss, and Maut, the three Brunzig men asked where they were going and then joined them. They all went outside to the chilly terrace and hastily lighted cigarettes. An SS man was ordered by Telesty to provide ashtrays. Clouds and fog lay in the valley below.

"How do we get out of the film?" said Gerhardt Brunzig under his breath. "I understand they'll play one."

"You've got an excuse!" said Telesty. "Tell him you want to check on the command cars. Tell him you don't want anything to go wrong tomorrow because the press were invited and the foreign attachés."

"Good thinking, Telesty! Call on me anytime in the future if you need me."

"I shall," said Telesty. "One day you'll regret you made the offer!"

At this point Morgenroth and Anneliese von Konsky joined them. They, too, were cigarette-starved. Morgenroth looked bored, while Anneliese von Konsky was her usual controlled self. She would stick with this evening if it took until dawn, because to her it was worth the investment.

When they returned to the salon, Hitler was still at his meeting, but Bormann was back, so Gerhardt Brunzig left Zoss as a hostage and the old boulevardier took it in stride. Brunzig, Maut, and Karl-Heinz then made a courtesy visit to the garage, after which they returned to the hotel. They found out next morning that the *Führer* had returned an hour later, and those who stayed had watched *Der Kongress Tanzt*, an ancient *schmaltzig* musical film about Vienna in the nineteenth century with waltzes and love songs and unending empty dialogue. Zoss fought hard to stay awake until three in the morning, when the *Führer* finally retired, Bormann in tow. Telesty then got the SS waiters to bring three bottles of champagne, and they had a late party until everyone gave up. Morgenroth got quite drunk, and Anneliese von Konsky had to help him to his room.

• • •

That night Karl-Heinz tossed and turned. It was one in the morning. Where was Hilde? Asleep? Out with friends? If he could have only spoken to her. He was confused. Hitler was totally unlike the man he had imagined. The *Führer* seemed oblivious to anyone's feelings, even snide about Göring, a close, old comrade. Then the disrespect, no, the insult to Dr. Maut and Gerhardt Brunzig, the talk of cadavers when guests were eating stew and allusions that his dog Blondi was more faithful than his guests?

The atmosphere at the Berghof was not one of affection and respect, but filled with cutting remarks, with innuendo and bitterness. It was a tense place. He would never again be able to see Hitler's face in portraits, on postage stamps, in the thousand ways and places it was displayed throughout Germany without thinking of the peevish, callous, and snide man on the other side of the dinner table.

At the ceremony on the SS parade ground those who had spent the last thirty-six hours eating, drinking, chatting, and discussing had become rigid puppets. Major von Totten, Telesty, and von Bernsdorfer, even Gerhardt Brunzig, Zoss, and Maut, walked, stood, and saluted like marionettes. Karl-Heinz, stiff in his uniform, was assigned to drive one of the G.F.W. 12s out of the garage and von Bernsdorfer drove the other.

On a certain spot in front of SS General Sepp Dietrich, and on a given signal, they stopped, got out of the cars, saluted, and yelled in unison, "For the honor of our *Führer* and Germany, may these vehicles be like the steeds of the knights of old!"

The small bulldog SS general had returned their salute. Karl-Heinz thought he detected a glimmer of recognition. The cars were then manned by SS drivers of the L.A.H. Finally, Kempka, the *Führer*'s personal driver, displaced one of the young SS men, the *Führer* got into the seat next to him, and they drove off in the direction of the Berghof, to the repeated shouts of "*Sieg Heil*" and the swirling flourishes of the SS band.

Now hours later, they were back in Munich at the Vier Jahreszeiten Hotel, in Gerhardt Brunzig's large suite, celebrating.

Brunzig raised his glass of champagne. "To von Bernsdorfer and Dorn and their brilliant cabaret rendition of that stuff about the knights of old! May your steeds always have iron cocks! And to Dr. Maut . . .'' He turned to the little engineer. ''Kempka liked it! Bravo, Maut, you succeeded beyond your wildest dreams. You pleased Kempka!''

Dr. Maut refused to acknowledge the toast. He mumbled, ''*Scheissidiot!* Goddam Kempka. Knows nothing about cars, but the *Führer* even falls asleep next to him on long trips. Kempka doesn't know the difference between a fart and a supercharger!''

Telesty said, ''Sometimes I think the further I keep away from the Berghof, the better off I am. What a *Drecksau* that Bormann is!'' Telesty's soft Austrian accent contrasted strongly with his vast body.

''Why do you dislike Bormann?'' asked Zoss. ''He's always been very cooperative.''

''When was the last time you asked him to work with you on something?''

''Two years ago.''

''Things have changed,'' said Telesty. ''Bormann is on the way up. That whole anti-Göring tirade you heard at dinner? That's Bormann's doing.''

''Why Göring?''

''Göring is the one the *Führer* admired most. War hero, intelligent, good family. Also an old fighter from the Munich days. So Göring is the one Bormann wants most to undermine. The only one he can't touch is Goebbels. The little propaganda minister is too clever for him and too dangerous. Bormann keeps a mistress in his own chalet near the Berghof, and he also has a family at home. In fact, the *Führer* was his best man! Goebbels knows about the mistress. Also, Goebbels is totally faithful to the *Führer* without ever kissing his ass.''

''Fascinating,'' said Brunzig. He raised his glass to Telesty. ''To you. You've got guts, *Mut*.''

Telesty smiled. ''What you mean,'' he said, ''is that I'll get my ass into a meat grinder by speaking this way? Don't worry about me! They need me to get their SS rough stuff organized. Same as Sepp Dietrich. The *Führer* needs scrappers. We're scrappers, Dietrich and I. I'll be around long after the others are through. Besides, I'm not one of them. Only the *Führer* knows that.''

''How do you mean, 'not one of them'?'' asked Zoss.

''I'm Austrian, just like Adolf Hitler. The others around

him are German, and—forgive me, gentlemen—Germans are different.''

"Totally," said Gerhardt Brunzig. "Now, *Herr Obersturm-bannführer*, why don't you come to an almost-German party at my house? There'll be a lot of non-Germans there, too."

"When?"

"Tomorrow."

"*Gemacht.* I'll be there!''

Brunzig said, "Everyone here is coming except Maut. He's too grouchy, and also he has to get back to one of his new *Kinder*."

"What sort of *Kind?*" asked Telesty.

"Can't tell you that. Not yet. Not even to the SS. But it'll be a beauty, won't it, Mautchen?"

"Excuse me," said Karl-Heinz to Brunzig. "May I speak to you for a few minutes alone?"

"Of course, Dornchen."

They stepped into the bedroom of the suite.

"*Herr* Brunzig," said Karl-Heinz. "I wonder if you could excuse me from coming to Ritterschwert tomorrow?"

"What's wrong?"

"*Na, also.* My wife and I are having a misunderstanding, not too grave . . . you know how these things can happen. She's in Nürnberg visiting her parents."

Gerhardt Brunzig nodded.

"So," Karl-Heinz continued, "I promised to go to Nürnberg after the Berghof and spend a few days with her. I asked *Herr* Zoss for permission before this trip. I would also like to ask your permission."

"Of course, Dorn. Go ahead. Get things *in Ordnung*. I never met your wife, but everyone says she's *prima*."

"Very grateful to you. Many thanks."

"*Hals und Beinbruch!* as the race drivers say for luck. Break a leg! And if it doesn't work, come join us at Ritterschwert. We'll be there for two or three days."

He was hungry for Hilde, horny like an *Oberprimaner*, a high school senior.

They sat and talked, his parents-in-law and Hilde and he. *Kaffeklatsch.* Coffee and cake. Whipped cream? No, thank you. Sugar? *Zwei, bitte.* He was not alone. Hilde had her knee against his, her bare foot massaging his leg. Would

Hilde and he like to come to a concert? Furtwängler conducting Bach. No, thanks. Too tired!

Finally, the Antmanns left, and the Dorns went to Hilde's old room, the place where she had lived from childhood to student days and where she had faced all the demons of growing up, and they made love to exhaustion, and when they thought they had no more strength to go on, they made even more love. Finally, drained, they fell asleep. An hour later they were awakened by shouts penetrating the double windows.

On the street in front of the house, torch-carrying platoons of S.A. storm troops yelled, "*Juda, verrecke!* Jews die!" and "Buy nothing from Jew pigs!"

That moment the phone rang and Hilde ran downstairs to pick up the receiver. Minutes later she was back. "Karle, that was Else calling from Berlin." Else, a former secretary at the Foreign Office, was now married and living in Charlottenburg. Hilde shook her head. "*Unglaublich!* Incredible! There have been the wildest anti-Jewish riots in Berlin. Storm troops, S.A., smashed the store window of every Jewish shop on Kurfürstendamm. They burned down the synagogue in the Fasanenstrasse and every other synagogue in the city. They also beat up Jewish people on the street, dragged them out of their stores and apartments and then made them clean up the broken glass and mess on their hands and knees. Some were even beaten to death!

"They started to smash up KaDeBe until their commanders were told that it is *Judenrein*, that there are no more Jews working there. Else tried to be careful, but she said that Jews were being hunted like animals and that very few people interfered with the S.A. Even the police were looking the other way. Else made it sound as if she was happy about the whole thing, but I know exactly what she really meant! She was almost in tears. So furious! So humiliated! Oh, God, I'm so happy Siegfried Schmidt isn't here to see all this."

The Antmanns returned long before they were due home. Hilde's mother was in tears.

"The S.A. rushed into the concert hall and pulled some people out into the street. Jews. Furtwängler stopped the concert. Now there are these rowdies all over Nürnberg, breaking windows, yelling for Jews to come out to beat them up. They're right outside now. I was scared to death until we ran through the door.'' She sobbed, and Hilde tried to calm her.

Professor Antmann walked into his study and reappeared with a hunting rifle. Hilde had not seen the weapon since she was a child, because he had long before given up shooting. "I'm going out there," he said. The women yelled "No!" and Karl-Heinz held out his hand for the weapon. He said, "I've got a better way."

"What way?"

"First, give me the rifle."

"All right. I'll put it away. Then what?"

"Wait! I'll be right back."

Upstairs, Karl-Heinz put on his N.S.K.K. uniform, and when he returned there was a moment of shock because the Antmann's had never seen him dressed this way. He told them to keep the door locked and then he went out into the raw November night.

Fifty meters away under a streetlight stood a squad of tan-uniformed S.A. troopers. They had formed a circle around their commander, who was scanning a sheet of paper. It suddenly occurred to Karl-Heinz that the only shop on the block might be owned by a Jew. "*L. Gross. Bäckerei*" in neat, small letters, a typical German shopkeeper's sign. It was a small bakery across from the Antmann home. Jewish? Not Jewish? Who could tell?

He quickly got his answer. The S.A. squad formed up and advanced in his direction, faces barely visible under the visors of their squat caps with chinstraps down. They carried wooden clubs, and several had rolls of paper under their arms. They came closer, talking loudly and peering at each house to locate their target. Then they spotted the tall officer in the black uniform and gleaming boots who raised his arm to stop them. "*Halt! Heilitla!*"

They stopped and saluted. "*Heilitla!*" Their corporal, an S.A. *Unterscharführer*, advanced, stopped at attention. "*Zu Befehl, Herr Hauptsturmführer!*" He was small, scrawny, probably a clerk during the day.

"What are you doing on this street?" Karl-Heinz asked sharply.

"That Jew pig, Gross the baker, we'll give him our message." His men grinned and murmured, cracking their clubs against their jackboots. They were raw-boned, probably factory workers.

"Here," said one of them. He handed Karl-Heinz a poster. It said, "Germans, defend yourselves! Buy nothing from Jew pigs!"

"Look, corporal," said Karl-Heinz. "I'll order Gross to stick up this sign in the morning."

"Captain, we have orders. This is our street, and we'll do the delivering ourselves." The corporal grinned. The others muttered. They had obviously been drinking.

Karl-Heinz had to finish it there and then, and he had learned the correct style at the Berghof. He beckoned to the corporal to step away from his squad. When they were alone, he said in a soft voice, "Corporal, the *Herr Brigadeführer* general and I"—he pointed vaguely at the dark house behind him—"have just returned from the Berghof. You know who lives at the Berghof?"

"The *Führer*," said the corporal, suddenly frozen at attention.

"Correct. Now I want no more noise, yelling, or other commotion on this street. The general and I are very tired. Take your men and get out of here at once before I report you to *Gauleiter* Streicher for disobedience!" He was genuinely angry and did not need much playacting.

After hesitating for a split second, the storm troop corporal cracked his heels together and raised his arm. "*Zu Befehl, Herr Hauptsturmführer. Heilitla!*" He was only a part-time S.A. trooper, outgunned by this tall officer in the black uniform. He marched off his men, their heels crashing on the medieval cobblestones. When they were out of sight, Karl-Heinz returned to the Antmann house.

"I got rid of them." He handed the poster to Hilde, which by itself seemed almost tame. "They were going to tackle the baker across the street."

"Gross?"

"Yes. He must be a Jew."

"I had forgotten," said Hilde.

The professor shook his head. "Gross came to me last week and said he was leaving. He apologized because from now on he could not guarantee the quality of the bread. *He* was apologizing! Some joke."

Hilde's mother said, "His daughter was at *Grundschule*

elementary school with Hilde. Beautiful child. She married someone in Leipzig. I wonder what happened to her?''

Hilde turned on the large Telefunken radio set with words like London, Hylversum, Luxembourg on its dial, tempting words, dangerous words. Minutes later, *Deutschlandsender* from Berlin made a special announcement.

A German embassy counselor in Paris, a certain Ernst vom Rath, had been assassinated by a Polish Jew named Grynszpan. ''The German people,'' said the announcer, ''are rising in their anger to protest this cowardly act. Spontaneous demonstrations are breaking out all over the country, mainly in the cities where Jewish vermin cluster.'' The government asked for ''calm and restraint.'' The announcement was followed by a military march.

''Vom Rath?'' said Hilde. ''I met him in Berlin long ago. A very decent man, and I am absolutely sure he was not a Nazi. He and I often discussed the anti-Jewish question, and he felt just as I did. That was before I was sent to London. I wouldn't be surprised if . . .'' She paused and shrugged.

''What?'' asked Karl-Heinz. ''Surprised if what?''

''Oh, I may be crazy,'' she said, ''but this would be one way to get rid of him. He probably became an embarrassment the way I would have, eventually.''

''Far-fetched,'' said Karl-Heinz, but he had begun to have his own doubts. The announcer had spoken of ''spontaneous'' demonstrations, but he had just held a prepared printed poster in his hands, and the S.A. troopers were obviously following a carefully prepared street-by-street drive. How ''spontaneous'' could that be? Vom Rath had been killed only that morning. It usually took twenty-four hours to muster these weekend troopers, but the S.A. were fully prepared. He shook his head. ''Let me get out of this uniform.''

He changed clothes mechanically. He could not get over the feeling he had been cheated. Not just the events of that evening, the S.A. bullies, the broadcast, and its transparent inconsistencies, but the ugly atmosphere at the Berghof and the small-spirited men at the top. Was Adolf Hitler a great man? Or was he the petty complainer and thoughtless egotist he had seen at that dinner table? What was Germany's future in the hands of this man? Was Hilde right? Had it all succeeded only because Germany was paying a bitter price?

Perhaps his father, Herbert Dorn, had found something in thirty-two that was really a myth? What now?

The chief rabbi was ready. He had said his evening prayers, his *maariv*, had packed his *tallis* prayer shawl, his *siddur* prayer book, and a few other essentials. Now he waited for them in his small, dark, old-fashioned Charlottenburg apartment. In his breast pocket were photos of his late wife and of his son in New York. There was nothing else he wished to take from this place where they had lived for so many years. He was glad he had turned down all chances to go to America.

He had waited this way before, but for some reason the SS had never chosen to arrest him. Since the beginning of this day, the ninth of November, since the phone call that told him the synagogues were burning and all the phone calls that followed, made from street corners, restaurants, hotels, anywhere a Jew could run, he had decided to stay put so that everyone, both Jews and SS alike, would know where to find him. He was still available to what was left of Berlin's shattered congregation, and thus, he also became available to the SS. It was a price he paid gladly.

Jewish history had reached out through the millennia, past the sham of assimilation and enfranchisement, Nobel Prizes, patents of nobility, wealth, titles, and honors, and was returning German Jews to their God. Being Jewish was no longer a courteous Friday night predinner ritual, a polite maneuver for "good" seats in the synagogue during the top-hatted High Holy Days, or a prissy "*Mosaisch*" on the line that asked for religious preference.

Now it was life and death, hard as a fist, painful as a wound, visible as blood. Once more *Adonai* had chosen to bring back his people. Once more, they were *Jews*.

Not since Torquemada's Inquisition had they been toppled from such lofty heights. German Jews were flabby, and still unable to face this bitter, brewing holocaust. He would have to help them if God would help him, here in Berlin, or out there, in the camps.

He heard a loud knock on the front door and a sharp voice. "*Aufmachen!*" He rose to unlock for them. These few steps had been destined since he was born.

• • •

The Eden Hotel restaurant was crowded and noisy. Couples were tangoing to a slick-haired, Latin-looking band, although the musicians were Berliners to their fingertips. The city seemed to have forgotten the riots of the week before, and the S.A. storm trooper squads had disappeared to their Neukölln and Moabit headquarters, their task done. The SS had stayed out of it.

"We got an order straight from *Reichsführer* Himmler," said von Bernsdorfer, "that any SS who participated in the street actions of November ninth would be severely reprimanded and even punished. I must say I sort of agree."

"Oh?" Karl-Heinz was puzzled.

"Well, it really isn't SS style to go around breaking store windows. I should hope that if we take action, we would do so in a more disciplined and meaningful way, not like a bunch of street *Raudies!*"

"Then you don't disagree with the principle?"

"Principle? You mean taking steps against the Jews? *Aber nein!* Solutions to that problem must be found! Everyone is faced with the Jewish question! Take my father: He was so involved with Jew bankers that I thought we'd go *pleite*, bankrupt. Fortunately, nothing happened, and the old bird got away with it. But every time I needed money to invest in something, his lousy Jew banker told him I had *Schnaps*-ideas."

Karl-Heinz did not want to pursue the subject. For the time being it was better to tread softly, to handle him, as they said in Berlin, "like a peeled egg." After all, von Bernsdorfer had made his feelings quite clear.

Dessert arrived, ice cream American style, an Eden specialty. Karl-Heinz asked about the Ritterschwert party.

"Ah, yes, the Ritterschwert party . . ." Von Bernsdorfer buried his face in his hands for a moment, and when he looked up, he was grinning. "*Na, ja*, let's say this: It was enormously interesting. Good thing for you that you were in Nürnberg."

"Explain."

"Very, very simple. Gerhardt Brunzig is a charming fellow, a great host, and a complete homosexual, totally *schwuhl*. He tackled every younger man at the party, including me, and I will say to his credit that he stayed completely charming whenever he got turned down. After two days of shopping for a bedmate he finally struck gold. Come to think of it, that's a

very exact description because he disappeared with the youngest of the Diestel boys.''

"Of Diestel steel, coal, zinc, copper . . .''

"Of Diestel steel, coal, zinc, copper. We never saw either
Brunzig or Diestel again that weekend. They took off for St.
Moritz, where Diestel owns a chalet.''

"And the others?''

"Telesty and Anneliese von Konsky started their own little
orgy together with a Milanese married couple. They had
adjoining bedrooms and you could hear the howls and grunts
and screams and furniture breaking all over their floor. Can't
tell who were the sadists and who were the masochists, but I
can guess, can't you?''

"Who took over as host?''

"Zoss, that old *homme du monde*. You really have the
most civilized boss. A bit of an opportunist, but civilized.''

Karl-Heinz was amazed. All this cynicism from bland,
blond *dumm* von Bernsdorfer! He made a mental note not to
take him lightly in the future. What luck that he, Karl-Heinz,
had not gone to Stuttgart. Perhaps Gerhardt Brunzig had
stayed charming with von Bernsdorfer, but Karl-Heinz Dorn
was a minor Brunzig employee and Gerhardt Brunzig might
have reacted differently to a refusal.

About Zoss, von Bernsdorfer was right. Zoss was a bit of
an opportunist, but after all, he *was* a salesman.

He was about to ask more questions, but decided not to.
The SS major's new "face" stopped him. He paid the bill,
and they left the restaurant.

Armin Zoss stretched his long legs, put his elbows on the
arms of his leather chair, and blew cigarette smoke toward the
crystal chandelier that hung on the ceiling.

"Von Bernsdorfer told you about Ritterschwert?''

"Yes,'' said Karl-Heinz.

"There's something I should explain. Most of us who are
close to Gerhardt Brunzig know his odd ways, but he has
never let anything interfere with his work. He is absolutely
erstklassig, first-rate. I promised his father long ago that I would
watch over Gerhardt, but I'm afraid that this time I failed.''

"How? No harm was done, according to von Bernsdorfer.''

"Wasn't there? There was an L.A.H. SS officer there, and
he made a pass at him.''

"Von Bernsdorfer won't say anything. He's a gentleman."

"Gentleman? You must be joking!"

"He comes of excellent background. And weren't you the one who got him into the SS?"

"That's only half true. He was dying to join the professional SS, but he did not want to start at the bottom. Besides, he despises his father. The old count is a tough bird who thinks his son is a lazy ne'er-do-well, a *Tunichtgut*. They hate each other. The old count is lucky that the boy hasn't had him sent away and taken over the estates."

"What does he have on his father?"

"Potentially, plenty. I'll tell you all about it soon, Dornchen. Why not come for a drive Sunday morning?"

"*Gemacht*. Ten o'clock?"

"Ten o'clock."

Sunday morning was crisp and beautiful, with a pure sky and a slight breeze. Although Christmas was only a few weeks away, there was not a hint of snow in the air, and the tall pine trees in the Grunewald forest stood evergreen against the clear blue overhead. Most Berliners were relieved that the Munich conference that previous September had defused the danger of a war. After fears that Adolf Hitler had overplayed his hand, everyone now admired the *Führer*'s patience and restraint. Berliners were never happy with the policies of confrontation. After the war, Berlin had suffered more than any other German city, and people knew the results of war.

The riots of November 9 (Berliners dubbed it "Reichs Crystal Night" because of the amount of broken glass on the streets) seemed to have shocked visitors from abroad, and many were leaving, but to the average Berliner life was sweet after the tensions of September and October and the portentous radio announcements that had accompanied each phase of the Munich negotiations. Church bells awakened the Dorns that Sunday, and, while Hilde was going to Mass, Karl-Heinz got ready to meet Zoss. He put on a Norwegian sweater and a ski jacket, a wise decision, because Zoss was downstairs in his beautiful convertible with the roof down.

Zoss, who wore a camel hair coat and tweed cap, pushed open the door. The red leather inside smelled like a saddle shop. The big engine roared into life. They circled Adolf Hitler Platz and aimed west on the wide Heerstrasse, which had often been used by troops on their way to war. They soon crossed the Müggelsee bridge, and Karl-Heinz thought back to that argumentative night with Hilde in the restaurant on the lake.

When they had passed the lake, Zoss stuck his foot to the floor, the supercharger whined into action, and the big car surged forward. The needle climbed the scale: 100, 120, 140, and settled at 165 kilometers. They flew past some small cars, and then they spotted a large black "Himmler *Panzer*" up ahead. When they drew close, Karl-Heinz recognized it, 1A-103777, one of Dr. Goebbels's staff cars. It was empty except for the driver and one young SS officer. They challenged the other Brunzig, and Zoss's blue convertible was faster, lighter, and better tuned. It was no contest. As they pulled past the black eight-seater, Karl-Heinz raised his hand and the SS officers smiled and responded. Obviously impressed by Zoss's blue convertible, they pursed their mouths and nodded approvingly.

Zoss kept tabs on the other car in the rearview mirror, and by the time they turned left onto the narrow country road to the village of Gatow, the SS car was already far behind and out of sight. Now they were on a narrow, tree-lined asphalt *Landstrasse* in open country. From time to time, they passed old farms, their yards enclosed by medieval stone walls. Each one had its own compost pile, and the smell of manure reminded Karl-Heinz of the farms near his grandparents' grain mill. They shot past horse-drawn haywagons and herds of dairy cows, and over slippery patches of mud on the road, but Zoss did not let up, and the speedometer still showed 160 kph.

"Good driving!" Karl-Heinz yelled into his ear.

Zoss's string-gloved hand pointed at a small chrome plaque on the dashboard that Karl-Heinz had not noticed. It read, "This car was built and finished for Armin Zoss, who won the unlimited class of the Targa Florio in Sicily, co-driving with Baron von Bernsdorfer zu Kehlsbach, 1930."

That explained his skill. And which von Bernsdorfer was this?

"Father?" yelled Karl-Heinz.

Zoss shook his head. "Uncle!"

They finally came to a sharp curve, where Zoss slowed down. "Death trap, this turn," he said. "We lost one of our best clients here a year ago, a good friend of mine. In fact, he owned this estate." They drove into a large property, past a gatekeeper's cottage, and then onto a straight elm-lined gravel road that led to the courtyard of an old manor house, flanked by stone stables, servants' cottages, and a carriage house. They were immediately challenged by a growling Weimaraner.

"*Guten Tag, Teufel*," said Zoss, and the dog calmed down at the mention of his name, having recognized this guest. An old manservant answered the door chimes and greeted Zoss with obvious pleasure.

"Do you wish to stay with us, *Herr* Zoss?"

"*Nein, danke*, Dahnfeld. My friend *Herr* Dorn and I just want a Sunday glass of brandy."

"Do come in, sir. It's been very quiet since the master's death. The *Gnädige Frau*, the *Baronin*, is in Paris."

"No, thank you again, Dahnfeld. Perhaps we could have it out here?"

"Of course, sir."

Dahnfeld disappeared.

"The inside gives me the shudders now that my friend is dead. We were quite close. Raced together at many hillclimbs. Shot skeet and sailed. I can't stand his widow, but I knew she was away, so I thought we'd have a *Zweites Früstuck*, a late breakfast, but without all that fattening food. Just brandy."

Dahnfeld appeared with two glasses and a bottle of Courvoisier.

The first swallow of cognac took away the chill. It was the perfect drink for that moment. Zoss always did things with style.

Zoss thanked the butler effusively. The old man beamed with pleasure and bowed after them as they turned back toward the road and the nearby lakeside village of Gross Glienicke. They drove slowly through the ancient main street, past church and schoolhouse, village hall and small shops. Then the cobblestones changed into a hard dirt road. They passed large villas, now closed for the winter, and finally stopped at the edge of a cathedral-like pine forest, its trees towering twenty meters into the sky, the ground covered by a thick blanket of dead pine needles.

Zoss shut off the engine, and there was silence, except for a cuckoo deep in the woods, a dog's bark far away in the

village, and the clock on the church tower chiming the half
hour.

All was still, as if the area was resting from its round of
summer parties, the laughing sailors on the lake, the crowds
of Berliners who vacationed here.

Armin Zoss pulled his coat tightly around his body, turned
up his collar, and stepped back out of the car, and Karl-Heinz
followed him. They took a narrow path across the potato
fields, which had recently been harvested and were now
waiting for winter and snow.

A rabbit scampered out of their way, and a brilliantly
plumed pheasant streaked across the path. When it took wing,
Zoss faked a shot. His form was excellent. Their breath could
be seen in the cool air. When they had gone about two
hundred meters from the car, halfway between the edge of the
woods and the road, Zoss stopped. He said, "Yesterday you
asked me a question about von Bernsdorfer."

"Which one?"

"What he had on his father, the old count."

"Right. And you said you would tell me."

"To do so, I have to bring up matters that must remain
confidential. At the risk of sounding overly dramatic, I shall
say things that are of importance to our country. What better
place to do so than right here, in a Prussian field, almost
within sight of Potsdam and Old King Frederick's palace?"

Was Zoss joking? But there was no irony in the man's
face. He was deadly serious.

"For certain reasons," said Zoss, "I don't think I have to
worry about your discretion." He stuck his hands in his coat
pockets, kicked at a pebble, and continued, "Old Count von
Bernsdorfer is one of a group of gentlemen who believe that
National Socialism is deeply harmful to our nation and will
have catastrophic results. He and some others are organizing a
group who wish to replace our present leadership." Zoss
paused. "It doesn't shock you?" he asked.

Karl-Heinz shook his head but said nothing.

"Perhaps," said Zoss, "you have your own doubts?"

Again, Karl-Heinz kept quiet.

"*Na, ja*," said Zoss, "never mind. I have reasons to
believe that you do have doubts. To continue: If young von
Bernsdorfer knew the truth about his father, he would not
hesitate for one second. He'd call the S.D., and it would be

all over. You don't realize, my dear boy, that he is SS, real
SS, part of the Adolf Hitler Bodyguard *Standarte*. He's not
just some nice, young lawyer or architect who has joined the
'weekend' SS because he wants to be chic. Von Bernsdorfer
is a professional. He may sound like an objective, witty
charmer, but he's really one of Himmler's boys. In a way,
old Sepp Dietrich is more human than our young major. At
least, Dietrich is all bluster and piss."

Karl-Heinz nodded and said, "I'm not quite as surprised as
I would have been a month ago. When von Bernsdorfer told
me about the Ritterschwert party, I suddenly got the idea that
he was not the bland fellow I always thought he was."

"Why? Did he say anything derogatory about Gerhardt
Brunzig or me? I'm not asking out of vanity, but to clear up
something."

"No. He spoke about *Herr* Brunzig's homosexuality and
his affair with Diestel."

"And what about me?"

"He said you were a great host and a man of the world."

"And?"

"*Na, also.*" Karl-Heinz was embarrassed. "He called you
a bit opportunistic."

"Good!" said Zoss. "*Prima!* That's first-rate. He obviously doesn't take me too seriously."

"What is so good about that?"

"I would prefer that he think of me as a lightweight. There
could be more dangerous things he might think about me."

"Such as what?" Karl-Heinz asked.

Zoss looked up at the sky, then hunched deeply into his
coat. He rocked to and fro on his feet and then, like someone
launching himself over a cliff, he said, very softly, "Because
I am part of the group being formed by the old count. There
are many of us. I shall bring up some names, only because I
want to convince you of the seriousness of this effort. Would
you be amazed if I told you that von Totten, Morgenroth, and
Anneliese von Konsky are part of our group?"

"Yes, except for Morgenroth. What about Telesty? He
seems friendly with all of them."

"Never. Telesty is not a Nazi in the true sense, but for as
long as the party is a political force, Telesty will use it. If the
N.S.D.A.P. collapsed tomorrow, Telesty would convince them
to let him hold their money. Then he would buy American

stocks and take a big commission for himself. Speaking of opportunists, he is *Nummer Eins!*''

Karl-Heinz looked around, but they were quite alone in the wide-open fields. ''You know,'' he said in a low voice, ''I am amazed that you trust me so completely.''

''Normally, my dear Karl-Heinz, I would look at you and say, 'Here's the perfect young National Socialist, the son of an early member, happy with his life and career. . . .' But someone very close to you has given me the go-ahead to talk to you: Hilde!''

Karl-Heinz was stunned. ''Is she also part of all this?''

''I am sure she will be when I ask her.''

''I should have known. She is such a determined girl and she has had her doubts about Adolf Hitler since long before I even met her.''

Zoss nodded. He said, ''A friend of mine, a former foreign service man who is in sympathy with us, and who also knew Hilde's views, found out you were working for me. He put Hilde in touch with our group.''

''Is it a very big organization?''

''No! It's not even an organization. Just a list of names, a cast of characters, as actors would say. Right now we're just trying to find people who are opposed to our government and who are willing to do something about it. Later we'll make plans and appoint leaders. I hope it's not too late.''

''For what?''

''War! We believe the *Führer* wants it. Germans are brave. We would acquit ourselves well, but eventually we'll get destroyed. I know the world out there. Most of the men around Hitler don't. Hitler thinks that little companies like Brunzig, Messerschmitt, and Heinkel can supply our military needs. He's wrong! We're not the Americans. I've been to Detroit, and make no mistake, America will eventually be in this thing. They'll swamp us!''

They walked back to the car and got in. ''From here on, to avoid problems, I'll use a code word when I want to talk about the resistance groups: I'll mention the word 'Otto.' When you hear me say 'Otto,' you will know. Zoss started the engine and headed back toward the village. Karl-Heinz was almost resentful. He was being initiated into a *Bruderschaft*, a fraternity, which he had not asked to join, being pointed on a dangerous course.

• • •

His world had suddenly become perilous and threatening.

When they passed the estate where they had stopped for cognac, Karl-Heinz asked, "Was your friend who died also in—er—'Otto'?"

"Yes!"

"That's why we stopped there?"

"A matter of sentimentality. He and I often spoke about the future in the same fields where I took you today. I felt as if I could sort of let him know that our cause is still alive."

Back on the Heerstrasse highway, Karl-Heinz kept looking behind.

Zoss grinned. "Looking for 1A-103777?"

Karl-Heinz was surprised. "How do you remember the number? I have to, but why do you?"

"Because I'm a very clever fellow! The car was probably on its way to Dr. Goebbels's country house in Schwanenwerder. No danger. They may mention that they saw us out for a Sunday drive. Quite natural for two Brunzig officials, don't you think?"

"*Natürlich*," said Karl-Heinz, but he was still worried.

Zoss slowed the car so that he could be heard better. "Look, Karl-Heinz," he said, "don't let this thing panic you. You'll get used to it. And frankly, so far Otto has done nothing. Most of all, don't be angry at Hilde when you get home. She wanted so much to tell you herself, but I absolutely insisted that she leave it to me. You must admit"—he smiled his old-fashioned tango-dancer smile—"the shock of hearing an honest piece of deep conviction from a dissolute old devil like me, now that was really something to remember!" He tapped Karl-Heinz on the shoulder with his fist, then opened the glove compartment and pointed at a silver flask. "Have a drink!"

"This was here all the time and you had that old butler bring us brandy?"

"*Na, ja*, von Bernsdorfer is right. It was free brandy, and I've always been an opportunist."

Back in the apartment, despite the request from Zoss, Karl-Heinz confronted Hilde.

"Karle," she said, "I just have to do something!"

"Do you think you can change a whole government? A whole party?"

"I must try."

"Don't you think I also love our country?"

"Of course you do, *Liebling*. But you're deceived. Before Hitler, you had miserable years. Then everything became good for you, and now, you're conservative. I can't blame you."

"And you?"

"I've never wanted for anything. Also, your father's life had much to do with your way of looking at things, and that's natural."

"Do your parents know about Otto?"

"Who's Otto?"

"A friend of Zoss."

"I don't know him."

"Do they know about your interest in the group Zoss spoke of?"

"No."

"How do you think they would feel if they knew?"

"Proud."

"*Wirklich?* Are you sure?"

"Absolutely. *Ohne Frage!* No question in my mind."

"Now tell me, Hildelein, what do you expect me to do?"

"That's up to you."

"Would you love me less if I did nothing?"

"Of course not!"

"Will you love me more if I join the group?"

"Perhaps. Who knows?"

"Some choice!"

"I won't love you any the less if you stay out of it, but I also know you're an honest, decent man and that you were shocked by that mess in Nürnberg in November. Also, you've been very quiet about your visit to the Berghof, so I imagine something there upset you. By now I know you. When you enjoy something, you love to talk about it."

Karl-Heinz shook his head. Finally at twenty-seven, he had everything he had dreamed of: marriage, security, position. "I have to think this through," he said, quite calmly, but inside he was cursing his fate.

• • •

The highway called the Avus was a curious hybrid: half racetrack, half commuter highway. It connected Berlin with the summer resorts at Wannsee Lake, less than an hour's drive from the city, but for a few days each year it became one of the world's fastest racetracks. It had two bolt-straight lanes one way and two lanes the other, divided by a narrow, grassy strip. At the Wannsee end, these roads were joined together by a wide, flat, looping horseshoe turn. At the Berlin end, there was a vertical, banked "kettle" turn, like those on a bobsled run, but much larger. At high speed, race cars stayed pressed against this steep slope by centrifugal force.

The pit area and spectator stands were at the Berlin end. One gray morning in the spring, about twenty people stood around, awaiting the new Brunzig *R-Wagen* (*R* for *Rekord*) that was to bring the road-speed record to Germany, and promptly at nine o'clock, a white Brunzig race-car transporter truck pulled into the pits. Its tail door rolled up, and they got their first glimpse of the *R-Wagen*'s shark snout with its large, red, Knight's Sword insignia. Two mechanics rolled it down a long ramp, a cross between race car and fighter plane, different from any previous Maut design. There was a small glass canopy over the cockpit and a tall horizontal stabilizer fin, with a swastika on each side. The long body was made of silver aluminum.

It was Morgenroth's first look at the monster he was to drive. The last time they had discussed it with him, it was still a quarter-scale clay model. This was not the usual Brunzig procedure. They were known for their meticulous testing, but this time many new products were ready to launch, all at the same time. Morgenroth was not worried. He was expected to get into this car, put his foot on the accelerator, and drive it in a straight line down the Avus. So far as he was concerned, that took no genius. It barely tested his skills and could have been done by a lesser driver, but Morgenroth was *Nummer Eins*, so it was a foregone conclusion that he would deserve this honor. Hannes Morgenroth was rather bored with the whole idea. He had always looked down on drivers like Sir Malcolm Campbell, whose only fame came from straight-line speed records. It could not compare with the virtuosity of wrestling a large, bucking, single-seater race car through the complicated streets of Monte Carlo or around the wild Nürburgring racetrack. Besides, he had never learned to appre-

ciate the streamlined appearance of these new cars, and he
preferred the lean bodies of the old racers. Of course, he had
to admit that these new cars were generations ahead. Still,
this thing, the *R-Wagen*, really looked vulgar.

Oh, well, *na, ja,* he would do what he had to do and if the
engine did not blow up, chances were that he would end the day
holding the world road-speed record. He would do his best. As
they said in Berlin, "*Wenn schon, denn schon!*" Might just as
well give it his best shot! One thing bothered him: those
embarrassing swastikas painted on the fin. He had an old bet
with most of the veteran foreign drivers. They were all sure
that sooner or later the party boys would paint this car full of
swastikas, just as they did with the new German drivers. So
he decided he would only be photographed standing in front
of the *R-Wagen*, next to the Ritterschwert emblem. If they
took shots while he was racing, they could not see it was he
inside the closed canopy.

Childish perhaps, but he would not forgive the patronizing
treatment he had received at the Berghof. This would be his
repayment for that evening. Hühnlein, the *Korpsführer*, and
national head of N.S.K.K., had called him about the racing-
school nonsense, but Morgenroth had stalled. Hühnlein was
an old Hitler pal, an *Alter Kämpfer*, which was his only
qualification for the motor corps job. Hühnlein could kiss his
ass.

Morgenroth's valet helped him into his white coveralls and
handed him his gloves, white cloth racing cap, and rubber-
rimmed goggles. He walked over to the car. As he suspected,
the steering wheel was tiny to save space. He would barely
have to use it anyway. One good thing: They had listened to
him and had given him more room to stretch out his arms.
They began to warm up the engine, sixteen cylinders; two
V-eight motors, one behind the other. Probably eight hundred
horsepower, and the aluminum body was light. He did some
quick calculations. He should easily be able to beat the old
record by 20 percent, from four hundred to five hundred
kilometers per hour. Better that way. It discouraged others
from trying.

The car made a fearful racket. His valet handed him earplugs.
Hannes knew Avus like his own bedroom because he had
raced there dozens of times, and also used it often to go to the
country. The trick would be to get this huge thing rolling,

because the starting gear would be like high gear in any other race car.

Maut came over and said something.

"Sorry, can't hear!" Morgenroth took out the earplugs. "Now . . ."

"What I was trying to say," Maut yelled, "was that all the punch will come in at about three thousand rpm, just as you go through the kilometer we marked off. At the end of the trap, you'll pass a flashing red light, and then you can lift your foot. It should stop you at the other end without much braking. Then turn around and do the same thing and that'll be it for the day. *Hals und Beinbruch*!"

Papa Hoegel, the racing manager, waddled over. "We need some photos," he said.

"Only from the front end," said Morgenroth.

"Don't give me that *Bockmist*, you old goat. I know why you don't want to be photographed alongside this thing. I can see right through you."

"Want me to drive? Photograph me my way. Otherwise, I shall develop a highly mysterious stomach cramp, probably an allergy to an old shithead like you."

All right, all right. Don't piss in your pants. *Mach Dir nicht in die Hosen.* We'll do it your way this time."

So they photographed:

Gerhardt Brunzig and Morgenroth.
Hühnlein and Morgenroth.
Von Bernsdorfer, Karl-Heinz Dorn, and Morgenroth.

Then came the people from the Reich's Propaganda Ministry, the people from the Reich's press office, the editors of two German illustrated papers, three foreign sports papers, the Berlin sports pages. It went on and on. The only two who did not wish to be photographed were Anneliese von Konsky and Dr. Maut.

Finally, they were ready to go. Morgenroth was hoisted into the tiny corsetlike cockpit and they closed the canopy.

He rolled off, careful not to stall the motor. As soon as he reached some semblance of speed, he fed more and more fuel until his foot touched bottom. The big, bellowing engine soon reached three thousand revolutions, and the beginning of the timing trap was in sight. The timers were waving and cheering, but he kept his eyes pointed straight down the immense metal snout and on the gray strip of road. There was no sensation of speed. In fact, it felt faster to drive an old-fashioned open-seater. Then the red light shot by, seen out of the corner of his right eye. He lifted his foot from the accelerator, and the car began to slue a bit when the engine compression got hold of the rear wheels. Nothing to worry about. He settled the *R-Wagen* with tiny instinctive movements of his hands. Heat came up from the vast hood, so, because the speed trap was long past, he opened the canopy from the inside and exhausted the fumes. Then he saw the end of the run. They were waving, jumping up and down. He came to a gentle halt and hoisted himself up until he stood on the seat. He slid down the side of the car and walked away. All of this had been almost soundless because his earplugs had kept out the motor's thunder. Now he pulled down his goggles, took off his cap, and unplugged his ears. The invasion of noise was incredible.

"You did it, you did it! Five ten, five ten . . ."

So, he had done five hundred and ten kilometers per hour. Good. It didn't take much to be a hero in this game!

The mechanics frantically prepared the car for the return run within the same time limit; otherwise the attempt would not be accepted by the International Federation.

Ten minutes later he was back in the cockpit. The engine was a bit balky this time, probably some fouled plugs, but he soon got it sorted out and by the time the speed trap hove into view, he was up to thirty-two hundred engine revolutions, faster than before. Just as he was about to enter the measured kilometer, he felt a sideways movement. Wind! A gusty breeze was blowing him off course. *Scheisse!* The big car edged toward the grass, and Morgenroth knew that this would not be easy. He concentrated fiercely. Gently, gently, ever so tenderly, he nursed the snout back into the right direction. The actual movement of his hands was so minuscule as to be almost undetectable, although the car had wandered three full meters off the true course. Hannes Morgenroth had shown why he was *Nummer Eins*, but this time he was breathing hard when the car came to a standstill. They opened the canopy from the outside, but he waved them away and stayed a few seconds to collect himself. This one had been close!

He had broken the old record. The average of the two runs

was just over five hundred and three kilometers an hour. Later, when everyone saw the films of the run, they could not believe the icy calm with which he had saved this berserk projectile.

The next afternoon Hannes Morgenroth was back on the Avus, which had resumed its tame role as public expressway. He was driving his beloved old 500C to Wannsee Lake, to spend the weekend with his old friends, the Forstmanns. When he passed the place of his near accident, he remembered those few seconds, but he had often come face to face with horror. Sooner or later, hospital beds and operating rooms appeared in each driver's life. Businessmen lost deals, soldiers got shot, and those who raced cars crashed. He had his rewards.

For Hannes Morgenroth, who had begun as a nobody, fame was vital. Externally, there was nothing exceptional about him. He was forty-five, had a smooth, unwrinkled face with heavy eyebrows and small eyes. His hair was parted high and slicked back. He could have been the reception clerk at a resort hotel or a headwaiter. He often seemed flip and superficial, like many shy people, but those close to him loved his honesty and courage. On or off the racetrack, the man was impeccable. He was a great champion. Some said the greatest ever.

The Forstmann's summer house right on Wannsee Lake was low and light gray, with white trim and tall French windows, surrounded by smooth lawns. To the side of the house, behind a tall fence, was the red clay tennis court. A small mahogany sloop was tied to their dock. Erich Forstmann was one of Germany's leading film directors, and his wife, Monika, was a great star until she retired to marry him.

When Morgenroth drove up, the Forstmann's beaming chauffeur took his bags and then reverently slid behind the seat of the famous convertible to drive it into the garage. Of course, the *Rennmeister* was his hero.

Morgenroth walked to the tennis court. A heated game of mixed doubles was in full swing, and no one noticed him. Erich Forstmann volleyed cross-court to Anneliese von Konsky, who half-volleyed a drop shot into the empty space ahead of her on the other side of the net. Monika Forstmann, unable to reach it, applauded Anneliese, clapping racquet against hand.

"*Fantastisch!* Anneliese, you're a devil."

Anneliese's partner was Fritz Scharn, the great romantic film star who still portrayed lovers although he was well into his fifties. Morgenroth knew Scharn. *Ein netter Kerl!* Nice fellow. He had seen his latest film, some nonsense about a *Luftwaffe* pilot of the German *Condor* squadron fighting in Spain and falling in love with a grandee's daughter. Unbelievable *Schiesse!* Poor Scharn. . . . But the Propaganda Ministry loved to tout *Luftwaffe* volunteers who fought for Franco. Anyone who produced films had to do it Goebbels's way, and the same thing went for actors.

They spotted Hannes, stopped the game, and rushed over. Shouting, "Congratulations! *Prima!* Terrific!" Forstmann pounded his back, Scharn shook his hand, the girls kissed him. The morning papers had reported his new world record on the front pages, and once again Hannes Morgenroth was Germany's hero.

"Was it tough?"

"No."

"How was the *R-Wagen?*"

"Ugly."

"Really?"

"Like a fat fish."

"You were shut into the cockpit? Looked that way in the photos."

"Completely. *Platzangst* . . . claustrophobic."

"Dangerous?"

"Not really. Stupid job, driving that thing. Next time one of the new boys can do it."

Erich Forstmann dried his face and said, "Let's go to the house for some drinks. Enough tennis, *gemacht?*" he turned to the players.

"*Gemacht,*" said Anneliese, "but I'm going to take a bath.

"Me, too," Monika chimed in. The two tall, slim women left, and Erich led the men to a veranda at lakeside.

He fixed three glasses of whisky and soda, the drink of that summer. Scharn wore a *frotte* terrycloth scarf around his neck. A lock of thick, black hair fell over his tanned forehead, and his celebrated blue eyes were cheerful. In his long white tennis flannels and a jersey suit he was still the ultimate screen idol, as handsome as the Americans like Gable, Cooper,

and Robert Taylor. Fortunately, he never took himself seriously and he laughed a lot, often at himself. He was once
again single (for the fourth time).

"Saw your flying film," said Morgenroth.

"Wasn't that *Mist?* Plain junk. But it paid well, and I love
making films in Spain. Good wine, good corridas, good
flamenco, good cunt. Only thing I missed is Hemingway. We
used to be great *Kameraden* before Franco. Now he's in
Florida. Many nice people left Spain when Franco took over."

"How about Germany? We've lost a lot of people, 'specially
in your field."

"Yes." Scharn looked around to see who was within
earshot. "And it shows. Our films are abominable! Erich,
you haven't directed one in three years, right?"

"*Stimmt schon,*" said Forstmann. "Quite right. For so
many reasons! The stuff they want me to direct, I'd rather not
touch. And anything I like they would call 'debauched' and
maybe even *Kulturbolschiwismus.* If I could only direct abroad,
but the government won't let me."

Scharn nodded. He understood. "Anyway," he said, "that
film about that flying hero shit? I did absolutely no flying.
But I drank a lot and fucked a lot. I also made very courageous faces."

"Wish I could learn to look as good as you," said
Morgenroth. "Every time they photograph me I look like
some bookkeeper in a racing suit."

"You don't need to make faces," said Scharn. "You're a
bona fide hero. I just act like one."

"Some hero!" said Morgenroth. "Yesterday I nearly wiped
out that expensive machine."

"You didn't mention that before."

"*Na, ja,* why scare the girls?"

Erich was concerned. Morgenroth had always seemed so
invulnerable. "How did it happen?"

"Gust of wind."

"At full speed?"

"Balls to the wall."

"Must have been close."

"*Aber wie.* You can say that again."

"Tell me truthfully," said Scharn, "were you scared?"

Erich Forstmann held his breath. This was not something
one asked Hannes Morgenroth. But Morgenroth was not upset.

He liked Scharn. "Yes, I was scared. It just made me concentrate harder. I react by being rational. It's the way nature built me. Nothing to brag about."

Erich had never heard Hannes speak about himself this way. *Interessant!*

The phone rang and Erich picked it up.

"Ja, Heilitla." He listened, obviously distressed. Then, reluctantly, *"Natürlich, Herr Doktor. Wir erwarten Sie.* Dinner is in an hour." Another pause. Then, "We'll take care of her if she arrives before you. *Auf wiederhören!"* He hung up.

"Goebbels," he said glumly. "Invited himself to dinner. He's bringing some *Pipimädchen,* one of his bimbos."

"Doesn't he own a house out here?"

Erich pointed across the lake to a small island. "On that island, Schwanenwerder. It used to belong to two crooks called the Barmat brothers. They went to jail, and now Goebbels has the house. As we shall see, the good *Doktor* often uses it for so-called special auditions."

An hour later, Goebbels's black Brunzig delivered Ella Marczova, a Czech film actress. She immediately proved that she had no talent. "Oh?" she said, eyebrows arched, "Hasn't the *Herr Minister* arrived yet? They came to pick me up in Berlin, and I was told he would be here." She tried to look helpless, lost. Unsuccessfully. She had obviously come straight from Goebbels house, not from Berlin. Ten minutes later, Goebbels arrived, and they acted out the rest of the scene.

Goebbels: "Did you have a good trip?"

Marczova: "Your driver is excellent."

Goebbels: "Sorry I was not here. My friends took good care of you?"

Marczova: *"Fantastisch!"* She spoke with a strong Slavic accent. She was a very juicy package: high cheekbones, dark, slanted eyes, mouth all lower lip, full bust, slim waist. Scharn, for one, would have made his move, but not against this sort of competition.

Goebbels immediately took over. He introduced the Czech girl to everyone, although they had all met her at various Berlin parties. She had not yet made a film in Germany. Her last one, something about espionage, was produced in France but never released in Germany. They said that Goebbels saw photos of all foreign actresses who applied for working papers, and when Marczova did so, he gave her a so-called private audience. They were together constantly until, it was rumored, Magda Goebbels had threatened a divorce. The *Führer* heard about the whole mess and had warned his propaganda minister. Now Goebbels tried to be more discreet. Obviously, this visit was staged to make it seem that he was introducing Ella Marczova to a famous director. Goebbels was "fulfilling one of his responsibilities as head of the German film industry." Any suggestion that Marczova was his bedmate was slanderous and therefore punishable.

Morgenroth had forgotten how tiny and ferretlike Goebbels was and how badly he limped, but the man had presence. He was a *Persönlichkeit*.

"*Herr* Morgenroth," said Goebbels, "all my admiration! That was an incredible feat of courage you performed yesterday. *Unglaublich!* According to my sources, the English, the French, and the Americans are busting their gut. And the *Duce* has blasted everyone at Alfa-Romeo, Maserati, and Lancia. Ciano told my press attaché in Rome that Mussolini's howls could be heard all the way from Villa Torlonia to Torino."

"*Na, ja, Herr Doktor,*" said Morgenroth in a deprecating tone, "driving these things is really not difficult. Any French, English, or American driver could have taken that Zeppelin down the Avus." Morgenroth shrugged.

"Very modest. But now it is *our* record." Goebbels pointed at his own chest, signifying that he represented the Reich. "And they"—he waved in the direction of the rest of the world—"can kiss our ass!" He looked around for applause, but only his Czech friend complied by nodding vigorously. Goebbels had a disconcerting habit of staring at her while speaking to others. "Scharn," he said, still looking straight at Marczova, "did you like making *Night Attack on Guérnica?*"

"I like filming in Spain. Good place."

"No, I meant the film. How did you like it?"

"*Na, ja,*" said the actor. "It's not exactly Shakespeare."

Now Goebbels turned his eyes on him. "What's wrong with it?" he asked bitingly. "I thought the film conveyed a very dramatic message: the courage of our *Luftwaffe* men in Spain and of Franco's Falangists."

"True," said Scharn in an even tone, "but why water it down with all that *kitschig* love stuff and mantilla flicking? The romantic *Dreck* took away from the story."

"Yes, you're right. It was not in good taste. But who said

it had to be? My dear Scharn, films like that are meant for them." He waved his arms toward the hypothetical masses, obviously the same direction where foreigners could be found. "We can't be concerned with a small, snobbish audience. Our message must be universal."

Erich Forstmann laughed and shook his head. "I'll always try to please *them*"—and he made the same sweeping gesture Goebbels had used—"by making them laugh. Thank God for comedy! I couldn't direct that big heroic stuff."

"Erich, do you mean that you would turn me down if I asked you to direct a film about, say, Frederick the Great?"

"Depends on the film. The Old Fritz might be a very amusing subject. According to Voltaire, who lived with the old boy at Sans Souci Palace, the king was a homosexual."

"Really?" Goebbels was fascinated. Even posthumous gossip could be of use.

"Yes," Forstmann continued. "When Voltaire was feuding with the king, Voltaire published a book in Paris that accused the old boy of affairs with every officer and groom in Potsdam."

Goebbels's eyes swung back to Marczova, but he was still speaking to Forstmann. "To get back to my original question, would you direct battle scenes for me?"

"As I said, I'm not very good at it."

"You'd do it for me, though, wouldn't you, Erich?"

"Badly."

"So long as you do it." Goebbels had won his Pyrrhic victory, making everyone uncomfortable. Then dinner was announced.

They moved to the dining room, where they found a typical cold summer buffet of the sort Berliners loved: cold fried herring, headcheese, Westphalian ham, potato salad. Conversation was strained, but fortunately Goebbels and his Czech friend soon left. They played their charade to the end, pretending that she was going back to Berlin. Dr. Joseph Goebbels's actions were always devious and convoluted. Although the original purpose of the visit might have been to "sell" Marczova to Erich Forstmann, something had made him back off, perhaps Forstmann's show of independence or possibly the inhibiting presence of Hannes Morgenroth. The race driver probably made him feel uncomfortable, and the little minister

hated situations and people he could not control. It was
difficult to threaten someone like Morgenroth.

Anneliese von Konsky had stayed in the background most
of the evening. After Goebbels had left, she went over to
Morgenroth, kissed his cheek, and said, "*Mein Süsser Hannes,*
you are really one of the world's good people! And so are all
of you!" Then she stood behind Morgenroth's chair, her arms
hugging his neck, her chin resting on his head. They were
very close. Old loves, old friends.

Scharn sighed. He had planned on the night with Anneliese,
but that was obviously not to be. *Na, ja,* he knew how to bow
out gracefully.

Morgenroth was up early the next morning. After breakfast-
ing alone, he went to the dock, climbed into the little sloop,
and rigged it. Soon he was close-hauled in a fair breeze. The
little boat handled well, and he enjoyed sailing at five kilometers an hour more than he did driving at five hundred kilometers on the Avus. The lake was still empty. There were no
motorboats out, and he could enjoy the silence, broken only
by the churning of his own bow wave. After an hour, he
aimed into the lee of a small, uninhabited island and anchored.
With sails furled, he stretched out in the hull of the boat,
lighted a cigarette, and watched the smoke disappear over the
transom. Little clouds overhead looked like fat sheep on a
field of blue, and wavelets slapped against the mahogany
hull.

How he had hated Goebbels! He resented the bastard's
attempt to intimidate Erich Forstmann and to push nice Fritz
Scharn to the wall. Good thing Goebbels did not talk about
automobile racing, or Hannes would have told him the truth
about the *Bockmist,* the manure being spread by the Propaganda Ministry. Nordic superiority? They obviously didn't
know about these dark-skinned, tough little Italian race drivers who could have outdriven everyone if they had better
cars. Some Nordics! And how about René Dreyfus, the French
champion with the Jewish name, who had wiped out the
combined German teams at Pau? Another Nordic specimen!
The whole official propaganda attitude caused him acute
embarrassment. Fortunately, no one in the international racing fraternity had blamed him, so far.

Most of all, he resented Goebbels's arrogance! When that

guttersnipe was still holding forth on street corners, he, Hannes Morgenroth, a German, was acclaimed all over Europe. His race cars were symbolic of *Deutschland* long before Hitler, that Austrian upstart, came to power. To many foreigners, Morgenroth was an authentic German hero. There were a few others, like von Cramm, the tennis star, and Schmeling, the boxer, but no one had demonstrated German courage and preserved German honor as long as he had.

Now these pigs wanted to lead Germany to war, he was quite sure of that. He was also sure that Germany had lost the last war through lack of judgment. The Nazis might yammer about treachery and deceit, but that was nonsense. Germany had tackled more than it could handle and got whipped.

There was no reason to fight the French, the English, the Americans. They were his friends, his *Kameraden*. Zoss was quite right. Something had to be done and *soon!* He would find out more about the "Otto" business.

Morgenroth lived in a permanent suite at the Eden, Berlin's most modern hotel, because it was more convenient for him than keeping an apartment. He traveled constantly, and the hotel housekept for him and took his messages and mail. They were very proud of their famous tenant, the *Herr Rennmeister* Morgenroth.

He invited Zoss and von Totten to come and dine there. After dinner he checked doors and curtains, closets and armoires. Then he said, "I've made up my mind about joining the Otto group. Germany is headed for deep trouble, and we must act now."

"*Prima,*" said Zoss. "Good. Glad we can count on you. Much will depend on the army people we can convince. We can't count on the *Luftwaffe*. They're all Göring's creatures. Some navy people feel as we do. The most important one is a senior admiral, but I don't want to use his name."

"Good!" said von Totten. "The fewer names, the less chance of compromising friends. Let's discuss only those in our immediate circle."

Morgenroth was surprised. Von Totten, the dry major, the cold aristocrat, seemed out of his element in this conspiracy. Morgenroth had never liked him. Too mechanical and dull. No charm. Why was this man involved? He had to find out.

"What got you thinking this way, Major?"

"What propelled me toward Otto?"

"*Ja. Es wundert mich.* I'm puzzled."

"Because I'm a professional soldier? Or because I'm from a *Junker* family?"

"Both."

"Precisely for those two reasons. We are led by amateurs. I can't stand that. They will bring us to harm. Also, they are the worst of street gangsters, and they disgrace us before the world."

"But you're a party member. I've seen you wear the badge."

"So I am, like many others. That includes Zoss." Zoss nodded in agreement. Von Totten continued, *"Na, ja . . ."* He counted off on the fingers of his right hand: "the Versailles Treaty, the Depression, the lousy *Reichstag* Parliament. Finally, fear of the future. These things once made me believe in Adolf Hitler. I was naïve and I admit it. In those days, I had not read *Mein Kampf*. Who the hell did?" He laughed bitterly. "Besides," he continued, "I was selfish. Hitler promised to build up the army. Good for us! Good for *me!* I was a professional, a lieutenant. A year after Hitler came, I was a captain, then a major. That's four ranks in three years in peacetime! Why, if war broke out, I'd be a staff general within two months." He stood up, uncharacteristically animated. "But I know we can't win. Not in the long run. Besides, Germany means more to me than my miserable career!" He turned his back for a moment, trying to deal with his emotions. Then, "Does that answer your question, Morgenroth?"

Morgenroth was contrite. "I did not mean to upset you."

"Not at all. You have every right to know whom you're taking into battle. Make no mistake. This is dangerous stuff."

"One more thing, Major," said Morgenroth. "How many officers would join us, so they could dump Hitler and get someone else to run the war?"

Von Totten nodded. "Yes, there are many opportunists. They want to get rid of *this* Hitler and appoint one of their own. It's a chance we have to take. We can't always expect purity."

Morgenroth asked, "What about the racial policies?"

"Mein lieber Morgenroth, let's face it: We German aristocrats are inherently anti-Semitic. I am, too. Nothing against

any special Jew, just a general feeling I was brought up with. I've known many Jews, titled and otherwise. There are even remote parts of my family intermarried with Jews. Speaking for myself, I'd rather not have Jewish in-laws. But then, I'd feel the same way about an Indian maharaja or a Japanese prince. We *Junkers* are a narrow-minded bunch. I admit it freely."

"Then you believe Hitler is right about the Jews?"

"*By no means!* I may have my personal little prejudices, but I can't condone a national policy of brutal suppression. We can't afford it. We're becoming the barbarians of Europe. I don't relish that."

Morgenroth held out his hand to von Totten, who shook it.

Zoss raised his eyebrows. "Before we all fall around each other's necks in tears of brotherhood, let's get to the real reason for this meeting. Whom can we bring into Otto?"

Morgenroth: "I have someone in mind, a wonderful man, a famous film director. Let me approach him."

Von Totten: "I shall have four names at our next meeting. Good men. True men."

Then Zoss: "The first one I have is a girl. You know her husband, Dorn. He works for me. Hilde, his wife, is absolutely first-class. She used to be in the foreign service, comes of an old Nürnberg family. I know her husband also has grave doubts about those brilliant men of the N.S.D.A.P."

"I only saw him that one night at the Berghof," said Morgenroth.

"He was chummy with Telesty, and later he was *kameradschaftlich* with that little swine von Bernsdorfer."

"Both true. But I'll still vouch for the fact that he's become quite disillusioned."

"Zoss, your word is good enough, although I shouldn't trust you with a woman." Morgenroth had seen the Brunzig man in action. "Is the young *Frau* Dorn beautiful? And are you screwing her?"

"Hannes, you're a great race driver and a total *Arschloch!* No." Zoss laughed. "I'm not laying Hilde Dorn! Although" —he shrugged—"under other circumstances it wouldn't have been a bad idea. . . ."

Von Totten said, "I could get Dorn a reserve commission and see that he gets assigned to a staff job with a *Panzer* group. He could be a good observer for us. Besides, I'd hate to leave him too close to von Bernsdorfer. After all, the *Sturmführer*'s father is one of our most important people. Too dangerous. About the girl, that's splendid! She could do wonderful work.''

The Kurfürstendamm's wide sidewalks were flooded with lunch-hour shoppers and even a few residues of pre-Hitler days: some *Nutten,* whores, blind beggars with their yellow armbands, and some queers, but in men's clothing, no longer in drag. To the disgust of the authorities, Berlin was slow to change its debauched ways.

Staring into shop windows and showcases were chic, young *Berlinerinen* and sturdy *Hausfrauen* with trilby hats and durable tweed suits. There were many service and party uniforms. Those shops that had been wrecked in Reichs "Crystal Night" had been rebuilt and were now under Aryan management. There were no more Jewish names on the Kurfürstendamm!

Karl-Heinz was delighted that he finally had a few hours to himself. He had spent weeks demonstrating the G.F.W. 12 to the *Wehrmacht,* party, press, and "friendly" foreign military attachés.

He was tempted to take lunch at the fashionable *Romanisches Cafe,* but he did not want to meet anyone he knew. No distractions! He had to think. He ordered a *Molle* of beer at one of the Aschinger *Bierstuben* and drank it standing up at one of their elbow-high tables. July heat came in through the open door, and it was time for the Friesian Islands and their beaches, time for Berlin's beloved *Sommerferien,* the summer vacations that emptied the city each August.

Yet he had a nagging feeling that this August might be the last carefree one for a long time to come. International tensions had sharpened dangerously since the Sudeten crisis. In March, the Reich had annexed all of Czechoslovakia. Several Czech engineers at Brunzig, first-class men, had quit and gone to England. They refused to work for a German firm.

Now the *Führer* insisted the Hanseatic port of Danzig had to rejoin the Reich. Then the British announced that they would defend Poland. Frightening . . . !

The *Spiesser,* the provincial hicks, probably liked all this talk of war, but not the Berliners. The *Führer*'s radio speeches sounded glorious, sure of the nation's support, but in Berlin there was anxiety and even fear.

Karl-Heinz finished his beer. Then he slowly walked past the towering Kaiser Wilhelm Church toward the zoo a few hundred meters ahead. It, too, was crowded. There were nannies pushing baby carriages, young soldiers and their girls, kids in Hitler Youth and B.D.N. uniforms, and many elderly people strolling in the sun.

He found an empty seat on a bench opposite the lions' enclosure, *Berliner Afrika* as they called it. The pretty girl sitting next to him, probably a stenographer on her lunch hour, eyed him expectantly, but when she spotted his wedding band concentrated on her *B.Z. am Mittag* paper. A tall *Schupo* policeman passed slowly, hands behind his back, his eyes sweeping the crowd, like a stern father watching over his brood. An old lady stopped him to ask a question, and he bent forward imperiously to answer her. Overhead, a Lufthansa *Junkers* droned toward Tempelhof airfield, and two new Heinkel *Luftwaffe* fighters sliced across the sky, their engines whistling. The high school boy on the next bench was chewing on his *Stulle,* the rye bread sandwich of the Berliner. Carrying a *Stulle,* usually with salami or lard, was so common that even businessmen and lawyers sometimes stowed them in their briefcases for nutritional first aid. Berliners had voracious appetites, and one never knew when hunger might strike!

Then a short man in a dark suit caught Karl-Heinz's eye. He was walking rapidly, head down, face almost covered by the brim of his hat. A yellow cloth star was sewn to the left front of his jacket. A Jew!

It shocked Karl-Heinz more than he could believe. He had read the new Jew-star regulation in the papers, but he had never actually seen anyone wearing it, probably because there were so few Jews left in Berlin. He pictured Siegfried Schmidt with a yellow star, branded like a medieval convict! Then, for the first time in years, the distinguished face of Adalbert Goldner, *"Der Olle,"* came to his mind's eye.

Karl-Heinz had still not joined Otto. Hilde would tell him nothing about the group, and he understood completely. There were others involved. Often, she disappeared for a few hours, and he asked no questions. With anyone other than Hilde, he would have been jealous, but she was so straightforward that it never occurred to him to question her absences.

Zoss had just thrown a dramatic new job into his lap: They wanted him to become an army officer. Hilde reacted quite uncharacteristically. Hilde, who had hated his N.S.K.K. uniform, said, "*Wunderbar*, Karle!"

When Zoss told him, Karl-Heinz was thunderstruck.

"An army commission? You must be joking!"

"Joking? Why?"

"I don't know anything about soldiering."

"Brunzig doesn't need you for soldiering. We need you as our liaison contact in the army!"

"But I don't even know how to salute or drill!"

"*Na, ja*, they'll teach you those necessary things. And then you won't be running an infantry company. You will be more concerned with the types of vehicles we supply to the *Wehrmacht*. Staff work. We'll prebrief you on all our newest equipment in Stuttgart before it gets shown to the army boys."

"One question. Has this anything to do with Otto?"

"Nothing. Obviously, we are being mobilized. Your work with the party no longer has priority. From here on, your responsibility is the *Wehrmacht*, and you can't work inside the army without a uniform. Remember, *mein Junge*, I'm the bastard who got you into the N.S.K.K. uniform. I'm sure Hilde must have loved that!"

"She was delirious."

"Newlyweds often are."

"Are you sending other Brunzig people into the military?"

"If you work out, we'll get people into the *Luftwaffe* and the navy. They would report to you."

"Isn't it tough to get me a commission?"

"We've got certain contacts. Anyway, why the hell should you care how we get you the commission? Besides, we'll pay you the difference between your army salary and your regular Brunzig salary. You'll be a very overpaid young officer."

"What rank?"

"*Na, ja*. I *knew* it! Ambitious! Tell me, *Hoheit*, your Highness, would captain be acceptable?"

Karl-Heinz shrugged. "It'll have to do! But it seems shabby considering my *fantastisch* military background."

"If it makes you feel better," said Zoss, "I'll buy you a regiment of toy soldiers so you can play colonel. Tell Hilde not to step on your troops!"

"Hilde! What the devil will she say?"

"She's no fool," said Zoss. "She knows the international situation. And she will prefer it to your work with the party."

"One more thing." Karl-Heinz had to clear the air about something. "I have not made up my mind about Otto. Not yet."

"*In Ordnung*. Never mind. Take your time. Whenever you're ready, tell me." Then Zoss held his finger over his mouth to put an end to any further talk. Even his office might be under surveillance.

The great power yacht *Destino* loomed above her smaller neighbors and dominated the harbor at Monte Carlo. Her forty-man deck crew was hard at work, preparing to weigh anchor early the next morning, but on the aft sundeck, above the fantail stern, all was languor and calm. Gerhardt Brunzig, who was stretched out in a deck chair, was hung over. He hoped that a combination of gin slings, sunshine, and rest could restore his usual, cynical humor. He had worked out special signals with the Chinese bar steward: one finger for more gin, two for more sun cream. The Chinese was very young and dressed in a short white mess jacket that showed off his slim hips. Gerhardt Brunzig took note of this despite his hangover. The French called it *mal aux cheveux;* "pain in the hairs," and that was exactly what he felt. He never had mornings-after, but Gerhardt was deeply depressed. He was sure war would come and despised the very thought of it. He hated giving up his friends, his travels. All of it was based on peace and freedom to go where he wanted and to see whom he wanted. Now he was on the yacht of an American friend, Jack Kingsley. The other guests were an Argentine, Pepe de la Carra; a Frenchman, the Baron André de Montrouge, a Jew whose great grandfather was Ernst Rothberg, the famed banker from Trier; and his baroness, a charming Syrian Jewess. Then there was Lord Andrew Bryston, a great, big, kind, dumb polo player, and Lady Bryston, who had the most beautiful taste and ran the most beautiful *ménage* in the most beautiful Georgian house in beautiful London. She had taught Bryston some civilization, and he could now talk of Picasso or Brecht, though somewhat in the manner of a trained dancing bear. He and Pepe shared a love for horses, dogs, guns, tarts, and supercharged sports cars.

André de Montrouge owned some of the world's finest

racehorses, and was a champion two-man bobsled driver and a devotee of the Cresta run at St. Moritz.

Their host, Jack Kingsley, was different. Like many truly rich Americans, he had made yet another fortune during the crash. When others had to dump, he was in a position to buy bargain stocks. Only coupon clippers, *nouveaux riches,* and the merely well-to-do got wiped out. People like the Kingsleys, the Vanderbilts, and the Carnegies did not.

Then, after thirty years of marriage with three grown children, Kingsley had settled a large sum upon his wife and had left her. He also left behind the kind of life he led in America, because he had grown reconciled to his own homosexuality and had finally stopped pretending. He moved to Europe, bought *Destino*, and became a sort of *grande dame* of international society's homosexuals. Everyone adored Jack. He was a gentle and loyal friend and a generous and forgiving host who was never offended by breaches of manners. The only thing that made him sad was to see friends unhappy, so he was truly distressed to find Gerhardt Brunzig in such obvious misery. He asked, "What is it, Gerhardt? I've never seen you so depressed."

Gerhardt sat up. "Dear, wonderful Jack. You're like a magician. You read minds. If you really want to know, and I hate to draw you into my personal swamp, I'm afraid this is the end of our happy days. I think there'll be war, and I just can't face it! I'll miss all of you so dreadfully, and I'll miss *Destino*, and oh, God . . ." he trailed off morosely.

"I'm sad to say I agree," said Kingsley. "My American friends in Berlin all say the same thing. And would you believe that Andy Bryston is absolutely on the side of the British declaration about defending Poland? He thinks your man Hitler needs to be curbed. It's the only thing Pepe and he fight about. Pepe is on Hitler's side, like most Argentinians."

"What about the Montrouges?"

"Well, because they're Jewish, it's an open-and-shut question for them. Montrouge has recently spent a fortune on Zionist settlements in Palestine, although he once used to hate the whole idea. I suppose now he feels it's the only place left for Jews from your country and Austria."

"Funny," said Gerhardt, "when I sit at dinner with the Brystons and the Montrouges, it simply never occurs to me that we might have differences. They're friends. I like them. I hope they like me. *Basta*."

"They're very fond of you, you know that. When I invited the Montrouges on this cruise, they specifically hoped you'd be along. And the Brystons adore you."

"Then why do we have to face this shit?" Suddenly Gerhardt's eyes filled with tears, and Jack Kingsley put his hand on the younger man's shoulder. He loved this bright, charming German as much as his own children.

"All right. Enough," said Gerhardt Brunzig, collecting himself. "What time do you want us for dinner?"

"Eight," said Kingsley.

"I'll go into town for a while, and I'll be back at seven, in time to change. Sorry I was such a bore."

One of *Destino*'s launches ferried him to the dock, and he walked slowly up the hill toward the Hotel de Paris. Monte was crowded. As soon as he entered the lobby of the hotel, a massive hand grabbed his shoulder from behind.

"Drink, *Herr Generaldirektor?*" It was Telesty, the SS colonel. He looked even larger in his red polo shirt, blue blazer, and white flannel trousers.

"Natürlich," said Gerhardt.

They found an outdoor table at the Café de Paris, overlooking the casino square from where Gerhardt had often watched the annual Monaco Grand Prix race. This was never Brunzig's favorite circuit because of its sharp curves and short straightaways. Brunzigs were big, powerful race cars. At Monte Carlo, they were like Great Danes trying to run around in a small room. Yet that genius Hannes Morgenroth had managed time and again to manhandle the big Brunzigs around the track at record speeds. Gerhardt was devoted to music, but his favorite sound was still the ear-shattering basso howl of a Brunzig racing engine. He loved his company, his cars, and the whole spirit of Brunzig. But to him Brunzig meant better passenger cars for more people, not military vehicles. A 900K in field gray was like a beautiful woman with a mudpack. Brunzigs were made for enjoyment, not for killing.

"What are you doing in this haven of debauch and degeneration?" he asked Telesty.

"I was in Italy, conferring with our respected and honored ravioli-scented allies," said the SS officer. "So I decided to make a small *Abstecher*, a side trip. This may be my last chance to lose money. Fortunately, I brought the two things I need: black-tie *smoking* suit and courage, so tonight the casino and I shall go *hart auf hart*."

"I'll bet on the Casino," said Gerhardt.

"I hate to agree with you, but you may be right. I just want to keep enough money to buy dinner for whatever lady I eventually fuck."

"Lucky at love . . ." Gerhardt shrugged.

"By the way," said Telesty. "I hear you are on the *Destino*. Everyone in Monte knows every guest aboard her. After all, she's the flagship of the Monte Carlo yacht fleet."

"What you're trying to say is that the Montrouges are aboard. And they're Jews. Well, to forestall you, I've known them for many years, and they did my father many favors. I believe in being loyal."

"Wait," said Telesty, "*langsam* my dear *Herr* Brunzig. I have nothing at all against your friends. I'm not your problem. Heydrich perhaps, but not I."

"Good. I am sure that even *Herr* Heydrich, as head of the S.D., will recognize my slim contributions to Germany. I do try to be useful to our *Führer* and our people, you know." Gerhardt had put on his most languorous British aristocracy voice. His eyes were half closed, and his hand made vague gestures.

Telesty was impressed. But he tried again. "This American who owns the *Destino*, Kingsley, is supposed to be an interesting fellow. I've never met him, of course, but everyone says that he gives exceedingly good parties."

"He does. Unfortunately, we're leaving early tomorrow for Capri, otherwise I would have asked you aboard." Gerhardt grinned to himself. Like hell he would have asked Telesty aboard. Never! What an insult it would be to the Montrouges and the Brystons. Andy would probably ask the bastard to step out on deck for a round or two. Pepe would be next. Not that Pepe had anything against the SS, but Andy Bryston was Pepe's friend and *noblesse oblige*.

Telesty was not deterred. "That young Diestel fellow, the one I met at Villa Ritterschwert when you gave the party, isn't he also a friend of Kingsley's?"

"A good friend. And a great friend of mine. We all stick together, you know, the *Warme Brüder*, the homosexuals. Is that what you're getting at, *Herr Sturmbannführer?*" he said

quite loudly, and people at the next table turned to look at the
tall, scarred man to whom the Nazi rank obviously applied.

Telesty ducked his head and his face flushed. This Brunzig
fellow was a viper. "All right," he said, "you don't have to
declare the German invasion of Monte Carlo. Yes. I was
trying to ask if Kingsley is a homo, but I didn't want to
produce a whole *confessio*."

"Then what was the point?"

"Just trying to make conversation. Just gossip. I love
gossip, don't you? That's what I like about the Berghof:
gossip."

"Yes. I like gossip. So long as it is lighthearted and
amusing. And so long as I'm not the victim. Anyway, there's
one thing, my dear Telesty, that you forgot to mention."

"Was denn?"

"You said you brought your dinner jacket and your courage.
Here's the rest." Gerhardt took a thick wad of money from
his wallet and put it under a plate, like a very large tip to the
headwaiter. "Do me a favor," he said. "Bet that for me
tonight. I won't be back in Monte. We'll share the winnings
fifty-fifty. If you win, pay me the next time you see me. If
you lose, don't complain to me. If there's one thing I can't
stand it's a whining SS officer!"

Telesty was speechless.

"Oh, and one more thing," said Gerhardt. "At the Berghof
you told me that you might have to ask me for a favor
sometime. Remember to keep your line of communications to
me open. We have long and tough years ahead, and industrial
people like me and the Krupps and the Diestels, we always
survive. Only politicians and soldiers don't."

He stood up, grinned, bowed, and left without paying.
Telesty felt the size of the wad of banknotes. It was a large
amount. He had been bought. His blackmail had failed. He
had been paid off like a gigolo. Oh, what the hell. *Na, ja,*
Gerhardt Brunzig was right. It was a big, tough world out
there and he, Telesty, owed his loyalties only to himself.

Gerhardt felt a lot better. He walked over to Cartier to buy
a gift for Jack Kingsley. After neutralizing a talky salesclerk,
he settled on some exquisite onyx and platinum cufflinks and
dress-shirt studs to match. Jack Kingsley loved onyx. There
was even a Sudanese masseur aboard *Destino*.

•   •   •

A launch from *Destino* was waiting for him at the dock. On the way back to the large white yacht, he remembered some hints Armin Zoss had thrown his way. He assumed that Zoss had connections with some anti-Nazi groups. Of course, Gerhardt was aware that there was some opposition to the Nazi regime. Certain of Germany's top industrial people who had given Hitler money in the beginning were now leery of him. Gerhardt guessed that making war against Poland would be easy. But would France and Britain be as simple? And what about Russia? Certain cynics believed that Hitler would soon negotiate a nonaggression pact with Russia, but that sounded insane. Russia and Germany? Although they used to call the S.A. storm troopers "beefsteaks" because they were "brown on the outside and red on the inside." Perhaps there was not much to choose between them. Certainly Hitler would do anything, anything at all, to fulfill his ambitions, even a deal with the Bolsheviks.

The launch fetched up smartly against *Destino*'s padded gangway, where a sailor took her bowline and held her until Gerhardt had stepped off.

Jack Kingsley stood on the promenade deck above him. He had obviously been waiting and worrying.

"Everything all right?" he asked.

Gerhardt looked up at him. "Nothing much has changed, but at least I feel better. I'll tell you about someone interesting I met at the hotel." He knew Jack Kingsley would love the story about Telesty.

After a happy, glorious, champagne-flooded week aboard *Destino*, Gerhardt Brunzig had to leave the great yacht and his friends. That last night in Capri he gave a dinner party at the Quisisana Hotel, high above *Destino*, anchored in the harbor with all her deck lights ablaze.

It was the first of August, nineteen hundred and thirty-nine, and they tried their best to ignore the growing threats of war.

By then, agonies later, Gerhardt had come to a reluctant conclusion: His personal anti-Nazi feelings were not as important as the company he loved. He dared not lose the helm of Brunzig by being caught in a compromising political situation. He was sure that only he could bring Brunzig through the disasters ahead.

He would explain this to Zoss, and surely his old friend and co-worker would understand.

He was right. Armin Zoss understood completely.

The Twelfth *Offiziersanwärter Übungskompanie* at Döberitz near Berlin trained officer candidates, mostly specialists like doctors, clergymen, cinematographers, and others who had to be in uniform. Karl-Keinz became *Ofz. Anw. DORN, K.-H.,* a cadet in the Twelfth. They wore infantry gear: stiff wool tunic, trousers, coat, and heavy black boots of the kind called *Knobelbrecher,* arch-busters. They lived in old-fashioned Prussian army barracks, one hundred men to a barrack. Bunks were lined up with geometric precision, and everything hung, stowed, rolled, or stacked according to regulations. Discipline was stiff, and even slight offenses brought harsh reprimands or extra duty. The training noncoms, all old soldiers, had ill-concealed disdain for this bunch of nonsoldiers, who would automatically become officers upon graduation. Karl-Heinz was treated with slightly more respect because he looked soldierly and managed to complete the daily run over the obstacle course, sweating in the August heat, but without huffing, puffing or dropping out. He also became a good marksman and qualified with pistol, rifle, and light machine gun.

Besides the use of weapons, Karl-Heinz mastered enough superficial army knowledge to act the part of an officer: the position of attention, thumbs at the trouser seam, elbows angled slightly to the front, chin tucked onto chest. The salute and return of salute. Where a junior officer must walk when he is with a senior officer. How the uniform is worn correctly. Where an officer is positioned in parade formations. How an officer speaks. How an officer signs a letter, and how an army communication must be composed. How to identify army units from the uniform and from markings on vehicles.

There was even a regulation way an officer held his glass when making a toast: at the level of the breast-nipple. And then, finally, the matter of personal conduct in battle: "Courage is the suppression of the cowardly animal inside oneself."

In many ways, the German army had not changed since the kaiser's day, except that the oath of allegiance was now given to "the *Führer und Reichskanzler* Adolf Hitler."

Despite side-shaven haircut, nights with his snoring barracks mates, bugles at five in the morning, and the howls of bull-necked *Feldwebel* training sergeants, Karl-Heinz rather enjoyed himself. Because he knew Döberitz quite well from their many G.F.W. 12 demonstrations, he could locate extra beer, cigarettes, and telephones. After dinner, washed free of dust and sweat, he would sit outside his barracks, with the wood-burning smell and evening sounds of an army post all around him. Men were singing, playing harmonicas. He was pleased with the camaraderie of his fellow soldiers, and he cheerfully took the misery of training, because at the end of the course he would be a captain with an officer's privileges. Most poor fellows joined the *Wehrmacht* and spent months in the ranks until they got the slim chance of becoming officer candidates. Then, if they passed the stiff course, they came out as lowly junior lieutenants.

Early in their training course, they formed up one morning to listen to the announcement that Germany and Soviet Russia had concluded a nonaggression pact. Incredible! Yet everyone in the Twelfth company, mostly men of great intelligence and education, took it in stride. They were convinced that Poland had provoked Germany endlessly and that the *Führer* had shown exemplary patience. Perhaps this pact would shut up the Poles. They were also relieved that the Russians would no longer be a danger, because everyone feared the Bolsheviks more than the English or the French. For those few, like Karl-Heinz, who had their doubts about the *Führer*, news of the pact was unwelcome. But what could they do?

On the day of graduation, Karl-Heinz put on his new captain's uniform: peaked cap, gray tunic, riding breeches, and his old black N.S.K.K. boots. He also pinned on his Italian ribbon. He was the only one of the newly minted officers to wear a decoration, and his old training sergeants were agog. It confirmed their opinion of him: The man would have made a fine "normal" officer had he not been commissioned as a vehicle specialist. He said good-bye to them, and they accorded him razor-sharp army salutes. *"Alles Gute, Herr Hauptmann!"*

That same day, September first, nineteen hundred and thirty-nine, at four-forty-five in the morning, the old German battleship *Schleswig-Holstein* opened fire on the Polish garrison near Danzig, and soon thereafter the first German army units crossed into Poland. On September third, Great Britain and France declared war on Germany.

Karl-Heinz, fit and trim, went home for one week's leave. Hilde hugged and kissed him and admired his uniform, but then burst into tears. She was devastated by the outbreak of war.

"Karle. How could those swine do this to Germany? Adolf Hitler wanted it and forced it and made it happen. There was no way out for England and France. They had to declare war. A friend at the Foreign Office said that even Göring begged the *Führer* not to do this. But Hitler just screamed at him."

"How do you know that?"

"He's the assistant to Weizsäcker, who is number two under Ribbentrop. He was just gossiping. He knows nothing about my sympathies. Seems Weizsäcker was right there when Göring and the *Führer* had their blowout."

Karl-Heinz held her tight. He was so sad for her. Then he said, "Now what? Our troops are cutting right across Poland. The Poles are surrendering, masses of them. And the English and French are doing nothing, just as the *Führer* predicted."

"I know, Karle. But this can't last. Oh, Zoss wants you to call him as soon as possible. And Morgenroth . . ."

"What about Morgenroth?"

"You haven't seen the papers?"

"No. Came straight here from Döberitz."

"He had an accident on the Avus. In his own car. He was drunk, Zoss said."

"Drunk?"

"Drunk. *Blau*. Plastered."

"Oh, my God. Is he badly hurt?"

"Here. Look for yourself." She handed him the *Berliner Tageblatt*. The report said "*schwer verletzt*, badly hurt." Karl-Heinz phoned Zoss.

"Happy to hear from you." Not the usual bouncy voice.

"I'll be home about six. I have much to tell you. I'll come up to your place."

"I heard about Morgenroth. Anything I can do?"

"Nothing. He's hanging on. Anneliese von Konsky is with him, and so is Erich Forstmann. Erich just called to say that it's very critical. Hannes may lose a leg, and he may have some brain damage."

"What happened?"

"I'll tell you later."

When Zoss arrived, he looked at the brand new captain and could not resist. "We're safe! Hilde, do not worry. We now have Captain Dorn to protect us. He will act as our guardian, our *Wacht am Rhein. Lieb Vaterland, magst ruhig sein!* Dear fatherland, stay calm!"

Then, somberly, he told the story of Morgenroth. "Apparently, he was with the Forstmanns in Wannsee when war was declared by England. They heard it on the radio. He got up, didn't say a word. They saw his old five hundred pulling out with the supercharger screaming. It seems he first stopped at a *Kneipe* and had a lot of *Schnaps.* The owner recognized him and, anyway, everyone knows his car. Then he drove toward the Avus. They said that when he got on it, he accelerated flat out, right up to the limit in every gear. He must have been doing over two hundred and thirty kilometers. The speedometer on the old car is in miles per hour, and it was stuck at one hundred and forty. He stayed flat out for miles. Other cars reported he absolutely flew past them. Then, a tire let go. One of the big rear ones. The 500-C is like a truck. It went into a wild skid, and then flipped end over end. He was thrown out and hit a fence. I swear to you, if he had been sober, he could have handled that skid. But he was very drunk. He *never* drove when he was drunk! He must have been in deep shock to get so loaded. He would have done anything to prevent our getting into a war. So many of his friends are French and English."

"Sounds," said Karl-Heinz, "as if he was trying to kill himself."

"Yes."

"God, I hope he pulls through."

"We all do." Zoss sighed, and for the first time, he looked his age. Then he said, "Karl-Heinz, you're going to Stuttgart so that our *Panzer* people can teach you about our newest stuff. Dr. Maut will be there, and Gerhardt Brunzig said you could stay at Ritterschwert. Hilde, dear, if you wish, you can join him for a week. After that, your captain will be off to one of the headquarters in the Saar."

Karl-Heinz asked, "How do you know my orders?"

"*Doovkopp!* The reason you're in that uniform is to work with Brunzig, so you'll be where *we* need you. *Capisce?*"

"*Capisce.*"

"Or would you rather be in the hands of the *Oberkom-mandeur der Panzertruppen?* The Commander of Armored Troops?"

"I think I'd prefer my old boss."

"The remarkable Armin Zoss?"

"The same."

"*Frau* Dorn," said Zoss with his old gallantry, "this young captain you've been sleeping with is dumb as hell. Hope he's at least good in bed, otherwise I'd get rid of him." But his attempt at banter was hollow. He was so obviously shaken. Aware of his distress, Hilde walked over to him and kissed his cheek. "Sorry that things are going so badly," she said.

"For all of us." He shrugged. "Sad times. But let's not give up. Perhaps our glorious *Führer* can continue his string of unbroken brilliance. After Poland, France, and England. Having achieved that, he can appoint Julius Streicher as future *Gauleiter* of New York. What would Streicher be without Jews? New York has several million. A lot of people are already saying that the French and English will soon make peace, and if they don't, we could take Paris in a few weeks. I wonder how many of those army officers who wanted to replace Hitler still feel the same? After this Polish adventure, Hitler looks better than Bismarck."

The Dorns decided to drive to Stuttgart because they heard the trains were jammed with military personnel, but the roads were also packed with *Wehrmacht* traffic, some going toward Poland and even more toward the "West Wall," the defense installations facing France.

Drowsy young soldiers on trucks and tanks braced into their version of stalwart fighting men when they spotted the captain and the pretty girl in the smart Brunzig convertible. It was slow going because long, motorized convoys moved ponderously, like circus elephants holding onto each other's tails. When they finally reached Coburg, halfway to Stuttgart, they had already driven five hours. So they decided to stay overnight in Nürnberg and continue the next day.

The Antmanns were happy to have them, startled by their son-in-law's new uniform, and deeply depressed by the war. They were also disheartened because some of their dearest friends, people they respected, were suddenly in full support

of the *Führer*. There had been several near-arguments, and
the Antmanns had to be careful to avoid such confrontations.
War fever had mounted. Success seemed to justify Adolf
Hitler's every move, and many skeptics became believers.

The four of them ate a quiet, glum dinner, and everyone
soon retired.

Nürnberg was blacked out, and when Hilde tried to peek
onto the street, a harsh voice yelled to "keep the *verfluchte*
goddam curtains closed. What the hell sort of a *Scheisswirt-
schaft* shit is going on in that house, anyway?"

Karl-Heinz was about to stop the loudmouth out on the
street, but Hilde kept him from putting on his tunic and cap.
"It's some little auxiliary policeman or block warden. They
have them by the dozen in Berlin. The real police are being
mobilized into the *Wehrmacht*."

After all those weeks of separation they made love frantically,
but it was hasty and careless. It was rare for their lovemaking
to fail, and they were upset, but they consoled each other and
finally went to sleep.

Getting up early did not improve their mood, but Karl-
Heinz had to attend meetings in Stuttgart, so they barely ate
breakfast, said a hasty *"Adeh!"* and drove off.

Hilde had never seen Ritterschwert. She found it overwhelming and depressing, but she finally met Gerhardt Brunzig,
who mock-saluted, army style. "*Na, ja, Herr Hauptmann*, at
last I see you accompanied by a pretty lady. You did say she
is your wife? *Prima!* Frankly, I was sick of seeing you with
that handsome SS horseman von what-ever-his-name. There
were ugly rumors about you two. . . ."

Hilde laughed. She liked Gerhardt Brunzig at once.

She said, "I really can't blame von Bernsdorfer! The *Herr
Hauptmann* Dorn has a certain appeal."

"Namely?"

"He looks good in riding breeches and boots. As you
know, that means a lot to von Bernsdorfer. As a matter of
fact, we all thought von Bernsdorfer was in love with a
certain little Arabian mare. I'm sorry to hear he switched to
Karle. . . . Horses are so much more dependable!"

Gerhardt Brunzig gave her a quizzical look and grinned.
This gal was pretty and certainly more worldly than her
husband. He said, "Mostly, I'm glad he belongs to you. He's
in luck. You are, too, I think."

Karl-Heinz stood by in silence and watched the exchange like a spectator at tennis. He finally spoke up. "I want to thank both of you, *Herr Generaldirektor* and *Frau Hauptmann* Dorn, for your deep concern with my sexual future. May I assure you that before I get engaged to any SS man, I shall inform both of you."

Then he excused himself to attend his first briefing at the proving grounds.

Karl-Heinz was studying the steel anatomy of *PZKW II Ausf. M.*, the latest tank, as built by Brunzig and modified by Dr. Maut. It was a brutal, slab-gray, grease- and oil-reeking monster with a revolving turret, high-speed, flat-trajectory gun, and two machine guns. He quickly realized how easily it could be immobilized.

"Looks very tough," he said, "but those exposed bogey-wheels could be jammed by all sorts of things: barbed wire or steel poles or just a high-explosive shell. Once this thing is stopped, surely one can do it harm. I watched them use flamethrowers in Döberitz, and this tank could be fried with everyone in it."

"Na, ja," said Maut, scratching his head, "you've put your finger right on the weak spot, my dear young captain. I hate to think that all along we've had someone that smart at Brunzig. Anyway, we're working on all those points. But the biggest tank problem is something else."

"Zum Beispiel?"

"All tanks, and I mean *all Panzers*. Doesn't matter whose they are, they have to stop to fire their main guns. It's like a pistol fight in one of those American cowboy films. The first tank to get the drop on the other tank has the advantage. Now we're trying to work on a stabilized, recoilless gun that can be fired in motion, like a miniature naval weapon." He took Karl-Heinz into the engineering office and showed him blueprints. They continued until seven, when they both realized that they were expected for dinner at Ritterschwert by eight.

While Karl-Heinz was at the factory, Hilde unpacked. Their bedroom overlooked some formal gardens. It was flanked by a dressing room and a large marble-sheathed bathroom with a mid-Victorian tub and gilded faucets. The bedroom floor was covered with oriental rugs and its furniture was massive, oaken, lavishly carved. There was a wide, sleigh-type bed and overstuffed velvet armchairs. The Dorns' small travel wardrobe disappeared in the suitcase-sized drawers and cavernous armoires.

Hilde decided to go for a walk. A tall butler at the foot of the stairs showed her the way out of Ritterschwert's labyrinthine passages. Outside, it was chilly. Newly fallen leaves covered the thick grass. A low cover of clouds, attached like a canopy to the mountains above the estate, extended to the far horizon. Not a sound was heard except for the crack of a snapping twig somewhere in the nearby forest and the squawking of a crow. She walked slowly around the big mansion. She tried to collect her thoughts.

Karl-Heinz seemed comfortable in his new role. The army had removed him from any distasteful contact with the Hitler entourage. If he was still unhappy, it was only for her, but she felt he was coming to terms with a disagreeable situation. He had not shown any wish to join Otto, and she suspected that he would not do so. Sad!

In the beginning he was so slow to see what was wrong with Hitler. Then he, too, had seen the evil. But now? Was he an opportunist? Or was he too phlegmatic? Probably a bit of each. She could not pass judgment. But something had come between them.

She heard someone knocking on a windowpane from inside the house: Gerhardt Brunzig, beckoning to her. She joined him in his study and they had cocktails.

"Your *netter Junge,* your nice chap, will be home soon. Dinner is at eight, although he's with Maut, and Maut has a knack of forgetting the hour. Why haven't you and I met before?" He was eager to be friends with this charming woman. In his own way, he really adored women.

"We haven't met because Karl-Heinz probably thought it wiser to keep me offstage and, thereby, out of trouble."

"Trouble? What kind? Sexual? Social?"

She laughed. "I hope not. No, that's not it."

"Then what?"

"Politics. Karl-Heinz knows I have very definite opinions about our country and that I have a forceful way of expressing them. In fact, *Einen grossen Mund,* a big mouth."

"If you don't always approve of our government, why take the chance of telling me? You don't know me."

"I know enough about you from enough people to take the chance."

"May I know who has been your informant?" He laughed.

"No. I keep my confidences."

"How long have you been married?"

"Three years."

"Planning a family?"

"None. Not the right time, don't you agree?"

"Oh, I don't know. I must admit that I'm always a bit dubious when people talk about the wrong time and the right time for having children. If people want them, anytime is the right time. But I mustn't be presumptuous. We're brand-new friends, after all."

"No, really. Do tell me! You seem to be a man of intuition. Why do you think we don't want kids?"

"Well, perhaps . . . how can I put it? Perhaps the two of you need to do a little adjusting. I felt the tension between you from the moment you arrived."

"That's easily explained. I despise this war, and I think my husband is beginning to accept it."

"Does he believe that we must defend ourselves against the Savage Poles?"

"No. I think he is under no illusion in that respect. But he feels that *Wenn schon, denn schon,* once we're committed, we have to go along without complaining."

Gerhardt Brunzig was about to answer, but stopped himself. He just shook his head.

Then they heard the voices of Dr. Maut and Karl-Heinz, returning from the factory.

All through dinner Karl-Heinz and Dr. Maut were so deeply involved in talk that they ignored the other two at the table. Gerhardt Brunzig looked on with a bored expression, but Hilde got more and more upset. Karl-Heinz sounded as if he was part of the war effort full steam ahead. Not that the subject was political. They spoke only about tanks. But he seemed to have lost sight of the ultimate purpose, like a marksman who cheerfully cleans his pistol and then shoots himself to death.

Dr. Maut, swept up in the younger man's interest, asked, "All right, what else is missing?"

"Snorkels."

"Like a U-boat?"

"Exactly. So that it can ford a river. Can we waterproof up to the lower gun ports?"

"Easily. But only for sweet water, not the ocean. Still, I think you're right. Excellent." He admired this inventive boy.

Karl-Heinz realized they had been discourteous. "*Tut mir leid.* So sorry. Hilde, don't be angry. It's a fascinating subject. Much more creative, in a way, than passenger cars, but without the emotional problem of styling."

Hilde just gave him a glum look, but there was an uncharacteristic edge to Gerhardt Brunzig's voice. "My dear boy, we may be temporarily busy with this military garbage, but let me remind you that our eventual future lies in the great passenger car, *with great styling!*"

Karl-Heinz blushed like a schoolboy caught masturbating. "I didn't mean to say . . ."

Gerhardt Brunzig cut across his explanation. "*Na ja,* I'm glad to hear that. We at Brunzig are first and foremost in the luxury automobile business, please remember that." He stood up abruptly, bowed to Hilde wordlessly, and left, ignoring the men.

Dr. Maut shook his head. "He can get that way sometimes, very tough, though fortunately not often. Something we said must have given offense."

"I'm afraid I did," said Karl-Heinz. "I should remember he loves only one thing: the Brunzig automobile."

"And," said Hilde, "if you'll forgive the intrusion, I think he's absolutely right."

Later in their bedroom, Karl-Heinz said ironically, "I'm so glad you sprang to my defense."

"I didn't."

"I know! And I thought I could always count on you."

"Not when you're behaving like an idiot."

"Idiot? Dr. Maut doesn't think so."

"Maut is an opportunist. He just wants to be famous and admired, 'Our genius Dr. Maut,' even if it's Goebbels who says so!"

"I still don't see why the things I told Maut made me into an idiot."

"*Zum Teufel noch mal,* why the devil can't you understand that it's the job of intelligent Germans to stop these insane people and their insane war?"

"Sabotage our country?"

"Sabotage? Don't you see that anyone who helps these pigs is sabotaging the real Germany? You yourself saw the whole thing on *Kristallnacht* in Nürnberg. And aren't you the one who came back from the Berghof sick of that Austrian gangster and the swine around him?"

"Quite true. But then we were not at war. The first thing we must do now is to fight this war. Later we can get rid of the Nazis. But our first duty is to defend ourselves."

"Defend ourselves? Who is attacking us? The Poles?"

"No. I'm quite sure that the *Führer* used so-called Polish atrocities as an excuse. But, on the other hand, *we* didn't declare war on England and France. *They* did."

"What did you expect?"

"Perhaps they had no choice. Still, we must remember what they did to us the last time we lost against them: the Versailles Treaty, inflation, those terrible reparations. They bled us dry. Perhaps Adolf Hitler has caused this whole mess, but now we're in it and we must prevent another Versailles. This time it will be even tougher. We've done such terrible things to the Jews, and there are so many of them everywhere. They'll see we get punished more severely than in 1918."

"What do you think will happen if Germany wins? How do you think you'll get rid of Hitler then?"

"I don't think we'll win. I think we must fight them to a halt and then try to talk peace. Things are different now with tanks and bombers. There won't be years and years of trench warfare. It'll be over quickly. But we mustn't get swamped."

"I can't believe you're saying all this."

"I have thought about it a great deal. I'm not alone. Many at Döberitz agree we shouldn't have been in this war, but now that it's here we cannot afford to get run over like squirrels on the highway. We must put up a good fight. There'll be a stalemate soon and armistice. Then we'll get rid of the people who got us into this."

Hilde felt abandoned.

The next morning she left for Nürnberg and then to Berlin. They were both angry. Hilde thought he was acting like a gullible fool, and Karl-Heinz was fed up with her constant criticism. Two days later, he was ordered to report to army headquarters in Saarbrüchen.

• • •

Miserable and discouraged, Hilde did not stay long with her parents. When she got home to Berlin, the empty apartment seemed to mock her, so she called Zoss.

As soon as he heard her voice, he guessed something was wrong. "I am having dinner with Morgenroth," he said. "Why don't you join us?"

"I'm so glad he's all right!"

"He is on crutches, but his mind is clear, and at least he is out of the hospital."

They met at Morgenroth's favorite *Kneipe* in Charlottenburg. His *Stammtisch* was a small alcove table in the back of the low-ceilinged dining room. Generations of Berlin drinkers had left the place with a permanent scent of cigars and beer, of frying lard and onions. The menu was predestined: beef liver, fried herring, pork shanks, chopped beef. They ordered the liver, pan fried with onions and apple slices, flanked by sliced fried potatoes, and backed up by beer. It was comforting to have those familiar surroundings, to eat the Berlin dishes. Even Hilde, the Nürnberger, had become addicted to Berlin.

She had never actually met Hannes Morgenroth, although she had heard much about him from Zoss, and she was amazed that a man who had suffered such terrible injury could be so insouciant. Morgenroth maneuvered on his crutches with skill, and his face had healed rapidly. He had brought Anneliese von Konsky, who eyed Hilde with some curiosity and soon decided that this was probably the more worthwhile of the two Dorns. For her part, Hilde was impressed by the tall *mondaine* whom Karl-Heinz had mentioned from time to time. The Chanel suit, the Cartier wristwatch, the gold-set, flat ruby pinky ring, and above all, the strong, decisive face with its high Marlene Dietrich cheekbones—all these quickly told her that the woman had "been everywhere and back" many times.

Zoss asked, "What about the new *Hauptmann?* How is he? How was Ritterschwert?"

"Karl-Heinz is fine, and he likes his army assignment."

"It's all right," said Zoss. "We can talk. We're all very close, and they're Otto." He bent his head in the direction of the other two. "Besides, this place is safe. These days, private apartments are worse than restaurants. The S.D. can wire our homes, but they can't wire every *Scheiss*-table in every *Scheiss*-restaurant in Berlin.''

"Please." She looked around the table. "We barely know each other. Only *Herr* Zoss and I know the whole story. So do not think ill of me when I speak of my husband. He's a wonderful boy and we have only this to disagree about, the political side. We just cannot seem to look at things the same way. So do not think me disloyal when I seem to speak ill of him.''

Anneliese and Morgenroth nodded. They understood and admired her frankness.

"Na, ja," said Hilde, "to be frank, you can forget about Karl-Heinz for Otto."

"Warum denn? Why?''

"Remember, he does not really know why you got him his army commission. He thinks that you really needed him as liaison.''

"That's quite true. We never told him anything else, but we thought he'd come around to Otto sooner or later, and then we'd have him there, available in the *Wehrmacht*.''

"He was finally convinced, just before war broke out, that we were right.'' She looked around, despite Zoss's assurances that the place was safe. "Then he was in Döberitz, training, when the first troops attacked Poland, and he came to this odd conclusion: If Germany lost, it would be even worse than the Versailles Treaty. He thinks that's because of the rotten way we treated the Jews. He believes every German must now fight to achieve a stalemate. Not victory, but a stand-off. He thinks the English and the French will make peace rather than fight a long war. For now, he wants no part of Otto. He thinks the time for that is later. It's an insane position. We had a terrible row. I left Ritterschwert after two days.''

"Does Gerhardt Brunzig know you had a fight?''

"I think so. Besides, Karl-Heinz made an idiotic remark about how much more fun it was to work on tanks than on passenger cars, and *Herr* Brunzig got very tough indeed and told him off. He said that this armaments nonsense was only temporary and that Brunzig would always be in the car business. He really rattled Karl-Heinz. Maut was there, but I don't think he gave a damn.''

Zoss nodded. "I couldn't get Gerhardt to join Otto. He

wanted to, but his only concern is the company. So, if Karl-Heinz said he loved tanks, Gerhardt must have cut him to ribbons.''

"As for Maut," said Anneliese von Konsky, "he is *ein Kotzmittel*, to vomit from.''

"And how!" said Morgenroth. "He's never given a damn about race drivers. He only cares about his cars. I've come into the pits choking on oil fumes, and all he's concerned with is if the engine got enough lubrication. When drivers get killed, he never writes their families or goes to their funerals. He's never come to the hopsital to visit me, and I've seen the inside of many hospitals. . . ." Morgenroth grinned and rubbed his leg.

"*Na*," said Zoss, "there's nothing we can do about Karl-Heinz. We'll just have to leave him in the army and give him the sort of technical stuff we supposedly have him there for. We can't cast him adrift. I'll let von Totten know how things are." Then he reached for her hand. "I'm sorry, Hildelein, I don't want to be insensitive. The fact is that you knew why we wanted him in the army. So we must discuss these things quite frankly.''

"Understood." Hilde nodded, feeling grim.

Hilde got back to the apartment at eleven. At eleven-fifteen, the phone rang: Karl-Heinz.

"Tried to call you all evening! I'm in Saarbrücken.''

"I had dinner with Zoss and Hannes Morgenroth and Anneliese von Konsky.''

"Morgenroth has recovered?''

"*Na, ja*. He's on crutches. He's obviously in pain, but one can't tell.''

"How is *Frau* von Konsky?''

"Charming! She seems to be nursing Morgenroth.''

"Good! She's terribly nice. They're old lovers.''

There was a long pause. Neither one knew how to carry on from there. Finally, Karl-Heinz said, "I'm sorry about the last night at Ritterschwert.''

"So am I.''

"I hope you will understand my point of view.''

"I'll try. But I doubt if I can agree with it.''

"*Na, also,* try to, please!''

"*Gemacht*, all right, I'll try.''

They hung up after halfhearted good-nights, and then Hilde began to weep, at first in sadness and finally in anger. Damn the things that had happened and that ruined their love. She poured herself a large glass of cognac and drank it down.

The phone rang again. She thought it was Karl-Heinz and so she sounded resigned. "Yes?"

But it wasn't her husband. It was von Bernsdorfer.

"Hilde, I know it's late, but I must discuss something. It's important."

"Karl-Heinz is in Saarbrücken."

"I know where he is. No, I have to talk to you, not to Karl-Heinz."

"Can't it wait until tomorrow? It's so late."

"No. It can't wait."

"*Na, ja,* if you must, then come up now."

"I'll be there in twenty minutes."

She had to sober up. Coffee! What could von Bernsdorfer want? Otto? Of course, Otto! She dialed Zoss. Many rings, then, finally, the sleepy voice of his butler. "Nein, *Herr Direktor* Zoss is not home yet." She tried the *Kneipe,* but it was closed. By now, it was past midnight. She could not shake off the cognac. Her fear increased. Then, suddenly, she felt brandy-laced courage, and her mood switched. She'd face this swine! To hell with him! She could not call Karl-Heinz for help. She did not even have his number in Saarbrücken. To hell with him, too!

When von Bernsdorfer walked in, he was in a new soldier-gray uniform with SS insignia. He was full of excuses.

"I know it's terribly late, but I spent all day trying to make up my mind."

"About what?" She looked for any threatening sign, but his face was bland, childlike, innocent.

"May I sit down?" he asked.

"Of course."

He stretched his slim figure into an armchair in one fluid, graceful motion. "Can I have a drink?"

"Cognac?"

"*Prima.*"

She poured some into a glass and gave it to him. "What is this all about?" she said. "Why the panic?"

"More quandary than panic. I've got a tough problem. I need your help."

He was very handsome. She hated to admit it, because he was a swine.

He went on, "I know certain things that trouble me deeply, and because I know them, I could be called disloyal."

She shook a tiny bit. Here it was. It had to come. He knew all about the Otto group. He was playing cat-and-mouse. Now she poured herself a drink. "Exactly what," she asked, "are you talking about?"

He stood up, very straight, wide-shouldered, slim-hipped. He emptied his glass and put it down on the table. Hilde tried to stay firmly in focus for that moment when her life would collapse, when all of them would be crushed by this menacing man. He looked almost angelic, an angel of death.

"Hilde," he said. "I cannot help myself. I am completely mad about you!"

The relief, the alcohol, the fear, the loneliness all came together, and when he bent to kiss her, she did not turn away.

They made love. He was intuitive, detached, skilled, cruel at times. He rode her like a dressage mare. He made her follow his every pressure, and he spurred her cruelly when she failed to respond. Soon she was exhausted, spent, drained by orgasm, and still he helped, guided, punished her through a haze of fatigue until she could come to him no more. Then, finally, the riding master released her, let her collapse into sleep.

Twelfth Army Headquarters was temporarily located in an old factory building in Saarbrücken. When Karl-Heinz arrived he checked into a hotel reserved for officers. Von Totten, now a colonel, collected him there and introduced him to a group of brand-new *Panzer* staff officers, as different from traditional *Generalsstabs Offiziere* as all modern armored troops were from old-fashioned horse cavalry. Their hero was a young general called Rommel, commander of the Seventh *Panzer* Division, which was stationed in the Rhineland to the north.

Rommel, a personal protégé of the *Führer,* was a World War I hero who had commanded the bodyguard that the army had assigned to the *Führer*. They said he was not at all shy about himself. In fact, many older and more aristocratic generals were suspicious of this *parvenu* whose picture appeared almost weekly in the illustrated news magazines. Yet they had to admit he was clever, and that his new book, *Infantry Attacks!*, had become a favorite of the *Führer*.

That May, the war seemed almost remote, although the enemy was but a few miles away. There had been no activity in the west, and the fighting in Poland was finished. German and French troops were often within plain view of each other, and both sides made massive propaganda efforts through huge signs and powerful loudspeakers. *"Franzosen, warum müssen wir uns bekämpfen?"* *"Allemands, nous sommes vos amis!"* Each side proclaimed its peaceful intentions. When Karl-Heinz visited a forward bunker, he could clearly see a bare-chested French soldier, scrubbing his face and neck in a bucket. The *poilu* was no more than two hundred meters away.

He asked the *Feldwebel* sergeant in charge of the bunker why the Frenchman seemed so oblivious to danger.

The sergeant shrugged. *"Na, ja,"* he said, "we just haven't been shooting at each other. No use starting it."

The morning of May 3, Karl-Heinz was plowing through long confidential lists of Brunzig-built vehicles assigned to army units in the west—tanks, trucks, staff cars, and G.F.W. 12s—when a *Feldwebel* sergeant in black tanker's uniform brought him an order to report immediately to the Seventh *Panzer* Division at Bad Godesberg. He was to contact the Division IA, its executive officer. A command car with Seventh *Panzer* Division markings was waiting for him, and within minutes he was on his breakneck way north. They covered the hundred and fifty kilometers in ninety minutes. Seventh Division's IA, the executive officer, a cheerful young lieutenant colonel, said, "Ah, yes, *Hauptmann* Dorn, the general wants to see you."

"Excuse me, *Herr Oberstleutnant,* you mean General Rommel?"

"Of course!"

So Karl-Heinz crammed himself into the sidecar of a motorcycle dispatch driver, and they raced to nearby Wahn, an army training area like Döberitz, and then over dirt roads, across open fields until they found the general's command tank. Rommel sat on the turret of his *PzKwIII*, his short legs dangling, staring through field glasses at some tank exercises about two kilometers away. He yelled into a microphone,

"*Verflucht noch mal,* dammit, tell that idiot on the right wing to keep up! Get his ass moving! *Los-los-los!* Go-go-go!"

A group of aides and dispatch riders were bunched around the tank.

Then he spotted the young captain who stood below him at stiff attention. Good-looking kid. One ribbon that looked Italian. Rommel wore breeches, boots, gray tunic with general's collar tabs. The fabulous blue cross of the kaiser era, *Pour le Mérite,* the "Blue Max," was at his throat. His face was tough, straight-nosed, with a strong jaw, and cement-colored eyes. He jumped down from his tank, agile, athletic, full of energy. When Karl-Heinz saluted, Rommel quickly touched his cap in response, as if to say, "Enough of that nonsense!"

"*Hauptmann,* I'm told that you worked for Brunzig and that you're now their man with us here."

"*Jawohl, Herr General.*"

"Good. Now I want to establish some liaison of my own with Brunzig. What do you think about that?"

"*Prima, Herr General.*"

"Glad you agree." He took the younger man by the arm and walked him a few steps, out of earshot of the others.

"*Nun, Hauptmann,*" he said. "I think you should bring it to the attention of your chiefs at Brunzig that we here, the Seventh *Panzers,* are their best testing unit for brand-new equipment. I think we can do the best job for Gerhardt Brunzig."

Karl-Heinz listened and nodded.

"So," said Rommel, "I expect you to suggest that the latest equipment should be earmarked for the Seventh *Panzer* Division, understood?"

"*Jawohl, Herr General.*"

"Oh, you're a Berliner?" said Rommel, suddenly catching Karl-Heinz's accent.

"*Aber wie!* And how, *Herr General!*"

"We both have accents we can't hide. Swabians like me and Berliners like you. Where did you get the Italian ribbon?"

"From the *Duce, Herr General,* when we delivered his first G.F.W. twelve."

"You were in on that? It's a good car. In fact, I have one myself." He pointed down a ravine where it stood and where Karl-Heinz had already spotted it. "Yes, *Herr General,* I saw it. It must be the first one we delivered to the Fourth Army.

Now the others have them, too, but I think Colonel von Totten told me you got the first one."

Rommel grinned. He liked this kid. One could talk sense to him. And one could keep him clear of the old staff fogies with the ancient titles, the *Uradligen*. He waved for one of his aides. "Here, bring the Leica. Let's take a picture for *Hauptmann* Dorn. That is your name, isn't it?"

"Yes, sir," said Karl-Heinz, amazed.

Rommel's aide snapped several photos of the general and the captain. Then Karl-Heinz was dismissed with a friendly smile.

Back in Saarbrücken that night, he reported Rommel's request to von Totten, who was just leaving for Berlin. The colonel grinned. "That, with respect, *Arschloch,* that asshole will do anything to get himself promoted. He's already stolen everyone else's equipment, and he's always on my tail. I'm glad you've got him now. What's more, he'll probably get to be a field marshal. Right now he's the *Führer*'s favorite general. I hope, for his sake, he never gets disappointed. By the way," he asked, "can I bring a letter to your wife?"

"No, thank you. Just tell her I'm all right," said Karl-Heinz.

On Saturday, May 10, at five-thirty-five in the morning, Rommel's Seventh *Panzers* and every other German division in the west launched an attack. "Plan Yellow," the invasion of France, Holland, Belgium, and Luxembourg, had begun.

The following Monday, Karl-Heinz joined the Sixteenth *Panzer* Division, which jumped off from Saarbrücken as an observer. On Tuesday morning, May 13, almost symbolically, he was a passenger in a *Kübelwagen* command car, part of a large convoy on a narrow, forest-lined mountain road in the Ardennes, near the village of Neufchateau. He was chatting with the young staff lieutenant next to him, a red-haired fellow with a freckled nose. Suddenly, the lieutenant's right cheek was peeled back as if by a knife, and the left side of his face, still intact, began to smile incredulously. Then his right hand reached up and when it touched the fearful mutilation, he screamed, as blood, bone chips, and teeth poured into his raised sleeve. His eyes rolled up and he slumped into a faint. They had heard no artillery, nothing Karl-Heinz could remember, and yet it was a piece of anti-tank shrapnel that had mangled the lieutenant's face. Their driver slammed on his brakes and pulled as near as possible to the high bank that bordered the deep woods. Karl-Heinz and the others lifted the wounded man to the ground and got doused with his gushing blood. A medical sergeant from the vehicle behind them came running to help. While he was being bandaged, the lieutenant regained consciousness and began to scream. The enemy antitank gun that had hit them fired again, but this round skipped off the road, leaving a long, black streak, and exploded against a tree. Karl-Heinz and the driver, a *Gefreiter* corporal with a stolid farmer's face, walked into the woods, ducking from tree to tree, hoping to find who was shooting at them, but they saw nothing. For the first time, Karl-Heinz held his Luger pistol in earnest, safety catch off, hands sweaty with tension, ready to fire. A machine gun began to stammer up ahead, but they could not tell if it was one of theirs. They soon returned to the command car, so they would not get separated from the others. A *Panzer* from the Sixteenth Division rolled past, clanking and squeaking, headed toward the shooting. Soon they heard the first report of its rapid-fire cannon, in between machine-gun bursts.

An ambulance pulled up, and the wounded officer, now sedated with morphine, was loaded aboard. The ambulance swung around, needing many passes to turn on the narrow road, and headed back toward the rear. The lieutenant's blood was on the asphalt, on the back seats of the command car, and on Karl-Heinz's uniform sleeve. Everything smelled like a butcher shop, and he wanted to puke, which he eventually did in some bushes. No one saw him.

The firing up ahead finally stopped, and a *Kradfahrer* motorcycle driver appeared to signal "all clear," so they drove on, now one man short.

Karl-Heinz had his baptism. He tried to ban the wounded lieutenant's face from his mind, but the stink of blood made it difficult. Two kilometers ahead, they slowed down for a column of German infantry soldiers of the Sixteenth who had taken prisoners, tall, pitch-black French colonial troops in gray-blue *poilu* uniforms. Even as prisoners, they seemed wild and dangerous. The German *Landser* soldiers, victors in their first firefight, were triumphant, showing off like schoolboys who had just won a soccer match, and their loud boasting voices echoed in the forest. Their black prisoners were glum, not even speaking to each other.

"Senegalese," said the driver. "We heard they were up ahead."

That night they stopped at a makeshift command post in the police office of a village. Karl-Heinz and two other officers found a nearby farmhouse and moved in, after trying to reassure the skeptical French peasants, *"Nous sommes des amis!* We mean no harm. . . ."* The grizzled Ardennes farmer and his black-mustached wife were not convinced, but what could they do? They shrugged and raised their hands and puffed air through their pursed lips. *"Eh, b'en, il faut qu'on se débrouille!"* and they accepted the inevitable. Three hated *chleux* were living in their small house, they hoped for only one night.

One of the three, a radio officer on his way to a forward unit, negotiated for three bottles of cognac, and Karl-Heinz and the others took deep, deep swallows. This had been their first taste of battle, and they had only just met, but now they were like brothers. Karl-Heinz loved them, loved himself, loved the farmhouse, loved being alive when death had been *so close,* carried on the razor edges of a screaming, whirring, slice of French steel. Though quite drunk, he found a water pump in the farmyard and tried to wash his blood-encrusted sleeve. He wrung out a pool of pink water, and soon the sleeve seemed cleaner. Then he hung up the tunic in the room they shared, but it still smelled of blood, and now there was also the stench of wet wool. They kept drinking brandy until after midnight. The third man was a staff officer who had to report at four-thirty next morning, but he was too drunk to set the alarm on his wristwatch. They fell into drugged sleep. Fortunately for the staff man, they were awakened by an insomniac rooster that crowed shortly after four in the morning.

By six, the convoy was back on the move. Karl-Heinz's tunic was still damp. He was hung over, shaking and shivering in the chill morning fog. Their command car pushed on past gray-green fields and clusters of woods. He had not shaved, and he hoped that no senior officer would see him. The fast world of armored Blitzkrieg was new to him, as it was to most men in the column, only a few of whom had been in the Polish campaign.

At a bend in the road, they crawled past a burned-out French tank. One of its dead crew members was halfway out of the hatch, black charred face and hands broiled to the

blistered steel and paint of the hulk. The stench of fried flesh
and grease was overwhelming, and Karl-Heinz came near to
throwing up again. The clock in a nearby church tower struck
seven in the morning as they headed deeper into France.

Hilde had heard nothing from Karl-Heinz, but the newspapers
were filled with triumphant reports from the west, and she
guessed that Karl-Heinz was somewhere in the midst of it.
She wrote twice to the Saarbrücken address Zoss had furnished,
superficial letters, as light as she could make them, considering what she felt. Von Bernsdorfer had disappeared that next
morning and had not called. She was relieved, because she
had no wish to see him again. She pushed all thought of him
into the cellar of her mind, where she hid the very few
memories that shamed her. Hilde was so straightforward that
she usually faced all things in the open light. But not this one!
It would stay in darkness, along with a short-lived lesbian
affair when she was a sixteen-year-old schoolgirl, and the lust
she once felt for a young priest.

She debated whether to tell Zoss, and she finally did. After
all, part of that night was her fear that von Bernsdorfer had
uncovered Otto. Zoss, always the *homme du monde*, was not
shocked. He tried to reassure her as she sat in front of him,
ein Häufchen Unglück, a bundle of misery, trying to crawl
into her own skin. "How," she wailed, "how could it have
happened?"

"*Na, ja,* don't do that to yourself, Hilde, you're human."

She began to sob angrily. "With that swine! With that
filthy swine!"

"Yes. Bad judgment. Should have been me."

She began to giggle despite her sobs. "You impossible, old
Scheisskerl!" she said.

"Old?" He looked aghast.

"All right, young *Scheisskerl*. How dare you make me
laugh when I'm trying to cry?"

"That's the trouble with virgins. They always cry."

"You made your point, Armin."

"Wish I had," he said wistfully. "By the way, Karl-Heinz
is fine. Von Totten came back from Saarbrücken and told me
that our young captain is the social lion of the *Panzer* generals.
Well, not all of them, but Rommel, that operator, found out

that Karl-Heinz has a direct connection to Brunzig, and he immediately tackled him for the latest equipment.''

"Rommel? Is that the general about whom there was a story in the *Berliner Illustrierte?*''

"In that and every other picture magazine.''

"*Na, ja,* I'm glad my husband is the new star of the *Wehrmacht*. It's what I always dreamed about. That, and this insane war.''

"Anyway, it looks as if France will surrender any moment. The British managed to get most of their troops out at the port of Dunkirk. Our troops will take Paris within days. I can get Karl-Heinz assigned to Paris, or do you want him here?''

"The truth?''

"Yes.''

"Paris.''

"I shan't try to get at the story behind that.''

"Nothing to do with von Bernsdorfer. That's over.''

"Good,'' said Zoss. "In that case, since Karl-Heinz is now of no use to Otto, I'll try to find things for him to do in Paris. As a matter of fact, I can use him for something, but he won't know he's being used.''

"Any danger?''

"None. The risk is all mine.''

"Careful, Armin.''

Gerhardt Brunzig arrived in Berlin and was staying with Zoss. That night they went to Horcher's. The restaurant was jammed with patrons in uniform, and they were almost the only guests in civilian clothes. Despite the *Führer*'s admonition to serve simple food (they now cooked only stews at the Berghof), Horcher's menu was as lavish as ever. The place quivered with the mood of victory, and diners' voices were loud and boisterous. Who could have guessed that German troops would wipe away the best armies in the world? Of course, they confided in each other, everyone had known all along! Was there ever any question? They had believed in the *Führer* from the beginning. Of course, they had!

A young, balding *Luftwaffe* general came into the dining room and was openly applauded. It was Kesselring, one of the first to win the Knight's Cross, the highest decoration. His dive bombers had cleared the way in Poland and were now supporting Rommel and the others in the west. These air force fellows were the envy of the senior army staff, because they were so mobile. Kesselring could leave his headquarters in France, fly to Berlin for a *Führer*-conference, have dinner at Horcher's, and fly himself back to France in the morning. *Sehr schneidig!* Very snappy!

Herr Horcher gave Gerhardt Brunzig an effusive greeting. Generals and politicians were important, but in the long run, luxury restaurants would still depend on captains of industry.

When they had settled at their table, Gerhardt Brunzig said, "I have a plan for Brunzig. It may fit in with your, er, other interests."

Armin Zoss nodded. He had to listen carefully because Gerhardt spoke so softly that he was almost drowned out by the voices of other diners. He continued, "When this is over, no matter what, we must keep our firm alive. They"—and he waved an elegant hand at the other diners—"they may think that this will be over in two months. But I don't."

"You don't sound optimistic."

Brunzig shook his head. "I received a confidential message from a friend, an American, who does a lot of business in Russia. He says the Russians expect to be attacked by us. He does not believe that we will invade England. I have no idea where he gets his information, but I've never known him to be wrong." Gerhardt Brunzig casually looked around the room. To others, he might have been dishing out gossip. Not many people recognized him. He was rather a mystical figure, hidden away in his large mansion, or on yachts, in private clubs, and in big hotel suites. Of course, Willy Horcher knew him, but generals who would have given a year's pay for an introduction failed to recognize him.

Gerhardt Brunzig went on, "I want you to go to America. It's important that you begin organizing for the postwar period. You will be paid through an Argentine bank. Naturally, your apartment here stays open. Rent and your servants will be paid by us."

"How do you explain my trip?"

"America is neutral. We at Brunzig want to learn some of their manufacturing techniques to help us with the war effort. I'll invite certain American automobile executives to visit us after we've sent you there. Some people in Detroit are pro-German and very anti-Roosevelt."

"What if the Americans get into the war?"

"We can bring you home by way of Argentina. I have friends there. Usually, in case of war people are given a day or two to clear out. I'm sure the Americans will behave correctly."

"What about you?" said Zoss.

"I shall stay here. That's my job," said Gerhardt, no playboy now.

Zoss nodded. He asked, "Would there be time for me to make a brief trip to Paris? The city will surrender any day now, and I want to get Dorn settled there."

"Certainly, if you consider it important. By the way, what about Dorn? Is he part of your group?"

"No. His wife, yes, but not Dorn. He . . . well, it doesn't matter. However, I do think he can be of some real use to Brunzig, because the army boys love him. As for my group, he may not be with us, but at least he's not against us."

"*Schon in Ordnung.* Whatever you say. And how about Hilde Dorn? I like her. She's *ein nettes Frauenzimmer*, really first-class."

"That she is. I think their marriage is in trouble." Zoss was tempted to tell about von Bernsdorfer, but it would have served no purpose.

Brunzig nodded. "So sorry to hear that. They were having a fight while they were staying at Ritterschwert."

"You won't believe this, Gerhardt, but Dorn has become Rommel's favorite new contact with Brunzig."

"Rommel? He seems to be on his way up."

"*Und wie!* And how! So I'd like to keep Dorn near Rommel." Zoss lowered his voice to a whisper. "Sooner or later, Rommel will fall out of favor. Meanwhile, he can be Brunzig's unpaid propaganda agent in the army."

"Zoss, you have the most devious mind since the Renaissance."

Zoss whispered, "Me? How about the Austrian corporal?"

Karl-Heinz had not seen Paris since Siegfried Schmidt had taken him there on a KaDeBe buying trip. Then they had stayed in a cozy little Gauloise-reeking hotel near the Place Vendome. Now things were different. *Hauptmann* Dorn was quartered in a requisitioned luxury apartment on the Place Victor Hugo near *Wehrmacht* headquarters.

Prewar French superiority and chauvinism seemed to have

disappeared. German troops had been in Paris only three weeks, but the French had already adapted themselves. Germans, *chleux* as they were called behind their backs, were regarded with a certain degree of reluctant admiration. They were accepted as a fact of life and as part of the foreseeable future. There was even legitimacy in collaborating with the conquerors. After all, *Maréchal* Pétain, one of France's most venerated men, had asked everyone to do so!

Karl-Heinz's ground-floor apartment, which he shared with a *Wehrmacht* medical officer, belonged to a retired Paris lawyer. The old man, a widower, had gone to live with his children in Neuilly and had left behind his housekeeper. That efficient woman *d'un certain âge* had the blowsy looks and superb culinary ability of a bordello madam. She soon performed Parisian marvels with their daily German army rations. Karl-Heinz and his roommate naturally assumed that she sold some of these foodstuffs on the *marché noir,* but they decided not to interfere as long as she kept their lives comfortable.

Zoss arrived at the apartment two days after Karl-Heinz moved in, and so did Colonel von Totten. Zoss carried a letter from Hilde, and Karl-Heinz excused himself at once to read it. He sat in a corner of the living room while the others poured cognac for themselves. Her letter was bland, noncommittal, banal. She wrote about the weather, her church, her work as a volunteer for war orphans, but the kernel of affection, the promise of love and continuity was missing. He tried to grab at straws because she had finished the letter with "Much love to you," but then he remembered that this was her standard south German way of ending letters.

Zoss, who saw his long face, said, "Come on, Dornchen, first we'll visit some French friends and then on to Fouquet's."

Zoss's friends, the Boucherons, were an attractive and well-to-do middle-aged couple. He had been deferred from the French army because he was assigned to the Ministry of War, so now he was home in Paris and not a prisoner of war like so many others. They owned a lavish apartment on Avenue Foch.

The old Rothschild mansion across the avenue had just been turned into Gestapo and S.D. headquarters, and the Boucherons adored gossip, so they immediately told of the many Parisians, mainly Jews, who had been locked up over there.

"Enfin," said Georges Boucheron raising his shoulders, *"les juifs* really did a lot of harm. They were, after all, *pas des vrais Français* and, not being really French, they controlled too much of our press and the banks."

Boucheron's wife, Natalie, slim and carefully groomed—a blue-eyed *normande*—nodded her complete agreement.

Boucheron continued, "We were manipulated into this mess by the Jews and the English. We could have stayed at peace! Who do you think made the real money out of our Maginot Line that was never finished? And all the guns and tanks we were supposed to have? Whose pockets got lined?" Boucheron pushed out his lower lip in that Gallic gesture that says, "I leave it to you to understand."

Zoss had known him for a long time, because Boucheron was once a Brunzig distributor. He tried to conciliate. "Well, at least it's over now. Do you think it will be difficult for you French to adapt yourselves?"

"Pas du tout, du tout!" Boucheron waved his hands for emphasis. "Of course not. That idiot de Gaulle is, *excuse moi*, Natalie, he is making *pipi* into the wind. Now let's have peace and start again to live like normal people. I think you will have our complete cooperation, *j'en vous assure!"*

Natalie Boucheron poured Dubonnets, and they drank. Then the three Germans excused themselves. They strolled slowly through the lovely July evening toward the tall Arc de Triomphe, where the eternal flame flickered over the Unknown Soldier buried there. Parisians were coming home from work, and traffic was amazingly heavy although gasoline was rationed. There were dozens of pretty girls on bicycles, and Zoss eyed each and every one enthusiastically. From time to time, Colonel von Totten and Karl-Heinz returned the salutes of German soldiers and of Paris policemen, the *flics*. As they rounded the Etoile at the top of the Champs Élysées, von Totten was saluted by a *Hauptsturmführer* of the SS Death's Head *Panzer* Division. The man flung up his arm in the party salute, and von Totten touched his cap in the traditional army way.

"*Herr Oberst,*" said the SS officer, "we've met before."

"Did we, captain?" They all stopped.

"At the Berghof. I am Colonel Telesty's adjutant."

Von Totten introduced Zoss and Karl-Heinz. The captain acknowledged each introduction with *"Heilitla!"* and a raised

arm, causing glances from passing Parisians. It was still new
to them!

"Is Telesty here?" asked von Totten.

"Yes. They're forming a new unit called *Brandenburg*,
and the *Herr Standartenführer* is here to find some men for
it."

"Was ist Brandenburg?"

The SS captain shrugged. "Sorry, can't tell you much
about it, colonel. It's Admiral Canaris's idea. Maybe it's a
Schnaps-idea. You know, the 'High C,' as we call Canaris.
He's quite unconventional. But my chief likes that. He hates
anything that goes according to regulations. Anyway, he can
explain the whole thing when you see him."

"Natürlich," said von Totten. "Tell him to contact me
through General Headquarters. I'm on the roster for as long
as I'm visiting here."

The SS captain left, and von Totten said: "The High C,
Admiral Canaris, is such an obscure man! I know he's chief
of all *Wehrmacht* Intelligence, but I also happen to know that
he's got his doubts about *Onkel* Adolf. He and Telesty! What
a combination! I don't know which one is the bigger
opportunist."

"I'll tell you in strict confidence," said Zoss, "that Telesty
tried to blackmail Gerhardt Brunzig in Monte Carlo last
summer. Gerhardt told him to go to hell and then *tipped* him,
like a headwaiter. Not bribed, tipped! I think we can buy
Telesty as soon as he gets the slightest doubt about his
brown-shirted friends."

He suddenly realized he had been talking Otto business in
front of Karl-Heinz. "Sorry, Dornchen, didn't mean to involve you in this."

Karl-Heinz said, "I heard nothing."

At Fouquet's, the old restaurant on the Champs Élysées,
they were shown to a big, front table. At first, they felt a bit
uncomfortable, but the French around them did not seem to
pay much attention so they settled down to enjoy their meal.
Besides, they were not the only Germans there. Three SS
officers were at the other end of the room, tall young men
with S.D. diamonds on their sleeves, obviously secret police
headquartered in the Rothschild mansion.

Von Totten shook his head. Speaking under his breath, he
said, "Armin, your friends the Boucherons sounded like

absolute swine! They've swallowed all that Goebbels nonsense. You know, old Petain reminds me of our old Marshall Hindenburg: senile. *Verkalkt!''*

"Na, ja,'' said Zoss. "You're quite right! Of course, the Boucherons were also kissing our asses, trying to ingratiate themselves. However, I get the impression that many French are more concerned with their pocketbooks than with their imperishable honor. And I can sympathize with that completely. It's better to live comfortably and in peace than to get your rearside removed by shrapnel. What I object to is the way they've adopted a lot of racial junk that Hitler once invented to appeal to our poor, beaten-up, inflation-ruined Germans of the 1920s. Goebbels's boys will have an easy time here.''

Karl-Heinz nodded sadly. "Yes,'' he said, "I suppose you're right about the whole party philosophy. Even my father found it appealing because he was one of those poor bastards you talked about. He was so happy when he first joined the party, but I think that he would be miserable by now, just like the two of you. By the way, I've been meaning to talk to you. This is as good a place as any.'' He looked around, making sure that no one was within earshot. "I once told Hilde that Otto should wait until we've won. I think we're now getting close.''

Zoss smiled ironically. "How much closer do you want us to get? If England falls, we'll never get rid of these *Schweine*. They'll tell us how to eat, sleep, defecate, and fornicate. The more they win, the more arrogant they get.''

Karl-Heinz shook his head. "I still don't think we *were* ready for Otto last year. But, I must admit, our country doesn't seem in any danger now, the way we could have been last September. The French caved in, and the English ran home. At least we won't have English Tommies kicking us off the sidewalks on Kurfüstendamm. But please, give me more time!''

Zoss said, *"Guter* Karl-Heinz Dorn, you must do what you think is right for yourself. Enough of that. Now I have something I want you to do for Brunzig.''

"Of course. Anything.''

"I want to see Rommel again. I want you to introduce me. He's in Paris on leave.''

"I'll try my best, but I'm only a captain. Colonel von Totten has better access with his rank.''

Von Totten smiled. "I admire your modesty, but I work
for the *Wehrmacht*, and Rommel knows you really work for
Brunzig. He'll be very, very accessible to you. *Keine Sorgen!*
Don't worry!"

The Ritz Bar was crowded, but instead of the usual English
and American regulars, now there were only French civilians
and German officers. The Italians stayed away. They got into
the battle at a suspiciously late time, and they could not count
on the same reluctant admiration many French felt for their
German conquerors. The Italians were *dégoûtants, affreux*, as
far as most Parisians were concerned.

Rommel stood at the entrance alone, a short man in a
well-tailored uniform and the top decoration from each world
war on his tunic. Every German in the bar recognized him,
but the French did not. Until now, the Rommel myth had
spread only inside Germany. His photos had not yet appeared
in the French press, although later the British would also
make a hero out of him, and even Churchill would eventually
pay him homage.

Karl-Heinz and Zoss got to their feet as Rommel walked
over to their table, as soon as he spotted the young captain
with the Italian ribbon. A few other decorations were now on
Karl-Heinz's tunic, including the Infantry Storm Badge and
the ribbon of the Iron Cross Second Class. Rommel made a
mental note to have the First Class Iron Cross awarded to this
young fellow who seemed to keep his promises. *For services
to the Seventh Panzer Division*.

"*Herr General*," said Karl-Heinz, cracking his heels together in classic style. "May I introduce *Herr Generaldirektor*
Zoss of Brunzig A.G.?"

"An honor, *Herr Generaldirektor!*" said Rommel, his turn
to crack heels. He took note of the party badge on Zoss's
navy blue business suit. Soon Rommel, sipping cognac, outlined the strength of the Seventh Division and what it could
do.

"But we've won, *Herr General*," said Zoss.

"No." Rommel shook his head. "There's still England."

"*Natürlich*, England." Zoss agreed. "Now for *that*
campaign, we may have something new to show you. But this
is not the place to describe it. Can I get you to Stuttgart?"

"Easy. I'll be going on a short trip to Berlin and Munich, and I can certainly stop off."

"Good. If you'll leave word with *Hauptmann* Dorn here. There is a chance I shan't be there, but Colonel von Totten, whom you know, and Captain Dorn can show you what we have in mind."

"Nebenbei," said Rommel, "just between us, I'd prefer that my visit to Brunzig be unofficial. My chief, Guderian, might not be keen on the idea. But you can depend on me to do my best for you in every way!" Then he pointed to Karl-Heinz. "And your young man here is very dependable. You can be proud of him."

"We are," said Zoss. "We are!"

Two A.M. by the wristwatch on Karl-Heinz's night table. He had turned out the light an hour earlier, bored with the latest novel someone had brought from Berlin. He was determined to get to sleep, but he was still wide awake.

Zoss was going to America, Zoss, his only link with Berlin and Hilde!

What was it Rommel had said? "You can be proud of this young man"? Was he proud of himself? According to Hilde, he had little to be proud of. Yet he was twenty-nine years old, an officer, seemingly well regarded. For a boy who had never gone to university and who had been very poor . . . What did they *expect* of him? What did Hilde, Zoss, von Totten want him to do? It was not in him to break rules, to rebel. He never had the arrogance to say he knew better than the majority. Since he was a child, he had done everything the way he had been told.

Had he done wrong? He could not remember a single vicious or mean thing. Perhaps, just perhaps, he let Schmidt's fate slide past him too easily. But Schmidt had landed on both feet in England, according to that letter to Hilde.

He knew now that the Hitler *Bonzen* were rotten! But what could he do about them? Germany was more important than the Nazis! He was still sure that first the war had to be won. Even the slightest danger had to be eliminated. The English had taken a thrashing, but they were still dangerous: troops all over the world and the vast British Empire to come to the island's defense. They had to be fought.

He missed Hilde.

• • •

Von Totten and Telesty met in an office at Paris *Wehrmacht* headquarters.

"Brandenburg?" Telesty shrugged his shoulders. "*Na, ja,* the *Brandenburgers* are a new unit, a tough bunch of bastards, and they'll be doing all sorts of specialized work. By the way, you've met Gellstein?" He pointed at the SS captain they had seen on the Champs Élysées.

"Yes," said von Totten, nodding at the SS man. "It all sounds very vague and interesting. By the way, I didn't know Gellstein is part of the Death's Head Division?" He pointed at Gellstein's sleeve stripe.

"He isn't," said Telesty, and Gellstein shook his head. He said, "Some Brandenburg people got permission to wear *Totenkopf* identification, because the division is around here now. It's a good cover."

"I still don't get it, Telesty. What in hell *is* Brandenburg?"

"I'll try to explain it. Canaris, you know him, decided we needed a small, mobile attack force of linguists and fighters who could do disruptive work. They'd know how to wear enemy uniforms, speak their language, use enemy weapons. At first it sounded crazy, but then I got to like the idea. It's an interservice outfit with members from the army, *Luftwaffe,* navy, and *Waffen*-SS. The reason for all the pretend identification is that we prefer not to be well known. All that I'm telling you is highly secret, and I had to get special permission to brief you, because there is someone I would like to recruit, and you know how I can get him."

"I won't ask you who right now. But I do want to say that the whole thing sounds highly illegal and against all international rules of warfare." Von Totten shook his head indignantly.

"Illegal? Are you kidding?" Telesty laughed. "The British invented the whole thing during the Boer War. And who cares? We're bombing the *Scheisse* out of London this week. By the end of this month they'll have flattened the whole of residential Whitechapel and all the Jews in it! Is that legal? Do you know what our wonderful SS *Sonderkommandos* are doing in Poland? Legal?" Telesty shook his large head. "Listen, my good von Totten." He pointed at Gellstein's *Totenkopf* sleeve band. "During the move through France, the *Totenkopf* boys captured a bunch of Tommy prisoners from the Royal Norfolk Regiment. Knöchlein, the *Totenkopf*

regimental commander, was in a hurry, so they machine-
gunned a hundred of 'em! The shit village where it happened
was called Le Paradis, would you believe it? The SS people
involved are a little nervous about the whole thing. It was not
quite cricket, as the English would say. But not one of them
has committed suicide. Legal? Hah!''

"All right. Whom do you want to recruit?''

"Dorn."

"Dorn?"

"Speaks languages. Knows his way around. Is a good,
athletic specimen.''

"I don't know," said von Totten. "He's Brunzig's boy.
And now Rommel's.''

"Rommel's?" There was respect in Telesty's voice.

"Yes. The general sort of adopted Dorn.''

"*Na, ja,* that's a pity. But try for me, would you? If you
fail, get me Gerhardt Brunzig. We could dress him up as the
Duke of Kent!'' Telesty pounded his knee, devastated by his
own humor.

Karl-Heinz was ordered to report to Place Trocadero, within
sight of the Eiffel Tower, where an honor company of infantry was lined up under a cloudless September sky, and where
he became one of thirty officers that morning who were
awarded the Iron Cross First Class. It was pinned on by a
blubbery little staff major from General Headquarters.

Drumroll. "In the name of the *Führer,* to *Hauptmann*
Dorn, K.-H., for valiant service in support of the Seventh
Panzer Division! By order of Lietuenant General Rommel,
Commanding General!''

Salute (the major).

Salute (Karl-Heinz).

Drumroll and on to the next officer to be decorated.

The major nearly stuck Karl-Heinz in the lower left rib
cage where the cross was pinned onto his tunic.

Paris spectators who lined the makeshift parade ground
looked on with envy, their own adored days of military
pageantry over for now. But *il faut qu'on avoue,* one had to
admit that *les chleux* did these things well.

Then came the "Deutschland" anthem, crashingly played
by the parade band, and finally the *"Horst Wessel"* song, the
party anthem, the *Führer*'s favorite.

Parade dismissed!

Later, as Karl-Heinz walked toward the Rondpoint on the Champs Élysées, a tall SS colonel came alongside. Telesty!

After Karl-Heinz saluted, Telesty put his arm around his shoulder. "Dornchen," he said, "do you know Gellstein?" The two captains exchanged army and SS salutes. "Come on," said Telesty, "Let's have a drink." His huge hand steered Karl-Heinz toward the cafe on the square ahead. Then he looked at Karl-Heinz's chest.

"*E.K. Eins?* When did you get it?"

"This morning."

"Congratulations! Now we really have something to celebrate!" They settled at a table on the outdoor terrace, and Telesty ordered champagne. "You know," he said, "they tell a story about this café: Just before the war, a rich Jew gets out of Berlin just ahead of the Gestapo, who had almost nailed him for *Devisenschieben,* for currency smuggling. He gets to Paris without a piss-pot to his name, and he slumps down at a table here in this café and tries to figure out what to do next. His whole life is in the dung heap. A small bird sitting up there in a chestnut tree"—Telesty pointed to the branches overhead—"this little bird shits . . . right on the Jew who's down here, moaning. To the Jew, this is the last straw. He looks up at the bird, shakes his fat fist and yells, 'For the *Goyim* . . . you *sing!*' "

Karl-Heinz could not help laughing because it was so unlikely that this tall SS colonel could do such a creditable imitation of a little Jew. Gellstein laughed, too, dutifully.

Karl-Heinz asked, "How do you know so much about a Jewish accent?"

"You must be joking," said Telesty. "I'm from Vienna, and we Viennese always lived surrounded by Yids. Why, half the slang words we Viennese use are Yiddish. You can imagine what happens when SS people arrive from Berlin and some blond, blue-eyed Aryan Austrian SS kid, who looks like he's straight from a propaganda film, says, '*Das macht mich vollkommen meschugge,*' or '*Das ist wirklich nebbich.*' The sow Prussians—pardon me, Dorn—the Prussians go mad when they hear us say *meschugge* or *nebbich.* Do I know Jews? Hah!" Then Telesty leaned his massive head close to Karl-Heinz and spoke softly, "Now, to other matters. It's a good thing we met. I've been meaning to talk to you. We're forming a new unit, an interesting one.''

''Yes,'' said Karl-Heinz, ''Gellstein mentioned that.''

''We could use you,'' said Telesty.

''Was that the Brandenburg outfit you mentioned?'' Karl-Heinz asked Gellstein. Gellstein nodded. ''What,'' he asked Telesty now, ''does the Brandenburg unit do?''

''Sabotage. Infiltration. Disruption. Hell-raising. All behind the enemy lines. Of course, England is next.''

''Hard to avoid being caught?''

''Not if you're wearing enemy uniform. But we can't discuss that here.''

''Sounds crazy!''

''*Ohne Frage*. No question about it.''

''I'll think about it.''

''I'll give you a week.''

''What if I say no?''

''I'd be very disappointed.''

''Did you speak to Zoss about this? They need me for Brunzig.''

''No. To von Totten.''

''What did he say?''

''That it was up to you. This is a voluntary assignment.''

Telesty was cordial and joking, but Karl-Heinz noticed that Gellstein stared like a maniac. They made his skin crawl.

The next morning Karl-Heinz phoned Rommel's aide, and an appointment was made in Rommel's suite at the Crillon Hotel.

Karl-Heinz stood at stiff attention. ''*Herr General*, I want to express my deep thanks for the great honor you have bestowed on me. The Iron Cross is so much more valuable because you, *Herr General*, have seen fit to recommend me.'' It was the second decoration he had received without performing any deeds of daring. One automobile delivery and one personal introduction. Should he be ashamed? To hell with it. He hadn't asked for either honor!

''*Na, ja*,'' said Rommel. ''*Schon gut*. That's all right.''

''*Herr General*, may I respectfully ask a favor? After we have visited Stuttgart together, may I be assigned to your staff? I would learn a lot, and I would try to be of help.''

''Why not? Good idea, Dorn! I'll have orders prepared.''

No harm having the Brunzig liaison man at his beck and call. A direct line to Stuttgart!

When Telesty called a week later, Karl-Heinz told him he had been assigned to the personal staff of General Rommel.

Two days later, he accompanied the general and Colonel von Totten to Stuttgart, where the general was the first outsider to see a new amphibious landing vehicle, capable of taking heavy surf, and able to crawl onto a pebble beach. Dr. Maut had designed it as the ideal infantry assault vehicle for *Seelöwe*, Sea Lion, as they had codenamed the invasion of Great Britain. Rommel looked impressed and asked that the prototype be sent to Boulogne so that he could conduct his own tests.

Life around Erwin Rommel, lieutenant general of *Panzer* troops, was exciting! The following week Karl-Heinz got into the film business. Dr. Goebbels had ordered the general to help produce a film called *Victory in the West,* the story of the lightninglike campaigns against France, Belgium, Holland, and Luxembourg. The general loved it. He moved troops, worked out the logistics, even directed French prisoners of war, both black and white, who had to reenact their surrender. The whole thing was as realistic as possible, and Karl-Heinz appeared in several heroic close-ups, eyes sweeping the horizon, profiled against the rising sun.

One night in a village near Sedan, he met two men in technical officers' uniforms, both with the rank of major. He recognized one immediately: Fritz Scharn, the actor. The other turned out to be Erich Forstmann, the famous film director. Scharn looked wonderful and the uniform suited him, but Forstmann was morose and tired. They were at dinner in a small *auberge* that had become a temporary film-production center. At first, they paid scant attention to the young captain who sat down at their long table and introduced himself.

Then Forstmann said, "Dorn? Are you a friend of Armin Zoss?"

"He's my chief at Brunzig. I'm here on General Rommel's staff."

"Then your wife is Hilde?"

"You know her?" asked Karl-Heinz, amazed.

"She came to our house in Wannsee," said Forstmann.

"Zoss brought her about a month ago. A delightful girl. My wife took a great liking to her."

"How did Hilde look? I'm told she works hard at the orphanage. I haven't seen her in many months."

"She looked wonderful. She's very pretty. You're a lucky man."

"I agree. Now, about this film you're making; it's been quite an adventure for me, but it must be lots of dull work for you."

"Na, ja," said Forstmann. "I suppose it's all necessary for morale on the home front." He seemed less than enthusiastic. Scharn shook his head. "Dr. Goebbels absolutely insists that Erich must direct battle scenes, and Erich hates doing them."

"Gott sei Dank, thank God," said Forstmann, "that your General Rommel is a better battle director than I am. I could have ruined thousands of meters of film, but your General Rommel had everything ready for the camera, even the poor Senegalese prisoners. They moaned and groaned like hundreds of King Lears, trying to act as if they were scared of us Germans. I had to tone them down. We were not making *Onkel Tom's Hütte!"*

Scharn and Karl-Heinz laughed. Every German kid knew the American story of *Uncle Tom's Cabin.*

"For me it's a pity this film stuff is over," said Karl-Heinz. "Now, I've got to go back to Boulogne for troop training. Miserable!"

"When you get to Berlin on leave, come out to Wannsee," said Forstmann. "And bring Hilde."

"Gemacht," said Karl-Heinz. "How about you, *Herr* Scharn? Will you be back in Berlin?"

"No idea, dear boy. I go wherever the good Dr. Goebbels sends me."

Armin Zoss told his butler to leave the cognac tray.

Then, when Hilde and he were alone, he told her that he was leaving for America. She was shocked. He meant a lot to her. He was friend, guide, confessor. She had told him all about the end of her marriage, and it was only at his urging that she had kept the charade alive. She did not wish to run home to her parents in Nürnberg. Berlin still had a semblance of freedom even in the middle of a war. There were still occasionally people who spoke their minds. Nürnberg, on the other hand, was completely taken over by the fever of victory and fervently National Socialist. Reading "through" her mother's carefully phrased letters, she could gauge the depth of her parents' frustration and their helplessness, but they had no choice but to stay. Their livelihood was in Nürnberg.

Shocked by Armin's announcement, stunned by her impending loss, she now put her face in her hands and wept. He gently moved her fingers, cupped her chin, and kissed her mouth. Then, for the second time since her marriage, Hilde made love to a man other than her husband.

This time it was neither lustful nor debauched. She was so happy to please him. It was her farewell gift.

S.S. *Sao Paolo,* a neutral Portuguese passenger ship, bound for Havana and Miami, was two days out of Lisbon when a navy station in the Azores picked up her distress signal. She had been torpedoed and was sinking fast. A German submarine had obviously mistaken her for another ship. The *Sao Paolo* closely resembled a British armed merchantman that had recently sunk submarine U-46 in the Bay of Biscay. Also, the *Sao Paolo's* captain had been slow to answer the U-boat's challenge. It was sad, but as they said, "Fortunes of war!"

When the killer torpedo tore into her port beam just below the waterline, Armin Zoss was in the bar, dead drunk. It was early in the afternoon, and he had swallowed the better part of a bottle of Scotch during the last half hour. Since he had not been in the mood for lunch, the liquor settled throughout him, insulating him from everything. He wanted very much to be drunk. He had been drunk both afternoons since they left port.

A very pretty young American girl, fascinated by him, had dogged his every footstep, but he cared not at all. For once, Armin Zoss failed to respond to an attractive woman, and it drove the American wild. She was a student, on her way home to her rich parents in Greenwich, Connecticut, after two years at the Sorbonne. This was her last bit of freedom before reentering the strict Protestant world of Round Hill. The more Zoss ignored her, the more she followed him. She was blond, tall, and tanned, having stopped at the unoccupied Riviera on her way to Lisbon.

At the moment of impact, the ship shuddered like a vast

oak under the axe. The engine stopped, silencing the pulse of the ship. There were alarm bells and claxon horns. The white-faced Greek bartender excused himself hastily and ran for his life jacket and then to man his station.

A drunken Zoss tried to adjust his out-of-focus eyes and brain. He stumbled to his cabin, tore the life jacket from an overhead rack, stuffed his passport and cash into his jacket pocket, and then lurched back out into the hallway and onto the promenade deck. The blond *Fotze,* the pretty cunt, the nuisance, could he help her? He saw her up ahead with a young ship's officer. Good! She didn't need him. He tried to remember his assigned lifeboat, but couldn't recall. Missing a step here and there, he climbed a companionway up to the boat deck.

Topside, there was panic! Many of the crew were still below decks, probably trapped or killed or trying to fight a fire that now sent thick smoke to the aft deck, pumped up through the brass ventilators. He stumbled toward the nearest lifeboat, where two small Portuguese sailors were trying to crank a balky davit to the outboard position, but they could not budge the winch. Zoss added his weight to the handle, and it began to move, the sailors sweating and cursing beside him. The davit was now in position. The two sailors manned the falls on one davit and, through the haze of liquor and smoke, Zoss found the catch that held the ratchet on his side. He loosened it, and the handle became fierce in his hands. He needed all his strength to keep it from running wild. The deck began to slant as the ship took more water, and thickening smoke blew down on him. Then a woman's voice behind him, choking, coughing: "Armin!" It was the American!

As he turned, startled, the huge handle got away from him, flailing at him with its thousands of pounds of torque. The first turn broke his right arm. The next pitched him forward where there was no lifeline, no railing under the lifeboat. He tried to hold on, but his right arm was now useless, and he slid overboard.

It took many days to report that he was missing and presumed drowned.

Most of them first heard the awful news of his death from Gerhardt Brunzig. He was one of the few to know Armin Zoss's exact travel arrangements and destination, and he was the first to be notified. Zoss had no close relatives. Brunzig was his real family.

Gerhardt had locked himself into his study at Ritterschwert for many hours, more shaken than when his own father had died. Armin Zoss had guarded him throughout his boyhood years and then guided him into the chairmanship.

Finally, his grief under control, he notified all his senior associates and then those close to Zoss, like Hilde, von Totten, Morgenroth, and Karl-Heinz. But guilt kept gnawing at him. What if he had not sent Armin on this mission?

When he reached Hilde in Berlin, she sensed the magnitude of his pain from his voice. She told him she was on her way to Ritterschwert.

"Why?"

"Because I would like to be there with you for a few days. Do you mind?"

"Of course not. You're always welcome here. I'll have someone pick you up at the station."

That first night they sat alone at dinner, wordless, lost in their own thoughts. Then slowly, during the next days, they began to speak about Armin Zoss, like two loving, orphaned children. Hilde and Gerhardt formed a deep and lasting friendship.

"*Gratuliere*, Anneliese!" Papa Hoegel grabbed her and bear-hugged her. "At last you converted that lousy bachelor." Anneliese von Konsky had become Anneliese Morgenroth the week before, very quietly, without newspapers and what the Berliners called *Tamtam* . . . fuss.

They were all in the lobby of the Oberhof, a sixteenth-century inn on the Ahr, a small stream that gurgled down the Eifel mountains. Since twenty-seven, when the beautiful and terrifying Nürburgring racetrack was first opened nearby, this little hotel had become *the* place for the international automobile fraternity. Twenty meters below the windows one could hook trout, and all around the inn terraced vineyards reached hundreds of meters toward the cloudy sky. The world's greatest race drivers were as familiar to the Oberhof as visiting royalty to the Hotel de Paris in Monte Carlo. The inn's owners had also accustomed themselves to the sad fact that their favorite guests might crash and die. How many times had they opened race drivers' rooms for glum friends and teammates who had packed the belongings of their fallen comrades? And yet, there was never the hint of any of this during the days of racing practice or on the morning before a grand prix. There were only animated, laughing, attractive people, drivers and their friends, as insouciant as golfers off to play eighteen holes.

It had been a full eighteen months since the Oberhof had last seen racing people. There was a war on, and all racing had been suspended for the duration. So it was with great joy that the desk clerk spotted the familiar, rotund Papa Hoegel and, within two hours, the great Hannes Morgenroth and his new wife. The walls of the *Weinstube* downstairs were lined with dozens of Morgenroth's photos. They began with the opening race in twenty-seven, which he had won in one of the old 330Ks, and ending with thirty-nine, still winning in one of the new low monsters of the last formula. What double joy, then, when a Brunzig racing transporter pulled into the narrow parking lot behind the inn. It was as if the war had never happened. A race car back at the Oberhof! *Yessus Maria!*

The official explanation was simple: A new fuel injector, something like a carburetor, had to be tested for use in tanks. What better way to test it than in a race car? What better man to test it than the great Hannes Morgenroth, now recovered from his terrible wounds of the year before?

The fact: Hannes had persuaded Gerhardt Brunzig that he had to find out if he could still drive at racing speeds. He could not afford to wait until the end of the war. Once his skills had rusted, he would never be able to regain them. Gerhardt was willing to do him the favor. He also wanted to retain Brunzig's number-one driver in near-efficient shape. As soon as the war was over, Brunzig would have to race again, and Morgenroth's skills would then be needed. So there was some selfishness in the machination that brought together race driver, car, racing manager, and several mechanics, and that caused the shuttered Nürburgring track to reopen. Fourteen miles a lap, over a hundred turns, every kind of surface, dip, straightaway, switchback, ridge, bump— the Nürburgring was a man-killer, but Hannes knew that it had to be the Nürburgring or nothing ever again. Although he had healed on the surface, he still felt constant pain from his mauled nerve endings and violated muscles, from stitches and scars. And, worse, it seemed to him, although he kept this to himself, that his vision, though good, was no longer as lightning fast. Even in simple road driving, things that were easy and instinctive before the Avus crash now demanded his concentration.

Something warned him that he might be finished when, as the Italian drivers would have said, it was *basta*. He was of half a mind to abort this return to the track. He had done it all before, after each crash, forcing himself back into the cockpit. But never before had he doubted his ability to shake off his wounds. Yet here was the car, the crew, Papa Hoegel, and, last but not least, his own considerable vanity.

Anneliese looked marvelous, fresh and perfumed, chic in sweater and slacks, *à la* Dietrich. She had just ordered an aperitif when she was called to the phone in the lobby. She returned minutes later, ashen-faced.

"Zoss is dead," she said without a preamble.

Papa Hoegel half rose. "How? *Um Gottes Willen,* how?"

"He was on his way to America for Gerhardt. His ship was torpedoed."

"Are they sure he's gone?"

"Quite sure. They searched for two days."

Hannes Morgenroth said nothing. Zoss and he went back a long way, the young race driver and the young Brunzig salesman. He slowly stood up. Now there was no way he could hide his physical pain. He limped over to the window and looked down at the Ahr River below. He stood there for a long time. Then he came back to the table and said, "I've decided not to try to drive again. I'm awfully sorry, Papa. I know I caused you a lot of trouble. I'll explain to Gerhardt as best I can. I just don't feel I'm fit. I have no right. Please give my apologies to the crew outside."

Then he took Anneliese's hand, and they both left the dining room.

Papa Hoegel understood. And he was relieved, because he had dreaded this day.

EUROPE

1940

THE AIR-RAID SIRENS started howling at eleven in the morning, but Londoners had grown used to them, and there was no change in their daily routine. They just went about their usual business. Siegfried Schmidt had been lucky. Many German Jewish refugees were arrested, sent to internment camps near Liverpool and the Isle of Wight, and then deported to Canada and Australia. The fear of a Fifth Column had taken hold. Many people who were probably genuine refugees from the Nazis could have been blackmailed through the relatives they left behind in Germany, and the British government did not wish to take any chances.

Siegfried Schmidt had finally managed to enlist in the Pioneer Corps, the only British army unit that accepted foreigners, once they had applied for British citizenship. Soon after he donned the drab wool battle dress of a greatly overaged "sapper," as privates were called in the Pioneer Corps, he was ordered into his commanding officer's presence. That good man, a major, could barely hide his grin, because Sapper Schmidt looked like a German army colonel in the wrong uniform. He told Sapper Schmidt that he had been posted to M.I. 5, the intelligence organization, and had been promoted to sergeant. He would be permitted to wear civilian clothes as part of his new duties.

Schmidt, who was proud of his British army gear, although

it itched him badly, was equally relieved to know that he could return to civvies without loss of dignity and without risking deportation. He was also gratified by his new rank. At M.I. 5 he became a resident expert on Berlin, since he knew every street, alley, corner, restaurant, and *Kneipe*. There were several Berliners in his section, and they formed an uncharacteristically boisterous group within the stately atmosphere of British army headquarters. Visiting officers were occasionally disoriented by the sound of booming Berlin voices telling dirty tales in German behind closed doors, followed by howls of laughter.

One Grenadier Guards colonel who was meeting someone for lunch said, "You chaps really treat German prisoners with a deucedly free hand, what?"

He was assured that every unseen Teuton voice belonged to a member of His Majesty's Armed Forces.

"Oh," said the colonel, "good show! You chaps are marvelous linguists!"

Schmidt's wife lived in Berkshire with friends, so he was not worried about her during air raids.

One day he was in one of the briefing rooms while a major with a paratroop badge and the green sleeve "flash" of the Intelligence Service put several photos in front of him. They all seemed to have been taken in Paris.

"We're trying," said the major, "to get to know as much as we can about this chap Telesty. He's a very wicked species, very clever, very tough. Here he is." He put down a regulation SS photo of an officer with a scarred face. "This came from his official file in Berlin."

Schmidt raised an admiring eyebrow. "That wasn't easy," he said. "I won't ask how you got it."

"Jolly good," said the major. "Because I certainly wouldn't tell you." He continued, "We're trying to establish associations with other factions. I know that sounds bloody complicated. Actually, we just want to know whom Telesty knows. I'll show you a photo taken in Paris about a week ago. Here is Telesty in a café with two men. Do you know who the others are?"

He put an enlarged snapshot in front of Schmidt. It was very grainy but in good focus. Telesty's back was to the camera, and two men were facing him. One was an SS officer. His sleeve was on the table: *"Totenkopf,"* the SS

Combat Division formed from the cadre of former concentration camp guards. The other man who was in army uniform, a captain with Iron Cross First Class, he was . . . *Karl-Heinz Dorn!* No question about it. Karl-Heinz was bareheaded, so, except for the army haircut, there was nothing to distract from his identification. It was Karl-Heinz all right!

"Know any of the other two chaps?" said the major's friendly voice.

Schmidt nodded. "Before I answer, sir, I realize it is my duty to tell you. Nevertheless, if it is at all possible, may I know if someone I identify is in grave trouble?"

"All right, old boy. I'll try my best. I'll fill you in if I can!"

"Well, sir, the army captain was an assistant of mine when I worked for a Berlin department store. His name is Karl-Heinz Dorn."

"National Socialist?"

"His late father was an old friend of mine. He became a member of the party when he was down and out. So far as I know, Karl-Heinz also joined the party, but he cannot really be considered a Nazi. It was opportune for him to join, that's all."

"Oh? How do you mean, opportune?"

"He went to work for Brunzig, and they suggested that all their executives join the party. It made all contacts with the government so much easier."

"What else do you know about his political leanings?"

"I know his wife. I could vouch that she is *anti*-Nazi. She came from a very liberal German family, very distinguished. In fact, she used to work here in London at the consulate, and they first met each other here at Walton's one night. I was there."

"Good show, Schmidt! Well, old boy, you're absolutely right, of course! We know all about Hilde Dorn. We have a full dossier on her. She's been very involved with certain people who are strongly anti-Hitler. We assumed that her husband was not a Nazi, so we were startled when we spotted him in this photo with Telesty. Of course, the whole thing might just be a coincidence. Perhaps *Hauptmann* Dorn is working for the anti-Nazi opposition. But Telesty is bad stuff. Absolutely dreadful chap! We've been trying to get at the bottom of a new thing he's brewing. Anyway, that's as much as I can tell you now. I'll get back to you, Schmidt, old boy.''

Schmidt could not believe that Karl-Heinz was working with a man like Telesty.

Then he thought back to the photo. Karl-Heinz, a captain. With an E.K. 1 on his chest! Old Herbert Dorn would have been so proud. . . . What irony!

Schmidt laughed. Sometimes he wished he did not understand so much, particularly about his former *Landsmänner*. The German soul was a burden, even for those who were not supposed to possess it!

Christmas 1940 was two weeks away, and the division had just been moved to Bordeaux. General Rommel had returned from leave to get them settled in their new sector, and had decided to stay with his men during Christmas, but Karl-Heinz got some leave so he took off for Berlin. After he boarded the train, he opened a letter that had just arrived from Hilde.

. . . expected at least some word from you about Armin's death. He was very good to you, and I cannot understand how you can just ignore this loss. Are you so taken up with your career or your new assignments that there is no time for normal feelings of decency? I am told that you are now an aide to General Rommel, whose face one knows because of the many articles about his victories and, also, because of his allegiance to the *Führer*. There was a recent Berlin article, calling him ''the *Führer*'s general.'' No doubt this is true. Anyhow, I still have no idea what I shall do for Christmas. Perhaps I shall visit my parents, since they are growing more and more isolated in Nürnberg. You will understand why. I spent a few days in Stuttgart with Gerhardt Brunzig to help him over his loss. Armin really took the place of his father in so many ways. Gerhardt and I have become good friends, which will no doubt please you. I confess that your behavior becomes more and more incomprehensible, and I would suggest that you should not plan Christmas here. I really would not know what to say to you, and all those hours we spent trying to adjust our differences seem to have vanished into thin air. I had some hopes, back there in Nürnburg, after the fuss out on the street, but you were obviously just showing off, partly because of your new uniform and also your adventures up in the mountains. Perhaps we can discuss all this sometime next year. Until then . . .

She finished with some superficial salutations.

Of course, he had written to her about Armin Zoss's death. And, of course, he was shocked. He was also ashamed to admit that he was slightly relieved, because Armin Zoss had loomed as his conscience. Zoss was Otto, and with Zoss's death he could shelve, for the time being, any decision about Otto. Nevertheless, and in part because of his shame, he was outraged by her letter. She was being "Saint Hilde" again, and he was tired of her holiness! He would continue on to Berlin, of course, and they would have it out, once and for all. Even if she had already left the city, he would find her. This might be their very last chance.

He had to change trains in Paris, and he took the first available train to Berlin with full instructions in case of enemy air attack, but they all knew it would never come. The R.A.F. fighters were much too busy over the Channel, holding off the *Luftwaffe*.

There was a happy Christmas mood in the compartment he shared with four other officers, and the closer they got to Germany, the more wine they drank, bought at each station along the way. It became a veritable *Tastevins* tour, starting with the Bordeaux, on to Burgundies, then Alsatian *vins gris* and finally, Rhine and Moselle wines. Although the train had many unexplained holdups, the passengers grew happier and drunker by the hour. The last part of the trip went quickly.

He was listening to some old dirty story his neighbor was telling when he looked up and they were already near his grandparents' grain mill. Then Potsdamn, Spandau, and finally, Berlin, lovely, familiar, cozy Berlin, the most *gemütlich* of all cities, as far as Karl-Heinz was concerned.

His solid, foul-mouthed, smiling, old taxi driver immediately informed him that he "wanted to congratulate *Herr Hauptmann* on his Iron Cross First Class but that he would still have to pay the fare!" Only Knight's Cross holders got free trips, and it was a good thing those heroes wore the Cross at the throat. That way, one could spot them and avoid them "like poison ivy up the rectum." Karl-Heinz felt at home.

They arrived at Adolf Hitler Platz, and he had almost moved his Iron Cross to the throat to make it look like a Knight's Cross so the driver would shit in his pants, but he was in a hurry, so he paid and took the snail's-pace elevator upstairs. There was a moment when he passed Zoss's floor . . . then he arrived at his own door.

He put the key into the lock and walked in. There was a letter on the floor. He picked it up. No Hilde. He set down his suitcase. The apartment was definitely closed up, no food in the refrigerator, and the beds had been stripped. Where had she gone? Nürnberg? Villa Ritterschwert?

The letter. "DELIVERED BY HAND."

Frau Hilde Dorn. Sender: SS *Standartenführer* von Bernsdorfer!

Should he open it? Of course. Von Bernsdorfer would write to Hilde only in order to reach him.

". . . so many months since we were together, and I cannot get that night out of my mind and body. I ache for you more than for any other woman I have ever had. . . ."

He phoned von Bernsdorfer and they met for late supper at the Eden Hotel. Von Bernsdorfer arrived ahead of Karl-Heinz. For a moment when he received the call from Karl-Heinz, von Bernsdorfer worried about his letter, but it was delivered days before and Hilde was certain to have read it by now. He had tried to phone her later, but could not reach her. Anyway, Karl-Heinz seemed at the top of his form, bubbly and cheerful, with a new E.K. 1 on his uniform.

Earlier in the evening von Bernsdorfer had been told that his staff days were over, and he welcomed the news. Sepp Dietrich's *Liebstandarte* Guards detachment was now a full-combat *Panzer* Division. *Herrlich!* Marvelous! He was fed up being a messenger boy. He wanted action, and he was impatient to get into the thick of things. He always felt the same way just before the start of his round in an international horse show, even better than sex: horseflesh through his knees and thighs, the long neck ahead of him, and the small brain for which he did the thinking, his decisions transmitted to the animal through a thousand little shifts and pressures. And then up to the tallest jumps! One final moment, and he would lift, yes, *lift* the ton of horse, leaning forward over the neck, looking ahead, past the ground, where they would land only to charge the next obstacle.

He sometimes came with the sheer joy of it, his erection held in place by the strap riders wore to avoid injury to their genitals.

Now he would enjoy these last evenings before joining the division. Champagne! Soon the England invasion would begin and he'd have the E.K. 1 *and* the Knight's Cross. The old cavalry song: *"Auf, auf Kameraden zu Pferd, zu Pferd . . . Im Felde da ist ja der Mann noch was wert. . . ."* "Comrades, mount up, mount up! In combat a man is still worthy. . . ." It sounded like Himmler-*Scheisse*, but something inside him wanted the taste of battle.

Karl-Heinz had never seen this other von Bernsdorfer, now no longer the controlled flunky.

"More champagne!" von Bernsdorfer yelled at the waiter. "And be goddamn quick! I shan't sit on my ass waiting for you! Nor will my friend here!"

A group of senior army officers at the next table turned to see who was making all the noise, and, of course, it was one of those SS idiots. Absolute swine, most of them. No manners. Army fellow with him . . . surprising!

Karl-Heinz would have cringed, but not this time. He said, "Didn't catch up with Hilde. She must have gone home to her parents for Christmas. But then, she didn't know I was coming home."

"Na, ja," said von Bernsdorfer. "Meantime you can have a good time in Berlin. I'm sure you didn't live like a monk in Paris, did you, *Bube?"*

"Oddly enough, I almost did. Hilde is quite extraordinary, you know?"

"Yes. I'm sure she is."

"But usually she's angry with me. Doesn't think that I'm principled enough."

"Principled?" von Bernsdorfer did not understand.

"She sometimes thinks I live too opportunistically. She has very high standards, you see."

"Very high, I'm sure." Von Bernsdorfer grinned. "But, you know, women were not created like us. We are naturally polygamous. It's the way of nature. I mean, what good would a fine stallion be unless one could put him to stud with many mares? And besides, I doubt if he could perform over and over, always with the same mare."

"Funny comparison, but there's something to it. Tough to keep getting horny over the same woman. Never happened to me until Hilde."

"Well, I'm sure that she's not completely holy. Women are just like all of us. Polygamy may not be natural to them, but now and then they get horny, too."

"Not Hilde. Funny you should say holy. I always call her that!"

"Oh? Well, perhaps you're right. I wouldn't know."

They drank on. By midnight they walked to a bar just off the Kurfürstendamm that looked almost like "old" Berlin: whores and drunks, although there were no queers. A pianist was playing prewar American *Schlager,* hit songs from the old movies, and French *chansons,* the sort of foreign music that the party frowned on.

"Paris," said Karl-Heinz, "that's where they still have good singers and good songs. Pity that Chevalier isn't performing, but a lot of the others are."

"Trouble is," said von Bernsdorfer, "that so many good songs were written by lousy Jews! Like all that *Scheisse* of Brecht and Weill, like *Three Penny Opera.* Even the old Dietrich songs. All Jew music, dammit. Have to admit it, though, they were good songs. 'In dreams I kiss your hand, madame . . . ,' 'Falling in love again . . .' " He hummed the old melodies: " *'Ich küsse Ihre Hand, Madame . . . ,' 'Ich bin vor Kopf bis Fuss auf Liebe eingestellt . . .'* " He was getting quite drunk. "Used to dance in the old Eden where we just ate. . . . There was a little Jew girl, her father was a banker and she could fuck, oh, how she could fuck! And she loved to be kicked around a little, to get the whip, like a good mare, screamed the damn house down when she fucked . . . came ten, twelve times each night. Jew women are good in bed, particularly when they're very young, seventeen, eighteen. Later they become flabby, fat, disgusting like all Orientals."

They kept on drinking, smoking, listening to the pianist, a fat Berliner, his bald head circled by a fringe of greasy, patent-leather hair. A stiff celluloid shirtfront dressed up his *smoking,* his tuxedo. When he sang prewar American songs, he seemed to speak English, but when Karl-Heinz asked him a question in English, the man said, *"Singen, ja. Sprechen, nein, leider!''* He confessed that he only knew words phonetically. Just like all the old-time Berlin jazz pianists! They learned the songs from American records.

"You speak good English, Dornchen," said von Bernsdorfer.

"Don't you speak it too?"

"Yes. The English riders taught me. And I also competed in London, at the Olympia Hall. Good sportsmen, the English! Hate to fight them, don't you?"

"Yes." Karl-Heinz was hoarse from smoking and trying to talk over the piano and the other voices. Anyway, it was time! "Let's get out of here," he said. "There must be some other place."

They walked out into the empty street. It was cold. Some light snow had fallen while they were in the bar. "I know a place," said Karl-Heinz, and they crossed the blacked-out Kurfürstendamm, their boots clicking on the pavement. Karl-Heinz aimed for Sybelstrasse, a quiet street nearby, and von Bernsdorfer followed him. He said, "You really know Berlin, don't you?"

"Born here," said Karl-Heinz. "Born two streets from here." They continued side by side, two uniformed men, marching in step. At a dark corner, Karl-Heinz stopped as if to find his way. Then he pulled a sheet of paper out of his pocket. "Here," he said. "This belongs to you." He handed it to von Bernsdorfer.

"What the hell is it?"

"I'll help you." Karl-Heinz flicked on his cigarette lighter, and then von Bernsdorfer knew that it was the letter to Hilde.

"Na, ja,'' he said. "I'm sorry. These things happen. Hate to sound ungallant, but, well, I was invited."

"Invited?"

"You know what I mean. I didn't look for it. It was offered. That's why I said what I did before, about women. They're not always so wonderful. You said so yourself."

"You're a real friend," said Karl-Heinz. "I'm so glad you're teaching me these things." Then he raised his open hand, kept it flat inside his army-gray leather glove, and slapped von Bernsdorfer's face as hard as he could. He could feel the man's nose crack sideways when the heel of his hand made contact, and even in the dim night he could see the instant flow of blood from both nostrils. Von Bernsdorfer's SS hat went flying into the gutter, and he reached up with both hands. He stood there, face hidden, legs spread, and began to sob like a small boy, his shoulders heaving. "*Scheisse, Scheisse, Scheisse!* Not my fault. Not my fault. Her fault. Didn't want to. She wanted to. Please, please! Please don't."

Karl-Heinz, anger waning, amazed by the collapse of this man, by his cowardice, had nothing to say. He turned on his heel and walked off. Von Bernsdorfer stood there, with his hands to his bleeding nose.

It began to snow harder.

He finally reached Hilde in Nürnberg. She was not as negative as he expected.

"I'm coming there," he said. "But I don't want to stay at your parents' house. We need time to ourselves. Please see if you can get a reservation in the Grand Hotel. You must have a lot of connections in Nürnberg. It's important."

"When are you coming?"

"Today."

She managed the impossible: a pompous suite in the Grand, opposite the railroad station, with a magnificent view of the old, walled city ascending toward the castle. At the focus of the living room was a heroic picture of the *Führer* in an open trenchcoat, held back by the hand on his hip to show the Iron Cross on his tunic. Obviously, the room had housed many Nazi *Bonzen*. The adjoining bedroom was cavernous.

Hilde walked in shortly after Karl-Heinz had checked in. She took a long look around.

"What?" she said. "No swastika bedsheets?"

Karl-Heinz shrugged. "The swastikas are all in the bathroom. Mainly in the toilet bowl."

"Do I detect a note of disgruntlement?"

"Mainly with the SS."

"Do they offend the army?"

"They offend me."

"Only you?"

"Particularly me."

"I don't follow your logic."

"I saw von Bernsdorfer."

She looked straight at him and said nothing.

He continued, "When I walked into the apartment, there was a letter from him to you. I opened it because I thought he was trying to reach me through you. But it was about your affair with him.''

''That's right.''

''Just like that?''

''No. Not just like that. I was at the bottom end of all black moods. You and I, in truth, had split up. I was heartsick. He called, and I let him come over only because he seemed to be threatening me and everyone else involved in Otto. On the phone he vaguely hinted at some secret he had learned. Actually, he was talking about having supposedly fallen in love with me, but I could not know that. Anyway, I slept with him, partly out of sheer relief that Otto was still safe, partly out of my own depression. . . . God knows why. It was only that one time. I'm not proud of it, but I also have no apologies. It happened. Now you must do as you think best.''

''I got your last letter as I was boarding the train.''

''You came, nevertheless.''

''Yes. I never took all your nagging seriously. It irritated me, but I put up with it. Inside, I started calling you 'Saint Hilde.' Now I found out you're not so saintly.''

''I never cheated on you before. But you let me down.''

''About Otto?''

''Partly. But that was only a symptom. I began to wonder if you would ever stand up for anything.'' She pointed at his Iron Cross. ''I see you got a decoration. Were you in combat? Is that how you won it?''

''I was in combat, but only by chance. I did not really get into the fight. I got the Iron Cross for being of help to Rommel. I managed to do him a favor at Brunzig, so he dished out an Iron Cross.''

''You're very honest. My compliments.''

''I believe you were equally straightforward with me just now.''

''Tell me about combat.''

''Nothing much to tell. I was in a car with another officer when we got attacked. Half his face was shot off, and I got covered with his gore. Then I went off into the woods, trying to find out who was shooting at us, but fortunately I never found out, else I might have joined the fellow who got mauled.''

''Is that the way it is in combat?''

''It was for me,'' said Karl-Heinz.

Hilde said, "I had word from Erich Forstmann that he met you. You made a great impression on him."

"He's crazy about you. Is he back in Berlin?"

"Yes. I think so."

"Let's take off tomorrow and visit him."

"I don't know."

"I'll phone him from here."

She did not answer.

"Look," he said, "here's the way it is: I know what I am. I agree, I'm an opportunist. But at least I've learned to recognize it. And you were quite wrong about me and Armin Zoss. I miss him terribly."

"Why didn't you write?"

"I did! Of course I did! It must have been lost."

"What happens next?"

"To us?"

"Yes."

"That's up to you," Karl-Heinz said. "You're the one with all the complaints."

"True. Maybe you're right. Let's visit the Forstmanns a few days. How long is your leave?"

"One week. Another four days."

They phoned, were invited, took the train, and got off at Potsdam, where Erich Forstmann came to collect them . . . in a BMW convertible just like the one they used to have! Like many summer resorts in the winter, Wannsee in December was cozy, and the lake was frozen.

The Forstmann house was filled with guests, including the Morgenroths. Karl-Heinz had not seen the *Rennmeister* since the Berghof, and he was shocked at how much he had aged. Anneliese was very solicitous of her new husband.

"How is business?" Karl-Heinz asked her.

"Gave it up. There are other things that matter more."

Karl-Heinz and Hilde kept to themselves the next few days. They took long walks in the snow-covered fields and skated on a pond. No one would have known that theirs was a last chance, a final effort. To the others the Dorns were the ideal couple. She had slimmed and hardened, and it became her. Karl-Heinz, at twenty-nine, began to show some premature gray hair, a heritage from his mother. They were an unusually good-looking couple even to the spoiled Wannsee crowd.

Several of the men were on leave after the Western

Campaign. The mood was odd. There was no denying that they were proud of the swift victory. This wealthy, successful group of resort dwellers, with their lavish homes, pools, tennis courts, Brunzigs, Mercedeses, Cadillacs, and motor launches, were not made of the stern stuff of the true National Socialist. Normally, they were too worldly and cynical to swallow every bit of the nonsense from the Propaganda Ministry, but, because of all that had happened, they were now "willing to give the devil his due." They shrugged off the vulgarity of the Nazi party bigshots who had become a new Wannsee presence, often by taking over Jews' houses, and who now swamped the clubs and parties. As for the Jews who used to own summer homes, surely they were all right, wherever they were? Anyway, it really was bad luck for them. And the Nazi *Bonzen?* Oh, well, in the old days there were also quite a few *nouveaux riches* and one had learned to put up with them!

One of the guests, a reserve quartermaster colonel, was home on leave from Brussels. He was a heavyset, tall man with handsome gray-white hair and the flushed skin of the habitual drinker. In civilian life, he had made a fortune as an importer of wines, and since the fall of France his Berlin company was booming. His wife was a Brunhilde-like Bavarian, wearing expensive French couture clothes. They had a large home nearby. Their blunt appearance was deceiving. Actually, they were worldly and knowledgeable, and good friends of the Forstmanns. The colonel spotted Karl-Heinz's Iron Cross. "Which division?" he asked.

"Rommel."

"What do you think of him, captain?"

"Exciting man," said Karl-Heinz, hedging his bets, glancing at Hilde to make her understand that he was stalling.

"Na, ja," said the colonel, "I'm not so bewitched with him. My job is to supply fuel and other things to that entire *Panzer-Korps,* and your man Rommel thought nothing of taking another division's provisions. He did it time and again. He obviously does not care about other commanders."

"I know what you mean," said Karl-Heinz. "You're right. He's, how can I put it, ambitious."

"Good boy! *Prima.*" The colonel laughed and patted Karl-Heinz's arm.

Hilde said, "You did not hear my husband criticize his

general, did you? I want him to come back to me without whip marks."

The colonel put his finger to his lips. "Not a word. We shall protect your handsome *Hauptmann* from his *verdammte* chief. But if I have any further trouble with Rommel, I'll know whom to call on his staff: *Hauptmann* Dorn!"

"How do you find things here in Wannsee?" asked Hilde. "Do you think it's changed a lot?"

"Not really," said the colonel.

"Aren't there a lot of new people?" she asked, probing.

"Yes. But I've been away in Belgium, so I haven't met many. My wife says they're mostly party people and from the south."

"Yes," said Hilde. "I'm from Nürnberg, myself. We sent them to you."

"Should I be grateful?"

"I'll leave that to you to decide," said Hilde. "What happened to all the Jewish houses? Karl-Heinz told me there used to be quite a few Jewish families who had summer homes here."

"*Na, ja,* they've left, of course, and sold their houses. We didn't know any of them personally, but we knew who they were, like the sons of the people who owned KaDeBe. What was their name?" He turned to his wife.

Karl-Heinz cut in. "Goldner," he said. "I used to work for them. The old *Kommerzienrath*—everyone called him 'Der Olle'—he was my first employer."

"Oh," said the colonel. "Of course! That's what they called him. . . . Well, they've left."

" 'Der Olle' killed himself," said Hilde.

"How long is your leave?" asked the colonel, changing the subject. Before Karl-Heinz could answer, Erich Forstmann told them dinner was served. From then on, the conversation stayed on secure ground, mainly about the occupation of the western countries and Berlin gossip. Erich Forstmann entertained them with tales of filmmaking, as produced and directed by Erwin Rommel. "In fact," he said, "you will find that our fine Captain Dorn has begun a career that will soon land him in Hollywood."

"Only," said Karl-Heinz, "if Lubitsch directs."

This caused a long pause in the conversation, until the colonel's tall wife, the most unlikely to do so, burst out laughing, and that released the others. As everyone in the room knew, the Jewish Ernst Lubitsch had gone to Hollywood long before. Hilde cocked an eyebrow at her husband. He went on like that for the rest of their stay. He no longer minced words, and several times he even dared to disagree with the official view of things.

Mostly he refused to let these spoiled Wannsee people forget that they used to have Jewish friends in their midst, as if he wanted some expression of doubt, some small admission of guilt, some slight regret. And he got it. Several people who would have preferred to ignore the subject eventually reminisced about Jewish neighbors. The Wannsee crowd was opportunistic and self-protective but not really cruel. Karl-Heinz recognized the symptoms.

He and Hilde found each other again. They were not the same people they had once been, but they began to like each other again, and once more they became lovers.

AFRICA AND GERMANY

1941

ON THE FOURTEENTH of February 1941, Karl-Heinz disembarked in Tripoli from a troopship. He was part of the newly formed *AfrikaKorps*, sent to Libya to bail the faltering Italian army out of a losing campaign. They wore a new, tan tropical uniform with pith helmets and British-style tunics, although their commander, General Rommel, was still dressed in field-gray wool. Karl-Heinz was part of the chief of staff's section, which moved into a pompous neo-Roman building. One of the first men he met in Tripoli was his old friend from Rome, the Marchese de Navone, still splendidly uniformed as part of the *Brigadi Imperiali*. Poor Navone! He was anxious to escape from a *maresciallo*, a very senior and sybaritic Italian field marshal, who used him as a pimp, butler, secretary, messenger, and wardrobe master. The handsome young marchese was bloated because of the rich bill of fare he was forced to provide for his demanding master.

"Dorn," he said, "*prego, prego* . . . get me assigned to become a liaison officer with you *Tedesci*. Perhaps with you Germans I can get my waistline back, and maybe I can even get into the war. The closest I've come to battle was when the British strafed our advance headquarters while I was taking a shit, and they hit the latrine hole next to me. Everyone thought I was wounded until they found out that I was only covered with dung. I stank for days and had to bathe in cologne.'' Karl-Heinz promised to try.

They went to an outdoor café and drank brutal North African red wine while Karl-Heinz told Navone how his unit was outfitted in Italy and then had some special training in Calabria, supposedly to learn tropical conditions. The biggest danger during training was not from heatstroke, but from gonorrhea. Calabrian girls were enchanted with the tall German soldiers, and *Wehrmacht* medical officers were kept busy battling V.D. On the troopship, a certain young lieutenant always came out of the lavatory with tears in his eyes and fire in his urethra. They named him *Flammenschwanz,* flame-tail.

"We heard that the *Führer* offered us troops earlier but that the *Duce* had refused them,'' said Navone.

"Apparently things are going badly for most of your divisions,'' said Karl-Heinz. ''Supposedly, your headquarters units are all that remain facing the Tommies.''

Navone blanched and ordered another bottle of wine. ''We had no idea! We thought our men were fighting superbly. Now it's even more important that I join you. Sheer self-protection!''

The white-djellabaed waiter, who spoke Italian with an Arabic accent, brought the wine. Navone poured two more glasses, finished his own at once, and quickly refilled it.

Two days later, when Karl-Heinz had his chief's ear for a few minutes, he ''respectfully suggested'' to the *Herr Oberbefehlshaber,* which was General Rommel's new title as supreme commander in Africa, that the Marchese di Navone, a brilliant young Italian officer and former aide to the *Duce,* could be of great use. Karl-Heinz knew that Navone would have much influence with the Italians by dint of Rommel's reputation. The general immediately saw the advantages of a direct back-door contact with the Villa Torlonia. But he had to make sure. ''Why is this Navone no longer with the *Duce?*''

"Herr General,'' said Karl-Heinz, inventing as quickly as he could, ''the marchese begged to be assigned to combat in Tunisia. He wanted to get away from the comforts of Rome when others were fighting in Tripoli. Instead, he was commanded to become the aide of a certain Italian field marshal whose name I'd rather not mention.''

"Why?''

"Because the marshal uses the marchese as a valet and procurer. The marchese is desperate to have a really meaningful assignment. You should have seen him, *Herr General,* when I promised to speak to you! He was beside himself. He is a great admirer of yours."

"*Na, ja,*" said Rommel. "I suppose we can do something." Dorn is a smart little bastard. All that flattery. But why not? This spaghetti aristo might work out fine. So far the Italians had not been too cooperative.

A request was made, and Navone got assigned to Rommel's headquarters. Soon he found himself on a Heinkel bomber, bound for Rome as a courier with a confidential message to Benito Mussolini.

Karl-Heinz's invented explanation had, fortunately, been correct. He still had back-door entrée to the *Duce*'s presence, so he managed to transmit Rommel's note in a confidential way. The sealed envelope contained a most flattering appeal to the *Duce*'s "indomitable fighting spirit," and named several Italian generals who were betraying their magnificent *Duce* by their laziness and cowardice, "a trait which is so completely out of character for the modern Fascist legions." Could the *Duce* replace them with men who were more "in his own image"? Navone, the born courier, had learned some of the contents of the message and fervently hoped that the fat marshal was on the list of victims.

Karl-Heinz now had to get down to the usual inventory and maintenance of motorized vehicles, mainly Brunzigs, only now, he dealt with the entire *AfrikaKorps*. He also managed to "divert" some brand-new, half-tracked Brunzig vehicles from *Panzer* Divisions in Europe. Even more critically, he got three of Dr. Maut's top assistants because the *AfrikaKorps*'s tanks were choking on dust, which clogged their carburetors and got into lubricant oils and track-bogeys. New filters and insulations were devised, and Rommel was absolutely delighted! He had made no error taking this boy Dorn along! And even Navone worked out fine. Some of the worst incompetents in the *Duce*'s army were unceremoniously kicked back across the Mediterranean.

Karl-Heinz learned to live in the desert through hundreds of miles of Libya and Tunisia: the broiling sun, and sandstorms whipping over bare rocks and through the wadis until men without goggles were blinded. Their nights were freezing cold, and they shivered in their lightweight uniforms. They all looked deceptively healthy in the *AfrikaKorps*, because their tanned faces and arms camouflaged dysentery and vermin bites and churning bellies from the chlorine-reeking water, besides stinking underpants, lice, and fungus-rotted toes.

But the German press saw another side. When the first magazines arrived from Berlin, they read about themselves: *"Heroic! Our blue-eyed eagles, our men of steel, Rommel's knights!"* What *Bockmist!* Goatshit!

The desert was not the desert they had come to expect from their boyhood films in the local *Flohkino* or from the adventure books of Karl May that they had all devoured as kids. No long stretches of rippling sand, no oases and palm trees and luxurious Arab tents. Instead, they saw the rocky desert of the Old Testament.

Karl-Heinz got close to the men for the first time. The *AfrikaKorps Landser*, the common soldiers, were good fellows, all in all. Kindhearted, helpful, and as gritty as soldiers had to be. They would do their job, and they would advance as long as they could, and longer than most.

There were Berliners throughout the divisions, loudmouthed and snotty, of course. After all, they were big-city boys, and they were not afraid to open their big Berlin traps. Their sardonic street humor traveled from mouth to mouth throughout the *Korps* and they got away with many things. One night, they had been through the hell of heavy British artillery, unable to move because they had run out of fuel, unable to defend themselves. Hundreds had been killed or were trying to keep from dying in field aid stations. The next morning a major from Berlin said to Karl-Heinz, "It turned out to be a wonderful evening after all." The line came from a story about a famous cabaret comic, a homosexual who was acidly anti-Nazi. One night, two storm troopers cornered him and started beating his bare buttocks with leather straps. "Oh," said his fag friends, "you poor, poor thing!" "No," said the comic, "it turned out to be a *wonderful* evening after all!"

They pushed through to the Mediterranean and, *Herrgott*, Oh God, there it finally was, the sea and the sun and the beach! They all undressed and got deloused. It was almost like a vacation, except for those damned patrols that still had to be taken out. Karl-Heinz, more and more involved with line soldiering, had learned to do patrol work. Once he nearly got his tail shot off by a Tommy fighter plane. As it was, he got sliced on the left arm by some splintered rocks, leaving him with a long scar. The major from Berlin caught it a few days later. At least he was a suntanned corpse! He had won a tanning competition during their few days on the beach.

They had wrecked the Americans at Kasserine Pass. The *Amis,* new to combat, were pathetic, unskilled, and soft, and they surrendered in droves. These were the first *Amis* in the war, and there had been so many rumors about them: that they were tough Texas cowboys, lumberjacks, and God knew what. But at Kasserine they turned out to be nothing much. There they were in their sand-colored field jackets, olive wool pants, tan leggings, and their piss-pot helmets, throwing away their new M-1 rifles and giving up without much fight.

Arschlöcher! Served them right!

And yet—like so many Berliners of his generation, Dorn had always admired Americans, first names like Johnny and Bobby, American dances and films, Josephine Baker, Douglas Fairbanks, American cocktails, Hollywood coats. Besides, a lot of Berliners had become famous names in the U.S.A., like Dietrich, Schmeling, Lubitsch, Emil Jannings, Conrad Veidt.

Along came these stupid American kids who tried to be soldiers. Why couldn't they stay out of it? After all the propaganda that came in over the radio from Cairo, they ended up getting their asses kicked.

Admittedly, it was wonderful and yet, to Karl-Heinz, almost a disappointment. They had grown to respect the Tommies. The English were good soldiers. Before Kasserine, Karl-Heinz had usually handed out a few discreet warnings about the Americans, and the others had shrugged. "What the hell can you Berliners know? You guys were always crazy for America."

Now he had to admit Americans were human after all. Their millions and their propaganda did them no good, not against Flak 18-88 guns, the "fuckin' Eighty-eights," as he heard the *Ami* prisoners call them. It was hard to believe that Germany's fabulous dual-purpose gun, the Eighty-eight, had sexual affinities. Yet he never heard it described without that adjective the American army used so freely. One of the regimental commanders had howled with laughter when Karl-Heinz translated G.I. slang. "What did you say they called it?'' asked the colonel. "Captain Dorn, did you really say *fickendes* Eighty-eight?"

The *Luftwaffe* gun crews who manned their Eighty-eights soon became known as the *"Fickers,"* which pleased them not at all. Their chief, a lieutenant, was a prissy little ex-schoolteacher from Saxony who pouted a lot.

Rommel was constantly on the move, and so were his aides. They drove, flew, and walked hundreds of kilometers each week, while their chief became the apple of Hitler's eye. They ate bad German field rations, captured British food, and even Italian army meat, which they soon called *"Asinus Mussolini."*

Then came incredible news. The headline in *Die Karawane,* the *AfrikaKorps* paper, told it this way:

> On the morning of June twenty-second, 1941, German troops crossed the border into Russia. This is the *Führer's* answer to constant and outrageous provocations by the Soviet government. Our troops are making rapid progress, and success is reported everywhere on the Russian front. Russian troops are retiring in confusion or surrendering by the thousands.

Added to Rommel's successful drive east, the Russian campaign seemed to prove once more that Germany was guided by one of the greatest military commanders in history.

The steel door slammed and shut out nearly all the light in the mildew-reeking cell. Colonel Eberan von Totten groped his way to the center of the small floor where he remembered a stool, seen in the second before they had pushed him forward.

At five that morning he had been harshly shaken awake in his room at headquarters by an SS officer who told him to get up and get dressed. The man wore S.D. on his sleeve and was accompanied by two other S.D. men. There was no doubting his purpose. They had obviously uncovered all or part of the Otto conspiracy, and he would have to try to keep the harm within limits, to betray no one and to be brave. Above all, to be brave. Eberan von Totten had no delusions. It was not heredity or family name or his honor as an officer that would help him now. It was his own, his personal capacity to resist the horrors he was to suffer. It was his sacred duty, his *Gottverdammte Plicht und Schuldigkeit*, to protect all the others who felt as he did: that Adolf Hitler was an abomination and the greatest curse Germany had ever suffered.

It was a clammy morning. He was not given time to shave or bathe. They would not even grant him privacy in the bathroom in case he might attempt suicide. He felt shamefully gritty, ill-groomed, slovenly, unwashed, which mattered to a man of his upbringing. Grooming had often helped to bolster his conduct in time of crisis. He would have shaved before facing the firing squad.

When they arrived at S.D. headquarters in nearby Potsdam, he was pushed into a small office where a short, young, SS *Obersturmführer* walked up to him and tore off his colonel's epaulets and wrenched the Iron Cross from his tunic. Then, with lightning speed, he slapped Eberan von Totten twice across the face, forehand and backhand. This was as expected, and von Totten had already blunted himself to it. These were only superficial things. He had been slapped many times before, by his father, by his governess, and as a cadet. Titled Prussian boys were accustomed to the ear-ringing crack of a hard hand. It had been a long time, but it still felt familiar.

So far he had said nothing. Nor had he been asked anything. The SS lieutenant now pushed him onto a wooden stool and stood in front of him, straddle-legged, fists clenched at the side of his waist, a small man, relishing the moment.

"*Na, Herr Oberst* von Totten—he rolled each word and tried for irony—"why don't you ask me what this is all about? Why don't you tell me that this is all a vast mistake? Why don't you threaten me with my superiors? We know you've been to the Berghof. Why don't you say you'll call *Reichsleiter* Bormann? Or the *Führer* himself?"

Eberan von Totten looked at the young fool and said nothing. There was a long pause, one of obvious disappointment for the SS man, who, temper boiling over, then screamed, "Swine! We'll teach gentry like you to do their duty. Do you hear me, *Herr* von Totten?" He emphasized the aristocratic "von."

Then von Totten was pushed, shoved, bludgeoned along corridors into the cell.

Eberan von Totten thought of his wife and two daughters, and bid them farewell. Then he commended his soul to the harsh, evangelical God of the Prussian *Junkers,* as the words of an ancient song of Frederick the Great's soldiers came back to him:

> Say farewell to me, my dear,
> For I march to fight the foe.
> When the enemy draws near,
> Frederick then will disappear,
> Melting as the winter's snow.
> Numberless as stars at night
> Or the sands on ocean's shore
> Come the enemies we fight.
> So then, if we judge aright,
> Say farewell for evermore.

AFRICA, EUROPE, AND AMERICA

1943

ROMMEL'S ELEPHANTINE command vehicle was captured from the British early in forty-one along with its original occupant, General O'Connor of the British army. To add to the enemy general's discomfiture, Rommel also requisitioned the man's wind-visor and wore it for the rest of the Africa campaign, adopting it as his trademark. The command truck was renamed "Moritz" after the famous German "Max and Moritz" children's books. It irked Karl-Heinz that "Moritz" was a British vehicle and not a Brunzig. He was still a Brunzig man rather than an army officer. But he understood. The newly promoted Field Marshal Rommel loved symbolism. Every senior captured British officer was brought to "Moritz," and every one of them knew that it once was British. Erwin Rommel was good at using this sort of ploy.

"Moritz," license number WH 819834, was now pulled up alongside a tall cliff in the deep shade, almost hidden from marauding enemy aircraft. Karl-Heinz, who had been ordered to report to the field marshal, had not seen his commander in chief for weeks. He wondered what had brought this special audience.

Rommel was perched on the top deck of "Moritz," elbows on the shiplike railing, chin resting on his fists. He watched Karl-Heinz approach and salute. Rommel returned the salute with a vague gesture and said, "Come in through the back entrance, Dorn."

Karl-Heinz entered and found himself in a small cabin with a large center table. He could hear a radio operator in the cubicle ahead of the main "room." One of the benches alongside the bulkhead was a convertible bunk, and there was a small lavatory in an enclosure against the other wall. Rommel had lived many days in "Moritz" since the long retreat from El Alamein.

The field marshal came down through an overhead hatch. He was much shorter than Karl-Heinz, who stiffened to attention, snapped his heels together, and almost cracked his head against the steel ceiling. The cabin reeked of gasoline, oil, and hot steel, just like the inside of a tank. English tanks smelled of diesel oil, like fishing boats. "Good morning," said Rommel. His new field marshal's insignia were shiny, the gold thread not yet dulled by sun, wind, and rain. Rommel's face was covered with sores, and he looked worn out. They had been on the run for weeks, and rumors were plentiful: Rommel was said to be on the slide, despite his promotion to field marshal. General von Arnim, the man who had slaughtered the Americans at Kasserine, was supposedly the man on the way up, but who could tell? Rommel was resilient and had often provided miracles to order. Besides, news from Stalingrad was disastrous, even worse than Africa.

Rommel wasted no time. He closed the peephole to the radio compartment. "Dorn, I sent for you to show you this." He drew an official envelope from his tunic pocket. He held it in his hand and gestured with it, emphasizing the next words. "It is absolutely imperative that you keep the contents of this message secret. It would be extremely dangerous for you if you did not. Is that clear?"

"Jawohl, Herr General Feldmarschall."

"I have your word as an officer?"

"You have my word of honor."

Karl-Heinz was completely puzzled. He wondered which burden would be saddled on him, but there was no way he could have hedged his promise of secrecy. He was handed the envelope. Inside was a document from Berlin on Gestapo and S.D. stationery:

Herr General Feldmarschall Rommel is hereby informed of the arrest, summary trial, and execution by hanging of a certain Colonel Eberan von Totten. The charge was High Treason against the *Führer* and the German people. This man was part of a group which conspired to assassinate the *Führer* and assume control of the Government in order to surrender to the enemy. It is suggested to the Field Marshal that there may be other members of this conspiracy who are presently in Africa and under the Field Marshal's command. It would be wise to find any officers who had previous connections, officially or privately, with the traitor von Totten. Similar confidential warnings are being dispatched to other Field Commanders. The *Führer* reiterates his wish that all traces of these vermin be eliminated ruthlessly.

It is also the *Führer's* direct command that all information regarding this group of traitors be kept completely secret, since such information would only further the purpose of certain defeatist elements.

It was signed by Kaltenbrunner, the man who had taken over from Heydrich as head of the Gestapo and S.D.

Karl-Heinz tried hard to keep his hands steady and to fold the message carefully. His heart was pounding. Otto had been discovered! Von Totten was dead! Hilde? Did they know about Hilde? Obviously not. Had they caught Hilde, they would have arrested him at once. And the Morgenroths? No. Unlikely. He would have heard the rumor. Von Totten had obviously managed to protect everyone. Incredible!

He was roused out of his thoughts by Rommel. "Dorn, I wanted to see you because I remembered something. In the early days in France you were assigned to this man von Totten. He had a lot of pull with Brunzig, and I had to kick him in the butt now and then to get some new stuff. Is that true?"

"*Jawohl, Herr General Feldmarschall.* My Brunzig chief, *Direktor* Zoss, wanted me in the army to take care of Brunzig's liaison. So he asked von Totten to arrange a commission, but I had nothing to do with von Totten."

"Good. Then you certainly are not involved. Whatever happened to Zoss? Are you still in contact with him?"

"Drowned at sea two years ago on his way to America.

His ship was sunk. He was going to Detroit to see some automobile people who are friendly to us."

"Pity! Good man, Zoss! *Na, dann,* the whole matter can be closed. Who is your contact at Brunzig now?"

"*Generaldirektor* Gerhardt Brunzig, sir."

"*Garnicht schlecht.* Not bad. Give him my very best when you write to him. Oh, and how is your spaghetti friend, Navone? I lost sight of him since we've been on the run."

"Dead. His command car was shot up by a Tommy fighter plane."

"Pity. I could have used him right now. I'm off to Italy in a week or so."

"Short trip, sir?"

"Haven't been feeling well. Going home for some checkups. Stopping to see the *Duce* along the way. Then the *Führer.*" He shook his head and mumbled almost to himself, "Certainly could have used that young Italian fellow. . . ." Then he looked up to dismiss Karl-Heinz. "That's all, Dorn."

Karl-Heinz stumbled out of "Moritz." He was horrified by what might have been, and blessing his lucky stars for having stayed out of Otto and also for Hilde's miraculous escape. He returned to the village near El Agheila where they had stopped on the way back west until they could turn once more to face Montgomery. A letter from Hilde awaited him. He almost tore it in two, so anxious was he to pull it out of the envelope. It said nothing. Not a hint, not an innuendo. She wrote about her daily life in subdued, quiet sentences. No feelings. Every complaint, even that she missed him, might have been misconstrued by a censor as "defeatist." Her words were as bland as a schoolchild's when he knew that her heart and her mind had to be filled to overflowing!

Karl-Heinz never saw Rommel again. The following week, they said in protest against the *Führer*'s recent refusal to accept his strategic judgment, Rommel left Africa and never returned. Eventually, they heard that he had checked into a hospital in Vienna.

On the first of November at many degrees below freezing in the fierce, wind-whipped snow on the banks of the Volga before Stalingrad, they were only two weeks from the great Russian counter-offensive that would finish the Germans under Field Marshal von Paulus. They were at a standstill, unable to budge the Russians. Supplies were stretched to a trickle, the *Luftwaffe* was immobilized both by the freezing cold and the Soviet air force, and Germany was about to suffer the greatest military defeat in its history. It would all end with a hysterical Adolf Hitler cursing his generals, and with generals damning the day they swore an oath of allegiance to "that Austrian upstart." They had all deluded themselves when the rash gambles of the western *Blitzkrieg* had succeeded so gloriously.

Ockert, the chauffeur, now an *Oberfeldwebel* staff sergeant in the Sixteenth *Panzer* Division, knew none of this. He knew only that his job was to drive a tank, and there was no more gasoline. He also knew that his cheeks and lips were cracked with frostbite, that he had tied a dead Russian farm woman's scarf around his head under his helmet to cover his ears, because many men had already lost their earlobes. He had not shaved in many days, his eyes were rimmed with red, and the eyeballs teared from the steely wind and the smoke of bursting Russian shells. He wanted to stand up and stamp some blood into his feet, but he dared not. Russian snipers were good and had the patience of true hunters.

His stomach was knotted with hunger. They were all starving, and there was nothing left to steal in the surrounding countryside, a shell-holed snowy waste. Ockert's tank stood nearby, immobile, its oil frozen solid since he could no longer crank up the big engine. He was afraid to take shelter inside it, because it was even colder there, and getting in and out also brought him into the sights of Russian snipers.

They had slaughtered one of the remaining horses from the supply column that had reached them the month before. The horse had to feed two companies. It was amazing how much sadness the end of that broken-down animal brought, while hundreds of men died as if it were a foregone conclusion. There was no pause in the bitter fights within the edge of Stalingrad, where familiar places assumed new guises. Shops, bedrooms, cellars, backyards, unrecognizable after months of bombardment and shelling, became gun emplacements, mortar positions, observation posts, or just places where wounded men crawled, hoping to live or die, almost without preference.

There were no more medical supplies, and each man knew that a wound would probably be fatal, since there was no way to stop infection and gangrene. Besides, they were too weak now.

His Anna and the kids and Berlin had long ago slipped into a world of his dreams. Perhaps it had never been. Sometimes he tried to remember details: the apartment over the garage, the old Brunzig down below, gleaming, the slow and stately trip from the villa to KaDeBe, the nice old gentleman on the back seat. Had it all been real? If not, why would he remember these details? He tried to blow heat into his hands, lifting the inside of his gloves. These were the gloves Anna had knitted. They were full of holes, raveled. He had saved them as best he could.

He knew he would never see his Anna again. They all knew they would never go home. Someone had gambled, staking all their lives, and had lost.

"Dorn!"
"Hier."
"Dorn, Captain, right?"
"Hauptmann."
"First name?"
"Karl-Heinz."
"Unit? *Einheit?*"
Silence.

"Never mind," said the American lieutenant-interrogator. "I can read. It says Fifteenth *Panzer* Division on your vehicles— and you're probably Eighth *Panzer* regiment, right?"
Silence.

"Achtes Panzer Regiment. Stimmts?" The American spoke perfect German with a Rhineland accent. Probably an emigrant, a Jew. They said there were many in the American army.

Karl-Heinz kept his tongue.

"Hell," said the American in English. "it doesn't matter worth shit anyway. Get over there with the others."

Karl-Heinz was a prisoner. He, Karl-Heinz Dorn, was a prisoner of the Americans. Of the Americans! Incredible! Yesterday the *Amis* had wiped out his company of PKW 3 tanks, those same Americans who were so useless back at Kasserine.

He walked over to the other prisoners, some thirty or forty German officers, who stood in front of a peeling stucco wall. He knew several of them. They all looked scruffy in their wrinkled, tan uniforms. Most of them wore Iron Crosses pinned to their tunics, and one major wore the *Ritterkreuz*, the Knight's Cross, around his neck. Berliners called it the "tin necktie." They also called the Russian Campaign Medal the "Frozen Meat Medal." Dorn grinned at the idea, though there was little to grin about.

The major with the Knight's Cross took it as a greeting and smiled back. "*Pech*," he said, shrugging. "Bad luck." He had a face like a small boy, but it was wrinkled. His blond hair was straight and short like a Roman centurion's.

"Von Werber," the major introduced himself and stuck out a gloved hand.

"Dorn."

Handshakes, quickly bowed heads, heels tapped lightly together, just like a dinner party in Berlin. Only no need for small talk, trying to find out what each was doing and where they were going next. Their social life for the immediate future was in the latrine, so to speak.

Separated from his army specialty, with Zoss dead, von Totten dead, and Rommel gone, Karl-Heinz had eventually become a soldier. Now that it was over, he was almost sad, but he also could not deny his relief. He was too old and too smart to get killed without purpose. He was neither hero, nor coward. Like most soldiers, he had grown accustomed to danger because it was daily. Combat had become as familiar as heavy traffic on the Kurfürstendamm. He knew his men called him a good guy, and he was a good soldier. No one paid any attention to the hogwash from Berlin. They, like soldiers everywhere, laughed at their own chiefs. Captured Tommies often made fun of Churchill, and the Italians were good at doing Mussolini imitations that began with "*Popolo d'Italia . . .*" and a lot of strutting.

Being part of a group, a unit, was the center of their spirit. They all knew that this was really of value, rather than the trash that came from the *Propagandaministerium*. They were German soldiers and he was one of them.

Major von Werber looked over at the interrogator and the tall American MPs who stood around aimlessly with their carbines slung.

He said, "How did the *Amis* pull it off? They're such slobs, such *Schlumpen*."

Karl-Heinz shrugged.

"Na, ja," said von Weber, "they're rich. They've got the equipment, and we don't, at least not here in Africa."

A loud-voiced American MP sergeant formed them into a column of threes, and they marched off. The MP called them "fucking Krauts." All noncoms were alike! A few days before, one of his own *Panzer* sergeants had yelled at the back of his car when he slowed down for some large rocks: "Hey *Arschloch,* get your shit wagon moving. You got round wheels, ain't ya?" All this in a Berlin dialect so broad you could kneel on it. Then the bastard had come around to the front of the command car, saluted him, and said, "Sorry, sir, didn't mean to be disrespectful." But he smiled as he said it, a low-down, dirty smile. Karl-Heinz tried not to show he was amused. It would have been bad form. He said, "Shut your loud yap, sergeant."

"Zu Befehl, Herr Hauptmann!" and the sergeant stood to attention. His voice was from Moabit, a lower-class district. Theirs was a classic confrontation: Moabit and Charlottenburg, the laboring class and the upper-middle class. *Plus ça change . . .*

The column of prisoner officers marched off, escorted by several MPs. The *Ami* sergeant yelled cadence, but the Germans had automatically fallen into step. Von Werber said, "Well, at least we don't have to worry about the clap for a while."

Good for him, thought Karl-Heinz, a *Ritterkreuz* winner with a sense of humor!

Von Werber said, "Odd little Jew, that *Ami* lieutenant." So he had spotted it, too.

Karl-Heinz nodded. "Yes, and how."

Von Werber said, "We could have used him. Seems clever." But he looked around when he said it. By now, they were all used to saying what they wanted, more or less, but usually only to people they knew.

They spent that night in an enormous P.O.W. compound near Bizerta. Soon they were joined by tens of thousands: the fragments of the *Afrika* Germans and the *Duce*'s Tripolitanian legions. It was over.

The Avus was closed to everything but military traffic, so they took the back roads out to Wannsee. The old man who was driving was not very steady. No matter. They had to get the kids out of Berlin. Hilde had finally, finally managed to borrow this old truck and to scrounge enough gasoline for two round trips. The kids were wonderful, seven little boys and six girls from three to six years old. They behaved like angels, but now and then Hilde had to hold and hug one or the other because their mummies had stayed in Berlin.

Wonderful Monika Forstmann was waiting for them in Wannsee, where the children would be safer. Now Berlin was bombed nightly, and even the days were dangerous.

They had taken out the first group of children early that morning, and this was their second trip. The old man stared at the needle on the gasoline gauge, which neared the "empty" mark although there were still a few millimeters between it and zero. Near Gatow, they pulled over to let a column of *Luftwaffe* trucks pass. The kids waved at the airmen on the trucks but got no response. In the old days, the men would have waved back, but since Stalingrad and Tripoli the mood had changed.

Finally, for the second time that day, they swayed and wheezed their way into the Forstmann driveway, and the children were lifted out and taken to their makeshift dormitories, four to each bedroom with mattresses on the floor. Now they would sleep in the fresh air that came in through the open windows instead of the cellar dampness of air-raid shelters in the city. Some of Wannsee's brightest young women had volunteered to help Monika with the nursing chores. The children had everything they needed except their mothers. That night, many a little boy tried manfully to suppress the sobs that would eventually overwhelm him, while the little girls clutched onto their dolls, hoping that this would make everything all right. The woman sat downstairs in the Forstmanns' living room, listening for any sounds from the little ones.

Monika Forstmann poured *Schnaps*.

"*Prost!*"

They drank.

"*Nochmal!* Another one!" said Monika, and they drank again, feeling a little less hurt by the pain they had inadvertently caused the children. But what was there to do? They would be so much safer in Wannsee.

Hilde asked, "Where is Erich?"

"I don't know," said Monika. "The last I heard he was doing combat filming in Russia. But that was a month ago.

Since then, nothing. The little *Doktor* called yesterday, a 'social' call. But I managed to avoid the bastard.'' She spoke under her breath so the others could not hear.

"Any word from Karin von Totten?''

"No. She would never call. She knows she might compromise me. She's a marvelous woman. Her son is an SS animal, somewhere in the east. Not *Waffen*-SS. Some police unit. Ugly! He is by her first marriage. They say he's the one who denounced his stepfather!''

"*Jesus Maria!* How dreadful! I never knew he had a stepson.''

"They hated each other!''

"I miss Armin Zoss.''

"So do I.''

"Where are the Morgenroths?''

"With Gerhardt Brunzig in Stuttgart.''

"Good. He's a clever man, and the *Bonzen* still respect him.''

"What will you do now, Hilde? Why don't you stay with me?''

"No. I have to be in Berlin. There's something I must do.''

"All right. I shan't ask questions.'' Monika hugged her.

Berlin had turned cold early in November, and one could see people's breaths on the chill air. Despite that, the old priest and Hilde sat on a bench in the small cemetery adjoining the church, and spoke softly about their dangerous task, the hiding of Jews. On the fifteenth, another fifty elderly Jews, both men and women, had been rounded up by the SS and shipped to Theresienstadt Camp, Transport Number 97, as it was offically called. On that same day Transport Number 44 left with seventy younger Jews for Auschwitz. These transports were smaller than the great roundups of late 1942, when they usually shipped out a thousand or more each week. It was pitiful, and finally, much too late for their reviving conscience, many Berliners had grown disgusted and sickened. The priest had a new ally at Gestapo headquarters in the Prinz Albrechtstrasse, an old Gestapo man called Tunnes whom he had known since they were both young, and the priest ministered to the criminals in a Moabit jail. Tunnes had passed several warnings about impending SS roundups.

"It's getting harder and harder," the priest now told Hilde. "Until last month, I could still buy food for registered Jews. But now, the shops have signs that say, 'No sale to Jews or to persons shopping for Jews.' "

"I saw the signs, Father," said Hilde. "Also, now they don't allow Jews into the air-raid shelters anymore. As soon as the blockwardens see the Jew stars, they keep them out."

"Na, ja," said the priest, "we still must do what we can. The priest from the Marienkirche in Charlottenburg said he can hide about ten or twelve more in the church basement. Have them take off their Jew stars and come into the church at intervals, one by one during the day, as if to worship. You'll have to teach them how to genuflect. If others are in the church, the Jews must look like Catholics."

"Like Aryans?"

"Like Aryans."

"Like our Lord Jesus Christ?"

The old priest grinned. "Yes," he said. "And Mary and Joseph." It helped to have a sense of humor as a Catholic priest in Protestant Prussia.

Hilde stood up and left after kissing the old man's cheek. She had been working closely with a group of women, young, old, rich, poor, from those of royal blood to the wife of the porter in their apartment house on Adolf Hitler Platz. They all hid Jews, saved them from the SS and the roundups. The women had found each other in a grapevine of decency.

Many Berliners now shared their sparse food rations with Jews and hid them in their rubbled, ruined apartments at the risk of their own lives. Construction workers shared their lunchtime *Stulle,* their beloved sandwich, with Jewish forced laborers, men from the professions, who were unskilled and lost in this harsh new work.

Much too late, Berliners became ashamed of the atrocities in their midst.

AMERICA

1942

EARLIER THAT YEAR, Siegfried Schmidt had arrived in Washington as one of ten British Intelligence officers who were to advise the brand-new United States Intelligence Service. It was freely admitted in U.S. staff circles that, when it came to intelligence work, "the Limeys were tops."

The overaged, German-accented, recently commissioned Lieutenant Schmidt was delivered via an R.A.F. "Dakota" transport. One of the mustachioed R.A.F. pilots told the American OSS captain who had come to collect Schmidt, "Marvelous chap, this Schmidt feller! Sounds a bit rum when he speaks English, but they say he's been doing absolutely wizard things against the Jerries."

The OSS man asked if they had a good crossing. Dakotas were twin-engined Boeings, slow and dependable, but not ideal for transatlantic hops in midwinter.

"Piece of cake!" said the R.A.F. man. "We had old Schmidt chatting to a U boat on our wireless near St. John. Very jolly! We steered the bastard straight at some Canadian destroyers and warned the Canadians there was a U-boat coming. Then we played poker and Schmidt suddenly yelled, 'Vat is goink on?' and ran forward to the flight deck. You see, we were *all* playing cards, my copilot and I, our radio fellow, and the passengers. The old Dakota was on automatic pilot, on 'George.' Back came Schmidt, pale as a ghost. He

287

said, 'No one is flyink zis sing!'' The flight lieutenant's
German accent was quite good. ''You see, we had left our
sweaty gloves glued to the control wheels, and you know how
the columns make little automatic moves. Well, poor old
Schmidt must have thought the spirit of Richthofen had taken
charge.''

The OSS moved Schmidt into a small hotel just off Connecticut Avenue. The other British officers were sent to Mary-
land and Virginia, where new intelligence training centers had
just been opened, but Schmidt's specialty was taught right in
the heart of Washington, in a small brownstone building, with
an innocuous brass plaque: CENTER FOR TRANSATLANTIC STUDIES.
No doubt about it, Area E, as the OSS called it officially, was
a center for just that. How to train people from America to
disappear inside a French village, an Italian city, or even a
German *Panzer* regiment. General Donovan's new Office of
Strategic Services, meant Espionage and Counterespionage,
Sabotage and Countersabotage, the unpleasant, distasteful,
brutal, backstairs part of the war.

The German armed forces were Schmidt's specialty, their
organization, uniforms, disposition, armaments, attitudes, and
even nicknames. Schmidt himself had several times disappeared inside Germany wearing a German army uniform,
speaking German army slang, while he made contacts and
obtained information. Now he was about to teach this craft to
others.

He soon became famous within the American intelligence
community. His super-Teutonic speech and appearance, his
occasional rages, and the whole mystery of his background,
which he steadfastly refused to clear up, all combined to
make him into a ''character.''

One asked OSS men:

''Did you study *mit* Schmidt?''

''Natürlich!''

''In ze Area E?''

''Selbstverständlich!''

''Egg-zellent.''

The so-called mit-Schmidt boys became the *crème de la
crème* of those Americans who functioned undercover against
the *Wehrmacht*. Those who were German Jewish refugees
had the Nazi-produced factor on their side: Most Germans
had no *real* way of identifying Jews! They could tell when a

man wore a yellow Jew star on his jacket. And they had also seen the vile caricatures in the *Stürmer,* Streicher's tabloid. But most Jews did not look like these caricatures, and under-cover men did not wear yellow stars!

Most lessons in undercover work came from Schmidt's own experience. The ribbon he wore on his British army tunic was the elite Military Cross.

There was a meeting at the Pentagon: Schmidt, Colonel Timmons of the OSS, a major from the Military Police, and another major from the U.S. Transportation Corps.

The *AfrikaKorps* had collapsed, and thousands of German *Landser* were about to be shipped to the United States as prisoners of war. To Schmidt it was like winning the sweepstakes! Finally, a chance to get large numbers of real German troops for the mit-Schmidt boys. Instead of simulat-ing Germans by using German refugee actors from Holly-wood in *Wehrmacht* uniforms, here were real Germans. What an opportunity to teach undercover work! Funneling mit-Schmidt men into these prisoner transports was the perfect way to test them.

"When do you expect the first ship?" asked Schmidt.

"About June tenth," said the Transportation Corps major.

"Arriving where?"

"Staten Island."

"Then what?"

"Then," said the Military Police officer, "we load them onto trains and send them to New Mexico under MP escort."

"Is that where they're building stockades?"

"Right."

"How long a trip?"

"Three, four days. We have to replenish supplies and get emergencies taken care of, like medical cases, although there will be no wounded aboard. They keep those in Italy."

Colonel Timmons asked, "Do you know what we're trying to do?"

"Not exactly, sir."

"I belong to a branch called the OSS. We're part of the War Department. We're an interservice organization that deals in undercover matters."

"Undercover?"

"Let's call 'em secret matters."

"Espionage?"

"That may be part of it." The colonel shrugged, obviously unwilling to continue this line of explanation. "Here's what we need," He said. "A group of German army men in their original organizations! And that's what we'll have, once the ships land these *AfrikaKorps* prisoners."

"Pardon me, sir, but what, if I might ask, will you use them for?"

In answer, Colonel Timmons handed printed forms to the Transportation and Military Police officers.

"Read and sign these forms," he said, "and I can give you some of the information you need to help us do this thing."

They signed the forms, which informed them that they were about to learn highly classified information.

"Why don't you explain, Schmidt?" said Colonel Timmons.

"We wish to use the transports as test runs for newly trained undercover men. They will be filtered onto the prisoner trains as German *Wehrmacht* men and forced to live with the Germans for three days without being detected."

"Pretty rough."

"Not really. Your transport commander and the C.O. of the MP escort will be informed of the identity of our men, of course, in total secrecy. Also, there is not much danger that our men will get hurt."

"Why?" asked the Military Police officer.

"Well," said Schmidt, "these prisoners have nothing to gain by killing our people. It's impossible to escape across the Atlantic. They're almost sure, by now, that they're losing the war. They know that we'll find out who did the killing and that they'll jolly well get their arses reamed until we do." The British terms sounded strange in his Berlin accent.

The others accepted his explanation reluctantly.

Schmidt continued, "There's only one real danger: if there are fanatics—*Waffen*-SS people or other SS units like the S.D., the secret police."

"How can we tell?"

"Firstly, there were no *Waffen*-SS units fighting in Africa. Secondly, just to make sure, when you screen them, raise their left arms. SS men have their blood type tattooed under the left upper arm."

"Regular German soldiers don't?"

"No. Nor do the *Luftwaffe* men."

"Lieutenant Schmidt . . ."

"We pronounce it *Leftenant*."

"We?"

"His Majesty's Armed Forces." Schmidt saw the grins around the table. "And I don't mean his Majesty Kaiser Wilhelm of Prussia."

"All right," laughed the Military Police officer. "I'm sorry. *Left*enant, tell us something about the German prisoners we'll be dealing with."

"They're the best of all German soldiers, and reasonably nonpolitical. They got licked because we could outsupply them and outbomb them."

"You sound very sympathetic to them."

"Don't mistake my realism for sympathy. You'll also find out that, contrary to the myth, German soldiers are inventive and highly intelligent. You can fairly much allow them to run themselves."

"Will there be some extra-tough outfits among them, and how can we tell who they are?"

"As I said, there are no SS. But there will be paratroops. They're part of the air force, the *Luftwaffe*. They wear tan army-style uniforms with baggy pants and side pockets, with the *Luftwaffe* eagle, which is different from the army eagle. You'll recognize it from the regular *Luftwaffe* uniforms, which are blue. Also, there's a *Luftwaffe* infantry outfit called "Hermann Göring." They're first-rate soldiers. Anyway, they're all tough. They've been in the desert for years, and they know how to handle themselves."

"How do they feel about Americans?"

"They like Americans."

"How about respect?"

"Well"—Schmidt shrugged—"that's different. You see, they took their beating from us British." There were more grins around the table. "The first time they ran into your fellows, they chewed them alive at Kasserine. So they really don't consider Americans killers. Don't get upset! You've only been in this bloody thing for a year. We've been at it since thirty-nine. Give yourselves time. You'll end up really being the winners with all your men and supplies."

It was not the most satisfying answer, but they had to accept it. They agreed to work out an agenda for Operation Barrymore, as they allusively decided to name it.

• • •

Lieutenant Harry Wolf, army of the United States, born Heinz Wolf in Frankfurt, was twenty-four years old and over six feet tall. With his tanned, lean face, paratroop helmet, gray eyes, and wide-shouldered body, he looked like an advertisement for the Eighty-second Airborne Division, but he was not really one of them. Like other OSS men, he wore their insignia and jump boots only because he had taken his paratroop training with them at Fort Benning, Georgia.

Wolf began his army career in a "line" infantry outfit and had just been selected for Officers' Candidate School when he was approached by the brand-new OSS. They sent him to parachute training and then for three months of stiff intelligence indoctrination in a special camp in Virginia. He was granted citizenship, so he could be commissioned a second lieutenant and he became one of the first mit-Schmidt boys.

Harry was an only child. He came to the United States with his parents in 1936 when he was seventeen. At his Frankfurt high school he felt the degradation of being Jewish, and he envied his Aryan schoolmates their new Hitler Youth uniforms and their immunity from insult and exclusion.

The Wolfs settled in New York's Washington Heights, a favorite district for many German Jewish refugees. Harry soon became estranged from his parents. He saw no reason to continue his Nazi punishment, and he thought, the hell with being Jewish! He was tall, good-looking, and armed with an innocuously nonreligious name. He wished to live without synagogues and refugee coffeehouses like the Eclair on West Seventy-second Street, where many refugees sat nightly, bemoaning their fate and criticizing the *Sacher Torte* or the *Streuselkuchen*.

Harry would bend New York to suit his new life. He moved from job to job, ever upward. He was a desk clerk, tennis coach—since he played stylish tennis—travel agent, foreign-car salesman, real estate broker, and he did well. He invested in a splendid wardrobe and big tips for the maître d's in New York's best places. He paid all his bills promptly, establishing more credit than he deserved. He was no fourflusher, but neither was he the international playboy he seemed. Nevertheless, from the Colony to El Morocco, from Voisin to the Stork, they were happy to see handsome Harry Wolf and to show him to a good table. Whenever he ran short of funds, he simply stayed away for a few weeks. Ever self-protective, he took out girls who were beautiful but not in the New York social swing, new faces, students from Columbia and Finch, magazine editors and young actresses, never girls who were in a position to snub him.

Early in forty-two, though not yet a citizen, he managed to enlist in the army. Everyone did. There were more private soldiers at the bar of the Stork Club than there were officers. What luck, then, that instead of a common place infantry commission, his status had been immeasurably improved by joining the very elite, very "social" OSS, instead of some dull "line" division from North Dakota or Oklahoma. OSS promised intriguing assignments, the stuff of which movies were made. OSS also offered a new world of contacts for postwar life.

He had barely spoken to his parents since he enlisted. Their reaction had been half horror, half pride, but he cared little. They were part of another life.

Schmidt had screened dozens of candidates for his group and accepted only a few, among them Harry Wolf. Most rejections had to do with language, appearance, and *acting*. An agent had to *become* the very person he pretended to be, if only for a few days. The "cover" had to be memorized like a Broadway stage role, and played with panache. Schmidt was sure Harry could work out, probably in the cover of a junior officer.

(Most mit-Schmidt men were educated and spoke the nonregional speech of upper-class Germans. For this reason most cover stories were "officer" stories. Few OSS men were capable of working-class dialect, and broad, raucous *Wehrmacht* slang. Also, an officer had greater mobility and had to answer fewer questions.)

At first, Schmidt's inelegance and seeming clumsiness annoyed Harry, but he soon changed his opinion. Schmidt might have looked like an oaf, but he knew his way around the big cities of Europe. Most of all, he understood the *Wehrmacht*. He knew each tiny detail of a uniform, the reputation of each unit, the gossip about their commanders, the markings on their vehicles, their latest training manuals, and even the slang contraction of each new headquarters. He was a living textbook.

He also knew about the group called Otto. He had worked closely with those who survived the von Totten purge. Schmidt wanted to train Harry as a liaison agent with Otto. Harry would be unknown to German Counterintelligence. They were not yet established in the United States. They had catalogued nearly every refugee in the small British Isles, but the American scene was comparatively unfamiliar to Abwehr, S.D., and Gestapo. They had no good "moles" in America.

Harry was ideal. He was a fine athlete who had done well in paratroop training. He also looked the part of a young *Wehrmacht* officer and, surprisingly, he still spoke very pure German with a Frankfurt inflection. Schmidt had one question: He considered Harry a bit of a fake. Could he handle stress, or would he collapse when faced with the real thing? Could he put his pretentiousness to good use by . . . *pretending?* And once he made his mark, would he overplay his hand by overacting? In truth, Siegfried Schmidt did not particularly like Harry Wolf, but he also understood many of the reasons. And, anyway, it had no bearing on his potential usefulness. So he prepared Harry for Operation Barrymore.

It was now three hours since Schmidt and Harry had begun this final session in a small soundproof room in the basement of Area E. Schmidt was relentless, pounding at Harry, forcing him to repeat the same answers, over and over, on and on.

"Sie sind?"
"Heini Winkelmann."
"Dienstgrad?"
"Oberleutnant."
"Einheit?"
"Sechszehnte Panzerdivision."

Harry "was" now *Oberleutnant* Heini Winkelmann, Sixteenth *Panzer* Division. He had never really served with the Sixteenth because he was on the way to join them in Russia as a replacement, but, because the division was encircled, he was ordered back to Germany. He never joined them, and they eventually surrendered at Stalingrad. Before then, he was in Paris on occupation duty. After Russia, he was sent to Italy to join the *AfrikaKorps*. He was never assigned to an actual Africa unit and knew no one there. Nor did he know anyone in the Sixteenth *Panzer*. He was born in Frankfurt. (They had chosen the same actual birth date as Harry Wolf, to give him two familiar fallbacks: hometown and birthday.)

The scriptwriters had concocted a near-perfect tale. It matched his *Wehrmacht* uniform and his pale, non-Africa face. It provided him with a lot of loopholes, allowed him a lot of leeway. Superficially, it was difficult to check on him. *Oberleutnant* Winkelmann had never been part of any unit long enough to play the "Did you know so-and-so?" game. Except for his time in Paris, but there were thousands of German officers in Pairs, and it was logical to say, "I didn't know him." They had also provided the correct uniform in every detail. He wore the ribbons of the "Frozen Meat Medal" because of his few weeks in Russia and the innocuous, standard Iron Cross, second class. His German army papers were impeccable, and his *Wehrmacht* German was now being slapped in place by the fierce Siegfried Schmidt.

"No, goddammit, one does not say *'Scheisse!'* in this case. One says *'Scheissdreck!'* And how many times do I have to tell you that to call a unit to attention you don't yell *'Das Ganze!'* You slur it into *'As Ganze!'* It's the same thing as calling troops to attention in your Yankee army. You don't yell *'Attention!'* You yell *'Ten-hut!'* "

Knowing that "Winkelmann" would probably have to march prisoners to and fro, since they were sometimes commanded by their own officers, Schmidt and Harry spent a lot of time on German army drill, and Harry's former experience in the U.S. Infantry was valuable.

They had been at it for one solid week, seven days, almost six hours each day.

How often did German officers get paid? *Monthly, if possible.*

How did they treat the clap? *They had no penicillin. They used prontosil or sulpha drugs.*

Were German officers permitted to drive army vehicles? *Yes. American officers were not supposed to drive except in special cases.*

When did German officers wear their steel helmets? *Rarely, compared with Americans.*

How did they feel about nurses? *Most German army nurses were ugly. The pretty ones were "Blitzmädchen," communication clerks.*

What was their favorite brand of cigarettes? *Anything. Preferably American.*

How much did *AfrikaKorps* people know about the disaster at Stalingrad? *Most of it. Not all of it.*

How far could he go making fun of Göring, Goebbels, the

Führer? Göring, all right. Goebbels, all right. The Führer?
Not a good idea.

Harry was insatiable. He wanted to be sure his Heini
Winkelmann was near-perfect. There might be some danger.
For the first time in months he thought of telephoning his
parents, but he knew it was only because he was scared, and
he decided not to call them. Harry kept to a certain code of
personal honor.

Early one June morning Karl-Heinz stood at that tiny section of ship's railing permitted for officer-prisoners on the
lumbering troop transport. The night before, they had anchored in the Lower Bay of New York Harbor. He woke
early, in the stifling, small hold that he shared with twenty
others. Now that the ship was at anchor, there was hardly any
ventilation. He stepped out on deck under the eyes of two
yawning American MPs who had just relieved the night guards.

It was still dark. He could vaguely make out some other
ships at anchor. Then, magically, the sun rose behind their
ship and there it was, the prow of New York City, towering,
gold-washed in the early light, and there, too, stood the
Statue of Liberty just ahead. He was stunned! He had seen
this view in films and photographs, but this, the real thing,
was *unglaublich! Erschütternd!* Overwhelming!

The two thousand German prisoners crammed below decks
were now awakened by a recorded U.S. army bugle and a
metallic, amplified announcement in English and German.
The ship weighed anchor and headed toward Staten Island,
where it would unload the prisoners.

Karl-Heinz knew only the few officers who were in his
hold. The daily shipboard routine of feeding, washing, and
sleeping was so involved that they had stayed separated from
the others aboard. He wondered if there were any familiar
faces?

Berlin seemed light-years away. And Hilde? Did she know
he was a prisoner, safe, here on a ship in New York Harbor?
How she would have loved this skyline scene!

The old MPs who had been with them on the transport had
served overseas. At dockside, there were other MPs, recruits
just out of basic training, filled with all manner of behavior
designed to intimidate these fierce Hitlerian warriors who

were about to be delivered into their charge. These brand-new, homefront MPs yelled and shouted and scowled and gesticulated.

By now, the German P.O.W.s knew that Americans were basically good-natured fellows, and so they looked at this new bunch of guards with a certain amused tolerance.

One baby-faced MP corporal from the deep South screamed at Karl-Heinz to "git the fuck over theah where the fuck you bee-long!" Karl-Heinz said nothing. He moved to his as-signed spot. But an old *AfrikaKorps* artillery sergeant, a Berlin original, said. *"Herr Hauptmann,* that *Ami* speaks En-glish like he's got someone's tongue up his ass."

"Trouble with you, *Feldwebel,*" said Karl-Heinz, "is that you've been spoiled by the way the Tommy soldiers speak. *Jetzt sind wir in Amerika,* and we have to learn things their way."

Many *AfrikaKorps* men were umbilically attached to their old enemies, the British, and had not yet accustomed them-selves to these new American fellows. For instance, why did all these MPs wear steel helmets? Who was going to fire shrapnel at them? They certainly had nothing to fear from the prisoners! It was over. All they wanted was fair treatment and, most of all, contact with their families. From the mo-ment they got to Sicily to be loaded on the transport, they had tried to contact home through the Red Cross. The Americans understood. Philadelphia, Tulsa, and Mobile were not getting bombed, and Germany's cities were. Each prisoner was mor-tally afraid of what might have happened at home.

Now they stared—incredulously—at these hysterical new American guards. Then they automatically formed platoons, automatically found noncoms and officers, automatically dressed ranks and counted off. Before the MPs knew it, the Germans, two thousand of them, were drawn up in three impressive battalions. Three senior officers then found the ranking Ameri-can MP officer and reported themselves and their men ready for orders. The Americans were impressed and also a bit frightened. They had never seen old combat soldiers face to face. This was the real thing. The Germans looked scruffy and badly in need of showers. Their uniforms were patched, faded, and worn, and they had slept in them for weeks. All of them smelled of disinfectant powder and had the bad breath of constipation, because they had been confined with-

out exercise. They looked older than the Americans, lined
and wrinkled, tanned and yellowed from the desert and from
fever pills. They were a sorry lot. And yet, drawn up in
ranks, instinctively able to present themselves as a military
unit, they were still impressive.

Their first sight of America was a dock, a dock like any
other. It could have been Hamburg or Bremen or Kiel.
Warehouses, sheds, railroad tracks, and freight cars. Hundreds of six-wheel U.S. army trucks and jeeps, jeeps, jeeps.
Not a horse in sight, which amazed the Germans. The German army still used many horse-drawn supply wagons. Marvelous food was now being ladled out to them at a makeshift
chowline! Generous portions, incredible variety, wonderful-
tasting. These men who had spent years on short rations were
starry-eyed. It was the beginning of their American experience,
and the deeper they penetrated into the vast country, the more
they realized that they could never have won, and could never
even have hoped to win! *Der Brocken war zu gross!* They had
chewed off too much. So thought most men in the ranks.

They were marched off to a large warehouse and told to
bed down for the night. Each one was issued two brown army
blankets with a "US" in the middle and a roll-up mattress.
After the cramped shipboard quarters, it was paradise.

The next morning they were examined by medical and
dental officers. They had long ago accustomed themselves to
the degrading military business of "milking" their penises for
signs of gonorrhea and bending over to spread their cheeks
for signs of piles. All armies were alike. Officers were sub-
jected to the same examination, but in a separate section of
the warehouse. According to the Geneva Convention on Prisoners of War, officers were dealt with separately.

"Na, ja," said one young paratroop lieutenant to Karl-
Heinz, "maybe the *Ami* doctor can look up my ass to see if I
need dental work. When that *Ami* dentist looked into my
mouth, he said, 'Asshole,' which I think means '*Arschloch.*' So
I asked him in English if he can see all the way through to my
rectum? He got quite angry. Anyway, maybe the ass-end
doctor can confirm the dentist's findings, but from the other
end."

The lieutenant sounded Viennese. They were also a breed
unto themselves, with their leisurely deprecatory humor, what
they called "Count Bobby" humor: Count Bobby, drunk,

strays into the ladies' restroom in a coffeehouse and starts to pee. An attendant bursts in and says, "Count, you mustn't use this place! It's for ladies. . . ." So Count Bobby points at his penis and asks, "And this is *not* for ladies?"

They were given tetanus shots and sent through a shower room that had been hastily rigged in one of the warehouses. Then they were issued razors, soap, toothpaste, toothbrush.

As they marched back to their warehouse barracks, something looked familiar about the back of an officer up ahead in another platoon. When they broke ranks to go indoors, he caught up with the man. *Von Bernsdorfer!* Von Bernsdorfer who was *Waffen*-SS in an ordinary army officer's uniform! The last he heard, von Bernsdorfer was assigned to one of Hitler's headquarters in the east.

The SS man spotted him and put a finger to his mouth. Silence! He mutely pointed at the man next to him. Gellstein! SS *Hauptsturmführer* Gellstein, Telesty's ass-kisser. Gellstein wore a *Luftwaffe* uniform. How did these two SS bastards get into this transport? How did they pick up their fake uniforms and, probably, fake identities to match? Why the deception? Karl-Heinz was sure they had never been in Africa.

He had heard that whenever *Waffen*-SS officers were in danger of getting captured, they usually tried to get plain army uniforms, because being SS was not exactly ideal when it came to Russian P.O.W. camps. It even made life tougher with the British and certainly with the Dutch, Belgians, Norwegians, and Danes. All of them had been kicked around by the SS. Some captured SS even tried to remove the blood-type tattoo from under their left upper arm. They burned it with a cigarette or a match, or asked a medic to cut away the little patch of skin. Anything to lose SS identity. Himmler would not have been too proud of his "black knights." They had heard that *Waffen*-SS in Russia were positioned behind army divisions so the army men, the ordinary *Landser*, couldn't retreat. There were even stories of SS officers who had orders to hang army officers who permitted anyone to surrender. Ever since Stalingrad, the *Führer* trusted no one except the SS.

On the prison ship they got *Stars and Stripes*, the U.S. army newspaper. At first it seemed that the story of Field Marshal von Paulus surrendering at Stalingrad with a quarter of a million men was Allied propaganda. But the more they read, the more it had to be the truth. *Unglaublich!* Incredible!

So, here were von Bernsdorfer and Gellstein, pretending to be army and *Luftwaffe* officers. Why?

In the transport commander's temporary office, things were fucked up, which was normal. The transport commander was an overaged, overweight major of Coast Artillery, an old National Guardsman from Oregon who was in the construction business in civilian life. When the National Guard was "federalized," he was assigned to the MPs, since he was classified as only fit for limited service due to a history of chronic piles. Now he was very much out of sorts, first because the Transportation Corps people were not cooperating by supplying a train and also because his accustomed affliction had come back to punish him. Never mind, he told himself, Napoleon had piles! He failed to remind himself that Napoleon was reputed to have lost Waterloo precisely because that day he was unable to sit astride his white horse. Napoleon had made all his decisions from a sitzbath, something the fat transport commander would have welcomed gratefully.

Now this son of a bitch young MP lieutenant comes to him with this fucking confidential memo about checking under all the prisoners' left armpits to find some possible SS men. What bullshit! Where did they get their ideas, some of those desk soldiers? Okay. He'd order the whole fucking Kraut transport to roll up its left sleeve. Why the hell couldn't they have thought of this one day earlier when the medics were up to their asses in stripped Krauts? After short-arm inspection and checking for piles, they could have all raised their left arms, if the B.O. didn't kill the examiners. The whole thing was stupid and embarrassing. Still, he'd get it done tomorrow, right before chow. Anyway, he had been told there was no train available for three days.

Next morning, the U.S. army stayed true to form. Just as the major was ready to give instructions for what he called Operation Armpit, he got a call from the embarkation officer at Fort Hamilton. A train would arrive at the docks in Staten Island by 0900 hours. The prisoners were to be ready to board by 0930 hours. He scrapped the inspection. The prisoners boarded promptly at 0930 hours, listening to the quiet commands of their own noncoms and paying scant attention to the bellowing MPs.

Seconds before he himself got on the train, the major received a sealed envelope, which he opened as the train started to roll. It informed him that there was an American undercover agent among the prisoners. The man's cover name was *Oberleutnant* Winkelmann.

How the hell was he going to find him among two thousand men? He would have to take a roll call, car by car, while they were under way. For now, his hands were tied unless he sent a man through the train yelling for an *Oberleutnant* Winkelmann. That would certainly make the shit hit the fan! God, how the fuck did the army manage to screw things up so royally?

Harry Wolf, alias *Oberleutnant* Winkelmann, sat quietly in a window seat of the second car from the front of the train. He looked down at his worn black riding boots and his scuffed, field-gray, winged breeches. Like several other officers, he had unbuttoned his tunic, something he would have been afraid to do until he saw the others do it. The carriage was unbearably hot because the windows were closed and locked. There were over a hundred officer prisoners, with an MP at each end of the car. The MPs were unarmed except for wooden police nightsticks, because it was standard procedure not to carry weapons when in close contact with prisoners. However, they could stop the train with the emergency cord and it would then be sealed off at once. The front and rear cars were filled with armed MPs.

The train smelled of stale cigarette smoke. It had been used to transport American troops, and eventually all soldiers leave the same residue of smells, jokes, and fears. The Germans had used up their cigarettes and started trading with the MPs: German ribbons and insignia for American Camels, Luckies, and Chesterfields.

The men from Bavaria, Würtemberg, Saxony, and Prussia stared out at this vast new country, the immense Pennsylvania farms where some of their ancestors had settled, the Allegheny Mountains where others had come to mine coal. Now their cynicism and bitter combat humor failed them. They were overwhelmed by what they saw, which was to "Winkelmann's" advantage. Nobody focused on the other prisoners. Their eyes were glued on the American landscape.

• • •

So far, Harry had not spoken a word. He stared at the floor, looked out the window, pretended to nap. He tried to tell himself that keeping still gave him a better chance to observe, but in truth he wanted to avoid the first test of his skills. Finally, at nightfall, while the train hurtled into the darkening countryside, he could dodge no longer.

A *Panzer* captain on the bench facing him offered him a blue box of French Gitanes. *"Rauchen Sie?"* he asked. "Do you smoke?"

"Ja, danke." Harry pulled a cigarette from the box and they lighted up. Like some of the others, the captain wore an *AfrikaKorps* ring engraved with palm and swastika.

The stench of harsh French tobacco rose from the Gitanes.

"Dreck," said the captain. "Crap. Hate these French things, but I had none, so I traded four or five packs on the transport. Wish I had *Ami* cigarettes. Camels. Lucky Strike." He pronounced Lucky with an *Umlaut* so it came out "Lurky." Harry's parents always made the same error. He finally gave up trying to correct them.

Harry nodded. *"Stimme bei.* Agree. Lousy stuff, this. But better than none."

The other laughed. "Bauer," he introduced himself. Captain Bauer was sand-colored. Tan skin. Sandy blond hair, sand-tinted eyes.

"Winkelmann," said Harry. "Thanks for the smoke."

Bauer asked if Harry had any of his men aboard.

"No," said Harry. "I had no command in Africa. I was only there one week. Then everything landed in the shit."

"Just as well," said Bauer. "I've got about thirty men somewhere on this train. Bastards. *Arschlöcher*. They're mad as hell at me because I can't wipe their asses and give them hot baths. One of my sergeants told me that I was a real shit and that they'd pay me back; goddammit, there's *verflucht* little I can do for them! The *Amis* have kept me away from them since we got on the ship."

"Have other officers found the same thing?"

"And how! The major over there"—he pointed at a reed-thin infantry officer on the other side of the car—"was threatened by some of his men. They're angry at him because he didn't want them to surrender without having used up their last rounds of ammunition. Personally, I think he was going a bit too far. *Schon Genug!* Enough is enough! Still, he was only doing his duty."

Harry shook his head, as if in disbelief.

"Na, ja," he said, "things were different in Russia."

"Were you there long?" asked Bauer, looking at the "Frozen Meat" Russia-ribbon on Harry's tunic.

"No. Just a few weeks. But everyone was close, officers and men."

"Like us, until Rommel went home."

"So I've heard. Of course, I got there after he left." Harry flicked out the top of his cigarette with his thumb, saving the butt, which he then pushed into his tunic pocket. He nodded at Bauer, folded his arms over his chest and pretended to go to sleep. His heart was pounding. He had passed his first test. Relief! Soon he really began to nod off, until an MP poked him with his nightstick.

"Hands," he said. "Get your fuckin' hands out. I want to see the fucking hands when you Krauts sleep."

Harry pretended not to understand.

"Hands," said the MP, pointing his stick at Harry's hand. *"Raus!"*

"Ach so!" said Harry. "Hands out!" And he showed them to the MP.

"You're fuckin' right," said the American.

How could he know that *Oberleutnant* Heini Winkelmann or Lieutenant Harry Wolf liked him a lot?

Captain Bauer looked over and shrugged sympathetically.

At seven in the morning, the train pulled onto a siding just west of Lexington, Kentucky, within easy view of one of the most magnificent horse-breeding farms in that state. The sleepy prisoners dismounted to stretch their legs, oblivious to the yelling MPs. They could relieve their full bladders at the side of the track, provided they did so in squads of twenty and under the scrutiny of a guard. Ahead of them, about a kilometer away, they could see thoroughbreds getting their morning workout. The thick grass, like a carpet spreading all the way to the horizon, was still wet with dew. After the harsh hills of North Africa, this was paradise to the prisoners. In the distance were elm and oak, painted white fences, horse barns, stables, and gabled houses. Kentucky bluegrass country was untouched by the horrors of war.

Karl-Heinz finished his pee and buttoned up his breeches. Then he saw von Bernsdorfer about five meters behind him. Karl-Heinz walked over and said, "*Warum denn?* Why?"

"*Na, ja.*" The SS man shrugged. "*Wir haben eben was zu erledigen.*"

"What in hell could you have to do?" Karl-Heinz whispered. "And in that uniform?"

"Can't tell you now. Maybe later."

"And Gellstein?"

"I'll discuss it with him. Maybe you can help us. You're the only man we know here."

"*Na, schön.* All right. I'll wait," said Karl-Heinz.

At lunchtime, the train stopped again, and an army style chowline was set up by a quartermaster crew from nearby Camp Campbell. The prisoners had been issued G.I. mess kits, and they had become experts at filling them. The G.I. cooks and chowline helpers, all recent army inductees, barely out of basic training, stared at this weathered residue of Rommel's heroes. They were fascinated, impressed, and could barely keep their minds on ladling out stew and potatoes.

To the ill-hidden joy of the *Landser,* their own officers were fed last, as they were in the American army. Since they were on the train, there had been no contact between German officers and their men. The *Landser* did not know that this was the doing of the Americans, who preferred to have German noncoms in charge, instead of German officers. Washington had warned that some *AfrikaKorps* officers were still fanatical, unwilling to accept defeat.

Karl-Heinz finished his meal and then dipped his kit with its attached spoon and fork (no knives) into the barrel full of hot water with disinfectant fluid at the end of the line. Then von Bernsdorfer and Gellstein came up behind him.

"We want to speak to you."

"*Wann?*"

"*Jetzt.* Now. We still have ten minutes here, before we load up again."

"I'm listening."

"You're a party member. We need you." Von Bernsdorfer spoke softly, while Gellstein stood by, screening them from others. "We're *Brandenburgers.* The outfit we wanted you for, remember?"

"I remember," said Karl-Heinz, thinking back to Telesty, Paris, and the café at the Rondpoint.

"We're told that a conspiracy called Otto has liaison people here in America," von Bernsdorfer said. "There were some traitors in the *AfrikaKorps* and there are also American agents right here on the transport, according to our sources. A certain Jew is now in Washington, a former Berliner. Anyway, this Jew-swine works for English Intelligence and is getting everything organized. We're supposed to find any traitor or American agent on this transport and we're to get rid of them. Berlin feels this sort of action will stop future nonsense of this kind. Then, we're to make our way to the Atlantic, where we'll be picked up by one of our U-boats. Trouble is, we're now heading too far west, so we have to do what we can while we can still reach the East Coast.

"Where in hell could a U-boat pick you up?"

"Several places. We know the spots. We spent weeks memorizing them. Also we studied enough English so we can say we're Amish from Pennsylvania. You know, the Swabians. They speak with German accents."

"*Lieber Gott*, the whole thing sounds like a real *Schnaps* idea," said Karl-Heinz. "Telesty must have been drunk when he came up with this one. Where the hell are you going to get civvies?"

"Look, we're wearing long pants, not breeches. And we have plain shirts under out tunics. His pants are gray. Mine are tan. We'll switch shirts. No one can tell these are uniforms. Eventually, we'll steal some civvies, or someone gets *umgelegt*, although it's a lot simpler if we don't have to kill anybody!"

Suddenly the plan did not seem quite so hash-brained, and Karl-Heinz shuddered. Otto! Hilde's Otto? So far she had stayed safe. Von Totten was dead, and even this swine's father, old Count von Bernsdorfer zu Kehlsbach, had lost his life, and still Hilde was untouched. Now these two would start all over again. He had to do something.

Karl-Heinz sat down next to Bauer, whom he had first met in the big prison "cage" in Bizerta. *Anständiger Kerl*. Nice fellow. Bauer told him about the trouble with his own men, and Karl-Heinz was amazed. The noncoms all seemed friendly, like that Berlin sergeant at the dock when the MP was yelling at him.

"By the way," said Bauer, "do you know Winkelmann?" He introduced Harry. Karl-Heinz and he went through the usual questions, and Harry trotted out his half-truths. Karl-Heinz did not give it much thought. Sounded very much like his own confused story. Then he asked, "Did you like Paris?"

"*Fantastisch*," said Winkelmann.

"Where did they quarter you?"

"Neuilly." Winkelmann did not pronounce Neuilly properly, *Noy-yii*. He said *Noily*. Strange! What with the two SS *Brandenburger* swine, Karl-Heinz was suddenly alert. "Where," he asked, "were your headquarters?"

"Place de la Concorde," said Harry.

Again, mispronounced. Not the way a German mispronounces French, but some other way. Yet Winkelmann looked real enough. Handsome boy, very young, early twenties. Karl-Heinz was now over thirty and getting gray. Whatever Winkelmann's story was, he did not want to pursue it then and there. He chatted with Bauer. Nothing vital. Bauer was from Hamburg, and like all Hamburg people, he was easygoing, relaxed, and almost English in style. They spoke about Bauer's wife. He had no word from her, but he said that he heard there would be Red Cross people in the prison camp. "Your wife is in Berlin?" he asked. "*Ja*, then we just have to wish each other luck, because Hamburg and Berlin are both being bombed." Bauer looked around. No one was listening. "I never thought we'd be prisoners while they're bombing our homes. *Scheisse!*" They both fell silent, and Karl-Heinz drifted back to his seat at the other end of the car.

The following evening they stopped near a small town in Oklahoma. They looked across miles of flat country, bright pink in the setting sun. Then two cowboys rode up. Actual cowboys! They were slim, middle-aged men in ten-gallon hats, tight shirts, neck bandanas, pointed, high-heeled boots, their legs encased in skintight, faded Levis. They rode next to each other on raw-boned pinto ponies, horses and men so completely in tune that they had almost grown together. Their lassoes were coiled at the fronts of their high-pommeled saddles and blanket rolls were strapped over the backs.

The Germans were goggle-eyed. This was the America of their dreams, the Wild West they all read about in their childhood books.

Bauer nudged Karl-Heinz. "There's Old Shatterhand and

Old Surehand.'' He was speaking of two legendary characters from Karl May adventure books. Every German boy knew them.

A tall MP stood nearby, watching the fascinated Germans. ''You boys like them wranglers?'' he drawled.

Speaking his fluent English, Karl-Heinz said, ''They're fantastic.''

''That's what I do for a living,'' said the MP. ''I'm from Texas. I work on a ranch.''

''You're a cowboy?''

''Waaal,'' said the MP, ''we don't rightly call it that. Like I said, we call 'em wranglers. It's the job. You kinda push the cattle around.''

An MP officer came by and the guard shut up. There was to be no chit-chat with prisoners.

Bauer had understood none of it, so Karl-Heinz translated for him. ''Winkelmann'' came over. He, too, seemed impressed by the cowboys. ''Real film stuff,'' he said. ''Gary Cooper.'' He pronounced it *Gahrie Coe-per,* the way most German filmgoers did. Karl-Heinz nodded.

Harry Wolf, alias ''Winkelmann,'' was quite pleased with himself. He had been on the train for two days, and he seemed to fit in. Bauer had become *kameradschaftlich,* chummy. Harry also liked Captain Dorn, the handsome guy with the E.K. 1. This wasn't really so tough! He was sure now he could pass muster with Germans. Still, he was glad Schmidt had hounded him. In retrospect, it was worth it. He still kept his mouth shut most of the time. He had listened to all their stories about Africa, picked up their slang, even about English and American men and weapons. ''Tommy'' meant English. *Ami* meant American. The feared Eighty-eight gun, their fantastic weapon, was never called the ''Eighty-eight.'' It was called *Flak.*

Germans usually moved briskly, purposefully, not at all like Americans. Americans ambled. Americans waved by passing their hand to and fro a few times, slowly. Germans raised the edge of their hands and shook them, Germans still ''braced'' for their seniors, drawing their heels together.

He tried to identify uniforms and insignia. It was all essentially like the mit-Schmidt course, and he was sure of himself until he saw two death's heads on the lapels of a short black jacket. SS? No. Just *Panzer*. The officer's eagle was on the right chest, like his own, not on the left sleeve, like the SS.

He wanted to join a game of rummy, not unlike gin rummy, but he suddenly realized he could not remember the German words for heart, spade, diamond and club. So he listened for a while. Quite soon he heard them say, *Herz, Pik, Karo, Treff,* and then he could finally join the game. He watched them slam down a winning card, the way they did at *Skat*, the German card game. Some of it came back from his boyhood.

Soldier talk: What was the word for hooker? *Nutte*. Cunt? *Fotze*. Cock? *Pimmel*. Vocabulary they had not studied in Area E, but which was part of this train. The clap? *Der Tripper*.

German officers were a different breed from their American counterparts. They were more remote from their men. In the German army, there were clear social distinctions. No "ninety-day wonders" or "gentlemen-by-Act-of-Congress" like most American officers. Many *Afrika* officers were titled or carried old names, "*von* this" or "*von* that." He was amazed how unconcerned they seemed with the comfort of their men. That was the noncoms' job!

Getting up to stretch his legs, Harry bumped into a slim, blond major. He had seen the man and another officer speaking to Captain Dorn during one of the stops. They seemed to know each other.

"*Pardon!*" he said using the the French word like many Germans.

The other man smiled and shook his hand. "*Schon in Ordnung*. We're all getting wobbly in the knees on this train. Where are you from? You sound like Frankfurt."

"Exactly right."

"Used to be," said the slim major, "that a Frankfurt accent often meant a Jew. There were so many Jews there."

Harry flushed. It was the first time since high school he had come face to face with a remark like that. He caught himself. "*Na*," he said, shrugging, "with me, that's not quite the case, is it, *Herr Major?*"

"Now don't get your ass end in an uproar, *Mein Guter*. It was just a joke! Yesterday, I stood next to you when we were taking out lunchtime leak, and I noticed you were circumcised. I was going to kid you then. Medical reasons, I suppose?"

"Exactly. Had an infection when I was very little. In those

days, the lousy Jew doctors were quick to slice things away. Makes it embarrassing at medical inspections, but so long as I don't try for the SS, I guess I'll be all right.''

The major laughed, patted him on the back, and continued on his way down the aisle.

"I'm absolutely sure,'' said von Bernsdorfer. Gellstein, Karl-Heinz, and he stood at the side of the train near Lubbock, Texas. "We have no more time. The man is a Jew. I spoke to him this morning, and he is an absolute fake. He's even circumcised. Let's get rid of him. We can distract some guards and throttle the pig. The MPs are getting sloppy. Look at them!''

He was right. MPs were smoking and talking to each other. They felt secure after three days with these disciplined Germans who certainly did not seem dangerous. Besides, they were only half a day from their final destination, Roswell, New Mexico, as they had just been told.

"*Grosser Scheissdreck*," said Gellstein. "We're way into Texas, I think. We'll have a hell of a time getting back to the East Coast.''

"*Na*, Gellstein, *beruhigen Sie sich doch*. Calm down. We'll get there. What about this *Hauptmann* Bauer? He and the Jew seem to be very chummy. Do you know him, Dorn?''

"Yes. We were captured together. Seems like a decent fellow.''

"We can still get the Jew. It will show these people that we're here and that we'll deal ruthlessly with Jew agents or with Otto swine. Frankly, I don't think Telesty expected anything more from us than a gesture. Will you help?''

Karl-Heinz nodded. "I'll do something.''

Karl-Heinz finally found Harry, who was half hidden by other prisoners.

"Winkelmann, I want to talk to you.''

"*Natürlich!*''

Karl-Heinz switched to English and whispered, "Look, I don't know who you are, but you are in danger. I can't tell you more. Just get yourself out of trouble right now. I'll try to play, how do you say, for time!''

Harry was stunned, but he was smart enough not to argue. Where had he failed? What did it matter now? He walked up to the tall Texas MP who stood nearby and said in English, under his breath, "Soldier. I'm Lieutenant Wolf, U.S. Intelligence. Get me to the transport commander at once."

The MP stared at him incredulously for a moment, but something about this Kraut speaking English the way he did made a believer out of him. "Come with me," he said. He walked Harry two cars back, where there was an MP sergeant.

"Sah-jint. This here fellow says he's an American officer. Guess you'd better take over."

Harry explained again, urgently. "Ask your C.O.," he said. "He'll tell you I'm aboard."

"Your name?"

"Lieutenant Wolf."

"That your Kraut name?"

"No. That's Winkelmann."

"Right. I was told to look for a guy called Winkelmann. But I didn't know why."

Harry was hustled into the last car, where he met the fat major.

"Jesus," said the major. "Glad I finally found you. I would have had my ass in a sling if anything had gone wrong! Sergeant." He turned to the MP noncom. "This is strictly confidential."

"Yessir."

"Oh," said Harry. "Stick around for a minute, sergeant." He turned to the major. "If that's all right with you, sir?"

"Anything you say, lieutenant."

"There's an officer called Captain Dorn in the second car who warned me I was in trouble. Can we have him brought here?"

"What's he look like, sir?"

"Tall, dark, some gray hair, has an Iron Cross pinned to his tunic."

They "arrested" Karl-Heinz. Then within ten minutes von Bernsdorfer and Gellstein were in handcuffs. To take the onus off him, and at his own suggestion, Karl-Heinz was also in handcuffs. Harry and he playacted a scene, shouting and ranting until the two thunderstruck SS people were taken away to be locked into a sealed, guarded compartment, where the transport commander visited them an hour later, Harry in tow.

"Strip," the major said.

Harry translated.

"Nude?" said von Bernsdorfer, ironically. "We know how sex-crazy you Jews are, but I didn't think you were homos."

Harry said, "Excuse me, sir," to the major. Then he hauled off, and once more von Bernsdorfer came apart when he got slapped. The two SS prisoners took off their shirts and raised their arms. They had not even bothered to remove their tattoos, which were still there.

"I'll be goddammed," said the major.

Harry hitched a ride back aboard an Air Force C-47 from Walker Air Force Base at Roswell, New Mexico, to Washington. He was crestfallen, unable to understand where he had failed, and also relieved that he had escaped unscathed. Schmidt told him to calm down.

"We got a message from London this morning about the two SS men. They are von Bernsdorfer and Gellstein, both part of the Brandenburg organization, and they're skilled intelligence operatives. They assumed that there would be OSS agents on the transports, mainly because of me."

"What's it got to do with you?" asked Harry.

"I'm afraid I'm rather well known in German intelligence circles. The *Abwehr* chaps certainly know me. And the Gestapo and S.D. have reasons to know me. Our little group of ex-Germans in British M.I. 5 and 6 is on every wanted list in Germany. We're their *bêtes noires,* so to speak. Don't forget we all entered England on German passports, and until the war we had to report twice a year to the German consulate general in London, else Britain would have considered us stateless. So the Germans had an easy time keeping tabs on us. Anyway, they must have guessed what I'm doing here in Washington, and they probably assume we'd use the prisoner transports and P.O.W. camps for training. They do it themselves. Deucedly many German agents"—a grin from Harry—"were filtered into camps where they held our prisoners."

"And that's how my cover got blown? Was I that unskilled?"

"Not exactly. You probably would have done fine with any normal group of Jerry officers. But it's hard to get past these Brandenburgers. Anyway, these two bastards were looking for someone just like you, old chap. The other prisoners weren't."

"What about Dorn?" said Harry.

"Did you say Dorn?"

"Yes," said Harry. "The fellow who warned me that I was in trouble was a German captain called Dorn."

"First name?"

"Don't know. Just *Hauptmann* Dorn. About thirty or a bit older. Infantry. Iron Cross First Class. Very handsome. Tall, maybe six feet. Getting a bit gray."

"Which accent?"

"Berlin, I think."

"Incredible!"

"What?"

"Nothing."

Harry continued, "I offered to bring him to Washington, but he insisted on staying with the others. So we worked out some sort of excuse why he had been separated from them."

"Did he seem to know the SS people personally?"

"Yes. I saw them talking the day before I got in trouble."

"That makes sense," said Schmidt, shaking his head in wonderment.

"What do you mean?"

"Doesn't matter for now." Schmidt's card-file mind remembered the Paris agent's photo of Karl-Heinz with Telesty and . . . an SS man called Gellstein! But there was no need for Harry Wolf to know any of this. At least, not now.

Roswell, New Mexico, was founded by Van Smith, a professional gambler from Omaha, who named the place after his father, Roswell Smith. Cattle king Chisum had his ranch there on the Pecos River, and the Mescalero Apaches, once described as the finest light cavalry in the world, had ended their last retreat up in the Sacramento Mountains and had settled there, seventy miles west of town. If anyone had planned to introduce a group of Germans to the American West he could not have chosen a more typical place. Roswell was only a hundred miles from Mexico, and the Spanish influence was strong in food, in language, and in the names of shops and streets.

How many German-language pulp westerns had these *Wehrmacht* soldiers gulped? "West of the Pecos," "East of the Pecos," *"Auf der Chisholm Trail."* Germans loved cowboy and Indian stories, and to think that the *"Kau-Bois"* and *Indianer* were right here and that their beloved *Apatschen*, as the Apaches were called in Munich and Bremen, were only one hundred kilometers away in the mountains! German boys knew terms like "How! I have spoken!" They knew who Manitou was. They knew wampum and smoking the *Friedenspfeife* and that a white man who got killed would probably be *skalpiert*.

And it was in Roswell, New Mexico, that Siegfried Schmidt and Karl-Heinz were to meet again in the old New Mexico Military Institute on Main Street. It was easier for Siegfried Schmidt. He knew what lay ahead: The captain's initials were K.-H., so there was no further doubt. Also, Schmidt had no questions about the purpose of his own life and his own war. He was possessed of a certain equilibrium Karl-Heinz lacked.

Karl-Heinz had been plucked from his barracks by a tough-talking MP and taken into a dark room. It took a few seconds to adjust his eyes after the dazzling, noontime light outside on the N.M.M.I. parade ground. At first, all he could make out was a hunched, burly figure. This failed to reassure him. Then he heard a familiar voice:

"Na, Karle, komm rein! Come on in, Karle!"

There was only one man it could be . . . Siegfried Schmidt! Schmidt stood up, and they embraced like father and son, still friends beyond all uniforms.

"Danke, Karle, for the help," said Schmidt.

"Help?"

"Winkelmann. You probably saved him from getting badly hurt or even killed."

"How did that help you? What did you have to do with Winkelmann? I see you're wearing a Tommy uniform."

"Winkelmann was one of my men."

"I see." Of course! This was the "Berlin Jew" von Bernsdorfer meant!

"Why did you help Winkelmann? I want to know for my own sake."

"I hate those two SS *Scheisskerle*," said Karl-Heinz.

"Personally?"

"Yes. And also as a *guter Deutscher*."

"I once saw a photo of you with Telesty in Paris, and Gellstein was also there. It was in a café at the Rondpoint."

"How the devil did you get my . . . oh, never mind. *Schon gut.*" Karl-Heinz had to smile. "Gellstein was Telesty's aide. Still is, I think."

"*Brandenburgers?*"

Startling! Schmidt knew a lot. The *Brandenburgers* were supposedly a secret organization. "They once tried to recruit me," he said. "In fact, that's exactly the moment when the photo was taken."

"And? Did you accept their offer?"

"That sort of thing is not for me. There are so many swine in that outfit, like Telesty and now von Bernsdorfer."

"Did you know von Bernsdorfer's father?"

"No," said Karl-Heinz. "But I heard what happened to him."

"You know who denounced him?"

"Yes, his beloved son."

"You could only know that if you know about Otto."

"I'm *not* part of Otto!"

"I know you're not. But Hilde is."

Again, Karl-Heinz was stunned. Obviously, Siegfried Schmidt was in complete touch with the people in Berlin. Absolutely *erstaunlich.* Astonishing!

"By the way," Schmidt continued, "as of yesterday, Hilde knows you're here. We got word to her. She knows you're safe."

"Who are 'we'?"

Schmidt shook his head. "*Tut mir leid.* Sorry."

"Still, thank you for contacting her. One question: Does she ever contact you?"

"Never. Her work no longer has any connection with us. Do you know what she has been doing for months?"

Karl-Heinz shrugged. He had no idea.

"Helping to hide Jews from the S.D. and the Gestapo, those few Jews left in Berlin, keeping them out of concentration camps. There are hundreds of Berliners risking their necks to do this, all Aryans."

"My God, that sounds like my Hilde. It must be so dangerous!"

"*Natürlich.*"

"She's fantastic. When she believes in something, she does it. Iron determination."

Siegfried Schmidt lifted the phone in front of him, and

seconds later, a Mexican brought two cups of coffee. There was a pause. They both had too much to say that very moment, so they kept still.

"Karle." Siegfried stood up and put his hands on the younger man's shoulders. "Would you work with me?"

"Doing what?"

"Helping to end this war. Come to Washington with me."

"Siegfried, it sounds so easy. But of all people you must understand who I am, what I am."

Schmidt raised his eyebrows, waiting for Karl-Heinz to explain.

"*Na, ja,*" said Karl-Heinz. "Let me try to tell you. I always turned down Hilde and the others when they asked me to join Otto."

Siegfried Schmidt smoked and listened.

"Do you know why?" Karl-Heinz continued. "Because I was unable to break the barriers. I am a creature of my background. Hilde is much more free. She had a brilliant education. Her parents are intellectuals, liberals. You knew my father. You know all about my life. I just couldn't get myself to step from my path. Can you understand that?"

"Yes. In one way it becomes you. In another, it is a great shame."

"Another thing, Siegfried. I have led a very opportunistic life under the N.S. regime. I had a good career, and I wanted nothing to disturb it. Hilde and I lived comfortably. I'm not proud of that, or of myself. Do you know when you smuggled a letter to us not long after you emigrated?"

Schmidt nodded.

Karl-Heinz continued, "It may not please you to know that I was absolutely panicked. I was aghast that someone might find out, and that it could cause me some difficulty. Hilde and I had a bitter argument. One of many. We almost split up completely until just before I got into the army. Then finally I began to see things her way. There was much about the party bigshots that made me sick, even about our 'sacred' *Führer!*"

"Did you meet him?"

"Yes. I spent time at the Berghof as a Brunzig liaison man and as an N.S.K.K. officer. It was nauseating."

"Well? Surely that should have convinced you."

"Convinced, yes. But would I do something about it? No. Instead, I was happy to get away from it all and into the army. Eventually Rommel became my sponsor. He liked to use me as a direct contact to Gerhardt Brunzig, because he wanted all the latest equipment. It was all a bit shady. Rommel is an ambitious swine, but that didn't bother me. At least I was away from the party *Bonzen* and from that whole Berghof atmosphere. Hilde and I got back together then, just before I went to Africa.''

''I still don't understand why you won't work with me.''

''Perhaps I can put it this way: I turned down the chance to help when I thought it was dangerous to me. So I feel I don't deserve the chance when it is completely safe. I have . . . Siegfried, don't laugh . . . some personal principles.''

''*Na, ja, aber,* are you turning me down completely?''

''*Nein.* I'll help, whenever you need specific information and when I know the answers. Of course, I'll help! But I won't come to Washington with you. Leave me here with my *Kameraden* as a prisoner. They're good fellows. They fought hard. I like them. They're fine Germans. A few of them are still crazy. They think they can get back into this war. But most of them know it's over.''

''Are you sure?''

''Absolutely! *Natürlich!* One look at this country, and anyone with eyes must know we can't win. Maybe if that *Saukerl* Hitler had not tackled the Russians, maybe we could have fought on even terms with this colossal country. But if you had been in Africa . . .''

''What about Africa?''

''In the beginning, we had the Tommies running like rabbits. Then the *Amis* came into it, and they were like little boys; and they got *umgelegt,* wiped out. Then, bit by bit, our *Luftwaffe* disappeared, and our gasoline disappeared, and our food, our ammunition. Then the *Ami* air force began to plaster us, and *Ami* tanks and their trucks were all over us, even if the Tommies often manned them. The idiots from Berlin kept telling us we were fine and that help was on the way and that supplies were coming from Italy, and *Gott weiss was!*''

''How did you feel about it?''

''*Na, ja,* Siegfried, I wasn't trained as a soldier. I was trained as a salesman for Brunzig, with the *Wehrmacht* as my sales territory. Then von Totten and Zoss, who got me my army job, both died.''

''I know.''

"And then, there I was, unskilled and untrained as a soldier. But these men, the others like the ones who are in the camp now, they helped me. They let me become a man, for the first time, the sort of man Hilde can be proud of. I became a good officer. I want to do no more *organisieren*, operating, no more maneuvering for jobs and opportunities. So, I really prefer to stay here until the end."

"And if I need you?" asked Schmidt.

"I'll always be open with you."

They embraced.

Karl-Heinz went back to the barbed-wire enclosure, under escort.

Many times during the next few weeks Karl-Heinz almost rued his decision to stay in Roswell, as the fearful monotony of stockade life took shape. Officers were prevented by international convention from doing manual labor while their men worked on local ranches, farms, and construction jobs. Nor did the officers have administrative duties because the American Military Police had taken complete charge. So they resorted to reading and writing and inventing sports, to playing music and cards, and, more often than not, to facing unutterable boredom.

Karl-Heinz decided to impose upon himself a strict program of physical fitness. He ran and did gymnastic exercises. He ate sparsely and grew dark brown in the New Mexico sunshine. His schedule soon bordered on the fanatic, and one day, after sinking into deep depression because he had forgotten a series of push-ups, he woke up to his own idiotic behavior. What was he doing to himself? Like so many prisoners before him, his daily exercises had become a veritable religion. From then on, the only routine he kept was not to keep a routine. He remained busy, but he made his plans day by day instead of month by month.

One morning in the latrine at the end of their G.I. barracks, he was pulled aside by Bauer.

"Karl-Heinz, they're actually trying to organize an escape."

"Who is?"

"Some of the kids. They're led by two young lieutenants, barely out of the *Hitlerjugend*. What'll we do?"

"Have you talked to anyone else about it?"

"Not yet. You're the first."

"How did you find out about it?"

"They approached me."

Several older officers, Karl-Heinz among them, decided to attend the first meeting of the *Fluchtgruppe,* as the escape committee dubbed itself. Perhaps they could defuse things. The ringleaders were, indeed, kids. The meeting was in a makeshift hall, where they usually held their religious services, so there were no guards present.

Leutnant "Eins": "We've got to get out of here!"

Leutnant "Zwei": "We'll flee one by one and meet at a rendezvous and then find our way through to the Louisiana swamp, the Bayou country, where we can hide. Then we can steal a boat and get into the Gulf of Mexico. He"—*Leutnant "Zwei"* pointed at *Leutnant "Eins"*—"has relatives in Honduras. They can get us onto a German ship."

"And then, I suppose," said the heavy, deep Berlin voice of a major in the paratroops, a solid, wide-shouldered man with ten ribbons on his chest and the Knight's Cross, "after that, I guess we all stick bamboo poles in our mouths, shove some shotgun cartridges up our asses, and fart our way over to the Azores, breathing through the bamboo and acting like submarines. Unless we fart too loud, in which case the *Ami* destroyers would sink us. I think you two kids must have been drinking aviation gasoline. For God's sake, use your heads!" He turned to the others. "I once heard a story from a captured Russki captain near Odessa. There was this little bird flying with its flock over the frozen Russian steppes. The poor little bird got colder and colder, and finally it fell to the hard ground and lay there all alone, freezing to death. Then a great big ox came over to it and—plop—shit on it. Pretty soon, the little bird got warmer, and it began to stir, and then it stuck its head up above the dung. But a falcon swooped down and snapped off its head! Do you know the moral, sonny?"

Leutnant "Eins" shook his head.

"The moral," said the major, "is, firstly, that not all people who shit on you mean you harm. Secondly, as long as you're warm, don't stir, even if you're in the middle of that shit!"

Leutnant "Zwei," red-faced, angry, shouted, "Sir, you're a traitor. Escape is our duty!"

The large paratrooper looked at him the way a bulldog

looks at a toy poodle and said, "Kiss my ass!" Then he left the hall, followed by Karl-Heinz, Bauer, and most of the others.

There was no further talk of escape.

By November 1943, Siegfried Schmidt had almost completed his American assignment, and he looked forward to returning to London. Then, at the last moment, he was given yet one more task.

Every Allied intelligence source on the mainland of Europe seemed to signal that things were not going well for Field Marshal Erwin Rommel and that he had lost the confidence of his *Führer*. After failing to hold together the Italian front he had openly criticized the conduct of the war. He had even been heard to say that the promised "secret weapons" were a myth! Now he commanded the Western defenses against a possible Anglo-American invasion. This seemed a job of extreme importance, but the real decisions were obviously made in Berlin. By now Rommel was only a figurehead, used as a symbol to sustain morale. Besides, the field marshal was in ill health and shuttled to and fro between his headquarters and various hospitals.

Then came this startling intelligence report:

Rommel had probably joined Otto! The anti-Hitler conspiracy, which had suffered nothing but setbacks, finally seemed ready, organized by no less than Admiral Canaris, the "High C," the chief of *Wehrmacht* Intelligence! Supposedly, several ranking generals were ready to support him, but with Rommel on their side, the resistance against the *Führer* would have new, dynamic impact.

Schmidt was instructed to find out as much as he could about Rommel through the *AfrikaKorps* men in American P.O.W. camps. Every small scrap of information was now vital. He immediately thought of Karl-Heinz.

A secret message mentioning Otto went to Karl-Heinz in Roswell. Schmidt needed help. Karl-Heinz had to come to Washington. Schmidt promised it would take only two days, and then Karl-Heinz could rejoin his comrades. If for no other reason than Hilde (and her part in Otto), Karl-Heinz agreed.

They devised a simple ruse. He was fed some pills that brought on symptoms of severe jaundice. Two medics collected him early one morning at his barracks. Promising to return soon, he waved cheerily from his stretcher, but he was clearly a yellow-faced victim of whatever liver disease beset him. Even the *AfrikaKorps* medical officer was concerned.

An ambulance, piloted by the fake medics, actually two Counter-Intelligence Corps agents, drove deep into the countryside behind the air base, where Karl-Heinz changed into a pair of dull-gray slacks, a blue shirt, maroon tie, and a tweed jacket. The CIC men took charge of his *AfrikaKorps* uniform. Thirty minutes later, he was on a twin-engine air force bomber for the long flight to National Airport, Washington. There he was hustled into a staff car, and that night he met with Schmidt and his American associate Colonel Timmons. Both Schmidt and the colonel were shocked by Karl-Heinz's ghastly yellow hue until they remembered the cover story. They showed him into a comfortable room with leather couches, framed hunting, and horseracing scenes, and wood-paneled walls.

Schmidt got right into the subject.

Karl-Heinz,'' he said, ''we hear that Rommel is in trouble and has fallen out with the *Führer*.''

''Since when?''

''The last few months. Recently he visited the *Führer*, who, they say, was most cordial and flattering, but was so shocked by Rommel's state of health that he immediately ordered him to the hospital. This did not help Rommel's cause. As you surely know, a lot of General Staff people hate Rommel, and since the field marshal had openly criticized the *Führer*, they are waiting to pounce.''

''*Na, ja*. The story was that because Rommel was not born a gentleman, the *Adligen*, the aristocrats on the General Staff, hate him. But that might be nonsense.''

''Any other rumors?'' asked the colonel, in German.

''*Ja natürlich*. Plenty! After all, Rommel was 'Hitler's general.' There seemed to be a lot of ass-kissing, as there is on most General Staffs, and so everybody was trying, as we say in Berlin, to creep into the *Führer*'s rectum.'' Colonel Timmons nodded. He seemed to understand German extremely well, and Schmidt grinned when he heard the old *''Im Asch kriechen''* expression.

Schmidt asked, ''How did you find Rommel? I mean, personally?''

''Quite charming. Very straightforward. But that is deceiving.''

"How do you mean?"

"*Na, ja,* he is an operator, meaning that when he sees a way of getting some advantages, he has no false pride. He is always trying to gain the edge over his competitors in the *Wehrmacht.*"

"Explain."

"He hired me for his staff because I had done him a favor. I had introduced him to one of the top people at Brunzig. So I asked him for a job, and he gave it to me. It was understood I would keep pursuing Brunzig for him."

"He wanted to have you on the payroll, as we say in America?" said Colonel Timmons. He reminded Karl-Heinz of Zoss.

"*Absolut.*"

"But he left you behind when he handed over command to General von Arnim?"

"Yes," said Karl-Heinz. "He left most of his people. By then I already had a feeling it was all over for him. We heard he was very ill, some sort of desert malignancy, perhaps *Krebs,* cancer. Then I joined the line *Panzer* Division. My influence-peddling days and liaison days were over. Anyway, two of my contacts were gone. You know one of them, Siegfried: Zoss, who got drowned in the Atlantic. He was on his way to the United States on some job for Gerhardt Brunzig. I believe he was secretly trying to recruit help for Otto, but I was not part of Otto, so I could only guess. The other was von Totten. And you know what happened to him."

Both Schmidt and Colonel Timmons nodded. Timmons said, "Executed."

"These were my two real contacts with Stuttgart and Brunzig and, thereby, my leverage with Rommel. I did not deal with Gerhardt Brunzig directly, although Rommel thought so."

Siegfried Schmidt stood up and walked around the room, his chunky Germanic figure still at odds with his British officer's tunic and Sam Browne belt. "Was there," he said, "any time, any moment when you thought he might be out of sympathy with the party?"

"*Na, mein guter Siegfried,* I was only a small fry. I probably spent a total of fifty full hours with the man between France, Stuttgart, and Africa. But if you ask me for an instinctive feeling, I'd say that for as long as the *Führer* and the party are of help to Rommel's career, he will stay loyal to them. But I do remember one thing that concerned me most directly. In fact, I thought it was the end of me and Hilde and everyone around us."

"*Was denn?*" Even Colonel Timmons, fascinated, suddenly spoke German.

"Early this year, I can't remember the exact month, I was told to report to Rommel directly. We were on the run, and everyone in our division was amazed that the *Herr General Feldmarschall* himself had sent for me. They didn't know much about my original association with Rommel. Anyway, I finally found 'Moritz.' You know what 'Moritz' was, don't you?"

"Yes, dammit," said Schmidt. Then he explained to Timmons, who seemed at a loss, " 'Moritz' was General 'Bull' Connor's command vehicle, which was captured along with him. Rommel had it repainted with *AfrikaKorps* insignia and made it into his own command vehicle. He named it 'Moritz.' "

Timmons said, "Like *'Max und Moritz'?*" He could not hide a grin.

"Right. There was also a 'Max' they had captured. Anyway, that's what my young friend here meant, blast it. Nothing to bring pride to a British officer!" Schmidt shook a mock-threatening finger at Karl-Heinz, the way he had many times in their KaDeBe days.

Karl-Heinz continued, "When I got to the *General Feld-marschall,* he swore me to secrecy and then showed me a directive from Kaltenbrunner of the *Reichs Sicherheits Hauptamt,* that Rommel was to arrest anyone associated with von Totten and the Otto conspiracy. Von Totten had just been executed. This was a direct *Führer*-order, with the usual jargon about 'ruthlessly eliminating these vermin' and so on."

"What happened?"

"Rommel acted as if I could not possibly have been part of any conspiracy. He accepted my half-baked explanations and said, *'Basta.'* I was sent back to my division."

"Why? Why do you think he let you go?" Timmons shook his head in disbelief.

"I have often tried to figure it out. Did he think I could still be of help to him? Or did he think Kalterbrunner was an *Arschloch* like most of the SS? After all, there were no SS units in Africa, and I would guess it was Rommel who kept them out. Did he just plain say, 'To hell with the bunch around the *Führer*'? Or, finally, did he see that it was time to join Otto and he thought of me as a future ally?''

Karl-Heinz counted off all these options on the fingers of his hand as he had obviously done many times before.

They adjourned for dinner in a small dining room on the same floor. The table was set for four, and the man who joined them, now in his paratroop uniform, was Harry Wolf, who greeted Karl-Heinz warmly. Of course, Timmons knew the whole story of the aborted "test run" on the prisoner transport. He said, "Trust Wolf to run into two trained SS undercover men."

"Wolf?" Karl-Heinz was puzzled.

"That's my real name, Harry Wolf," said Harry. "The Winkelmann was part of my act. Not a very good act, I'm afraid."

He spoke English and so, without thinking much about it, did Karl-Heinz. Schmidt was amused. "When Karl-Heinz worked for me in thirty-one, thirty-two—oh, you didn't know how long we've known each other?" Timmons and Harry Wolf shook their heads. "Anyway," Schmidt went on, "I used to be infuriated because this boy could speak English better than I. We traveled to England, and for him it was the first time and, by Jove"—grins around the table—"he got along better than I. Even found a marvelous girl. Married her, in fact."

"Is she English?" Harry asked.

"No," said Karl-Heinz. "She worked in the German consulate general in London."

"Where is she now?"

"Berlin, I'm afraid."

Knowing that Berlin was under heavy bombardment, the others said nothing. Then Schmidt broke the silence. "Karl-Heinz, may I tell them about Hilde?"

Karl-Heinz nodded.

"A marvelous girl," said Schmidt. "Fine old academic family from Nürnberg. Thoroughly opposed to the whole bloody Nazi movement, since the very beginning. Extremely involved in the underground resistance. Right now she is helping to hide Jews from the SS. I daresay that one of the reasons my friend Karl-Heinz is here is because he wants to do everything to protect his wife. Correct?''

"Correct."

"But forgive me," said Colonel Timmons. "You yourself never joined the Otto movement?"

"No. Many reasons. Schmidt can tell you more. On the other hand, I suppose I have never really been a good National Socialist. In fact, if I were a Nazi, would I be here?"

"And would he have saved my tail?" said Harry. "Forgive me, sir, but I think there must be more to the story."

"Again"—Karl-Heinz shook his head and smiled—"I refer you to my British army friend here. He knows me almost as well as my own father did. But now I wonder if I may be allowed to ask something?"

"Of course," said Colonel Timmons.

Karl-Heinz turned to Harry Wolf. "What is the reason you are here in an *Ami,* excuse me, American uniform? You must be twenty-two, -three years old."

"Twenty-four."

"Why did you come here?"

"Believe me," said Harry, "it wasn't my idea. It was the idea of your great *Führer und Reichskanzler* and his racial laws."

"Jewish?"

"Jewish."

"Full-blooded?"

"Full-blooded."

Karl-Heinz shook his head and looked at Siegfried. "The longer I live, the more I see what *Unfug,* what nonsense the movement tried to teach the German people. How could we afford to lose boys like this?" He pointed at Harry.

Harry laughed. "My father, who served in a Hessian regiment in World War One, is glad you lost me! He only wishes the American army would also lose me. He's not too fond of armies. He made it all the way to *Unteroffizier,* a sergeant. He finally got badly wounded in Cambrai."

"Where is he now?"

"Here in America, in New York, with all the other German Jewish refugees, moaning how bad the *Streuselkuchen* tastes in America. We don't talk much. He and my mother think I'm from some strange new breed. Germans are funny, as you know. Even Germans who've been told they're not Germans."

Karl-Heinz looked unhappy. *"Was für 'ne Scheisse!"* he said, to Siegfried Schmidt. It was the old German army way of saying, "What a stinking mess!"

The next day, true to his promise, Siegfried Schmidt was ready to ship Karl-Heinz back to Roswell, but Karl-Heinz was still quite yellow in the face. So he stayed another thirty-six hours, so the German army doctor in Roswell would see he was completely cured.

Colonel Al Timmons had grown extremely fond of Schmidt during their many months together. Timmons, a first-rate international lawyer in civilian life and a close friend of the founder of OSS, Colonel Donovan, had studied in Germany and lived there for years, representing American firms. He spoke almost perfect German and felt he understood Germans. In fact, he was quite fond of them. Now he thought of them as an ill nation and, therefore, irrational.

He asked Schmidt if he might have a crack at recruiting Karl-Heinz.

"Go ahead," said Schmidt. "But I doubt if you'll get anywhere. I couldn't and I know him well. He can be very stubborn. But I can't tell you why he won't work for us. Maybe he will. I gave my word. That's why he's here."

Nevertheless, Al Timmons wanted to speak to Karl-Heinz in the privacy of his small office on the top floor of Area E.

"Herr Dorn, there's something I simply cannot reconcile with everything I have learned about you."

Karl-Heinz listened.

Timmons continued, "When you speak of the Nazi *Bonzen*, you do so with disdain. For instance, when you described the Kaltenbrunner order with the *Führer*'s typical jargon, you obviously despise it."

"I do."

"Also you're willing to stick out your neck and save one of our men. And you agreed to come here and help us in the Rommel matter. Then Siegfried Schmidt tells us about that wonderful wife of yours who is very anti-Hitler, and is risking her life right now to help Jews."

"All correct."

"Then, won't you join us? Won't you help free your own country from this evil?"

Karl-Heinz looked down at his folded hands. Then, as if to himself, he said, "Didn't Siegfried say why I feel this way?"

"No. He refused to tell me."

"Wonderful Siegfried. He is the most loyal of men. Look, *Herr Oberst*, Hilde, my wife, hated the Nazis from the beginning. I didn't. I thought they were good for Germany. Actually, I had quite a career because I became a party member, and, in fact, I was working close to party *Bonzen*. It took a while until I finally got the feeling that this Nazi heaven might not be as glorious as I had once thought. By the time I got to Africa, my days of sympathy for the party were over. But I am a conventional man. It is hard for me to join the resistance. Instead, I decided to take my chances as an ordinary infantry officer and to do my best. Later, I'd help rebuild."

"May I ask you this: Were you ever really a Nazi?"

"Do you mean if I denounced and beat Jews or sent them to concentration camps? Never! Of course not. I could never feel any hatred for them the way every good German was supposed to. But I must admit I was damn glad I wasn't a Jew!"

"Frank talk," said Al Timmons, quietly thinking that he had often felt the same way when he heard that this or that prominent Jew had been barred from joining a good club. Damn right he understood, though he wasn't too proud of it.

"And so," Karl-Heinz said, "I'll stay with my comrades in the camp until it's all over. Then I'll go back to my poor Germany and help. Do you see?"

"I think so."

"Frankly, I feel that joining you would be opportunistic, and the man you're looking at has been guilty of too much opportunism in his life."

"All right." Al Timmons nodded, but sadly.

The next day Karl-Heinz was taken sightseeing in Washington like any tourist. He made the rounds from the Washington Monument to the outside of the White House and the imposing Capitol Dome, and he was impressed. But it was not until he stood in front of the vast, brooding figure of Abraham Lincoln looking out over the city from inside his memorial that he really began to feel a sense of discovery. He read the Gettysburg Address on the wall. Someday he would learn more about America, but not from the inside of a prison camp, and not while Germany was fighting for her life.

He was back in his own old uniform and with the others the next evening. They greeted him as if he had miraculously returned from the grave.

As soon as he spotted Karl-Heinz getting out of the ambulance, the paratroop major shouted. *"Da kommt ja unser Chinese*, here comes our Chinese." A colorful reference to the recent shade of Karl-Heinz's face. Then he said, "And the son of a bitch didn't even bring an *Ami* nurse with him! Dorn, you're a *Scheisskerl!* I'm getting a callus on my hand from jerking off!"

Later the major took Karl-Heinz aside. "Karle," he said, "I finally had word from the Red Cross. Berlin is in terrible shape! They can't find out anything. They're being hit day and night. *Scheiss*-Göring and his *Scheiss*-bragging! And our beloved *Führer* is probably hiding out down in his bunker, reading dispatches from the little *Doktor. Verdammt nochmal!"*

He quickly wiped a massive hand over his eyes.

The chilly night of November 23 forecast a long north German winter. Shivering Berliners had been ducking into and out of air-raid shelters as American Flying Fortresses by day and British Lancasters by night rained bombs onto their miserable city. Yet they kept up a reasonable sense of humor and wit, even though the city's houses were collapsing around and on top of them.

By eight that evening, the sirens had started to wail. Once, they had been a warning. Now they were only like the howl of a suffering animal.

Hilde Dorn got on her bicycle in front of the damaged apartment house on Adolf Hitler Platz and began the long, dangerous journey down bomb-cratered Masurenallee, toward Charlottenburg. Vast fires were burning in the north of the city, and she could hear flak from the western air defenses. The cold wind brought tears, which ran down her cheeks, and she thought of her poor skin, ravaged by weeks of cold weather. Would she ever again be able to sit in a beauty parlor?

Just then, the first British planes were high overhead in the black sky, and searchlights from the Grunewald probed for them, like long, slim fingers, while flak burst in a display of deadly fireworks. Despite the brutal noise and the hell all around, Hilde grinned, remembering the gentle hands of her old beautician. She pedaled on. When this war was over, she'd have legs like a weight lifter!

Up ahead, near the Funkturm tower, a blockbuster bomb had torn a deep, new crater into the pavement, and firemen were trying to douse a burning gas main. She had to walk her bike around the mess. No one paid much attention to her. The firemen seemed quite old, mostly in their sixties. Most younger men were in the *Wehrmacht*. There were also some teenage boys helping out. She felt sorry for them, but they seemed to enjoy themselves. It obviously made them feel important, and they yelled to each other in mock-manly voices.

Further along, on Kantstrasse, an apartment house was burning and, as usual, there were wounded people being brought out of their ruined flats. Amazing! After all the raids, destruction, and death, there were still many Berliners who would not go into the cellars, because they preferred to take their chances in their own flats. After all, it would not happen to them. *"Menschenskind, mir könn se' Alle!"* It was their Berlin way of saying, while pointing their thumbs in the direction of the bombers above, "Go screw yourselves."

An old woman was propped against the curb, whimpering. She was bleeding from some body wound, and her wool-stockinged legs were flooded with red ooze, which formed a puddle around her. She rocked to and fro, muttering *"Um Jottes willen . . ."* Oh, my God, Hilde wanted to help, but she had to keep going. Then the woman screamed. Hilde had seen it often: The shock had worn off, and now the pain came with a thousand knives. A policeman leaned over her. He said, *"Na, Mütterchen . . ."* and shook his head. What could he do?

Hilde finally reached Mommsenstrasse, near where Karl-Heinz had once lived. She had to find it by instinct in that nightmare of flash and noise and darkness.

Then she turned toward Sybelstrasse, where she found the house she was looking for. Thank God, it was still untouched! She walked her bike into the entranceway and knocked at the door, as hard as she could, three times. It opened, and the porter's wife, a fat, disheveled woman, took her bike and led her into her ground-floor apartment.

Someone said, "Hilde?"

"*Ja.*"

A tall woman stood silhouetted in the gloom. "We have the whole family," she said. Her voice was calm. "*Frau* Balinsky here has been wonderful. We couldn't have done it without her." She obviously meant the fat woman, who grumbled, "*Na, ja,* it was nothing! I'll keep your bike here, *Frau* Dorn."

"I'm ready," said Hilde. "Shall we get going?"

From a door in the back of the room, barely seen except in the occasional flash of flak shells, like lightning during a thunderstorm, there emerged a man, a woman, and two small girls. Jews. The fat woman opened the front door for them and then Hilde led the way on foot toward a church about three hundred meters away. The tall calm woman brought up the rear. No one paid much attention to them, and there were quite a few people on the street, all busy saving their own or others' lives and belongings, dodging for new shelter, or looking for relatives. There were also drunk soldiers on leave and, incredibly, whores soliciting them. Charlottenburg, after months of round-the-clock air attacks, stayed true to its bordello history. It would survive, no matter what!

They reached the church. The side door was open, and the four Jews were quickly led to a basement room.

While the tall woman waited, Hilde then walked toward the dark altar, genuflected and crossed herself. She was not alone. There were many people sitting quietly in the pews, although the cold wind blew through shattered stained-glass windows above them.

Hilde rejoined her companion and the priest, a short man. She introduced the tall woman. "Father, do you know the *Baronin* von Tessold?" The priest acknowledged by nodding his head. "Bless you both," he said. "Bless you! Would you like to stay here?"

"No thank you," said the baroness. "We have to meet some others. This is a good night for it. Everyone is busy. Our little Hilde"—she gave Hilde a hug—"bicycled all the way from the west. She's a brave girl!"

They left the church and aimed toward the Kurfürstendamm, where they had a rendezvous with several other "helpers" in Fasanenstrasse, not too far away. As they got nearer, they saw that the Kaiser Wilhelm Memorial Church, the huge cathedral at the end of the Kurfürstendamm, was in flames.

Incredible! More than anything they had seen, this proved that Berlin was now mortally wounded. The Kaiser Wilhelm Church was the true Berliner's symbol of his city, more so even than the Brandenburg Gate. It was clearly too late to save it, and the firemen had given up. The spire burned like some vast, macabre torch.

They stopped for a moment, riveted by the sight. An old policeman behind them said, *"Was würde seine Scheiss-Majestät Kaiser Wilhelm dazu sagen?* What would his shit-majesty Kaiser Wilhelm say to all this?"

"What?" asked the baroness. "What would he say?"

"He'd say"—and he trotted out the propaganda slogan of the early Hitler days when all seemed rosy—"he'd say, 'You can thank your *Führer* for all this!' "

In a nearby flat, they met with their group, women who ranged from a countess to a washerwoman, all good Germans, several of them real *Berliner Pflanzen,* "Berlin plants," as the Berlin woman was called. How did the old song go?

> *Denkst de' denn, denkst de' denn*
> *Du Berliner Pflanze*
> *Denkst de' denn ick heirat dir,*
> *Weil ick mit dir tanze?*
>
> You've got the wrong slant,
> you Berlin plant.
> Don't dare suppose
> That I'll propose.
> Dancin' is dancin'
> Not serious romancin'!

It seemed so very long ago since Berlin's music-hall singers used to belt it out.

Their hostess, a doctor's wife, arm badly burnt in a recent air raid, even served cups of scarce ersatz coffee, made of God knows what. She had to heat the water with wood. There was no gas because of the danger of explosion.

By midnight the raid had ended, and the Baroness von Tessold and Hilde set out back to the flat on Sybelstrasse, because Hilde had to get her bike. Kaiser Wilhelm Church was still burning. Ambulances and fire engines were chasing to and fro, and people were still emerging from their cellars to see what evil surprises this night had brought. Was their apartment still there? Did Grandfather Hugo make it to the shelter? Did all the warm clothes get stolen?

As they walked along, the baroness said, "Any news of your husband?"

"Yes, finally! He seems to be all right. He's a prisoner in America."

"Are you sure?"

"Absolutely." Hilde asked, "What about your son?"

The baroness shrugged. "In Italy, somewhere. But, as you know, we've kept precious little contact. He's SS, and he hates me for whatever I stand for. His father has been dead for years. In a way, I suppose, it's all my fault."

"Why? How can you be blamed?"

"*Pensionat*. Boarding schools. No contact. No warmth. No affection. No kisses. Our Prussian code: so-called manliness. He was always a sickly boy. His father thought boarding school would toughen him. We *Junker* families pamper no one. And I went along, although I knew it was wrong."

"Forgive me for presuming to give advice," said Hilde. "But I don't believe it ever happens that way. If he could only see you now, he'd have to admire you. He'd be proud of you."

"For hiding out Jews?" The baroness shook her head. "He knows we have some Jewish blood, his great-aunt on my mother's side, and he's never forgiven me. What's more, he hates himself for that tiny bit of Jewish blood. He thinks it makes him impure. He's petrified the SS will find out. I wouldn't be surprised"—the baroness shook her head—"if that is the only thing that keeps me out of Dachau. I'm sure he knows I'm working underground, but he's afraid that if he denounces me, I might talk about his one Jewish great-aunt!"

Almost an hour later, after riding her bike or walking or waiting while blocked streets were cleared, at nearly two in the morning, Hilde had almost reached home. She was on the Masurenalle, opposite the same spot where a bomb had fallen earlier that night. The big Rundfunk broadcast building was on her right, and she had to dodge some firetrucks, one of which overtook her. Its headlights were blacked out except for tiny slits, and the driver missed her by only centimeters because he did not see the rear reflector on her bike. It was a close call, and she was very scared.

Then it all came to an end. Probably it was an incendiary bomb that had penetrated the pavement earlier and had finally set off a gas main below. The ground came up to hit her, and there was darkness or light or vile sound or total silence. Who could know what Hilde felt in the dreadful, final surprise of sudden, violent death?

The fire engine that had just passed her came to a halt, and firemen ran toward her. They had seen her spraddled flying figure silhouetted in the flash of the explosion. Then they found her many meters away on the sidewalk, they shook their heads, long ago resigned to the sight of death.

This was the night of November 23, nineteen hundred and forty-three, only ten short years after Hitler's takeover.

At last Siegfried Schmidt had completed his assignment in America. He had packed and was finally within a day of going home to London. Then, through his usual clandestine sources, he received word of Hilde's death.

Immediately he used every bit of leverage he could muster to hitch an air force ride to Roswell, knowing that if there were hold-ups he could easily lose his seat on the flight home to Britain.

And so they met again in that dark room in the New Mexico Military Institute, and this time they both wept.

Karl-Heinz returned to the stockade and shut himself away behind a wall of sorrow. Bauer and the paratroop major tried their best, but for many weeks he lived in his private purgatory. If only he had not let her down! He had such hopes for them, such plans. Then, slowly, he rejoined the others, and they welcomed him.

GERMANY

1946

KARL-HEINZ'S REPATRIATION began in 1946. At first they were all shipped from Roswell to Boulogne, where they were held for several months in P.O.W. camps while Allied authorities tried to figure out their future. Several thousand *Landser* were sent to the south of France to help with the harvest, but officers were eventually released with special identification cards as former P.O.W.s. Karl-Heinz, Bauer, and the Berlin paratroop major managed to get on a train to Cologne, where Bauer left them. He was off to Hamburg to find his family. When Karl-Heinz saw the lanky figure disappearing at the end of the ruined station platform, he felt unutterably sad. Bauer had been like a brother.

"Na, mein Guter," said the major. *"Auf-auf nach der Reichshauptstadt!"* which was, at best, comical, because Berlin was certainly no longer the capital of Germany nor even one of the world's great cities. From all they had heard, it was a heap of rubble. Yet, somehow, Karl-Heinz did not care. What was there in Berlin for him? Then he kicked himself. The major's family was still there, and that blunt man was hiding his anxiety behind his usual front of snottiness and humor.

But Karl-Heinz decided not to accompany the major. Instead, he set off to Stuttgart. He had read accounts of Gerhardt

Brunzig's short trial and knew that Brunzig was back at Villa Ritterschwert, or what was left of it.

Gerhardt was happy to see him and to offer him work and a home. Karl-Heinz moved into Ritterschwert. There were no servants, but he was quite content. After Roswell, the biggest luxury was a room of his own. Privacy.

When Zummer the mechanic first saw Karl-Heinz, he looked at him almost happily and said, "*Herr* Dorn! Where the hell have you been? They told me you had *abjenubbelt*, that you had 'bought it' in Africa?"

"I was in America. A prisoner. Since forty-three."

"*Na, ja,*" said Zummer, his large paw gesturing at the devastation outside and, by implication, at the last five years of inferno. "*Da habn se' och nischt vamisst!*" In the broadest of Berlinese, this meant, "You didn't miss a fuckin' thing." As a Berliner, he refused to let anything impress him, not even the loss of Germany.

For the first time since he came home, Karl-Heinz stood in front of the spot where their apartment house had once been. Now he could see straight across from the former Adolf Hitler Platz, now Theodor Heuss Square, to the Berlin Skating Club, which had, ironically, stayed untouched. Yet, although it was January and snow covered the sidewalks and the rubble, no one was skating. The sound of puck hitting hockey stick had long disappeared, along with most things. In his mind's eye, there stood Zoss's beautiful Brunzig and their little BMW convertible, ready for weekends at Wannsee.

It was 1949, over five years since the night Hilde had died. Ignoring the cutting wind, he walked back toward the wide Masurenalle until he reached the spot where they said it had happened, but he could find no special sense of sanctity. It was simply a piece of roadway in front of the long, bomb-scarred Broadcast House. The old Funkturm tower stood behind his right shoulder, miraculously unscathed, and beyond that the famous banked north turn of the Avus, and memories of Morgenroth, the Forstmanns, Fritz Scharn, and Zoss.

He had tried to find them all to make contact. Then, in some cases with amazing ease, and slowly in others, they had reappeared, like the cast credits of an old UFA film; the quick picture of a smiling Richthofen in the cockpit of his plane, and then: "Richthofen: FRITZ SCHARN." Hannes Morgenroth and Anneliese were alive. They spent the last years of the war as exiles in Switzerland. Now they were back in Berlin as guests in someone's Dahlem villa. Morgenroth limped and looked old, but he spoke about racing again, and when Karl-Heinz quickly looked at Anneliese to see if she agreed, he found no sign of disapproval.

Gerhardt Brunzig was arrested for war-crimes trials in 1947. He was accused of having employed slave labor. It was true, of course, that conscripted foreigners were part of Brunzig's wartime work force.

With the help of many people, including the American Jack Kingsley, Lord and Lady Bryston, and even the very distinguished Jewish Baron Montrouge, Gerhardt could prove his lack of sympathy for the Nazis. Besides, he had employed known resistance fighters like the late Armin Zoss and was closely associated with the executed Otto martyr, Major von Totten.

There seemed no question about his feelings.

"Why then, *Herr* Brunzig," asked the prosecutor, "Why then did you not give up the chairmanship of Brunzig? Surely you knew that the longer you were involved, the more you would identify yourself with certain Nazi crimes, like forced labor?"

"Because, my dear sir," said Gerhardt, almost bursting with uncharacteristic forcefulness, all his languor discarded for the moment, "because I felt it was necessary to save the great company my father had founded! Because I knew all along that when all this was over, when these dreadful people were gone and buried, Germany would still be there. And because Brunzig can help to rebuild Germany's *Wirtschaft,* its economy. Our poor Germany! We need to help our country now. I am ready, and so is Brunzig A.G."

Many anti-Nazi German spectators and witnesses in the courtroom clapped their approval.

Gerhardt Brunzig was freed by the tribunal.

Villa Ritterschwert still stood, its outside scarred by bombs, its inside stripped by Allied occupation troops. After negotiating with the military government, Brunzig was allowed to move back into his old home. Down in the valley, the city of Stuttgart had disappeared, flattened by a giant steamroller. Gerhardt set about the rebuilding of Brunzig, and within six months, the first Brunzig chassis, tubular-steel creations, based on a new design, began to emerge, because, wonder of wonders, Dr. Maut had also survived. He was never even arrested. Besides, Gerhardt Brunzig had requested him.

The Forstmanns had survived and were in Munich. Erich was preparing his first postwar production at the Geiselgasteig studios. Handsome Fritz Scharn was also in Munich, married to a wealthy Argentine woman, who was somewhat his senior.

Papa Hoegel had spent the last part of the war in Spain, as the guest of friends from the old racing days. Now he was on his way back to Stuttgart, hoping to help Morgenroth talk Gerhardt Brunzig into a new race car. Considering the times, this seemed absurd, but Gerhardt Brunzig was quite aware of the publicity value of racing. Besides, rumor had it that the Russian-dominated German factories in the Eastern Zone were ready to launch a sports car for international racing. They employed several talented German designers from the prewar days.

Von Bernsdorfer and Gellstein were still under arrest in Nürnberg, waiting for their turn to be tried. They were only minor Nazi functionaries, and their trial would come as soon as the cases against the superiors had been disposed of.

The amazing thing was how many had survived!

Sadly, the Antmanns had not. Hilde's parents were killed one week after their daughter, when a bomb cut through their old Nürnberg house like a meat cleaver. News of their death came as a dull echo to the sadness within Karl-Heinz. But how could he have helped them to face Hilde's death when he himself had not learned to bear it?

He tried to find the whereabouts of Hilde's sister, but there was absolutely no trace of her. Finally, he heard that she had managed to get to Argentina.

Telesty?

No one knew where Telesty was hiding. Even Allied intelligence authorities had almost given up. His only arrest "category" was his senior rank in the SS. Beyond that, he was not known to have committed any war crimes in the technical sense, such as the killing of prisoners, the execution of Jews, the use of slave labor. So Telesty, whom Karl-Heinz considered an archcriminal, could not be criminally accused within context of the Nürnberg trials, and eventually, the hunt for him was suspended.

•   •   •

The real reason Karl-Heinz was back in Berlin in 1949 stood near the north turn of the old Avus: a tiny, oval loaf of a silver-colored racing coupe, powered by a small version of an aircraft engine. It had no chassis. Instead, the whole thing was composed of a network of featherweight steel tubes covered by a thin aluminum skin, again in the manner of a plane. The car weighed a third of the old bellowing prewar monsters, but the new engine and body, together with a tricky independent suspension, promised much better acceleration, braking, and handling. Dr. Maut had planned this machine for years.

Despite the cold, the Avus was clear of snow, and anyway, the car was a closed coupe. They had to begin testing there and then, because the first international racing season was upon them, and Avus was the only test track available to them, because it was in fair shape. Other tracks had been ruined by bombs or were closed by bad weather and neglect. But the mayor of Berlin was anxious to help. Since the airlift Berliners felt invigorated.

A familiar cast was assembled: Papa Hoegel, trilby-hatted, fat, unchanged. Morgenroth, limping, overweight, in his white prewar coveralls. He still wore his white cloth helmet and goggles. Anneliese, chic in U.S. air force leather jacket and corduroy slacks, was tying her husband's polka-dot ascot, his characteristic trademark. Zummer checked tire pressures. Karl-Heinz stood by with stopwatches and clipboard. Dr. Maut squatted, but a fancied oil leak turned out to be a puddle of melting snow. The day was clear, perfect for the birth of 190X, the first experimental race car Brunzig had produced since the war.

The engine came to life with a silky purr, completely unlike the bellowing monsters of old. After a final puff on his cigarette, the old champion ducked into the low coupe and started his run. The car performed brilliantly: arrow-straight, steady, and very, very fast. In the turns it was glued to the road. At the end of the first hour of testing, Morgenroth got out, smiling widely, and said, *"Unglaubliches Ding! Erstklassig!"*

He was right. This was an unbelievable, a first-rate vehicle, but Anneliese, Dorn, Zummer, and Papa Hoegel were not concentrating on the 190X. Their concern was its pilot, and, although Morgenroth limped and had difficulties folding himself into the modern cockpit, he seemed cheerful and capable. Admittedly, compared with the old cars, 190X was easy to drive, but, for now, it looked as if Morgenroth's skills were still intact.

Papa Hoegel even shouted out the famous prewar two-line poem about his Number one:

> *Der Hannes,*
> *Der kan es!*

Or, loosely:

> Wow!
> Hannes knows how!

The only one there who seemed to care little about Morgenroth was Dr. Maut. His head was deep in the car's engine compartment.

Nothing had changed his priorities.

BERLIN

1951

KARL-HEINZ DID not return to Berlin until 1951, when he met with Dr. Rottmann, his new chief. It was a spring day, and they went to a café on Kurfürstendamm. They found a table on the sunny outdoor terrace.

"You Berliners are absolutely incredible," said Uwe Rottmann. He pointed at the ruined tower of the Kaiser Wilhelm Church, which had become a permanent memorial, looming over them as a grim reminder. "Do you know what my taxi driver called that church tower? 'The Hollow Tooth!' And it does look like an immense dead molar." Dr. Rottmann was in his late forties, slim and gray-haired, suntanned and cheerful, and he was the new managing director and chief of Hubertus Brunzig A.G.

Rottmann was typical of his generation of German business leaders, a welcome contrast from the classic heavy-bellied, cigar-smoking prewar *Generaldirektor*. Rottmann had served as a tank officer in Russia and France. He was captured during the Allied invasion but was soon released. He was an automobile man, a graduate engineer, and an enthusiastic amateur racer and rallyist. Before the war, like Zoss in Berlin, Rottmann had run Brunzig's Munich operation. After Gerhardt Brunzig's death, he was everyone's favorite choice for the chairman's office.

Karl-Heinz smiled and agreed. "Yes, Berlin is still unique.

But I hate to admit that it has become provincial. After all, it's isolated here in the middle of the Eastern Zone.''

"That's the reason I'm here. I feel we ought to let Berlin know that we at Brunzig haven't forgotten it. I want to set up a marketing center here." He used the English word *marketing*. "We must create large displays. I want more of the Berlin taxi fleet to be Brunzigs, maybe our new diesels. And the rental people, like the American Hertz Company, we want to make sure they have plenty of Brunzigs. I want to encourage Berlin businessmen to buy Brunzigs. I want to hold more tests on the Avus. Everything to show the Knight's Sword to Berliners.'' He shook his fist in a mock-combative gesture. "Or do I sound a touch pompous?'' He grinned, deprecating his words.

Karl-Heinz shook his head. "Of course not. I agree wholeheartedly.''

"You're a Berliner, right?'' said Rottmann.

"Born five minutes from here.''

"Would you like the job?''

"Which job, sir?''

"Of running the Berlin show for Brunzig.''

Karl-Heinz was taken aback. He had wondered why he was told to fly to Berlin and to meet with the big boss. Karl-Heinz had avoided Berlin. After Morgenroth's crash at Le Mans, there was even less to bring him to the city. Two of the three 190Xs had done magnificently, taking first and third. After they took the flag, running far behind the others, on his final lap in the pouring rain, an outclassed, bone-weary Hannes Morgenroth had skidded off the road on the long curve after the pits. When they pried him out of the tubing and aluminum, he was dead. Shortly thereafter, Anneliese Morgenroth had moved to Italy.

"Herr Generaldirektor," Karl-Heinz said, "please understand that I am extremely flattered. You pay me a great compliment. At thirty-nine it's a dream job. Now I hope you shan't think me ungrateful, but I'd rather not be back in Berlin.''

Rottmann nodded. Obviously, Karl-Heinz's answer did not come as a total surprise. "They told me,'' he said, "that you might feel this way. I hope you don't think I tried to pry into your private affairs, but I know you lost your wife.''

"Na, ja, Herr Doktor, that and several others like Zoss,

who was one of my best friends. It's difficult for me to be happy here."

"Zoss was a marvelous man. He was also my great friend, and he really boosted my career," said Rottmann. "Without him I wouldn't have had the Munich job. For that matter, I wouldn't have the job I now have."

"And Hannes Morgenroth," said Karl-Heinz. "He was wonderful. If Anneliese were still living here . . . but she's moved away. Anyhow, there are so many things!"

"*Schon in Ordnung.* I understand completely." Rottmann accepted Karl-Heinz's point of view gracefully. "Then I've got another proposal for you. You speak excellent English, I'm told."

"*Einiger Massen.* Fairly well," said Karl-Heinz.

"How would you like to join our new American staff? We're opening an office in New York on Park Avenue. I can't give you the top job, of course. Dr. Erdmann will get that. Do you know him?"

"No, sir, I don't."

"Good man, Erdmann. Not a marketing fellow, but an engineer. For now we have to be sure that our cars are serviced properly and that we build a network of dealers who understand Brunzigs. That's the reason we need a technical man at the top. What I was thinking of for you was rather more in the marketing line."

"*Herr Doktor*, I was in America for over two years as a prisoner. I like Americans. We get along well. So I would absolutely love to go back there. *Fantastisch!*"

"Good." Rottmann was pleased. He went on, "Here's what I have in mind: After Le Mans, and after the Mille Miglia and the Targa Florio and all the other races in which we did all right—"

"All right? We won every damn race!"

"Yes," said Rottmann. "You're right, but I'm just back from setting up our offices in London, so I'm still getting over attacks of English understatement. Anyway, within two years we'll start delivering replicas of the 190X. We want to sell lots of them in America. There's a whole new group of sports car enthusiasts there and they have lots of money."

"*Prima!*"

"So, if you join Erdmann, you would have to organize a

special marketing effort so that we can have everything lined up when we go into production.''

''Would that be a permanent assignment?''

''As permanent as you want to make it.''

''That suits me fine.''

''Meantime, you can begin by getting around in New York, Chicago, and Los Angeles, meeting people, going to clubs, attending sports car races. There's a new international race at Sebring in Florida. The Italians are sending their teams there. I'm told it's a big-time sales and publicity opportunity. The English have been selling M.G.s like crazy because of these sports car races, but of course we'll be in a much higher price bracket. So you'll have to get to know the so-called''—Rottmann ducked, feigning embarrassment— ''upper crust, the *Besseren Schichten*. I have a hunch you won't find it too hard.'' Rottmann thought, With this fellow's looks, and charm . . .

''It all sounds very 'Armin Zoss'!'' said Karl-Heinz.

''Aber wie!'' said Rottmann. ''And how!'' He continued, ''There is one unpleasant situation overseas. I inherited it, but still, it is now my responsibility. Last month I checked into our Argentine setup. I had not been there, nor had I met the men who are our distributors.''

''Surely,'' said Karl-Heinz, ''from all one hears, it's doing well. So it must be run by people who are close to Perón?''

''Quite right,'' said Dr. Rottmann. ''In fact, since the war ended, Argentina has been one of our best export markets. Gerhardt Brunzig was delighted with it. However, there is one thing about it that I cannot believe he knew.'' Dr. Rottmann shook his head, hesitating, then continued, ''An old Argentinian friend wrote to me in confidence, asking me if I knew the real agent behind our business in the Argentine and the government.''

''And?'' said Karl-Heinz.

''The real *Organisator*, the man who makes a big profit for us and also for himself is *Jan Telesty!*''

''That son of a bitch? Really?''

''Yes. He has wormed his way into an invulnerable position. For now, we have no way of dumping him.''

''Herr Brunzig despised him.''

''So I hear. But apparently he's safe. The Argentinians

won't let him be extradited. I'm told the War Crimes Tribunal hasn't even tried.''

"Sometime, *Herr Doktor,* I'll tell you the whole story as Zoss told it to me. It was connected with the Berghof and a party at Ritterschwert, and then Monte Carlo. Are we really stuck with him?''

"Yes. For now. I told you about him in case he makes contact about the Sebring race. The Argentinians are very keen to race there.''

"Thanks for warning me.''

Then they parted company. Rottmann had to attend meetings with the *Oberbürgermeister,* the mayor of Berlin, the great Ernst Reuter.

For the first time in years, Karl-Heinz was ecstatically happy. Even the mention of Telesty could not dampen his mood. Now, finally, he had been dealt a winning hand. He felt as he did at eighteen when he found out that he has passed his *Abitur* final examinations with honors. He started drifting toward Mommsenstrasse, where he and his father had lived. At the intersection of Fasanenstrasse and Kurfürsten-damm, he stood next to a tall, slim, gray-haired woman. She looked straight at him, so he smiled and said, *"Guten Tag!"* Then he crossed the avenue.

Baronin von Tessold followed his disappearing back with her eyes. Who was that? Why did she think she knew that tall, handsome boy? Why? Then, suddenly, it came to her! *Karl-Heinz Dorn!* Hilde had shown her his pictures so many times. Their albums with snapshots of sunny prewar days, his photos as a young officer. Karl-Heinz Dorn. Too late. She crossed the avenue, looking for him, but he was gone. She tried the hotels, but no one by the name of Dorn was registered. Karl-Heinz had flown in that morning and left that evening. He had not checked into a hotel.

NEW YORK

1954

TELL ME, DORN, how you joined the goddam party?" For two long evenings, Aaron Kornberg had heard the story of Charly Dorn. The lawyer cajoled, threatened, and even flung insults, while the German tried to tell about his life, and to answer that one harsh question.

Then it became easier, and Dorn spoke without prodding. Yet how do you condense a life into a few hours?

Kornberg seemed unconcerned with motives. He would not accept feelings. He wanted only solid facts for the defense of this man, and he finally got them, almost at the end of the whole story. Hilde, Zoss, von Totten, von Bernsdorfer, Gellstein, Rommel—these were the pawns in his game of chess. But Timmons, Wolf, and Schmidt—above all, Schmidt— they were his moves, his strategy.

So far, Kornberg had tried not to judge. Anyway, he would never have done so professionally. His concern was with the law, not the moral aspect. This German had finally given him the stuff of which a defense could be built.

Dorn *sounded* anti-Nazi. He *claimed* the friendship of active anti-Nazis, and he said his wife was a saint. Perhaps it was all true. One would have to wait and see. But the actions concerning Wolf, Colonel Timmons, and Lieutenant Schmidt, these could be documented at once.

"Dorn," he said, "now that I've listened to you, I've

344

decided I'll take your case. No, don't thank me. I don't know if I can get you out of this lousy mess."

Dorn did as he was bid. He shut up.

Kornberg went on, "I don't even know if you're a goddam liar or not. If you're a liar, let me tell you now, you're a good one! Meantime, I have to be in Washington tomorrow, so I'm going to stop in at the Immigration and Naturalization Service. I'll speak to some people I know. I want the department to postpone your case for three months. I think they'll do it for me. The bastards owe me. In fact, the whole fuckin' Department of Justice owes me."

"Do you really think . . .?" said Dorn, but Kornberg cut him off.

"Yes," he said, "I think!" Then he sat down at his desk and for the next thirty minutes he wrote down the exact descriptions, names, and last known addresses of every personality Dorn had mentioned and of the three star witnesses: Schmidt, Timmons, and Wolf. Fortunately, Dorn had stayed in touch with Schmidt, and Timmons and Wolf would be easy to locate.

Kornberg lighted an old worn-out pipe. So that was the smell in the office!

"Here is the procedure," he said. "Once we get the postponement"—Dorn liked the "we"—"we'll ask for a Board of Special Inquiry, usually three Immigration officers. We'll submit our evidence to them. In this case, because of the way the case came to them, they'll probably get their Investigation Division very busy checking out everything we claim. There might even be a Department of Justice prosecutor on the board. Just as well. They're usually good men. There's also a Board of Immigration Appeals, as a last resort, but I hope we shan't need that." His pipe had gone out, and he did not bother to relight it. Dorn was still listening, quietly.

"I'm amazed," Kornberg said, "that you didn't ask me about the way the case came to them."

"I was going to," Dorn said. "But I didn't want to interrupt."

"There's a certain congressman. Young. Tough. You were going to ask me if he was Jewish, weren't you?"

"No," said Dorn. "I wasn't going to ask that." Paranoia,

he thought. But understandable. The opposite of Paul Stern. Or was it?

Kornberg continued, "Now, this congressman, he's a pain in the ass, but bright as hell. He's going to run for bigger and better things soon, and the one thing he uses to build his reputation is Nazi-hunting. He's the one who got the facts on you to the Department of Immigration. He's a New Yorker, so he needs a lot of Jewish votes. Personally, I have nothing against Nazi-hunting. Did some myself in the old German-American *Bund* days before the war. But I've got a gut feeling this young bastard is more concerned with glory than with justice. I can't even blame him for that." Kornberg sank back into a deep, shabby leather couch at the side of his desk. "Except when it concerns a client of mine. Particularly if my client is unjustly accused and being railroaded. You know what I mean by railroaded?"

"Yes."

"That is, unless my client is a fucking liar, which we shall find out in the next few weeks, during our goddam postponement. Now, get out of here! I'll call you beginning of next week."

"Before I go," said Dorn, "Do I tell my boss at Brunzig?"

"Not yet."

"Will I need a lot of money to pay for this?"

"We'll talk about that later."

"And. . . . thanks."

"Aw, go screw yourself!" said the lawyer. When Dorn's tall figure had left his office, Aaron Kornberg said to himself, "Aaron, when will you stop being a shmuck?" Originally, he had no intention of being in Washington the next day.

He had to tell Carla, so he phoned her.

The American long-distance operator needed every word spelled out, and even then, she pronounced Milano *My-Layno*.

Finally, there, warm, sweet, excited, and deliciously audible despite the cruel scratches in thousands of miles of wires, was Carla.

"*Caro!* How wonderful. How sweet of you to call! I miss you terribly. Everyone here—"

"What did you say, darling?"

"I said everyone here wants to meet you. I've talked about nothing but my *Tedesco*."

"Carla, I miss you like mad. I am *miserabile* without you. But I have to tell you something that is not pleasant."

"Go ahead, *caro*."

"The American government says that because I was technically a member of the Nazi party and because they have photos of me with the *Führer* and the *Duce,* I can no longer stay in this country. That would ruin all of our plans."

"Oh, poor darling, you must be so unhappy."

"For both of us. But I've gone to a famous lawyer who specializes in these immigration matters."

"What did he say?"

"He decided to take my case, and he said that we stand a chance of getting it all put aside."

"That sounds wonderf—" *Static. Static.*

"Darling, Carla! Carla . . .!"

"—sure it was just a mistake!"

"Oh, thank God, you're back on the line. There are some things I have not told you, things that would now be in my favor. Anti-Nazi things. Anyway, I wanted you to know right away. . . . This may postpone our plans! But even if we win my case, I'll be almost bankrupt, because it will cost a lot of money. I certainly can't ask you to marry me until I can afford it!"

"You must be *pazzo!* What do I care about money? I can get the money for your defense. My brothers will advance it, and we can always pay them back later."

"Why should you bother them with this?"

"The exact same thing has happened to one of our relatives here in Italy who was in the party and even had a high rank. But he was never a real Fascist. We always knew that. He hid our Jewish relatives, those who survived. And he helped so many others. Anyway, we're taking care of his defense. So my brothers know all about this sort of thing."

"I would feel ashamed to borrow from them. And from you."

"Idiot! I love you. I'll try to come over next week! We'll be together. I don't want you to be alone when you've got all this trouble."

"I wish I had the courage to tell you to stay away. But I haven't."

"I love you."

"I love you."

Scratch, hiss, scratch.

The operator: "Are you through, sir?"

"Yes, thank you." But he felt he was not through at all!

Dorn and Aaron Kornberg had an appointment with Dr. Erdmann, who assumed it was about Dorn's naturalization. Kornberg winced when he saw the chrome and aluminum Knight's Sword on the wall outside Dr. Erdmann's office. Kornberg's heart was still with the Abraham Lincoln boys in Madrid. He had never forgiven the Germans, and he would rather have choked than drive one of their cars. But that was neither here nor there.

There was another moment of antipathy when he was introduced to Dr. Erdmann. To him, the man looked just like a goddam German officer. Kornberg was a simple man. No shadings, only sharp contrasts. He admitted it. He was prejudiced. Of course, never against *decent* people! But that was personal, and he had learned to shelve these feelings for the sake of his work.

Dr. Erdmann, in turn, was taken aback by the rumpled appearance of his visitor, but offered his customary courtesy. He gestured the lawyer and Dorn to armchairs and leaned forward expectantly. Kornberg quickly told him the harsh facts. Erdmann showed unexpected calm and resolve, and Dorn, who had dreaded the moment, was impressed.

"Look," Erdmann told Kornberg, " as a German, I know a great deal about these matters. Things that may now look dreadful were completely understandable at that time. I myself never joined the party, only because I never got boxed into a corner. I heard someone use that expression yesterday, and I think it is so . . . *genau.*"

"Exact," Dorn translated for a puzzled Kornberg.

"I am very happy, *Herr* Erdmann," said the lawyer, "that you understand. Mr. Dorn felt that we ought to let you know the facts so you can inform your company if you wish. We got a postponement. Nothing will happen for several months. Dorn, here, can go on working as before, and I think we can avoid all publicity."

"I appreciate that. You really had no obligation to tell me now, because this is still *Herr* Dorn's private matter. But I have always thought of him as a fine person, and this proves

it. Did he tell you that we just offered him the national sales
managership for Brunzig-America?''

''No.''

''That's typical of him. I think we made the right choice, at
the risk of flattering him to his face.''

After Kornberg left, Dr. Erdmann asked Dorn back into his
office. He said, ''Karl-Heinz—may I call you that? I will try
my best to help you. I cannot believe that you did anything
criminal. But I must inform Dr. Rottmann.''

''*Natürlich.*''

''It will stay completely confidential between the chief,
myself, and you. But you do understand: The final decision
will be up to him.''

Charly Dorn need not have worried. The next day Dr.
Erdmann told him what the chairman had said on the phone,
verbatim: ''Tell Karl-Heinz not to worry. We are one hundred
percent behind him. And also ask him if he knows a Baroness
von Tessold. She is an old friend of my mother's, and she
asked me the other day if I knew a man called Dorn who used
to work for Brunzig. I told her yes and gave her your name.''

Von Tessold? Charly had no idea. He had never heard of
her, but he would certainly try to find out who she was once
this miserable thing was over.

Margarete Rottmann had a special guest in her beloved
little flat in Berlin-Wilmersdorf. She was chubby and cheerful
and mad about her only son, Uwe. She poured some coffee
and said, ''*Na, ja,* let's not wait. I'm *starved!* I love that new
Apfeltorte from Kempinsky. And I also have *Moonkuchen* with
all those fantastic poppyseeds. But that may be too sweet for
you!''

Margarete and the Baroness Gertrud von Tessold had known
each other since childhood. Margarete was born a von
Traunstein and then, to her parent's horror, she married a
Bürgerlichen unbetitled engineer, Erno Rottmann. Now that
her husband was dead, her son Uwe was all the family she
had, but you wouldn't know it to hear her.

''Where in the devil is that Uwe? Just because he's good-
looking and because he's now the high and mighty boss at
Brunzig, he thinks he can be late. He doesn't get to Berlin so
often! I'll kick him right in the *popo* when he arrives.''

''There he is! *Zum Teufel,* Uwe, you're late, and I need my coffee and cake, and *Tante* Gertrud is also at the end of her endurance!''

Uwe Rottmann laughed. ''Sorry, Mama!'' He gave her a kiss on the cheek and then kissed the baroness's hand. ''Frankly,'' he said to his mother, ''you don't look as if you're at starvation's door.'' This earned him a mock slap on the cheek.

''*Tante* Gertrude,'' he said to the baroness, ''I sent your message to Karl-Heinz Dorn. He'll probably contact you through me.''

''He doesn't know me, Uwe.''

''Doesn't know you? How's that possible? I thought he did.''

''He can't. He's never met me. You see, I knew his wife, Hilde, an absolutely adorable girl and like a daughter to me. She and I worked together at the end of the war. She was the most courageous and gallant little thing. She belonged to some marvelous old family in Nürnberg, and they must have been proud of her.''

''What did you do?''

''We got Jews away from the Gestapo and from the *verdammte* SS. We hid them anywhere we could. This was in the last two years of the war. Your mother knows many of the women who were in our group.''

''Incredible! In the middle of the air raids?''

Gertrud von Tessold shrugged. ''That was just it. Poor Hilde got killed one night after she and I hid some people in a Catholic church near here. She was going home on her bicycle at two in the morning, when there was an explosion. I was heartbroken. Anyway, she often showed me her husband's picture. She simply adored him. Then, a while back, here in Berlin, I thought I once saw him in the Kudamm. But he certainly knows nothing about me.''

Uwe Rottmann shook his head in disbelief. He ignored the coffee and cake his mother had put before him.

''*Tante* Gertrud, this is an incredible coincidence! Yesterday I had a call from my associate in New York. Now I'm going to tell you something in complete confidence, and then you can do as you wish.'' And he told her about Karl-Heinz Dorn's problem.

•   •   •

The documents arrived in Aaron Kornberg's office with amazing speed. The first was delivered by a B.O.A.C. executive within three days of Kornberg's telephoned request.

Note: The author of this Affidavit is Siegfried Schmidt, M.C., C.B.E., a former British Intelligence officer, with a distinguished war record, holder of the Military Cross and decorated by the Crown as Companion of the Order of the British Empire for contributions to the war effort. Mr. Schmidt, a naturalized British citizen, is presently Chairman of an Import-Export Company in London. He was born in Berlin in 1890 of Jewish parents.

Respectfully submitted,

Aaron Kornberg
Attorney-at-Law

AFFIDAVIT

Sworn to before Alan Seagrave, Solicitor at Law, in London, United Kingdom, on 3 December 1945.

I, Siegfried Schmidt, a British subject, do hereby declare that I have known Karl-Heinz Dorn, originally of Berlin, Germany, since he was an eleven-year-old boy, an only child living with his widowed father. I obtained his first job for him, and he worked under my supervision at the KaDeBe department store in Berlin until I had to leave Germany. He and his wife were my warm friends. After my emigration to England, Karl-Heinz Dorn left KaDeBe and joined Brunzig A.G. through Armin Zoss, their International Sales Director. Zoss was a well-known member of an anti-Hitler organization and died during an anti-Nazi mission to America. Karl-Heinz Dorn joined the N.S.D.A.P. and the N.S.K.K., probably at the suggestion of Zoss, who wanted to create a deep contact within Hitler's Berghof and among the leading Nazis. Dorn could not have functioned close to the Hitler coterie without party membership and without some uniformed party affiliation. N.S.K.K. must not be confused with the SS. Their uniforms were similar, but N.S.K.K. was only a national motoring organization. During this time, Dorn also became associated with Major Eberan von Totten, a heroic anti-Hitler conspirator, who was executed by the SS in 1943. Dorn was also on the staff of Field Marshall Rommel in Africa, and Rommel once protected him from the Gestapo.

Hilde Dorn, his wife, was a courageous member of the anti-Nazi resistance. She helped to organize a group of Berlin women who saved hundreds of Jews from being sent to extermination camps, and she died on one of these heroic missions. For the purpose of this affidavit, I have been given permission by H.M. Government to reveal these facts:

Later, when Karl-Heinz Dorn became a P.O.W. in the United States, he saved the life of an American intelligence agent and assisted in the arrest of two German SS agents. Later, he was extremely helpful to our intelligence organizations.

It is my absolute belief that Karl-Heinz Dorn was not a true National Socialist and that he joined the party and the N.S.K.K. without any real political convictions. I shall be proud to testify on his behalf in an American court of law.

Siegfried Schmidt

Similar affidavits from Colonel Timmons and Harry Wolf were delivered within days. Alan Timmons was an executive with a Boston bank, but living in Washington. His papers came by hand.

Harry Wolf, now with a New York advertising agency, brought the papers himself.

Both men gave their unqualified support to Dorn and provided Kornberg with gilt-edged evidence.

Then a letter arrived from Berlin, accompanied by a legal deposition.

Berlin-Dahelm.
Fichtenstrasse 2.
5 Dezember 1954.

Mein Lieber Herr Karl-Heinz Dorn!
You might have heard my name from Uwe Rottmann,

who is the son of one of my oldest friends. Now I am writing to you although I risk betraying a confidence because Uwe told me what was happening to you and it distresses me deeply. I was told that the Americans are accusing you of sympathies for the old N.S. regime.

You see, my dear Karl-Heinz (forgive me for calling you that, but once one has passed seventy-five, one takes certain liberties), your wonderful Hilde was like a daughter to me. We worked together for those last terrible years, and your dear, gallant, courageous, and beautiful Hilde did such *heroic* things! Because you were part of her, you will understand the depth of her courage and convictions.

The night God took her from us, she and I had walked through heavy bombardment to lead a Jewish family, poor wretches, from a basement on Sybelstrasse to the Marienkirche, where the priest hid them and many other Jews. It was the night of November 23, when the Kaiser Wilhelm *Gedächtnis Kirche* was destroyed. You could not have known how close she was to me and how much I loved her. I knew your face because she had shown me your photo so often. She had spoken with such love and admiration about you that now I think of you with much affection.

Through Uwe, I was referred to a Dr. Erdmann in New York, whom I telephoned. He was charming and referred me to Mr. Kornberg, your lawyer. Mr. Kornberg asked me to supply what he called an affidavit, which I enclose herewith. You will have to get it translated. My old family lawyer here in Berlin does not have an English-language stenographer.

Do not be angry at me, my dear Karl-Heinz. I am usually not an interfering woman.

All my warmest affection and greetings to you, and the blessings of our God upon you. From your friend in Berlin whom you have never seen.

Gertrud von Tessold

N.B.
Could I have seen you, one day, crossing the Kurfürstendamm, about 1951? I asked Uwe Rottmann, and he said he had met with you about then in Berlin.

Note: The author of the attached affidavit, *Baroness Gertrud von Tessold*, 77, a German citizen, is a resident of the American Sector of Berlin. She has been called one of Germany's great anti-Nazi heroines, since she helped to save hundreds of German Jews from certain death in concentration camps. She did so daily, at the risk of her life, hiding her activities from her son, an SS officer who was later killed in Russia.

In recognition of these courageous acts, the baroness was decorated in 1952 with the Star of the Grand Cross of Merit of the Federal Republic of Germany, her country's highest honor. It is also understood that special ceremonies for her are now being planned by the Israeli Government, although she is still unaware of these. The undersigned obtained this information through the Israeli Embassy in Washington.

Respectfully submitted,

Aaron Kornberg
Attorney-at-Law

The undersigned certifies that the following translation from German is true and correct.

Adeltrud Wallrahm

Vice Consul,
Consulate General of the
Federal Republic of Germany

December 10, 1954 New York   New York

AFFIDAVIT

Having heard about the charges brought against KARL-HEINZ DORN by the United States Government, I hasten to his aid. I was closely associated with his wife, HILDEGARD DORN, née ANTMANN, during the final years of the war. She was my colleague and courageous helper in those activities which were carried out by a group of Berlin German women to save German citizens of the Jewish faith from arrest, incarceration, or worse. For two years, until her death, HILDEGARD DORN risked her life to this end, despite heavy Allied bombardments, and the SS, Gestapo, police, and other Nazi organizations.

She often spoke to me of her husband, who was fully aware of her anti-Nazi activities. He knew that she belonged to a powerful anti-Nazi organization long before he joined the Army and while he was a member of the N.S.D.A.P. and the N.S.K.K.

Had he been a Nazi, he certainly would have kept her from these activities or even denounced her, since interfamily treachery in Nazi times was quite common. Those living outside Germany could not have known the many pressures on German men. In many cases, party membership did not signify agreement or sympathy. There were even Nazi party members who helped with the work HILDEGARD DORN and I were doing.

I shall be proud to testify in person on the behalf of this young man who was married to my heroic, courageous comrade, the late HILDEGARD DORN, killed the night of November 23, 1943, after having helped to hide a family of Jewish Germans in the basement of a Catholic church. I am convinced that KARL-HEINZ DORN could at no time have been a National Socialist, in sympathy with that abominable regime.

Respectfully:

Gertrud Baronin von Tessold

Carla and he walked, hand in hand, into Aaron Kornberg's office past his old-maid secretary who once was ready to disapprove of them: He was too good looking; and she smelled of too much perfume. Besides he was . . . German! But Dorn had remembered her name, Miss Ida, and had brought her a set of linen handkerchiefs with embroidered "I." She was enchanted. Carla said, "Thanks for taking care of my Charly."

"I think Mr. K. has good news for you." She could not resist. She wanted to tell them something to make them feel good.

So the great news was not a complete surprise.

The rumpled Kornberg said, "The Department of Immigration and Naturalization!" He waved a piece of paper. "Sit down. Don't stand there. Sit down, goddam it. Sorry, Miss Roselli.'' Then he came around his desk, bouncy, cheating on his usual air of boredom. "Basically they have decided to suspend the proceedings against you. If they find nothing new within another six months, they will permit your application for First Papers to be processed, so you can be a goddam red, white, and blue genyoo-wine citizen of this here idiot nation of ours within five years. How does that grab you, chum?''

Carla looked puzzled, but Dorn said, "Marvelous. Terrific. Now, give me a chance to explain to Miss Italy."

"Is she really Miss . . .?''

"No.''

"Save me from your Kraut humor.''

"Too fast for you?''

"Oh, shut up.''

Dorn explained their victory to Carla, and she threw her arms around Aaron Kornberg.

"I could learn to like this,'' he said.

"It's part of your fee,'' said Dorn.

"I'll collect the rest later! Now listen, there's one important thing I still have to do, or else there's a chance that someone could throw a clinker into this.''

"Clinker?'' Dorn asked.

"I keep forgetting you're a goddam foreigner. I mean someone could foul things up!''

"Who?''

"I'll tell you later. This one I have to handle my own way. Anyway, I'll call you.'' Dorn's face clouded over with fresh worry and Kornberg said, "Don't get upset, Charly. Leave it to me. I'll handle it. You can go home now. Just leave me Miss Italy.''

It was Dorn's turn: "Screw you!'' Berliners learned fast.

The King Cole Room at the St. Regis requested "gentlemen only'' at lunchtime, like an old-fashioned club, and the clientele, carefully graded by table placement, was unvarying.

Whenever he was midtown, Aaron Kornberg lunched there.

On the far wall there was an enormous painting of the enthroned King Cole, flanked by his two sly-looking jesters. St. Regis regulars said that the quizzical look on their faces was easy to explain: The old king had just farted.

Aaron Kornberg sat at "his'' banquette, the second down

from the entrance, which was rated "Double A" by cognoscenti. There was only one "Triple A" table, the one dominating the entrance, and it was reserved for movie stars, senators, the mayor, or Henry Ford II.

Aaron was waiting for Leon Schloss, United States congressman from the Seventeenth or "Silk Stocking" District of New York. It was Leon Schloss and his well-financed staff who had alerted the Department of Immigration and Naturalization to the case of Karl-Heinz Dorn.

Gino, the maître d', brought him to the table. Gino liked to have congressmen at the King Cole Room. He liked governors and senators even better, but Congressman Schloss was the best there was today, and he got the full escort treatment not accorded to lesser "members."

Aaron and the congressman greeted each other with the inborn antagonism of two champions separated by their generations. In a way, they were alike: both liberals, both Jewish, both quintessentially New Yorkers. But Schloss considered Kornberg a fossil, stuck in the La Guardia-Roosevelt era, and Kornberg thought of Schloss as a superficial, opportunistic, Johnny-come-lately, a liberal now that it was fashionable. But he admired Schloss's brain and was not about to underrate him.

The congressman, short of body, quick of movement, was dressed in Brooks Brothers gray flannel with blue button-down shirt, navy knitted tie, and a Bronze Star decoration bar in his buttonhole. As a New York Jewish liberal congressman during those recent McCarthy days, it was smart to demonstrate evidence of some wartime heroism, and he still wore the Bronze Star insignia on all his jackets although McCarthy had finally been scuttled. What harm? He'd keep wearing them. As a very young infantryman he saw action in Okinawa, right at the tail end of the war, and he deserved his Bronze Star. Every G.I. on Okinawa did.

Schloss looked very young, although he was now twenty-nine and had been in office for several years. He was elected by the young veterans, and the antiques who ran the political machinery were forced to give way to this tough new constituency. What's more, they grumbled, Schloss was a stubborn bastard who did things his own way.

Schloss had done a great deal of reading about the Nazis, but he had never been to Germany. Then, through a constituent, a German Jewish refugee, he began to hear about former Nazis who were entering the United States illegally.

It was beyond belief! He was genuinely aghast. With the help of other refugees, he discovered first one, then another German Nazi, who had managed to slip past the Immigration people. He was amazed by the acclaim that came through these cases. The newspapers loved the story, and he found himself a hero. To his credit, he did not exploit the publicity, but several people who knew the political game convinced him not to play Sir Lancelot. Eventually he assumed the mantle of Nazi-hunter.

Still, Leon Schloss occasionally took stock and questioned his own motives. He knew how easily he could destroy himself by becoming a cardboard figure, yet the cause was true. It *was* shameful that Nazis were getting into the United States. It had to be stopped!

Now Leon Schloss's own sense of proportion helped Aaron Kornberg's cause more than the lawyer's fancied skill as a negotiator and wheeler-dealer.

"Leon, I'm working for Karl-Heinz Dorn. I'm his attorney."

"Dorn? Fellow who works for Brunzig, right?"

"You ought to know. You're the one who went for his jugular."

"Hold it, Aaron. I didn't invent these things we gave to the Immigration people. He was a member of the Nazi party, right?"

"Right."

"And in the SS?"

"Wrong. He was in a reasonably harmless outfit that had a similar uniform."

"Photographed with Hitler and Mussolini?"

"Correct."

"Then, good Aaron, what in hell do you mean by all this 'going for the jugular' crap? It's not as if I'm accusing Rabbi Steven Wise of having collaborated with the Gestapo."

"I'm going to ask you to hold everything while we order drinks and lunch because nothing, but nothing, must stand in the way of my martini and the corned beef, which is their special of the day, according to Gino."

They both ordered corned beef, but Schloss had a bottle of beer.

Aaron continued, "Leon, you know I haven't always been your biggest booster."

"Oh, how can you say that?" asked Schloss with a cheerful irony. "You almost busted my hump drumming up support for that brokendown pal of yours during the election." Aaron had supported one of New York's oldest liberals, a man who had been in politics for thirty years. They owed each other. Besides, Aaron couldn't stand this wet-behind-the-ears kid.

Aaron said, "Well, anyway, I have to admit that you've really turned out to be good at what you're doing."

Leon was suspicious of praise from Aaron Kornberg. What next? he thought.

Kornberg handed him a manila folder.

"Here are certified copies of some papers I submitted to the Immigration and Naturalization people. They've had them for over a month. They just informed me that, barring any unforeseen developments, they will allow Dorn to go ahead with his application for First Papers. Leon, no matter what you think of me, do you have any doubts about my patriotism?"

"That's a stupid question," said Schloss. "I think you can be an awful shit, but of course I'm absolutely convinced that you would never do anything you might have to be ashamed of. Why the hell did you ask that?"

"Then you know goddam well that I would never allow a true German Nazi to be in our country. We've got enough trouble with our own brand."

"Go on."

"Read these documents. They're not long-winded. Then check on them. If you still think Dorn is a Nazi, in the real sense of the word, I've misjudged you."

"All right. I'll take 'em back to the office."

"No. Read 'em now."

"Now?"

"Now, Leon!"

While Schloss began to read, Kornberg drank his martini. He noticed that Schloss did not touch his beer. When the food was delivered, Schloss ignored it. Aaron tried not to disturb him. He searched the room for faces he knew. There were several, but he avoided waving at them so that Schloss could concentrate.

Schloss finished, stacked the papers into a neat pile, and

returned them to their folder. "These, I suppose, are my copies?"

"They are."

"Aaron, I must tell you that, as you know, I always felt antagonistic toward you. For that matter toward many of your contemporaries. I thought you fellows were far behind the times and, well, naïve."

Aaron Kornberg nodded. This was nothing new to him, but it was the first time he had heard it said out loud.

"Now, about Dorn. Frankly, Aaron, I think, well, you may have saved my tail. Normally, I would have raised a tremendous stink if the Immigration people had put aside the case against him and I had found out about it. I would have hit the roof and accused them of everything under the sun." Schloss finally took his first bite of corned beef. Kornberg had been eating steadily, undaunted by any tension he might have felt.

Schloss went on, "Then they would have handed me these documents and I would have yelled, 'Fake! These affidavits are phony!' Well, I have a strong hunch these affidavits are valid, and that makes Dorn into pretty good material for American citizenship. In fact, a lot better than some of the shits in the Klan."

"I can promise you," said Kornberg, "they're real and good as gold. I had to make very sure before I stuck out my neck in Washington."

"Obviously. Also, the Immigration boys weren't born yesterday. Anyway, you saved me from making a damn fool of myself. Picture the whole thing: 'New York Jewish congressman condemns anti-Nazi hero whose wife was killed saving the lives of hunted Jews!' Something like that. Anyway, it wouldn't have been my favorite moment."

They shook hands.

"Okay, okay, let's talk money. If you insist on it, let's do that."

"I insist," said Charly. "It's been over three months. So let me settle with you, Aaron."

"Here's the fee." Kornberg wrote something onto a piece of notepaper and pushed it over to Charly.

"Ridiculous," said Charly. "Five hundred dollars? You put in weeks and weeks and trip after trip. Please, Aaron, I appreciate what you're trying to do, but you're not in the *Heilsarmee,* what do you call them, the Salvation Army."

"No. I'm not. But there are certain things I really wish to do, and this is one of them." He scratched his messy hair, pulled on the tip of his nose, massaged his forehead with his fingertips, anything to help him get over an embarrassing explanation. "Let's say that I'm doing this for someone I've grown close to, and I didn't even know her!"

"Hilde? She was every bit as wonderful as you think. All right, Aaron. If you insist. You'll have my check in the morning. One thing, though."

"What now?"

"If someone else from Germany, *na, ja,* gets into a mess of this sort, and gets accused of things, and really wasn't as guilty as they say, will you take their case? I'll help. I'll give advice, money, anything I can. Also, I'll help shake out the fake ones."

"You got yourself a deal, Charly, my friend. Now that it's over, pal, look me straight in the eye and tell me how you feel about yourself. Straight! Just you and me! Man to man!"

"Lucky."

"Is that all?"

"Well, that's the whole point. I know I'm lucky because I'm not sure I deserve everything that is happening."

"Now you tell me you were a goddam Nazi?"

"No. Not that. The things in the affidavit are substantially true. All in all, they told the truth. Except for one thing."

"Specifically?"

"What do you mean, specifically?"

"I mean—was there one time when you really were a Nazi?"

"No. The sin I mean was being an opportunist. I confess to that. I also confess to complacency. Laziness. Being what we Germans call *Faul.*"

"You mean the stuff Schmidt wrote about Zoss and Totten wanting you in the party as a contact was not true?"

"It was true from their point of view. For my part, as they say in America, I just went along for the ride. I never actively tried to help them, or even Hilde. Didn't have the courage. Not until the prisoner train!"

Aaron was startled. For weeks now he had been so close to this man's life and still, it seemed, he had missed things about him. "Charly," he said, "let me tell you something. I'm just as guilty as you are." He shook his head. "God-dammit, there are so many things about which I should have stood up on my hind legs and raised hell. But I didn't. Our lousy jails. Our screwed-up system of plea-bargaining. Clubs that won't admit Jews. I should have taken them on, all of them, as a matter of principle. I have rich clients who flatter me when their fucking English butler needs an extension on his visa and yet I know they're the worst anti-Semites in the world. I should really tell them to shove it, but instead I soak them. I take their dough and think I've shafted them. But inside, I know that isn't so."

Dorn nodded. Of course, Aaron was trying to make things easier. He was a wonderfully kind man.

Things were working out. Carla and he started househunting in Manhattan. Dr. Erdmann was delighted by the outcome in Washington, and Dorn was now national sales director. Dr. Rottmann had sent a warm letter, confessing that it was he who had told the whole story to Baroness von Tessold.

The brothers Roselli were on their way to New York, and Marge Allery and Carla were making their wedding plans. Where would it be? At Marge's maisonette? Or Marge's house in Southampton? Even Vivier got involved. Dorn had phoned Siegfried Schmidt and written to the Baroness von Tessold. He had also spoken to Al Timmons. Then he lunched with Harry Wolf. It turned out the Wolfs lived within four blocks of him, on Park and Sixty-ninth. They planned dinner.

Only one thing had flawed these weeks: Paul Stern was leaving Brunzig. He gave several reasons. Some official: He "wanted to enter other fields of communications." Some unofficial: "The movie business beckons." Then finally, after many drinks on Saturday afternoon at Twenty-one, Paul Stern told Dorn the truth.

He was just back from Stuttgart, where Brunzig had held a meeting of their advertising and P.R. people. One night he had dinner with some of his German colleagues.

"Paule," said one of them, "*Na, Mensch,* you really have those New York and Hollywood Jews by the balls! You people in America are *fantastisch!*"

"So," Paul Stern said to Charly, "What did I do about it? Did I get up and slap him silly? Did I say how dare you? *I'm one of those New York Jews!* Did I go to Dr. Rottmann and complain? No. I did nothing, because I realized that it wouldn't have done any good. No one there had disapproved of what was said. Tacitly, they all agreed!''

''Why in God's name didn't you speak to Dr. Rottmann? You know how he came through for me?''

''Yes, he's a *fabelhafter Kerl,* a marvelous guy. But he can't regulate his people's feelings. The men at the table felt that way, and that's that! They weren't drunk and saying stupid things. They were dead sober. I knew then and there, Charly, that I had no business working for Brunzig. I had kidded myself that my being a Jew made no difference. Not so! Worse: I had expected Germans, today's Germans to be better, to be *above* all that. I don't know why I dared expect it. I did, though. As I told you, there's plenty of anti-Semitism here in America, but somehow I can take that. I don't like it, but I can take it. But when it comes from Germans . . . now, in 1954 . . . after all that shit! Well, it makes me vomit. Anyway, it's hard to explain. And particularly to you. Or perhaps it's easiest with you. But I *must get out!*''

''You can't judge a whole corporation, a whole country, by a few idiots at a dinner table!''

''Charly, you're right. Okay, okay. I'm not being rational. Why the fuck should I be? Why are Jews always expected to be the rational ones?''

''Why Germans?''

In answer, Paul Stern raised his glass and clinked it against Charly Dorn's. ''Because,'' he said, ''because we're both so fucking brilliant, the Krauts and the Jews!''

Then he burst into laughter and so did Dorn. But Paul Stern left Brunzig anyway.

There was a small synagogue on East Fifty-sixth Street, tucked away between a large apartment house and an office building. Paul Stern had passed it a hundred times without noticing, but because he was loafing a few days with nothing to do until he flew to Los Angeles, he paid more attention. On a whim, despite the vitriolic nagging of his inner voice, he walked in.

He was in a narrow hallway that smelled like stale onion soup. To one side was a shelf with prayer books and *yarmulkes,* skullcaps. Ahead of him was the main part of the synagogue, a narrow room about sixty feet long housing fifteen rows of benches. Eleven or twelve men stood, deep in prayer, facing the Ark with its Torah, wearing their *tallis* prayer shawls, bobbing and weaving in the antique prayer ritual while their lips murmured, chanted, spoke the Hebrew litany. They were like Oriental transplants, and, to Paul Stern, as much out of context with Western American life as a Zen Buddhist temple or a Shinto shrine. But he took a prayer book and put on a *yarmulke* and then, strangely, out of his grandfather's rabbinical past, he found himself touching his lips to the book before he opened it. The hieroglyphics of Hebrew stared at him, and yet, here and there, he remembered things from his early and useless bar mitzvah training, useless since he had never been confirmed. The symbols that said *Adonai* meant God. *Shem* meant a name, *Meloch*, a king. To his surprise, he could read the stuff! Not much, he admitted, nor could he make any sense of it, but a few words here and there. Once you've ridden God's bicycle. . . . He laughed at himself.

Then he looked at the men around him. They were quite old, except for one young fellow, red-haired, with ritual *peyes*, the side curls of the Hassidic Jews, which once were the earmark of Nazi caricatures. The young man threw his whole body into the prayer, as if flailed by some giant wind. Paul was in awe, until he noticed that the man was only performing the ritual, vigorously doing God's calisthenics, but he was not nearly as involved as he had seemed at first. He looked at Paul with obvious curiosity. His eyes were ice-blue, Teuton, Hunnish, Goth, Visigoth, Celt. Who knew which rape or love or conquest or surrender had brought these blue eyes to this young orthodox Jew in New York?

Paul stayed only a few more minutes. This was not for him, not his world. But then, what was? What came after the delusion of his personal assimilation? Never mind the others who had tried it. He, dammit, had succeeded. Until Stuttgart. And even there, he could have shut up and accepted the ugly compliment. No one would have been any the wiser, except he himself.

Where was his world? He could have worked with a man like Dorn for the rest of his career. They could have been like brothers. They were the perfect team.

No. It had nothing to do with individuals. Perhaps it was caused by their need to cluster, to adhere, to be part of a tribe, a "better than thine" tribe. Now he would try to join his own changed, modified, restructured, redesigned section of Jewry. But where the hell could he find *that?*

Not long thereafter, when Charly Dorn got to his office one morning he found an airmail envelope marked *"Streng persönlich. Bitte nicht öffnen.* Very personal. Not to be opened." The stamp was Argentinian, postmarked Buenos Aires.

It looked vulnerable, so Dorn used his letter opener. The paper inside was also lightweight, and the message was typed in German:

Lieber Karl-Heinz!

Certain people have informed me about your troubles in America, and I hasten to contact you. The last word I had about you was *"Alles in Butter,"* that all was going fine. I even heard that Erdmann was going to promote you. Now, this shit comes along! According to Gellstein, who is in jail in Germany, you nearly got caught earlier. You were lucky!

Anyway, you will probably get kicked out by your beloved Americans, and neither Rottmann nor your boss, the kindly Dr. Erdmann, can do a *Scheiss* thing to help you! So, come to Argentina! Come to work for me. As you know, I run Brunzig here, and I mean *run.* The Argentine government and I are very close. But there are other things I have in mind for you. Some in Egypt, some in Spain, some even back in our bombed-out, democratized "new" *Vaterland.* I must admit, I was never able to persuade you before, but I have a feeling that with your imminent departure from the land of the Jewish skyscrapers, you will be a little more benevolently inclined toward an old friend.

Jan Telesty

Buenos Aires
13 February 1955.

Contact me by writing to *Brandenburg,* P.O. Box 1932, Buenos Aires, Argentina.

Charly Dorn, aghast, read and reread it, and he knew what to do. First, he made a complete translation of Telesty's letter and typed it himself. Then he went downstairs to a public Xerox machine and had several copies made, of the original and his translation.

Back in his office, he put a copy into an envelope to Siegfried Schmidt in London, attached a note and marked it AIR—SPECIAL DELIVERY.

Then he put another copy and the translation into his own briefcase to show to Carla. But the original and the translation went into the breast pocket of his suit. Then he called Aaron Kornberg's office.

"Aaron, I have something important to show you. I think it's something you may want to hand to Congressman Schloss. This time he can really try to nail someone, although it will take some doing. I'll help! You can count on me."

BIBLIOGRAPHY

Acheson, Dean. *Present at the Creation*. New York: Norton, 1969.

Bailey, G. *Germans*. New York: World Publishing Co., 1972.

Baker, Leonard. *Days of Sorrow and Pain*. New York: Macmillan Publishing Co., 1978.

Bender, R. J. and Larm, R. *Afrikakorps*. Mountain View, Calif.: R. J. Bender Publishing, 1971.

Bender, R. J., and Taylor, H. P. *Waffen SS*. Mountain View, Calif.: R. J. Bender Publishing, 1971.

Bergner, Elisabet. *Bewundert viel und viel Gescholten*. Munich: Goldmann Verlag, 1978.

Borgeson, G. "In the Name of the People," *Automobile Quarterly* 18, no. 4.

Bower, Tom. *The Pledge Betrayed*. New York: Doubleday, 1982.

Buchein, L. *Das Boot*. Munich: Piper Verlag, 1973.

Buxa, W. *Der Kampf um Leningrad*. Dorheim, Germany: Podzun Verlag, 1971.

Collier, Richard, *Duce!* New York: Viking, 1971.

Davis, Bryan Leigh. *German Uniforms of the Third Reich*. New York: Arco Publishing Co., 1973.

Deakin, F. W. *The Brutal Friendship*. New York: Harper & Row, 1962.

Elon, Amos. *Herzl*. New York: Holt, Rinehart & Winston.

Essame, Maj. Gen. H. *Normandy Bridgehead*. New York: Ballantine Books, 1970.

Flemming, H. *Uber den Umgang mit Berlinern*. Berlin: Kleiber Verlag, 1954.

Friedrich, O. *Before the Deluge*. New York: Harper & Row, 1972.

Gehendes, F., and Whiting, C. *Jener September*. Düsseldorf: Droste Verlag, 1979.

Goebbels, J. *The Goebbels Diaries*. New York: Eagle Books, 1948.

Grunfield, F., and Trevor-Roper, H. *The Hitler File*. New York: Random House, 1974.

Hamilton, Nigel. *Monte*. New York: McGraw-Hill, 1981.

Hansen, T. *Der Hamsun Prozess*. Hamburg: Knaus Verlag, 1979.

Heiden, Conrad. *Hitler*. London: Constable, 1936.

Herzstein, R. *The Nazis*. New York: Time-Life Books, 1980.

Hitler, A. *Mein Kampf*. Munich: Franz Eher Verlag, 1925.

Infield, Glen B. *Hitler's Secret Life*. Felthams England: Hamlyn, 1979.

———. *Skorzeny*. New York: St. Martin's Press, 1981.

Irving, D. *The Trail of the Fox*. New York: Dutton, 1977.

Kahn, Leo. *Nuremberg Trials*. New York: Ballantine Books, 1972.

Katcher, Leo, *Post Mortem*. New York: Delacorte Press, 1968.

Kiaulehn, W. *Berlin*. Munich: Biederstein Verlag, 1958.

Kirkpatrick, I., *Mussolini—A Study of Power*. New York: Hawthorn Books, 1964.

Konsalik, H. *Stalingrad*. Bayreuth, Germany: Goldmann Verlag, 1979.

Laqueur, Walter, *Weimar*. New York: G. P. Putnam's Sons, 1974.

Lorant, S. *Sieg Heil!* New York: Norton, 1974.

Luft, G. *Heimkehr ins Unbekannte*. Wupperthal, Germany: Peter Hammer Verlag, 1977.

Macksey, Maj. Kenneth. *Afrika Korps*. New York: Ballantine Books, 1968.

Manchester, W. *Krupp*. Munich: Heyne Biographien, 1964.

Marrus, M., and Parton, R. *Vichy France and the Jews*. New York: Basic Books, 1981.

Maser, Werner. *Adolf Hitler, Ende der Führerlegende*. Düsseldorf: Econ Verlag, 1980.

———. *Hitlers Briefe und Notizen*. Düsseldorf: Econ Verlag, 1973.

———. *Nuremberg*. New York: Charles Scribner's Sons, 1979.

Michaels, M. *Mussolini and the Jews*. New York: Oxford University Press, 1978.

Morris, James. *Farewell the Trumpets*. New York: Harcourt Brace Jovanovich, 1978.

Mosley, Diana Mitford. *A Life of Contrasts*. New York: Times Books, 1977.

Nelson, W. *The Berliners*. New York: David McKay, 1969.

Organisationsbuch der N.S.D.A.P. Munich: Zentralverlag der N.S.D.A.P., 1943.

Pem. *Heimweh nach dem Kurfürstendamm*. Berlin: L. Blaufelt Verlag, 1962.

Persico, J. E. *Piercing the Reich*. New York: Viking, 1979.

Picker, H., Hoffman, H., and Lang, J. *Hitler Close-up*. New York: Macmillan Publishing Co., 1974.

Piekalkiewicz, J. *Secret Agents, Spies and Saboteurs*. London: William Morrow & Co., 1973.

Pomrehn, A., Sanger, H., and Schaeffer, H. *Der Weg der 79, Infanterie Division*. Dorheim, Germany: Podzun Verlag, 1971.

Pryce-Jones, D. *Paris in the Third Reich*. New York: Holt, Rinehart & Winston, 1981.

Reiners, Ludwig. *Frederick the Great*. New York: G. P. Putnam's Sons, 1960.

Sellenthin, H. G. *Geschichte der Juden in Berlin*. Berlin: Berliner Jüdische Gemeinde, 1959.

Siewert, C. *Schuldig?* Dorheim, Germany: Podzun Verlag, 1968.

Shirer, W. *The Rise and Fall of the Third Reich*. New York: Simon and Schuster, 1960.

Smitz, G. *Die 16. Panzer Division*. Dorheim, Germany: Podzun Verlag, 1971.

Speer, Albert. *Infiltration*. New York: Macmillan Publishing Co., 1981.
———. *Inside the Third Reich*. New York: Macmillan Publishing Co., 1970.

Tetens, T. H. *The New Germany and the Old Nazis*. New York: Random House, 1961.

Toland, John. *Adolf Hitler*. New York: Doubleday, 1976.
———. *Hitler*. New York: Ballantine Books, 1976.
———. *The Last 100 Days*. New York: Random House, 1965.

Tutas, H. E. *N.S. Propaganda und Deutsches Exil*. Worms, Germany: Georg Heintz Verlag, 1973.

Von Eckardt, W., and Gilman, S. *Bertolt Brecht's Berlin*. Garden City, N.J.: Anchor Press, 1975.

Von Lang, Jochen. *The Secretary*. New York: Random House, 1979.

Von Staden, W. *Darkness Over the Valley*. New York: Ticknor and Fields, 1981.

Werlich, R. *Orders and Decorations*. Washington, D.C.: Quaker Press, 1974.

Wykes, A. *Goebbels*. New York: Ballantine Books, 1973.

Zaloga, S. J. *Blitzkrieg*. Carrollton, Texas: Squadron-Signal Publications, 1980.

Ziemke, Earl F. *Battle for Berlin*. New York: Ballantine Books, 1968.

Phonograph recording, O. Joost, "Oscar Joost in Eden Hotel, Berlin, 1931–34" Electrola, 1934.

Bestselling Books